THE BLACK TULIP

By

ALEXANDRE DUMAS

MELLIFONT PRESS LTD.
1 FURNIVAL STREET, LONDON, E.C.4

THE BLACK TULIP

CHAPTER I

A GRATEFUL PEOPLE

On the 20th August, 1672, the city of the Hague, always so lively, so neat, and so trim, that one might believe every day to be Sunday; with its shady park, with its tall trees, spreading over its Gothic houses, with its canals like large mirrors, in which its steeples, and its almost Eastern cupolas are reflected; the city of the Hague, the capital of the Seven United Provinces, was swelling in all its arteries with a black and red stream of hurried, panting, and restless citizens, who, with their knives in their girdles, muskets on their shoulders, or sticks in their hands, were pushing on to the Buitenhof, a terrible prison, the grated windows of which are still shown, where, on the charge of attempted murder, preferred against him by the surgeon Tyckelaer, Cornelius De Witt, the brother of the Grand Pensionary of Holland, was confined.

If the history of that time, and especially that of the year in the middle of which our narrative commences, were not indissolubly connected with the two names just mentioned, the few explanatory pages which we are about to add might appear quite supererogatory; but we will, from the very first, apprise the reader—our old friend, to whom we are wont on the first page to promise amusement, and with whom we always try to keep our word as well as in our power—that this explanation is as indispensable to the right understanding of our story, as to that of the great event itself on which it is based.

Cornelius De Witt, warden of the dykes, ex-burgomaster of Dort, his native town, and member of the Assembly of the States of Holland, was forty-nine years of age, when the Dutch people, tired of the republic such as John de Witt, the Grand Pensionary of Holland, understood it, at once conceived a most violent affection for the Stadtholderate, which had been abolished for ever in Holland, by the "Perpetual Edict" forced by John de Witt upon the United Provinces.

The brothers De Witt humoured Louis XIV, whose moral influence was felt by the whole of Europe, and the pressure

of whose material power Holland had been made to feel in
that marvellous campaign on the Rhine, which, in the space
of three months, had laid the power of the United Provinces
prostrate.

Louis XIV had long been the enemy of the Dutch, who
insulted or ridiculed him to their hearts' content, although
it must be said, that they generally used French refugees for
the mouth-piece of their spite. Their national pride held him
up as the Mithridates of the republic. The brothers De Witte,
therefore, had to strive against a double difficulty,—against
the force of national antipathy, and, besides, against that
feeling of weariness which is natural to all vanquished people,
when they hope that a new chief will be able to save them
from ruin and shame.

This new chief, quite ready to appear on the political stage,
and to measure himself against Louis XIV, however gigantic
the fortunes of the Grand Monarch loomed in the future,
was William, Prince of Orange, son of William II, and
grandson by his mother, Mary Stuart, of Charles I of
England. We have mentioned him before as the person by
whom the people expected to see the office of Stadtholder
restored.

This young man was, in 1672, twenty-two years of age.
John De Witte, who was his tutor, had brought him up with
the view of making him a good citizen. Loving his country
better than he did his disciple, the master had, by the " Perpetual Edict," extinguished the hope which the young Prince
might have entertained of one day becoming Stadtholder.
But God laughs at the presumption of man, who wants to
raise and prostrate the powers on earth without consulting
the King above; and the fickleness and caprice of the Dutch
combined with the terror inspired by Louis XIV, in repealing
the " Perpetual Edict ", and re-establishing the office of
Stadtholder in favour of William of Orange, for whom the
hand of Providence had traced out ulterior destinies in the
hidden map of the future.

The Grand Pensionary bowed before the will of his fellow-
citizens; Cornelius De Witte, however, was more obstinate,
and notwithstanding all the threats of death from the
Orangist rabble, who besieged him in his house at Dort, he
stoutly refused to sign the act by which the office of Stadtholder was restored. Moved by the tears and entreaties of
his wife, he at last complied, only adding to his signature the
two letters V. C. (*Vi Coactus*), notifying thereby that he only
yielded to force.

It was a real miracle that on that day he escaped from the doom intended for him.

John De Witte derived no advantage from his ready compliance with the wishes of his fellow-citizens. Only a few days after, an attempt was made to stab him, in which he was severely, although not mortally, wounded.

This by no means suited the views of the Orange faction. The life of the two brothers being a constant obstacle to their plans, they changed their tactics, and tried to obtain by calumny what they had not been able to effect by the aid of the poniard.

How rarely does it happen that, in the right moment, a great man is to be found to head the execution of vast and noble designs; but it as rarely happens that, when the devil's work is to be done, the miscreant is not at hand who readily and at once enters upon the infamous task.

· The wretched tool in this instance was Tyckelaer, a surgeon by profession. He lodged an information against Cornelius De Witte, setting forth that the warden—who, as he had shown by the letters added to his signature, was fuming at the repeal of the "Perpetual Edict"—had, from hatred against William of Orange, hired an assassin to deliver the new republic of its new Stadtholder; and he, Tyckelaer, was the person thus chosen; but that, horrified at the bare idea of the act which he was asked to perpetrate, he had preferred rather to reveal crime than to commit it.

This disclosure was, indeed, well calculated to call forth a furious outbreak among the Orange faction. The Attorney-General caused, on the 16th of August, 1672, Cornelius De Witte to be arrested; and the noble brother of John De Witte had, like the vilest criminal, to undergo, in one of the apartments of the town prison, the preparatory degrees of torture, by means of which his judges expected to force from him the confession of his alleged plot against William of Orange.

But Cornelius was not only possessed of a great mind, but also of a great heart. He belonged to that race of martyrs who, indissolubly wedded to their political conviction, as their ancestors were to their faith, are able to smile on pain: whilst being stretched on the rack, he recited, with a firm voice, and scanning the lines according to measure, the first strophe of the "Justum ac tenacem" of Horace; and, making no confession, tired, not only the strength, but even the fanaticism of his executioners.

The judges, notwithstanding, acquitted Tyckelaer from every charge; at the same time sentencing Cornelius to be deposed from all his offices and dignities; to pay all the costs of the trial; and to be banished the soil of the republic for ever.

This judgment against not only an innocent, but also a great man, was indeed some gratification to the passions of the people, to whose interests Cornelius De Witte had always devoted himself: but, as we shall soon see, it was not enough.

The Athenians, who, indeed, have left behind them a pretty tolerable reputation for ingratitude, have, in this respect, to yield precedence to the Dutch. They, at least, in the case of Aristides, contented themselves with banishing him.

John De Witte, at the first intimation of the charge brought against his brother, had resigned his office of Grand Pensionary. He, too, received a noble recompense for his devotedness to the best interests of his country, taking with him into the retirement of private life the hatred of a host of enemies, and the fresh scars of wounds inflicted by assassins, only too often the sole guerdon obtained by honest people, who are guilty of having worked for their country, and of having forgotten their own private interests.

In the meanwhile, William of Orange urged on the course of events by every means in his power, eagerly waiting for the time when the people, by whom he was idolized, should have made of the bodies of the brothers the two steps over which he might ascend to the chair of Stadtholder.

Well, then, on the 20th of August, 1672, as we have already stated in the beginning of this chapter, the whole town was crowding towards the Buitenhof, to witness the departure of Cornelius De Witte from prison, as he was going to exile; and to see what traces of the torture of the rack had left on the noble frame of the man who knew his Horace so well.

Yet all this multitude was not crowding to the Buitenhof with the innocent view of merely feasting their eyes with the spectacle: there were many who went there to play an active part in it, and to take upon themselves an office which they conceived had been badly filled—that of the executioner.

There were, indeed, others with less hostile intentions. All that they cared for was the spectacle, always so attractive to the mob, whose instinctive pride is flattered by it:—the sight of greatness hurled down into the dust.

"Has not," they would say, "this Cornelius De Witte been locked up, and broken by the rack? Shall we not see him pale, streaming with blood, covered with shame?" And was not this a sweet triumph for the burghers of the Hague, whose envy even beat that of the common rabble; a triumph, in which every honest citizen and townsman might be expected to share?

"Moreover," hinted the Orange agitators interspersed through the crowd, whom they hoped to manage like a sharp-edged, and, at the same time, crushing instrument,—"more-over, will not, from the Buitenhof to the gate of the town, a nice little opportunity present itself to throw some handfuls of dirt, or a few stones, at this Cornelius De Witte, who not only conferred the dignity of Stadtholder on the Prince of Orange merely *Vi Coactus,* but who also intended to have him assassinated?"

"Besides which," the fierce enemies of France chimed in, "if the work were done well and bravely at the Hague, Cornelius would certainly not be allowed to go into exile, where he will renew his intrigues with France, and live with his big scoundrel of a brother, John, on the gold of the Marquis de Louvois."

Being in such a temper, people generally will run rather than walk; which was the reason why the inhabitants of the Hague were hurrying so fast towards the Buitenhof.

Honest Tyckelaer, with a heart full of spite and malice, and with no particular plan settled in his mind, was one of the foremost, being paraded about by the Orange party like a hero of probity, national honour, and Christian charity.

This daring miscreant detailed, with all the embellishments and flourishes suggested by his base mind and his ruffianly imagination, the attempts which he pretended Cornelius De Witte had made to corrupt him; the sums of money which were promised; and all the diabolical stratagems planned beforehand to smooth for him, Tyckelaer, all the difficulties in the path of murder.

And every phase of his speech, eagerly listened to by the populace, called forth enthusiastic cheers for the Prince of Orange, and groans and imprecations of blind fury against the brothers De Witte.

The citizens ran along faster and faster, cocking their muskets, brandishing their hatchets, and looking death and defiance in all directions.

No violence, however, had as yet been committed, and the file of horsemen who were guarding the approaches of the Buitenhof remained cool, unmoved, silent, much more threatening in their impassibility, than all this crowd of burghers, with their cries, their agitation, and their threats. The men on their horses, indeed, stood like so many statues, under the eye of their chief, Count Tilly, the captain of the mounted troop of the Hague, who had his sword drawn, but held it with its point downwards, in a line with the straps of his stirrup.

This troop, the only defence of the prison, overawed by its firm attitude not only the disorderly riotous mass of the populace, but also the detachment of the burgher-guard, which, being placed opposite the Buitenhof to support the soldiers in keeping order, gave to the rioters the example of seditious cries, shouting:

"Hurrah for Orange! Down with the traitors!"

The presence of Tilly and his horsemen, indeed, exercised a salutary check on these civic warriors; but, by degrees, they waxed more and more angry by their own shouts, and as they were not able to understand how any one could have courage without showing it by cries, they attributed the silence of the dragoons to pusillanimity, and advanced one step towards the prison, with all the turbulent mob following in their wake.

In this moment, Count Tilly rode forth towards them single-handed, merely lifting his sword and contracting his brow whilst he addressed them:

"Well, gentlemen of the burgher-guard, what are you advancing for, and what do you wish?"

The burghers shook their muskets, repeating their cry:

"Hurrah for Orange! Death to the traitors!"

"'Hurrah for Orange!' all well and good!" replied Tilly, "although I certainly am more partial to happy faces, than to gloomy ones. 'Death to the traitors,' as much of it as you like, as long as you show your wishes only by cries. But, as to putting them to death in good earnest, I am here to prevent that, and I shall prevent it."

Then, turning round to his men, he gave the word of command:

"Soldiers, ready!"

The troopers obeyed orders with a precision which immediately caused the burgher-guard and the people to fall back, in a degree of confusion which excited the smile of the cavalry officer.

"Halloa!" he exclaimed, with that bantering tone which is peculiar to men of his profession: "be easy, gentlemen, my soldiers will not fire a shot; but, on the other hand, you will not advance by one step towards the prison."

"And do you know, sir, that we have muskets?" roared the commandant of the burghers.

"I must know it, by Jove, you have made them glitter enough before my eyes; but I beg you to observe, also, that we on our side have pistols, that the pistol carries admirably to a distance of fifty yards, and that you are only twenty-five from us."

"Death to the traitors!" cried the exasperated burghers.

"Go along with you," growled the officer, "you always cry the same thing over again. It is very tiresome."

With this, he took his post at the head of his troops, whilst the tumult grew fiercer and fiercer about the Buitenhof.

And yet, the fuming crowd did not know, that at the very moment when they were tracking the scent of one of their victims, the other, as if hurrying to meet his fate, passed, at a distance of not more than a hundred yards, behind the groups of people and the dragoons, to betake himself to the Buitenhof.

John De Witte, indeed, had alighted from his coach with a servant, and quietly walked across the courtyard of the prison.

Mentioning his name to the turnkey, who, however, knew him, he said:

"Good morning, Gryphus, I am coming to take away my brother, who, as you know, is condemned to exile, and to carry him out of the town."

Whereupon the jailer, a sort of bear, trained to lock and unlock the gates of the prison, had greeted him and admitted him into the building, the doors of which were immediately closed again.

Ten yards further on, John De Witte met a lovely young girl, of about seventeen or eighteen, dressed in the national costume of the Frisian women, who, with pretty demureness, dropped a curtesy to him. Chucking her under the chin, he said to her:

"Good morning, my good and fair Rosa; how is my brother?"

"Oh! Mynheer John, sir," the young girl replied, "I am not afraid of the harm which has been done to him. That's all over now."

"But what is it you are afraid of?"

"I am afraid of the harm which they are going to do to him."

"Oh! yes," said De Witte, "you mean to speak of the people down below, don't you?"

"Do you hear them?"

"They are indeed in a state of great excitement; but when they see us, perhaps they will grow calmer, as we have never done them anything but good."

"That's unfortunately no reason, except for the contrary," muttered the girl, as on an imperative sign from her father she withdrew.

"Indeed, child, what you say is only too true."

Then, in pursuing his way, he said to himself:

"Here is a damsel who very likely does not know how to read, who, consequently, has never read anything; and yet, with one word, she has just told the whole history of the world."

And with the same calm mien, but more melancholy than he had been on entering the prison, the Grand Pensionary proceeded towards the cell of his brother.

CHAPTER II

THE TWO BROTHERS

As the fair Rosa, with foreboding doubt, had foretold, so it happened. Whilst John De Witte was climbing the narrow winding stairs which led to the prison of his brother Cornelius, the burghers did their best to have the troop of Tilly, which was in their way, removed.

Seeing this disposition, King Mob, who fully appreciated the laudable intentions of his own beloved militia, shouted most lustily:

"Hurrah for the burghers!"

As to Count Tilly, who was as prudent as he was firm, he began to parley with the burghers, under the protection of the cocked pistols of his dragoons, explaining to the valiant townsmen that his order from the States commanded him to guard the prison and its approaches with three companies.

"Wherefore such an order? Why guard the prison?" cried the Orangeists.

"Stop," replied the Count; "there you at once ask me more than I can tell you. I was told: 'Guard the prison,' and I guard it. You, gentlemen, who are almost military men yourselves, you are aware than an order must never be gainsayed."

The mob answered only by redoubled clamour and horrible threats, to which the Count opposed the most perfect urbanity.

"Gentlemen," he said, "uncock your muskets; one of them may go off by accident, and if the shot chanced to wound one of my men, we should knock over a couple of hundreds of yours, for which we should, indeed, be very sorry, but you even more so; especially as such a thing is neither contemplated by you, nor by myself."

"If you did that," cried the burghers, "we should have a pop at you too."

"Of course you would, but suppose you killed every man

Jack of us, those whom we should have killed would not, for all that, be less dead."

"Then leave the place to us, and you will perform the part of a good citizen."

"First of all," said the Count, "I am not a citizen, but an officer, which is a very different thing; and secondly, I am not a Hollander, but a Frenchman, which is more different still. I have to do with no one but the States, by whom I am paid; let me see an order from them to leave the place to you, and I shall only be too glad to wheel off in an instant, as I am confoundedly bored here."

"Yes, yes!" cried a hundred voices, the din of which was immediately swelled by five hundred others; "let us march to the Town-hall; let us go and see the deputies! Come along! come along!"

"That's it," Tilly muttered between his teeth, as he saw the most violent among the crowd turning away; "go and ask for a meanness at the Town-hall, and you will see whether they will grant it: go, my fine fellows, go!"

The worthy officer relied on the honour of the magistrates, who, on their side, relied on his honour as a soldier.

"I say, Captain!" the first lieutenant whispered into the ear of the Count, "I hope the deputies will give these madmen a flat refusal; but, after all, it would do no harm if they would send us some reinforcement."

In the meanwhile, John De Witte, whom we left climbing the stairs, after his conversation with the jailer Gryphus and his daughter Rosa, had reached the door of the cell, where, on a mattress, his brother Cornelius was resting, after having undergone the preparatory degrees of the torture. The sentence of banishment having been pronounced, there was no occasion for inflicting the torture extraordinary.

Cornelius was stretched on his couch, with broken wrists and crushed fingers. He had not confessed a crime of which he was not guilty; and now, after three days of agony, he once more breathed freely, on being informed that the judges, from whom he had expected death, were only condemning him to exile.

This was just at the very moment when the mingled shouts of the burgher-guard and of the mob were raging against the two brothers, and threatening Captain Tilly, who served as a rampart to them. This noise, which roared outside the walls of the prison, as the surf dashing against the rocks, now reached the ears of the prisoner.

But threatening as it sounded, Cornelius appeared not to deem it worth his while to inquire after its cause; nor did he get up to look out of the narrow grated window, which gave access to the light and to the noise of the world without.

He was so absorbed in his never-ceasing pain, that it had almost become a habit with him. He felt with such delight the bonds, which connected his immortal being with his perishable frame, gradually loosening, that it seemed to him as if his spirit, freed from the trammels of the body, were hovering above it, like the expiring flame which rises from the half-extinguished embers.

John tenderly kissed his brother on the forehead. "Cornelius, my poor brother, you are suffering great pain, are you not?"

"I am suffering no longer, since I see you, my brother."

"Oh, my poor dear Cornelius, I feel most wretched to see you in such a state."

"And, indeed, I have thought more of you than of myself; and whilst they were torturing me, I never thought of uttering a complaint, except one, to say ,'Poor brother!' But, now that you are here, let us forget all. You are coming to take me away, are you not?"

"I am."

"I am quite healed; help me to get up, and you shall see how well I can walk."

"You will not have to walk far, as I have my coach near the pond, behind Tilly's dragoons."

"Tilly's dragoons! What are they near the pond for?"

"Well," said the Grand Pensionary, with a melancholy smile which was habitual to him, "the gentlemen at the Town-hall expect that the people of the Hague would like to see you depart, and there is some apprehension of a tumult."

"Of a tumult?" replied Cornelius, fixing his eyes on his perplexed brothr; "a tumult?"

"Yes, Cornelius."

"Oh! that's what I heard just now," said the prisoner, as if speaking to himself. Then, turning to his brother, he continued:

"Are there many persons down before the prison?"

"Yes, my brother, there are."

"But, then, to come here to me——"

"Well?"

"How is it that they have allowed you to pass?"

"You know well that we are not very popular, Cornelius," said the Grand Pensionary with gloomy bitterness. "I have made my way through all sorts of by-streets and alleys."

"You hid yourself, John?"

"I wished to reach you without loss of time, and I did

what people will do in politics, or on sea when the wind is against them—I tacked."

In this moment the noise in the square below was heard to roar with increasing fury. Tilly was parleying with the burghers.

"Well, well," said Cornelius, "you are a very skilful pilot, John; but I doubt whether you will as safely guide your brother out of the Buitenhof in the midst of this gale, and through the raging surf of popular hatred, as you did the fleet of Van Tromp past the shoals of the Scheldt to Antwerp."

"With the help of God, Cornelius, we'll at least try," answered John; "but, first of all, a word with you."

"Speak!"

The shouts began anew.

"Hark, hark!" continued Cornelius, "how angry these people are. Is it against you? or against me?"

"I should say it is against us both, Cornelius. I told you, my dear brother, that the Orange party, whilst assailing us with their absurd calumnies, have also made it a reproach against us that we have negotiated with France."

"What blockheads they are!"

"But, indeed, they reproach us with it."

"And yet, if these negotiations had been successful," they would have prevented the defeats of Rees, Orsay, Wesel, and Rheirberg; the Rhine would not have been crossed, and Holland might still consider herself invincible in the midst of her marshes and canals."

"All this is quite true, my dear Cornelius, but still more certain it is, that if in this moment our correspondence with the Marquis de Louvois were discovered, skilful pilot as I am, I should not be able to save the frail barque which is to carry the brothers De Witte and their fortunes out of Holland. That correspondence, which might prove to honest people how dearly I love my country, and what sacrifices I have offered to make for its liberty and glory, would be ruin to us if it fell into the hands of the Orange party. I hope you have burnt the letters before you left Dort to join me at the Hague."

"My dear Brother," Cornelius answered, "your correspondence with Monsieur de Louvois affords ample proof of your having been of late the greatest, most generous, and most able citizen of the Seven United Provinces. I doat on the glory of my country; and particularly do I doat on your glory, John—I have taken good care not to burn that correspondence."

"Then we are lost, as far as this life is concerned," quietly said the Grand Pensionary, approaching the window.

"No, on the contrary, John, we shall at the same time save our lives, and regain our popularity."

"But what have you done with these letters?"

"I have entrusted them to the care of Cornelius Van Baerle, my godson, whom you know, and who lives at Dort."

"Poor honest Van Baerle! who knows so much, and yet thinks of nothing but of flowers and of God who made them. You have entrusted him with this fatal secret; it will be his ruin, poor soul!"

"His ruin?"

"Yes, for he will either be strong or he will be weak. If he is strong, he will, when he hears of what has happened to us, boast of our acquaintance; if he is weak, he will be afraid on account of his connection with us: if he is strong, he will betray the secret of his boldness; if he is weak, he will allow it to be forced from him. In either case he is lost, and so are we. Let us, therefore, fly, fly, while there is yet time."

Cornelius De Witt, raising himself on his couch, and grasping the hand of his brother, who shuddered at the touch of the linen bandages, replied:

"Do not I know my godson? have I not been enabled to read every thought in Van Baerle's mind and every sentiment in his heart? You ask whether he is strong or weak. He is neither the one nor the other; but that is not now the question. The principal point is, that he is sure not to divulge the secret, for the very good reason that he does not know it himself."

John turned round in surprise.

"You must know, my dear brother, that I have been trained in the school of that distinguished politician John De Witte; and I repeat to you that Van Baerle is not aware of the nature and importance of the deposit which I have entrusted to him."

"Quick, then," cried John, "as there is still time, let us convey to him directions to burn the parcel."

"Through whom?"

"Through my servant, Craeke, who was to have accompanied us on horseback, and who has entered the prison with me, to assist you down stairs."

"Consider well before having those precious documents burnt, John!"

"I consider, above all things, that the brothers De Witt must necessarily save their lives, to be able to save their character. If we are dead, who will defend us? Who will have fully understood our intentions?"

"You expect, then, that they would kill us, if those papers were found?"

John, without answering, pointed with his hand to the square, from whence, in that very moment, fierce shouts and savage yells made themselves heard.

"Yes, yes," said Cornelius, "I hear these shouts very plainly, but what is their meaning?"

John opened the window.

"Death to the traitors!" howled the populace.

"Do you hear now, Cornelius?"

"To the traitors! that means us!" said the prisoner, raising his eyes to heaven and shrugging his shoulders.

"Yes, it means us," repeated John.

"Where is Craeke?"

"At the door of your cell, I suppose."

"Let him enter then."

John opened the door; the faithful servant was waiting on the threshold.

"Come in, Craeke, and mind well what my brother will tell you."

"No, John; it will not suffice to send a verbal message; unfortunately, I shall be obliged to write."

"And why so?"

Because Van Baerle will neither give up the parcel, nor burn it, without a special command to do so."

"But will you be able to write, poor old fellow?" John asked, with a look on the scorched and bruised hands of the unfortunate sufferer.

"If I had pen and ink you would soon see," said Cornelius.

"Here is a pencil, at any rate."

"Have you any paper? for they have left me nothing."

"Here, take this Bible, and tear out the fly leaf."

"Very well, that will do."

"But your writing will be illegible."

"Just leave me alone for that," said Cornelius. "The executioners have indeed pinched me badly enough, but my hand will not tremble once in tracing the few lines which are requisite."

And, really, Cornelius took the pencil and began to write, when through the white linen bandages drops of blood oozed out, which the pressure of the fingers against the pencil squeezed from the raw flesh.

A cold sweat stood on the brow of the Grand Pensionary. Cornelius wrote:—

MY DEAR GODSON,

"Burn the parcel which I have entrusted to you. Burn it without looking at it and without opening it, so that its contents may for ever remain unknown to yourself. Secrets of this description are death to those with whom they are deposited. Burn it, and you will have saved John and Cornelius De Witte.

"Farewell, and love me,

"August 20th, 1672.　　　　　　　　　DE WITTE."

John, with tears in his eyes, wiped off a drop of the noble blood which had soiled the leaf; and, after having handed the despatch to Craeke with a last direction, return to Cornelius, who seemed overcome by intense pain, and near fainting.

"Now," said he, "when honest Craeke sounds his old coxswain's whistle, it will be a signal of his being clear of the crowd and of his having reached the other side of the pond. And then it will be our turn to depart."

Five minutes had not elapsed, before a long and shrill whistle was heard through the din and noise of the square of the Buitenhof.

John gratefully raised his eyes to heaven.

"And now," said he, "let us be off, Cornelius."

CHAPTER III

THE PUPIL OF JOHN DE WITTE

Whilst the clamour of the crowd in the square of the Buitenhof, which grew more and more menacing against the two brothers, determined John De Witte to hasten the departure of his brother Cornelius, a deputation of burghers had gone to the Town-hall to demand the withdrawal of Tilly's horse.

It was not far from the Buitenhof to Hoogstraat (Highstreet); and a stranger, who since the beginning of this scene had watched all its incidents with intense interest, was seen to wend his way with, or rather in the wake of, the others towards the Town-hall, to hear, as soon as possible, the current news of the hour.

This stranger was a very young man, of scarcely twenty-two or three, with nothing about him that bespoke any great energy. He evidently had his good reasons for not making himself known, as he hid his face in a handkerchief of fine Frisian linen, with which he incessantly wiped his brow or his burning lips.

With an eye keen like that of a bird of prey, with a long aquiline nose, a finely-cut mouth, which he generally kept open, or rather which was gaping like the edges of a wound; this man would have presented to Lavater, if Lavater had lived at that time, a subject for physiognomical observations, which at the first blush would not have been very favourable to the person in question.

He was plainly dressed, and apparently unarmed; his arm was lean but wiry; and his hands dry, but of aristocratic whiteness and delicacy, and he leaned on the shoulder of an officer, who, with his hand on his sword, had watched the scenes in the Buitenhof with eager curiosity, very natural in a military man, until his companion drew him away with him.

On arriving at the square of the Hoogstraat, the man with the sallow face pushed the other behind an open shutter, from which corner he himself began to survey the balcony of the Town-hall.

At the savage yells of the mob, the window of the Town-hall opened, and a man came forth to address the people.

"Who is that on the balcony?" asked the young man, glancing at the orator.

"It is the deputy Bowelt," replied the officer.

"What sort of a man is he? Do you know anything of him?"

"An honest man; at least I believe so, Monseigneur."

Hearing this character given of Bowelt the young man showed signs of such a strange disappointment and evident dissatisfaction, that the officer could not but remark it, and, therefore, added:

"At least people say so, Monseigneur. I cannot say anything about it myself, as I have no personal acquaintance with Mynheer Bowelt."

"Well," the young man muttered half to himself and half to his companion, "let us wait, and we shall soon see."

The other officer bowed his head in token of his assent, and was silent.

"If this Bowelt is an honest man," His Highness continued, "he will give to the demand of these furibond petitioners a very queer reception."

The nervous quiver of his hand, which moved on the shoulder of his companion, as the fingers of a player on the keys of a harpsichord, betrayed his burning impatience, so ill-concealed at certain times, and particularly at that moment, under the icy and sombre expression of his face.

The chief of the deputation of the burghers was then heard

addressing an interpellation to Mynheer Bowelt, whom he requested to let them know where the other deputies, his colleagues, were.

"Gentlemen," Bowelt repeated for the second time, "I assure you that in this moment I am here alone with Mynheer d'Asperen, and I cannot take any resolution on my own responsibility."

"The order! we want the order!" cried several thousand voices.

Mynheer Bowelt wished to speak, but his words were not heard, and he was only seen moving his arms in all sorts of gestures, which plainly showed that he felt his position to be desperate. When, at last, he saw that he could not make himself heard, he turned round towards the open window, and called Mynheer d'Asperen.

The latter gentleman now made his appearance on the balcony, where he was saluted with shouts, even more energetic than those with which, ten minutes before, his colleague had been received.

This did not prevent him from undertaking the difficult task of haranguing the mob; but the mob preferred forcing the guard of the States—which, however, offered no resistance to the sovereign people—to listening to the speech of Mynheer d'Asperen.

"Now, then," the young man coolly remarked, whilst the crowd was rushing into the principal gate of the Town-hall, "it seems the question will be discussed indoors, Captain. Come along, and let us hear the debate."

"Oh, Monseigneur! Monseigneur! take care!"

"Of what?"

"Among these deputies, there are many who have had dealings with you; and it would be sufficient, that one of them should recognise Your Highness."

"Yes, that I might be charged with having been the instigator of all this work; indeed you are right," said the young man, blushing for a moment from regret of having betrayed so much eagerness. "From this place we shall see them return with or without the order for the withdrawal of the dragoons, and then we may judge which is greater, Mynheer Bowelt's honesty, or his courage."

"But," replied the officer, looking with astonishment at the personage whom he addressed as Monseigneur, "but Your Highness surely does not suppose for one instant that the deputies will order Tilly's horse to quit their post?"

"Why not?" the young man quietly retorted.

"Because doing so would simply be signing the death-warrant of Cornelius and John De Witte."

"We shall see," His Highness replied, with the most perfect coolness; "God alone knows what is going on within the hearts of men."

The officer looked askance at the impassible figure of his companion, and grew pale: he was an honest man as well as a brave one.

From the spot where they stood, His Highness and his attendant heard the tumult and the heavy tramp of the crowd on the staircase of the Town-hall. The noise thereupon sounded through the windows of the hall, on the balcony of which Mynheers Bowelt and d'Asperen had presented themselves. These two gentlemen had retired into the building, very likely from fear of being forced over the balustrade by the pressure of the crowd.

After this, fluctuating shadows in tumultuous confusion were seen flitting to and fro across the windows: the council-hall was filling.

Suddenly the noise subsided; and as suddenly again it rose with redoubled intensity, and at last reached such a pitch that the old building shook to the very roof.

At length, the living stream poured back through the galleries and stairs to the arched gateway, from which it was seen issuing like water from a spout.

At the head of the first group, a man was flying rather than running, his face hideously distorted with satanic glee: this man was the surgeon Tyckelaer.

"We have it! we have it!" he cried, brandishing a paper in the air.

"They have got the order!" muttered the officer in amazement.

"Well then," His Highness quietly remarked, "now I know what to believe with regard to Mynheer Bowelt's honesty and courage; he has neither the one nor the other."

Then, looking with a steady glance after the crowd which was rushing along before him, he continued:

"Let us now go to the Buitenhof, Captain; I expect we shall see a very strange sight there."

The officer bowed, and, without making any reply, followed in the steps of his master.

There was an immense crowd in the square and about the neighbourhood of the prison. But the dragoons of Tilly still kept it in check with the same success and with the same firmness.

It was not long before the Count heard the increasing din

of the approaching multitude, the first ranks of which rushed
on with the rapidity of a cataract.

At the same time, he observed the paper which was waving
above the surface of clenched fists and glittering arms.

" Halloa!" he said, rising in his stirrups and touching his
lieutenant with the knob of his sword; " I really believe these
rascals have got the order."

" Dastardly ruffians they are!" cried the lieutenant.

It was indeed the order, which the burgher-guard received
with a roar of triumph. They immediately sallied forth,
with lowered arms and fierce shouts, to meet Count Tilly's
dragoons.

But the Count was not the man to allow them to approach
to within an inconvenient distance.

" Stop!" he cried, " stop, and keep off from my horse, or
I shall give the word of command to advance."

" Here is the order," a hundred insolent voices answered
at once.

He took it in amazement, cast a rapid glance on it, and said
quite loud :

" Those who have signed this order are the real murderers
of Cornelius De Witte. I would rather have my two hands
cut off than have written one single letter of this infamous
order."

And, pushing back with the hilt of his sword the man who
wanted to take it from him, he added:

" Wait a minute, papers like this are of importance, and are
to be kept."

Saying this, he folded up the document, and carefully put
it in the pocket of his coat.

Then, turning round towards his troop, he gave the word
of command:

" Tilly's dragoons, wheel to the right!"

After this, he added in an undertone, yet loud enough for
his words to be not altogether lost to those about him:

" And now, ye butchers, do your work!"

A savage yell, in which all the keen hatred and ferocious
triumph, rife in the precincts of the prison, simultaneously
burst forth, and accompanied the departure of the dragoons,
as they were quietly filing off.

The Count tarried behind, facing to the last the infuriated
populace, which advanced at the same rate as the Count
retired.

John De Witte, therefore, had by no means exaggerated
the danger, when, assisting his brother in getting up, he
hurried his departure. Cornelius, leaning on the arm of the

Ex-Grand Pensionary, descended the stairs which led to the courtyard.

At the bottom of the staircase, he found little Rosa trembling all over.

"Oh! Mynheer John," she said, "what a misfortune!"

"What is it, my child?" asked De Witte.

"They say, that they are gone to the Town-hall to fetch the order for Tilly's horse to withdraw."

"You do not say so!" replied John. "Indeed, my dear child, if the dragoons are off, we shall be in a very sad plight."

"I have some advice to give you," Rosa said, trembling even more violently than before.

"Well, let us hear what you have to say, my child. Why should not God speak by your mouth?"

"If I were in your place, Mynheer John," the young girl said, "I should leave by the postern, which leads into a deserted by-lane, while all the people are waiting in the High-street to see you come out by the principal entrance. From thence I should try to reach the gate by which you intend to leave the town."

"But my brother is not able to walk," said John.

"I shall try," Cornelius said, with an expression of most sublime fortitude.

"But have you not got your carriage?" asked the girl.

"The carriage is down near the great entrance."

"Not so," she replied. "I considered your coachman to be a faithful man, and I told him to wait for you at the postern."

The two brothers looked first at each other and then at Rosa, with a glance full of the most tender gratitude.

"The question is now," said the Grand Pensionary, "whether Gryphus will open this door for us."

"Indeed he will do no such thing," said Rosa.

"Well, and how then?"

"I have foreseen his refusal, and just now, while he was talking from the window of the porter's lodge with a dragoon, I took away the key from his bunch."

"And you have got it?"

"Here it is, Mynheer John."

"My child," said Cornelius, "I have nothing to give you in exchange for the service you are rendering us, but the Bible which you will find in my room: it is the last gift of an honest man; I hope it will bring you good luck."

"I thank you, Master Cornelius, it shall never leave me," replied Rosa.

And then, with a sigh, she said to herself, "What a pity that I do not know how to read!"

"The shouts and cries are growing louder and louder," said John; there is not a moment to be lost."

"Come along, gentlemen," said the girl, who now led the two brothers through an inner lobby to the back of the prison. Guided by her, they descended a staircase of about a dozen steps; traversed a small courtyard, which was surrounded by castellated walls; and, the arched door having been opened for them by Rosa, they emerged into a lonely street where their carriage was ready to receive them.

"Quick, quick, my masters, do you hear them?" cried the coachman in a deadly fright.

Yet, after having made Cornelius get into the carriage first, the Grand Pensionary turned round towards the girl, to whom he said:

"Good-bye, my child, words could never express our gratitude. God will reward you for having saved the lives of two men."

Rosa took the hand which John De Witte proffered to her, and kissed it with every show of respect.

"Go—for Heaven's sake, go," she said; "it seems they are going to force the gate."

John De Witte hastily got in, sat himself down by the side of his brother, and, fastening the apron of the carriage, called to the coachman:

"To the Tol-Hek!"

The Tol-Hek was the iron gate leading to the harbour of Schevening, in which a small vessel was waiting for the two brothers.

The carriage drove off with the fugitives at the full speed of a pair of spirited Flemish horses. Rosa followed them with her eyes, until they turned the corner of the street, upon which, closing the door after her, she went back and threw the key into a well.

The noise which had made Rosa suppose that the people were forcing the prison door, was indeed owing to the mob battering against it after the square had been left by the military.

Solid as the gate was, and although Gryphus, to do him justice, stoutly enough refused to open it; yet it could not evidently resist much longer, and the jailer, growing very pale, put to himself the question whether it would not be better to open the door than to allow it to be forced: when he felt someone gently pulling his coat.

He turned round and saw Rosa.

" Do you hear these madmen?" he said.

" I hear them so well, my father, that in your place——"

" You would open the door?"

" No, I should allow it to be forced."

" But they will kill me?"

" Yes, if they see you."

" How shall they not see me?"

" Hide yourself."

" Where?"

" In the secret dungeon."

" But you, my child?"

" I shall get into it with you. We shall lock the door, and when they have left the prison, we shall again come forth from our hiding-place."

" Zounds, you are right there!" cried Gryphus; " it's surprising how much sense there is in such a little head!"

Then, as the gate began to give way amidst the triumphant shouts of the mob, she opened a little trap-door, and said:

" Come along, come along, father."

" But our prisoners?"

" God will watch over them, and I shall watch over you."

Gryphus followed his daughter, and the trap-door closed over his head, just as the broken gate gave admittance to the populace.

The dungeon where Rosa had induced her father to hide himself, and where for the present we must leave the two, offered to them a perfectly safe retreat, being known only to those in power, who used to place there important prisoners of state, to guard against a rescue, or a revolt.

The people rushed into the prison, with the cry of—" Death to the traitors! To the gallows with Cornelius De Witte! Death! death!"

CHAPTER IV

POPULAR JUSTICE

The young man, with his hat still slouched over his eyes, still learning on the arm of the officer, and still wiping from time to time his brow with his handkerchief, was watching in a corner of the Buitenhof, in the shade of the overhanging weatherboard of a closed shop, the doings of the infuriated mob, a spectacle which seemed to draw near its catastrophe.

" Indeed," said he to the officer, " indeed, I think you were right, Van Deken; the order which the deputies have signed, is truly the death-warrant of Master Cornelius. Do you hear

these people? They certainly bear a sad grudge to the two
De Wittes."

"In truth," replied the officer, "I never heard such shouts."

"They seem to have found out the cell of the man.
Look, look, is not that the window of the cell where Cornelius was locked up?"

A man had seized with both hands, and was shaking the
iron bars of the window, in the room which Cornelius had
left only ten minutes before.

"Halloa, halloa," the man called out, "he is gone."

"How is that? gone?" asked those of the mob who had
not been able to get into the prison, crowded as it was with
the mass of intruders.

"Gone, gone," repeated the man in a rage, "the bird has
flown."

"What does this man say?" asked His Highness, growing
quite pale.

"Oh! Monseigneur, he says a thing which would be very
fortunate if it should turn out true!"

"Certainly, it would be fortunate if it were true," said the
young man; "unfortunately it cannot be true."

"However, look——" said the officer.

And indeed, some more faces, furious and contorted with
rage, showed themselves at the windows, crying:

"Escaped, gone, they have helped them off!"

And the people in the street repeated with fearful imprecations:

"Escaped! gone! Let us run after them, and pursue
them!"

"Monseigneur, it seems that Mynheer Cornelius has really
escaped," said the officer.

"Yes, from prison perhaps but not from the town; you
will see, Van Deken, that the poor fellow will find the gate
closed against him, which he hoped to find open."

"Has an order been given to close the town gates, Monseigneur?"

"No, at least I do not think so; who could have given such
an order?"

"Indeed, but what makes your Highness suppose——?"

"There are fatalities," Monseigneur replied, in an off-hand
manner; "and the greatest men have sometimes fallen victims
to such fatalities."

At these words the officer felt his blood run cold, as somehow or other he was convinced that the prisoner was lost.

At this moment the roar of the multitude broke forth like

thunder, for it was now quite certain that Cornelius De Witte was no longer in the prison.

Cornelius and John, after driving along the pond, had taken the large street which leads to the Tol-Hek, giving directions to the coachman to slacken his pace, in order not to excite any suspicion.

But when, on having proceeded half-way down that street, the man felt that he had left the prison and death behind, and before him there was life and liberty, he neglected every precaution, and set his horses off at a gallop.

All at once he stopped.

" What is the matter?" asked John, putting his head out of the coach-window.

" Oh! my masters," cried the coachman, " it is——"

Terror choked the voice of the honest fellow.

" Well, say what you have to say!" urged the Grand Pensionary.

" The gate is closed, that's what it is."

"How is this? It is not usual to close the gate by day."

"Just look!"

John De Witte leaned out of the window, and indeed saw that the man was right.

" Never mind, but drive on," said John; " I have with me the order for the commutation of the punishment, the gate-keeper will let us through."

The carriage moved along, but it was evident that the driver was no longer urging his horses with the same degree of confidence.

Moreover, as John De Witte put his head out of the carriage-window, he was seen and recognised by a brewer, who, being behind his companions, was just shutting his door in all haste to join them at the Buitenhof. He uttered a cry of surprise, and ran after two men before him, whom he overtook about a hundred yards further on, and told them what he had seen. The three men then stopped, looking after the carriage, being, however, not yet quite sure as to whom it contained.

The carriage, in the meanwhile, arrived at the Tol-Hek.

" Open!" cried the coachman.

" Open!" echoed the gatekeeper, from the threshold of his lodge; " it's all very well to say open, but what am I to do it with?"

" With the key, to be sure!" said the coachman.

" With the key! Oh, yes! but if you have not got it?"

" How is that? Have you not got the key?" asked the coachman.

" No, I haven't."

" What has become of it?"

" Well, they have taken it from me."

" Who?"

" Someone, I dare say, who had a mind that no one should leave the town."

" My good man," said the Grand Pensionary, putting out his head from the window, and risking all for gaining all; " my good man, it is for me, John De Witt, and for my brother Cornelius, whom I am taking away into exile."

" Oh! Mynheer De Witt, I am indeed very much grieved," said the gatekeeper, rushing towards the carriage; " but upon my sacred word, the key has been taken from me."

" When?"

" This morning."

" By whom?"

" By a pale and thin young man, of about twenty-two."

" And wherefore did you give it up to him?"

" Because he showed me an order, signed and sealed."

" By whom?"

" By the gentlemen of the Town-hall."

" Well, then," said Cornelius calmly, " our doom seems to be fixed."

" Do you know whether the same precaution has been taken at the other gates?"

" I do not."

" Now, then," said John to the coachman, " God commands man to do all that is in his power to preserve his life; go, and drive to another gate."

And whilst the servant was turning round the vehicle, the Grand Pensionary said to the gatekeeper:

" Take our thanks for your good intentions; the will must count for the deed; you had the will to save us, and, in the eyes of the Lord, it is as if you had succeeded in doing so."

" Alas!" said the gatekeeper, " do you see down there?"

" Drive at a gallop through that group," John called out to the coachman, " and take the street on the left; it is our only chance."

The group which John alluded to had, for its nucleus, those three men whom we left looking after the carriage, and who, in the meanwhile, had been joined by seven or eight others.

These new-comers evidently meant mischief with regard to the carriage.

When they saw the horses galloping down upon them, they placed themselves across the street, brandishing cudgels in their hands, and calling out:

"Stop! stop!"

The coachman, on his side, lashed his horses into increased speed, until the coach and the men encountered each other.

The brothers De Witte, inclosed within the body of the carriage, were not able to see anything; but they felt a severe shock, occasioned by the rearing of the horses. The whole vehicle for a moment shook and stopped; but immediately after passing over something round and elastic, which seemed to be the body of a prostrate man, set off again amidst a volley of the fiercest oaths.

"Alas!" said Cornelius, "I am afraid we have hurt someone."

"Gallop! gallop!" called John.

But, notwithstanding this order, the coachman suddenly came to a stop.

"Now then, what is the matter again?" asked John.

"Look there!" said the coachman.

John looked. The whole mass of the populace from the Buitenhof appeared at the extremity of the street along which the carriage was to proceed, and its stream moved roaring and rapid, as if lashed on by a hurricane.

"Stop, and get off," said John to the coachman; "it is useless to go any farther: we are lost!"

"Here they are! here they are!" five hundred voices were crying at the same time.

"Yes, here they are, the traitors, the murderers, the assassins!" answered the men who were running after the carriage, to the people who were coming to meet it. The former carried in their arms the bruised body of one of their companions, who, trying to seize the reins of the horses, had been trodden down by them.

This was the object over which the two brothers had felt their carriage pass.

The coachman stopped, but, however strongly his master urged him, he refused to get off and save himself.

In an instant, the carriage was hemmed in between those who followed and those who met it. It rose above the mass of moving heads like a floating island. But in another instant it came to a dead stop. A blacksmith had, with his hammer, struck down one of the horses, which fell in the traces.

At this moment the shutter of a window opened, and disclosed the sallow face and the dark eyes of the young man, who with intense interest watched the scene which was preparing.

Behind him appeared the head of the officer, almost as pale as himself.

"Good heavens, Monseigneur, what is going on there?" whispered the officer.

"Something very terrible, to a certainty," replied the other.

"Don't you see, Monseigneur, they are dragging the Grand Pensionary from the carriage, they strike him, they tear him to pieces."

"Indeed, these people must certainly be prompted by a most violent indignation," said the young man, with the same impassible tone which he had preserved all along.

"And here is Cornelius, whom they now likewise drag out of the carriage—Cornelius, who is already quite broken and mangled by the torture. Only look, look!"

"Indeed, it is Cornelius, and no mistake."

The officer uttered a feeble cry, and turned his head away; the brother of the Grand Pensionary, before having set foot on the ground, whilst still on the bottom step of the carriage, was struck down with an iron bar which broke his skull. He rose once more, but immediately fell again.

Some fellows then seized him by the feet, and dragged him into the crowd, into the middle of which one might have followed his bloody track, and he was soon closed in among the savage yells of malignant exultation.

The young man—a thing which would have been thought impossible—grew even paler than before, and his eyes were for a moment veiled behind the lids.

The officer saw this sign of compassion, and, wishing to avail himself of the softened tone of his feelings, continued:

"Come, come, Monseigneur, for here they are also going to murder the Grand Pensionary."

But the young man had already opened his eyes again.

"To be sure," he said. "These people are really implacable. It does no one good to offend them."

"Monseigneur," said the officer, "could not one save this poor man, who has been your Highness's instructor? If there be a means name it, and if I should perish in the attempt——"

William of Orange—for it was he—knit his brows in a very forbidding manner, restrained the glance of gloomy malice which glistened in his half-closed eye, and answered:

"Captain Van Deken, I request you to go and look after my troops, that they may be armed for any emergency."

"But am I to leave your Highness here, alone, in the presence of all these murderers?"

"Go, and don't you trouble yourself about me more than I do myself," the Prince gruffly replied.

The officer started off with a speed which was much less

owing to his sense of military obedience than to his pleasure at being relieved from the necessity of witnessing the shocking spectacle of the murder of the other brother.

He had scarcely left the room, when John—who with an almost superhuman effort had reached the stone steps of a house, nearly opposite that where his former pupil concealed himself—began to stagger under the blows which were inflicted on him from all sides, calling out:

"My brother—where is my brother?"

One of the ruffians knocked off his hat with a blow of his clenched fist.

Another showed to him his bloody hands; for this fellow had ripped open Cornelius and disembowelled him, and was now hastening to the spot in order not to lose the opportunity of serving the Grand Pensionary in the same manner, whilst they were dragging the dead body of Cornelius to the gibbet.

John uttered a cry of agony and grief, and put one of his hands before his eyes.

"Oh! you close your eyes, do you?" said one of the soldiers of the burgher-guard; "well, I shall open them for you."

And saying this, he stabbed him with his pike in the face, and the blood spurted forth.

"My brother!" cried John De Witte, trying to see, through the stream of blood which blinded him, what had become of Cornelius; "my brother, my brother!"

"Go, and run after him!" bellowed another murderer, putting his musket to his temples and pulling the trigger.

But the gun did not go off.

The fellow then turned his musket round, and, taking it by the barrel with both hands, struck John De Witte down with the butt-end. John staggered and fell down at his feet, but raising himself with a last effort, he once more called out:

"My brother!" with a voice so full of anguish, that the young man opposite closed the shutter.

There remained little more to see; a third murderer fired a pistol with the muzzle to his face; and as this time the shot took effect, blowing out his brains, John De Witte fell, to rise no more.

On this, every one of the miscreants, emboldened by his fall, wanted to fire his gun at him, or strike him with blows of the sledge-hammer, or stab him with knife or sword; every one wanted to draw a drop of blood from the fallen hero, and tear off a shred from his garments.

And after having mangled, and torn, and completely stripped the two brothers, the mob dragged their naked and bloody bodies to an extemporised gibbet, where amateur executioners hung them up by the feet.

Then came the most dastardly scoundrels of all, who, not having dared to strike the living flesh, cut the dead in pieces, and then went about in the town selling small slices of the bodies of John and Cornelius at ten sous a piece.

We cannot take upon ourselves to say whether, through the almost imperceptible chink of the shutter, the young man witnessed the conclusion of this shocking scene; but at the very moment when they were hanging the two martyrs on the gibbet, he passed through the terrible mob, which was too much absorbed in the task so grateful to its taste, to take any notice of him; and thus he reached unobserved the Tol-Hek, which was still closed.

"Ah! Sir," said the gatekeeper, "do you bring me the key?"

"Yes, my man, here it is."

"It is most unfortunate that you did not bring me that key only one quarter of an hour sooner," said the gatekeeper with a sigh.

"And why so?" asked the other.

"Because I might have opened the gate to Mynheers De Witte; whereas, finding the gate locked, they were obliged to retrace their steps."

"Gate! gate!" cried a voice which seemed to be that of a man in a hurry.

The Prince, turning round, observed Captain Van Deken.

"Is that you, Captain?" he said. "You are not yet out of the Hague? This is executing my orders very slowly."

"Monseigneur," replied the Captain, "this is the third gate at which I have presented myself; the two others were closed."

"Well, this good man will open this one for you; do it my friend."

The last words were addressed to the gatekeeper, who stood quite thunderstruck on hearing Captain Van Deken addressing by the title of Monseigneur this pale young man, to whom he himself had spoken in such a familiar way.

As it were, to make up for his fault, he hastened to open the gate, which swung creaking on its hinges.

"Will Monseigneur avail himself of my horse?" asked the Captain.

"I thank you, Captain, I shall use my own steed, which is waiting for me close at hand."

And, taking from his pocket a golden whistle, such as was generally used at that time for summoning the servants, he sounded it with a shrill and prolonged call, upon which an equerry on horseback speedily made his appearance, leading another horse by the bridle.

William, without touching the stirrup, vaulted into the saddle of the led horse, and, setting his spurs into its flanks, started off for the Leyden road. Having reached it, he turned round and beckoned to the Captain, who was far behind, to ride by his side.

"Do you know," he then said, without stopping, "that those rascals have killed John De Witte as well as his brother?"

"Alas! Monseigneur," the Captain answered sadly, "I should like it much better if these two difficulties were still in your Highness's way of becoming *de facto* Stadtholder of Holland."

"Certainly, it would have been better," said William, "if what did happen had not happened. But it cannot be helped now, and we have had nothing to do with it. Let us push on, Captain, that we may arrive at Alphen before the message which the States-General are sure to send to me to the camp."

The Captain bowed, allowed the Prince to ride ahead, and, for the remainder of the journey, kept at the same respectful distance as he had done before his Highness called him to his side.

"How I should like," William of Orange malignantly muttered to himself, with a dark frown and setting spurs to his horse, "to see the figure which Louis will cut when he is apprised of the manner in which his dear friends De Witte have been served!"

CHAPTER V

THE TULIP FANCIER AND HIS NEIGHBOUR

While the burghers of the Hague were tearing in pieces the bodies of John and Cornelius De Witte, and while William of Orange, after having made sure that his two antagonists were really dead, was galloping on the Leyden road, followed by Captain Van Deken, whom he found a little too compassionate to honour him any longer with his confidence, Craeke, the faithful servant, mounted on a good horse, and little suspecting what terrible events had taken place since his departure, proceeded along the high road lined with trees, until he was clear of the town and the neighbouring villages.

Being once safe, he, with a view of avoiding suspicion, left his horse at a livery-stable, and, quietly continuing his journey on the canal-boats to Dort, soon descried that cheerful city at the foot of a hill dotted with windmills. He saw the fine red brick houses, mortared in white lines, standing on the edge of the water, and their balconies, open towards the river, decked out with silk tapestry embroidered with gold flowers, the wonderful manufacture of India and China; and near these brilliant stuffs, large lines set to catch the voracious eels, which are attracted towards the houses by the garbage thrown every day from the kitchens into the river.

Craeke, standing on the deck of the boat, saw, across the moving sails of the windmills, on the slope of the hill, the red and pink house which was the goal of his errand. The outlines of its roof were merging in the yellow foliage of a curtain of poplar trees, the whole habitation having for background a dark grove of gigantic elms. The mansion was situated in such a way, that the sun, falling on it as into a funnel, dried up, warmed, and fertilised the mist which the verdant screen could not prevent the river-wind from carrying there every morning and evening.

Having disembarked unobserved among the usual bustle of the city, Craeke at once directed his steps towards the house which we have just described, and which—white, trim, and tidy, even more cleanly scoured and more carefully waxed in the hidden corners than in the places which were exposed to view—enclosed a truly happy mortal.

This happy mortal *rara avis* was Doctor Van Baerle, the godson of Cornelius De Witte. He had inhabited the same house ever since his childhood; for it was the house in which his father and grandfather, old-established princely merchants of the princely city of Dort, were born.

Mynheer Van Baerle, the father, had amassed, in the Indian trade, three or four hundred thousand guilders, which Mynheer Van Baerle, the son, at the death of his dear and worthy parents, found still quite new, although one set of them bore the date of coinage of 1640, and the other that of 1610, a fact which proved that they were guilders of Van Baerle the father, and of Van Baerle the grandfather; but we will inform the reader at once, that these three or four hundred thousand guilders were only the pocket-money, or a sort of purse, for Cornelius Van Baerle, the hero of this story, as his landed property in the province yielded him an income of about ten thousand guilders a year.

When the worthy citizen, the father of Cornelius, passed from time into eternity, three months after having buried his wife, who seemed to have departed first to smooth for him the path of death as she had smoothed for him the path of life, he said to his son, as he embraced him for the last time:

"Eat, drink, and spend your money, if you wish to know what life really is; for as to toiling from morn to evening on a wooden stool, or a leathern chair, in a counting-house or a laboratory, that certainly is not living. Your time to die will also come; and if you are not then so fortunate as to have a son, you will let my name grow extinct, and my guilders, which no one has ever fingered but my father, myself, and the coiner, will have the surprise of passing to an unknown master. And least of all imitate the example of your godfather, Cornelius De Witt, who has plunged into politics, the most ungrateful of all careers, and who will certainly come to an untimely end."

Having given utterance to this paternal advice, the worthy Mynheer Van Baerle died, to the intense grief of his son, Cornelius, who cared very little for the guilders, and very much for his father.

Cornelius then remained alone in his large house. In vain his godfather offered to him a place in the public service; in vain did he try to give him a taste for glory. Cornelius Van Baerle, who was present in De Ruyter's flagship, "The Seven Provinces," at the battle of Southwold Bay, only calculated, after the fight was over, how much time a man, who likes to shut himself up within his own thoughts, is obliged to waste in closing his eyes and stopping his ears, whilst his fellow-creatures indulge in the pleasure of shooting at each other with cannon-balls. He, therefore, bade farewell to De Ruyter, to his godfather, and to glory; kissed the hands of the Grand Pensionary, for whom he felt a profound veneration, and retired to his house at Dort, where he possessed every element of what alone was happiness to him.

He studied plants and insects, collected and classified the Flora of all the Dutch islands, arranged the whole entomology of the province, on which he wrote a treatise, with plates drawn by his own hands; and at last, being at a loss what to do with his time, and especially with his money, which went on accumulating at a most alarming rate, he took it into his head to select for himself, from all the follies of his country and of his age, one of the most elegant and expensive—he became a tulip-fancier.

It was the time when the Dutch and the Portuguese, rivalling each other in this branch of horticulture, had begun to idolize and almost worship that flower, which originally had come from the East.

Soon people from Dort to Mons began to talk of Mynheer

Van Baerle's tulips; and his beds, pits, drying-rooms, and drawers of bulbs were visited, as the galleries and libraries of Alexandria were by illustrious Roman travellers.

Van Baerle began by expending his yearly revenue in laying the ground-work of his collection, after which he broke in upon his new guilders to bring it to perfection. His exertions, indeed, were crowned with a most magnificent result: he produced three new tulips, which he called the "Jane," after his mother; the "Van Baerle," after his father; and the "Cornelius," after his godfather; the other names have escaped us, but the fanciers will be sure to find them in the catalogues of the times.

In the beginning of the year 1672, Cornelius De Witte came to Dort for three months, to live at his old family mansion; for not only was he born in that city, but his family had been resident there for centuries.

Cornelius, at that period, as William of Orange said, began to enjoy the most perfect unpopularity. To his fellow-citizens, the good burghers of Dort, however, he did not appear in the light of a criminal who deserved to be hanged. It is true, they did not particularly like his somewhat too austere republicanism, but they were proud of his valour; and when he made his entrance into their town, the cup of honour was offered to him, readily enough, in the name of the city.

After having thanked his fellow-citizens, Cornelius proceeded to his old paternal house, and gave directions for some repairs, which he wished to have executed before the arrival of his wife and children; and thence he wended his way to the house of his godson, who, perhaps, was the only person in Dort as yet unacquainted with the presence of Cornelius in the town.

In the same degree as Cornelius De Witte had excited the hatred of the people, by sowing those evil seeds which are called political passions, Van Baerle had gained the affections of his fellow-citizens by completely shunning the pursuit of politics, absorbed as he was in the peaceful pursuit of cultivating tulips.

Van Baerle was truly beloved by his servants and labourers; nor had he any conception that there was in this world a man who wished ill to another.

And yet it must be said, to the disgrace of mankind, that Cornelius Van Baerle, without being aware of the fact, had a much more ferocious, fierce, and implacable enemy than the Grand Pensionary and his brother had among the Orange party.

At the time when Cornelius Van Baerle began to devote himself to tulip-growing, expending on this hobby his yearly revenue and the guilders of his father, there was at Dort, living next door to him, a citizen of the name of Isaac Boxtel, who, from the age when he was able to think for himself, had indulged the same fancy, and who was in ecstasies at the mere mention of the word tulips.

Boxtel had not the good fortune of being rich like Van Baerle. He had, therefore, with great care and patience, and by dint of strenuous exertions, laid out, near his house at Dort, a garden fit for the culture of his cherished flower; he had mixed the soil according to the most approved prescriptions, and given to his hotbeds just as much heat and fresh air as the strictest rules of horticulture exact.

Isaac knew the temperature of his frames to the twentieth part of a degree. He knew the strength of the current of air, and tempered it so as to adapt it to the wave of the stems of his flowers. His productions also began to meet with the favour of the public. They were beautiful, nay, distinguished. Several fanciers had come to see Boxtel's tulips. He had even started a tulip which bore his name, and which, after having travelled all through France had found its way into Spain, and penetrated as far as Portugal; and the King, Don Alphonso VI—who, being expelled from Lisbon, retired to the Island of Terceira, where he amused himself, not, like the Great Condé, with watering his carnations, but with growing tulips—had, on seeing the Boxtel tulip, exclaimed: "Not so bad, by any means!"

All at once, Cornelius Van Baerle, who, after all his learned pursuits, had been seized with the tulipomania, made some changes in his house at Dort, which, as we have stated, was next door to that of Boxtel. He raised a certain building in his courtyard by a story, which, shutting out the sun, took half a degree of warmth from Boxtel's garden, and, on the other hand, added half a degree of cold in winter: not to mention that it cut the wind, and disturbed all the horticultural calculations and arrangements of his neighbour.

After all, this mishap appeared to Boxtel of no great consequence. Van Baerle was but a painter, a sort of fool who tried to reproduce, and disfigure on canvas, the wonders of nature. The painter, he thought, had raised his studio by a story to get better light, and thus he had only been in the right. Mynheer Van Baerle was a painter, as Mynheer Boxtel was a tulip-grower; he wanted somewhat more sun for his paintings, and he took half a degree from his neighbour's tulips.

The law was for Van Baerle, and Boxtel had to abide by it. Besides which, Isaac had made the discovery that too much sun was injurious to tulips, and that this flower grew quicker, and had a better colouring, with the temperate warmth of morning, than with the powerful heat of the midday sun. He, therefore, felt almost grateful to Cornelius Van Baerle for having given him a screen gratis.

Maybe this was not quite in accordance with the true state of things in general, and of Isaac Boxtel's feelings in particular. It is certainly astonishing what rich comfort great minds, in the midst of momentous catastrophes, will derive from the consolations of philosophy.

But, alas! what was the agony of the unfortunate Boxtel on seeing the windows of the new story set out with bulbs and seedlings of tulips for the border, and tulips in pots; in short, with everything pertaining to the pursuits of a tulip-fancier.

There were bundles of labels, cupboards, and drawers with compartments, and wire-guards for the cupboards, to allow free access to the air whilst keeping out slugs, mice, dormice, and rats, all of them very curious fanciers of tulips at two thousand francs a bulb.

Boxtel was quite amazed when he saw all this apparatus, but he was not as yet aware of the full extent of his misfortune. Van Baerle was known to be fond of everything that pleases the eye. He studied nature in all her aspects for the benefit of his paintings, which were as minutely finished as those of Gerard Dow, his master, and of Mieris, his friend. Was it not possible that, having to paint the interior of a tulip-grower's, he had collected in his new studio all the accessories of decoration?

Yet, although thus consoling himself with illusory suppositions, Boxtel was not able to resist the burning curiosity which was devouring him. In the evening, therefore, he placed a ladder against the partition-wall between their gardens, and, looking into that of his neighbour, Van Baerle, he convinced himself that the soil of a large square bed, which had formerly been occupied by different plants, was removed, and the ground disposed in beds of loam mixed with river mud (a combination which is particularly favourable to the tulip), and the whole surrounded by a border of turf to keep the soil in its place. Besides this, sufficient shade to temper the noonday heat; aspect S.S.W.; water in abundant supply, and at hand; in short, every requirement to ensure not only success but also progress. There could not be a doubt but that Van Baerle had become a tulip-grower.

Boxtel at once pictured to himself this learned man, with a capital of four hundred thousand, and a yearly income of ten thousand guilders, devoting all his intellectual and financial resources to the cultivation of the tulip. He foresaw his neighbour's success, and he felt such a pang at the mere idea of this success, that his hands dropped powerless, his knees trembled, and he fell in despair from the ladder.

And thus it was not for the sake of painted tulips, but for real ones, that Van Baerle took from him half a degree of warmth. And thus Van Baerle was to have the most admirably-fitted aspect, and, besides, a large, airy and well-ventilated chamber, where to preserve his bulbs and seedlings; whilst he, Boxtel, had been obliged to give up for this purpose his bedroom, and, lest his sleeping in the same apartment might injure his bulbs and seedlings, had taken up his abode in a miserable garret.

Boxtel, then, was to have next door to him a rival and successful competitor; and his rival instead of being some unknown, obscure gardener, was the godson of Mynheer Cornelius De Witte, that is to say, a celebrity.

Boxtel, as the reader may see, was not possessed of the spirit of Porus, who, on being conquered by Alexander, consoled himself with the celebrity of his conqueror.

And how if Van Baerle produced a new tulip, and named it the John De Witte, after having named one the Cornelius? It was indeed enough to choke honest Isaac with rage.

Thus Boxtel, with jealous foreboding, became the prophet of his own misfortune. And, after having made this melancholy discovery, he passed the most wretched night imaginable.

CHAPTER VI

THE HATRED OF A TULIP-FANCIER

From that moment Boxtel's interest in tulips was no longer a stimulus to his exertions, but a deadening anxiety. Henceforth all his thoughts ran only upon the injury which his neighbour would cause him, and thus his favourite occupation was changed into a constant source of misery to him.

Van Baerle, as may easily be imagined, had no sooner begun to apply his natural ingenuity to his new fancy, than he succeeded in growing the finest tulips. Indeed, he knew better than any one else at Haarlem or Leyden—the two towns which boast the best soil and the most congenial climate—how to vary the colours, to modify the shape, and to produce new species.

Mynheer Van Baerle and his tulips, therefore, were in the mouth of everybody; so much so, that Boxtel's name disappeared for ever from the list of the notable tulip-growers in Holland, and those of Dort were now represented by Cornelius Van Baerle, the modest and inoffensive savant.

Engaging, heart and soul, in his pursuits of sowing, planting, and gathering, Van Baerle, caressed by the whole fraternity of tulip growers in Europe, entertained not the least suspicion that there was at his very door a pretender whose throne he had usurped.

He went on in his career, and consequently in his triumphs; and, in the course of two years, he covered his borders with such marvellous productions, as no mortal man, following in the tracks of the Creator, except, perhaps, Shakespeare and Rubens, have equalled in point of numbers.

And also if Dante had wished for a new type to be added to his characters of the Inferno, he might have chosen Boxtel during the period of Van Baerle's successes. Whilst Cornelius was weeding, manuring, watering his beds; whilst, kneeling on the turf-border, he analysed every vein of the flowering tulips, and meditated on the modifications which might be effected by crosses of colour or otherwise—Boxtel, concealed behind a small sycamore which he had trained at the top of the partition-wall in the shape of a fan, watched, with his eyes starting from their sockets, and with foaming mouth, every step and every gesture of his neighbour; and, whenever he thought he saw him look happy, or descried a smile on his lips, or a flash of contentment glistening in his eyes, he poured out towards him such a volley of maledictions and furious threats, as to make it indeed a matter of wonder that this venomous breath of envy and hatred did not carry a blight on the innocent flowers which had excited it.

When the evil spirit has once taken hold of the heart of man, it urges him on without letting him stop. Thus Boxtel soon was no longer content with seeing Van Baerle. He wanted to see his flowers too; he had the feelings of an artist; the masterpiece of a rival engrossed his interest.

He, therefore, bought a telescope, which enabled him to watch, as accurately as did the owner himself, every progressive development of the flower, from the moment when, in the first year, its pale seed-leaf begins to peep from the ground, to that glorious one when, after five years, its petals at last reveal the hidden treasures of its chalice. How often had the miserable jealous man to observe, in Van Baerle's bed, tulips which dazzled him by their beauty and almost choked him by their perfection.

And then, after the first blush of the admiration which he could not help feeling, he began to be tortured by the pangs of envy, by that slow fever which creeps over the heart and changes it into a nest of vipers, each devouring the other and ever born anew. How often did Boxtel, in the midst of tortures which no pen is able fully to describe—how often did he feel an inclination to jump down into the garden, during the night, to destroy the plants, to tear the bulbs with his teeth, and to sacrifice to his wrath the owner himself, if he should venture to stand up for the defence of his tulips.

But to kill a tulip was a horrible crime in the eyes of a genuine tulip-fancier; as to killing a man, it would not have mattered so very much.

Yet Van Baerle made such progress in the noble science of growing tulips, which he seemed to master with the true instinct of genius, that Boxtel at last was maddened to such a degree as to think of throwing stones and sticks into the flower-stands of his neighbour. But, remembering that he would be sure to be found out, and that he would not only be punished by law, but also dishonoured for ever in the face of all the tulip-growers of Europe, he had recourse to stratagem; and, to gratify his hatred, tried to devise a plan by means of which he might gain his ends without being compromised himself.

He considered a long time, and at last his meditations were crowned with success.

One evening he tied two cats together by their hind-legs with a string about six feet in length, and threw them from the wall into the midst of that noble, that princely, that royal bed, which contained not only the " Cornelius De Witte," but, besides, the " Beauty of Brabant," milk white, edged with purple and pink; the " Marble of Rotterdam," colour of flax-blossom, feathered red and flesh colour; and the " Wonder of Haarlem," dark dove colour, tinged with a lighter shade of the same.

The frightened cats, having alighted on the ground, first tried to fly each in a different direction, until the string by which they were tied together was tightly stretched across the bed; then, however, feeling that they were not able to get off, they began to pull to and fro, and wheel about with heart-rending caterwaulings, mowing down with their string the flowers among which they were disporting themselves, until, after a furious strife of about a quarter of an hour, the string broke and the combatants vanished.

Boxtel, hidden behind his sycamore, could not see anything, as it was pitch dark; but the piercing cries of the cats told the whole tale, and his heart, overflowing with gall, was now throbbing with triumphant joy.

Boxtel was so eager to ascertain the extent of the injury, that he remained on his post until morning to feast his eyes at the sad state in which the two cats had placed the flower-beds of his neighbour. The mists of the morning chilled his frame, but he did not feel the cold, the hope of revenge keeping his blood at fever heat. The chagrin of his rival was to pay for all the inconvenience which he incurred himself.

At the earliest dawn the door of the white house opened, and Van Baerle made his appearance, approaching the flower-beds with the smile of a man who has passed the night comfortably in his bed, and has had happy dreams.

All at once he perceived furrows and little mounds of earth on the beds, which only the evening before had been as smooth as a mirror; all at once he perceived the symmetrical rows of his tulips to be completely disordered, like the pikes of a battalion in the midst of which a shell has fallen.

He ran up to them with blanched cheek.

Boxtel trembled with joy. Fifteen or twenty tulips, torn and crushed, were lying about, some of them bent, others completely broken and already withering, the sap was oozing from their bleeding bulbs; how gladly would Van Baerle have redeemed that precious sap with his own blood!

But what were his surprise and his delight! what was the disappointment of his rival! Not one of the four tulips which the latter had meant to destroy was injured at all. They raised proudly their noble heads above the corpses of their slain companions. This was enough to console Van Baerle, and enough to fan the rage of the horticultural murderer, who tore his hair at the sight of the effects of the crime which he had committed in vain.

Van Baerle could not imagine the cause of the mishap, which, fortunately, was of far less consequence than it might have been. On making inquiries, he learned that the whole night had been disturbed by terrible caterwaulings. He, besides, found traces of the cats, their footmarks and hairs left behind on the battlefield; to guard, therefore, in future against a similar outrage, he gave orders that henceforth one of the under-gardeners should sleep in the garden in a sentry-box near the flower beds.

Boxtel heard him give the order, and saw the sentry-box put up that very day; but he deemed himself lucky in not having been suspected, and, being more than ever incensed against the successful horticulturist, he resolved to bide his time.

Just then the Tulip Society of Haarlem offered a prize for the production of the large black tulip without a spot of colour, a thing which had not yet been accomplished, and was considered impossible, as at that time there did not exist a flower of that species approaching even to dark nut-brown. It was, therefore, generally said that the founders of the prize might just as well have offered two millions as a hundred thousand guilders, since no one would be able to gain it.

The tulip-growing world, however, was thrown by it into a state of most active commotion. Some fanciers caught at the idea without believing it practicable; but such is the power of imagination among florists, that, although considering the undertaking as certain to fail, all their thoughts were engrossed by that grand black tulip, which was looked upon as chimerical, as the black swan or the white raven were reputed to be in those days.

Van Baerle was one of the tulip-growers who were struck with the idea; Boxtel thought of it in the light of a speculation. Van Baerle, as soon as the idea had once taken root in his clear and ingenious mind, began slowly the necessary sowings and operations to reduce the tulips, which he had grown already, from red to brown, and from brown to dark brown.

By the next year he had obtained flowers of a perfect nut-brown, and Boxtel espied them in the border, whereas he had himself, as yet, only succeeded in producing the light brown.

Boxtel, once more worsted by the superiority of his hated rival, was now completely disgusted with tulip-growing, and, being driven half mad, devoted himself entirely to observation.

The house of his rival was quite open to view: a garden exposed to the sun; cabinets with glass walls, shelves, cupboards, boxes and ticketed pigeon-holes, which could easily be surveyed by the telescope. Boxtel allowed his bulbs to rot in the pits, his seedlings to dry up in their cases, and his tulips to wither in the borders, and henceforward occupied himself with nothing else but the doings at Van Baerle's.

But the most curious part of the occupation was not performed in the garden.

It might be one o'clock in the morning when Van Baerle went up to his laboratory, into the glazed cabinet whither Boxtel's telescope had such easy access; and here, as soon as the lamp illuminated the walls and windows, Boxtel saw the inventive genius of his rival at work.

He beheld him sifting his seeds, and soaking them in liquids which were destined to modify or to deepen their colours. He knew what Cornelius meant, when heating certain grains, then moistening them, then combining them with others by a sort of grafting—a minute and marvellously delicate manipulation—he shut up in darkness those which were expected to furnish the black colour; exposed to the sun or to the lamp those which were to produce red; and placed between the endless reflection of two water mirrors those intended for white, the pure representation of the limpid element.

This innocent magic, the fruit at the same time of child-like musings and of manly genius—this patient untiring labour, of which Boxtel knew himself to be incapable—made him, gnawed as he was with envy, centre all his life, all his thoughts, and all his hopes, in his telescope.

For, strange to say, the love and interest of horticulture had not deadened in Isaac his fierce envy and thirst of revenge. Sometimes, whilst covering Van Baerle with his telescope, he deluded himself into a belief that he was levelling a never-failing musket at him; and then he would seek with his finger for the trigger to fire the shot which was to have killed his neighbour. But it is time that we should connect with this epoch of the operations of the one, and the espionage of the other, the visit which Cornelius De Witte came to pay to his native town.

CHAPTER VII

THE HAPPY MAN MAKES ACQUAINTANCE WITH MISFORTUNE

Cornelius De Witte, after having attended to his family affairs, reached the house of his godson, Cornelius Van Baerle, one evening in the month of January, 1672.

De Witte, although being very little of a horticulturist or of an artist, went over the whole mansion from the studio to the greenhouse, inspecting everything, from the pictures down to the tulips. He thanked his godson for having joined him on the deck of the Admiral's ship, "The Seven Provinces," during the battle of Southwold Bay, and for having given his name to a magnificent tulip; and whilst he thus, with the kindness and affability of a father to a son, visited Van Baerle's treasures, the crowd gathered with curiosity, and even respect, before the door of the happy man.

And all this hubbub excited the attention of Boxtel, who was just taking his meal by his fireside. He inquired what it meant, and on being informed of the cause of all the stir, climbed up to his post of observation, where, in spite of the cold, he took his stand, with the telescope to his eye.

This telescope had not been of great service to him since the autumn of 1671. The tulips, like true daughters of the East, averse to cold, do not abide in the open ground in winter. They need the shelter of the house, the soft bed on the shelves and the congenial warmth of the stove. Van Baerle, therefore,, passed the whole winter in his laboratory, in the midst of his books and pictures. He went only rarely to the room where he kept his bulbs, unless it were to allow some occasional rays of the sun to enter, by opening one of the movable sashes of the glass front.

On the evening of which we are speaking, after the two Corneliuses had visited together all the apartments of the house, whilst a train of domestics followed their steps, De Witte said in a low voice, to Van Baerle:

"My dear son, send these people away, and let us be alone for some minutes."

The younger Cornelius bowing assent, said aloud:

"Would you now, sir, please to see my dry-room?"

The dry-room, this pantheon, this sanctum sanctorum of the tulip fancier, was, as Delphi of old, interdicted to the profane uninitiated.

Never had any of his servants been bold enough to set his foot there. Cornelius admitted only the inoffensive broom of an old Frisian housekeeper, who had been his nurse, and who, from the time when he had devoted himself to the culture of tulips, ventured no longer to put onions in his stews, for fear of pulling to pieces and mincing the idol of her foster-child.

At the mere mention of the dry-room, therefore, the servants who were carrying the lights, respectfully fell back. Cornelius, taking the candlestick from the hands of the foremost, conducted his godfather into that room, which was no other than that very cabinet with a glass front, into which Boxtel was continually prying with his telescope.

The envious spy was watching more intently than ever.

First of all he saw the walls and windows lit up.

Then two dark figures approached.

One of them tall, majestic, stern, sat down near the table on which Van Baerle had placed the taper.

In this figure, Boxtel recognised the pale features of Cornelius De Witte, whose long hair, parted in front, fell over his shoulders.

De Witte, after having said some few words to Cornelius, the meaning of which the prying neighbour could not read in the movements of his lips, took from his breast pocket a white parcel, carefully sealed, which Boxtel, judging from the manner in which Cornelius received it, and placed it in one of the presses, supposed to contain papers of the greatest importance.

His first thought was that this precious deposit enclosed some newly-imported bulbs from Bengal or Ceylon; but he soon reflected that Cornelius De Witte was very little addicted to tulip growing, and that he only occupied himself with the affairs of man, a pursuit by far less peaceful and agreeable than that of the florist. He, therefore, came to the conclusion that the parcel contained simply some papers, and that these papers were relating to politics.

But why should papers of political import be entrusted to Van Baerle, who not only was, but also boasted of being, an entire stranger to the science of government, which, in his opinion, was more occult than alchemy itself?

It was undoubtedly a deposit which Cornelius De Witte, already threatened by the unpopularity with which his countrymen were going to honour him, was placing in the hands of his godson; a contrivance so much the more cleverly devised, as it certainly was not at all likely that it would be searched for at the house of one who had always stood aloof from every sort of intrigue.

And, besides, if the parcel had been made up of bulbs, Boxtel knew his neighbour too well not to expect that Van Baerle would not have lost one moment in satisfying his curiosity and feasting his eyes on the present which he had received.

But, on the contrary, Cornelius had received the parcel from the hands of his godfather with every mark of respect, and put it by with the same respectful manner in a drawer, stowing it away so that it should not take up too much of the room which was reserved to his bulbs.

The parcel thus being secreted, Cornelius De Witte got up, pressed the hand of his godson, and turned towards the door, Van Baerle seizing the candlestick, and lighting him on his way down the street, which was still crowded with people who wished to see their great fellow-citizen getting into his coach.

Boxtel had not been mistaken in his supposition. The deposit entrusted to Van Baerle, and carefully locked up by him, was nothing more nor less than John De Witte's correspondence with the Marquis de Louvois, the war minister of the King of France; only the godfather forbore giving to his godson the least intimation concerning the political importance of the secret, merely desiring him not to deliver the parcel to anyone but to himself, or to whomsoever he would send to claim it in his name.

And Van Baerle, as we have seen, locked it up with his most precious bulbs, to think no more of it after his god-father had left him; very unlike Boxtel, who looked upon this parcel as a clever pilot does on the distant and scarcely per-ceptible cloud which is increasing on its way, and which is fraught with a storm.

Little dreaming of the jealous hatred of his neighbour, Van Baerle had proceeded step by step towards gaining the prize offered by the Horticultural Society of Haarlem. He had progressed from hazel-nut shade to that of roasted coffee; and on the very day when the frightful events which we have related in the preceding chapters, took place at the Hague, we find him about one o'clock in the day, gathering from the border the young suckers, raised from tulips of the colour of roasted coffee, which, being expected to flower for the first time in the spring of 1675, would, undoubtedly, produce the large black tulip required by the Haarlem Society.

On the 20th of August, 1672, at one o'clock, Cornelius was, therefore, in his dry-room, with his feet resting on the foot-bar of the table, and his elbows on the cover, looking with intense delight on three suckers which he had just detached from the mother bulb, pure, perfect, and entire, and from which was to grow that wonderful produce of horticulture, which would render the name of Cornelius Van Baerle for ever illustrious.

"I shall find the black tulip," said Cornelius to himself, whilst detaching the suckers. "I shall obtain the hundred thousand guilders offered by the Society. I shall distribute them among the poor of Dort; and thus the hatred which every rich man has to encounter in times of civil wars will be soothed down, and I shall be able, without fearing any harm either from Republicans or Orangists, to keep, as heretofore, my borders in splendid condition. I need no more be afraid, lest on the day of a riot the shopkeepers of the town, and the sailors of the port should come and tear out my bulbs, to boil them as onions for their families, as they have sometimes quietly threatened when they happen to remember my having paid two or three hundred guilders for one bulb. It is, there-fore, settled I shall give the hundred thousand guilders of the Haarlem prize to the poor. And yet——"

Here Cornelius stopped, and heaved a sigh.

"And yet," he continued, "it would have been so very

delightful to spend the hundred thousand guilders on the enlargement of my tulip-bed, or even on a journey to the East, the country of beautiful flowers. But, alas! these are no thoughts for the present times, when muskets, standards, proclamations, and beating of drums are the order of the day."

Van Baerle raised his eyes to heaven, and sighed again. Then, turning his glance towards his bulbs—objects of much greater importance to him than all those muskets, standards, drums, and proclamations, which he conceived only to be fit to disturb the minds of honest people, he said:

"These are, indeed, beautiful bulbs; how smooth they are, how well formed! there is that air of melancholy about them which promises to produce a flower of the colour of ebony. On their skin you cannot even distinguish the circulating veins with the naked eye. Certainly, certainly, not a light spot will disfigure the tulip which I have called into existence. And by what name shall we call this offspring of my sleepless nights, of my labour and my thoughts? *Tulipa nigra Barlœensis.*"

"Oh! these darling bulbs!"

"When my tulip has flowered," Baerle continued in his soliloquy, "and when tranquillity is restored in Holland, I shall give to the poor only fifty thousand guilders, which, after all, is a goodly sum for a man who is under no obligation whatever. Then, with the remaining fifty thousand guilders, I shall make experiments. With them, I shall succeed in imparting scent to the tulip. Ah! if I succeeded in giving it the odour of the rose or the carnation, or, what would be still better, a completely new scent; if I restored to this queen of flowers its natural distinctive perfume, which she has lost in passing from her Eastern to her European throne, and which she must have in the Indian Peninsula at Goa, Bombay, and Madras, and especially in that island which in olden times, as asserted, was the terrestrial paradise, and which is called Ceylon—Oh, what glory! I must say, I would then rather be Cornelius Van Baerle than Alexander, Cæsar, or Maximilian."

"Oh, the admirable bulbs!"

Thus Cornelius indulged in the delights of contemplation, and was carried away by the sweetest dreams.

Suddenly the bell of his cabinet was rung much more violently than usual.

Cornelius, startled, laid his hands on his bulbs, and turned round.

"Who is here?" he asked. "Sir," answered the servant, "it is a messenger from the Hague."

"A messenger from the Hague! What does he want?"

"Sir, it is Craeke."

"Craeke! the confidential servant of Mynheer John De Witt? Good, let him wait."

"I cannot wait," said a voice in the lobby.

And at the same time forcing his way in, Craeke rushed into the dry-room.

This abrupt entrance was such an infringement of the established rules of the household of Cornelius Van Baerle, that the latter, at the sight of Craeke, almost convulsively moved his hand which covered the bulbs, so that two of them fell on the floor, one of them rolling under a small table, and the other into the fireplace.

"Zounds!" said Cornelius, eagerly picking up his precious bulbs, "what's the matter?"

"The matter, sir!"—said Craeke, laying a paper on the large table, on which the third bulb was lying—"the matter is, that you are requested to read this paper without losing one moment."

And Craeke, who thought he had remarked in the streets of Dort symptoms of a tumult similar to that which he had witnessed before his departure from the Hague, ran off without even looking behind him.

"All right! all right! my dear Craeke," said Cornelius, stretching his arm under the table for the bulb; your paper shall be read, indeed it shall."

Then, examining the bulb which he held in the hollow of his hand, he said, "Well, here is one of them uninjured. That confounded Craeke! thus to rush into my dry-room; let us now look after the other."

And without laying down the bulb which he already held, Baerle went to the fireplace, knelt down, and stirred with the tip of his finger the ashes, which, fortunately, were quite cold.

He at once felt the other bulb.

"Well, here it is," he said. And looking at it with almost fatherly affection, he exclaimed, "Uninjured, as the first!"

At this very instant, and whilst Cornelius, still on his knees, was examining his pets, the door of the dry-room was so violently shaken, and opened in such a brusque manner, that Cornelius felt rising in his cheeks and his ears the glow of that evil counsellor which is called wrath.

"Now what is it again," he demanded; "are people going mad here?"

"Oh, sir! sir!" cried his servant, rushing into the dry-room, with a much paler face, and with much more frightened mien than Craeke had shown.

"Well!" asked Cornelius, foreboding some mischief from this double breach of the strict rule of his house.

"Oh, sir, fly! Fly, quick!" cried the servant.

"Fly! and what for?"

"Sir, the house is full of the guards of the States."

"What do they want?"

"They want you."

"What for?"

"To arrest you."

"Arrest me? arrest me, do you say?"

"Yes, sir, and they are headed by a magistrate."

"What's the meaning of all this?" said Van Baerle, grasping in his hands the two bulbs, and directing his terrified glance towards the staircase.

"They are coming up! they are coming up!" cried the servant.

"Oh, my dear child, my worthy master!" cried the old housekeeper, who now likewise made her appearance in the dry-room, "take your gold, your jewellery, and fly, fly!"

"But how shall I make my escape, nurse?" said Van Baerle.

"Jump out of the window."

"Twenty-five feet from the ground!"

"But you will fall on six feet of soft soil."

"Yes, but I should fall on my tulips."

"Never mind, jump out."

Cornelius took the third bulb, approached the window, and opened it, but seeing what havoc he would necessarily cause in his borders, and, more than this, what a height he would have to jump, he called out, "Never!" and fell back a step.

In this moment they saw across the banister of the staircase the points of the halberds of the soldiers rising.

The housekeeper raised her hands to heaven.

As to Cornelius Van Baerle, it must be stated to his honour, not as a man, but as a tulip-fancier, his only thought was for his inestimable bulbs.

Looking about for a paper in which to wrap them up, he noticed the fly-leaf from the Bible, which Craeke had laid upon the table, took it without, in his confusion, remembering whence it came, folded in it the three bulbs, secreted them in his bosom, and waited.

At this very moment the soldiers, preceded by a magistrate, entered the room.

"Are you Doctor Cornelius Van Baerle?" demanded the magistrate (who, although knowing the young man very well, put his questions according to the forms of justice, which gave his proceedings a much more dignified air).

"I am that person, Master Van Spennen," answered Cornelius, politely bowing to his judge, "and you know it very well."

"Then give up to us the seditious papers which you secrete in your house."

"The seditious papers!" repeated Cornelius, quite dumb-founded at the imputation.

"Now don't look astonished, if you please."

"I vow to you, Master Van Spennen," Cornelius, replied, "that I am completely at a loss to understand what you want."

"Then I shall put you in the way, doctor," said the judge; "give up to us the paper which the traitor Cornelius De Witte deposited with you, in the month of January last."

A sudden light came into the mind of Cornelius.

"Halloa!" said Van Spennen, "you begin now to remember, don't you?"

"Indeed I do; but you spoke of seditious papers, and I have none of that sort."

"You deny it then?"

"Certainly I do."

The magistrate turned round, and took a rapid survey of the whole cabinet.

"Where is the apartment you call your dry-room?" he asked.

"The very same where you now are, Master Van Spennen."

The magistrate cast a glance at a small note at the top of his papers.

"All right," he said, like a man who is sure of his ground.

Then, turning round towards Cornelius, he continued: "Will you give up those papers to me?"

"But I cannot, Master Van Spennen; those papers do not belong to me, they have been deposited with me as a trust, and a trust is sacred."

"Doctor Cornelius," said the judge, "in the name of the States I order you to open this drawer, and to give up to me the papers which it contains."

Saying this, the judge pointed with his finger to the third drawer of the press, near the fireplace.

In this very drawer, indeed, the papers deposited by the

Warden of the Dykes with his godson were lying; a proof that the police had received very exact information.

"Ah! you will not," said Van Spennen, when he saw Cornelius standing immovable and bewildered; "then I shall open the drawer myself."

And, pulling out the drawer to its full length, the magistrate at first lighted on about twenty bulbs carefully arranged and ticketed, and then on the paper parcel, which had remained in exactly the same state as it was when delivered by the unfortunate Cornelius De Witte to his godson.

The magistrate broke the seals, tore off the envelope, cast an eager glance on the first leaves which met his eye, and then exclaimed with a terrible voice:

"Well, justice has been rightly informed after all!"

"How," said Cornelius, "how is this?"

"Don't pretend to be ignorant, Mynheer Van Baerle," answered the magistrate, "follow me."

"How's that, follow you?" cried the Doctor.

"Yes, sir, for in the name of the States I arrest you."

Arrests were not as yet made in the name of William of Orange, for he had not been Stadtholder long enough for that.

"Arrest me?" cried Cornelius, "but what have I done?"

"That's no affair of mine, Doctor, you will explain all that before your judges."

"Where?"

"At the Hague."

Cornelius, in mute stupefaction, embraced his old nurse, who was in a swoon; shook hands with his servants, who were bathed in tears; and followed the magistrate, who put him in a coach, as a prisoner of State, and had him driven at full gallop to the Hague.

CHAPTER VIII

THE FAMILY CELL

The incident just related was, as the reader has guessed before this, the mischievous work of Mynheer Isaac Boxtel.

It will be remembered that, with the help of his telescope, not even the least detail of the private meeting between Cornelius De Witte and Van Baerle had escaped him. He had, indeed, heard nothing; but he had seen everything, and had rightly concluded that the papers entrusted by the Warden to the Doctor must have been of great importance, as he saw

Van Baerle so carefully secreting the parcel in the drawer where he used to keep his most precious bulbs.

The upshot of all this was, that when Boxtel—who watched the course of political events much more attentively than his neighbour Cornelius was wont to do—heard the news of the brothers De Witte being arrested on a charge of high treason against the States, he thought within his heart, that very likely he, Boxtel, needed only to say one word, and the godson would be arrested as well as the godfather.

Yet, full of hatred as was Boxtel's heart, he at first shrank with horror from the idea of informing against a man whom this information might lead to the scaffold.

But there is this terrible in evil thoughts, that evil minds soon grow familiar with them.

Besides this, Mynheer Isaac Boxtel encouraged himself with the following sophism:

" Cornelius De Witte is a bad citizen, as he is charged with high treason and arrested.

" I, on the contrary, am a good citizen, as I am not charged with anything in the world, and as I am as free as the air of heaven.

" If, therefore, Cornelius De Witte is a bad citizen—of which there can be no doubt, as he is charged with high treason and arrested—his accomplice, Cornelius Van Baerle, is no less a bad citizen than himself.

" And as I am a good citizen, and as it is the duty of every good citizen to inform against the bad ones, it is my duty to inform against Cornelius Van Baerle."

Specious as this mode of reasoning might sound, it would not, perhaps, have taken so complete a hold of Boxtel, nor would he, perhaps, have yielded to the mere desire of vengeance which was gnawing at his heart, had not the demon of envy been joined by that of cupidity.

Boxtel was quite aware of the progress which Van Baerle had made towards producing the grand black tulip.

Doctor Cornelius, notwithstanding all his modesty had not been able to hide from his most intimate friends that he was all but certain to win, in the year of grace 1673, the prize of a hundred thousand guilders offered by the Horticultural Society of Haarlem.

Just this certainty of Cornelius Van Baerle caused the fever which raged in the heart of Isaac Boxtel.

If Cornelius should be arrested, there would necessarily be a great upset in his house, and, during the night after his arrest, no one would think of keeping watch over the tulips in his garden.

Now, in that night, Boxtel would climb over the wall, and, as he knew the place of the bulb which was to produce the grand black tulip, he would steal it; and instead of flowering for Cornelius, it would flower for him, Isaac: he also, instead of Van Baerle, would have the prize of a hundred thousand guilders, not to speak of the sublime honour of calling the new flower *Tulipa nigra Boxtellensis*—a result which would satisfy not only his vengeance, but also his cupidity and his ambition.

Awake, he thought of nothing but the grand black tulip; asleep, he dreamed of it.

At last, on the 19th of August, about two o'clock in the afternoon, the temptation grew so strong that Mynheer Isaac was no longer able to resist it.

Accordingly, he wrote an anonymous information, the minute exactness of which made up for its want of authenticity; and posted his letter.

Never did a venomous paper, slipped into the jaws of the bronze lions at Venice, produce a more prompt and terrible effect.

On the same evening the letter reached the principal magistrate, who, without a moment's delay, convoked his colleagues early for the next morning. On the following morning, therefore, they assembled, and decided on Van Baerle's arrest, placing the order for its execution in the hands of Master Van Spennen, who, as we have seen, performed his duty like a true Hollander, and who arrested the doctor at the very hour when the Orange party at the Hague were roasting the bleeding shreds torn from the corpses of Cornelius and John De Witte.

But, whether from a feeling of shame, or from craven weakness, Isaac Boxtel did not venture that day to point his telescope, either at the garden, or at the laboratory, or at the dry-room.

He knew only too well what was about to happen in the house of the poor doctor, to have felt any desire to look into it. He did not even get up when his only servant—who envied the lot of the servants of Cornelius just as bitterly as Boxtel did that of their master—entered his bedroom. He said to the man:

"I shall not get up to-day; I am ill."

About nine o'clock he heard a great noise in the street, which made him tremble; at this moment, he was paler than a real invalid, and shook more violently than a man in the height of fever.

His servant entered the room; Boxtel hid himself under the counterpane.

" Oh, sir! " cried the servant, not without some inkling that, whilst deploring the mishap which had befallen Van Baerle, he was announcing agreeable news to his master—" oh, sir! you do not know, then, what is happening at this moment?"

" How can I know it?" answered Boxtel, with an almost unintelligible voice.

" Well, Mynheer Boxtel, at this moment your neighbour Cornelius Van Baerle is arrested for high treason."

" Nonsense! " Boxtel muttered, with a faltering voice; " the thing is impossible."

" Faith! sir, at any rate that's what people say; and, besides, I have seen Judge Van Spennen with the archers entering the house."

" Well, if you have seen it with your own eyes, that's a different case altogether."

" At all events," said the servant, " I shall go and inquire once more; you remain quiet, sir, I will let you know all about it."

Boxtel contented himself with signifying his approval of the zeal of his servant by dumb-show.

The man went out, and returned in half an hour.

" Oh, sir! all that I told you is indeed quite true."

" How so?"

" Mynheer Van Baerle is arrested, and has been put into a carriage, and they are driving him to the Hague."

" To the Hague?"

" Yes, to the Hague; and if what people say is true, it won't do him much good."

" And what do they say?" Boxtel asked.

" Faith, sir, they say—but it is not quite certain—that by this hour the burghers must be murdering Mynheer Cornelius and Mynheer John De Witte."

" Oh!" muttered, or rather growled, Boxtel, closing his eyes at the dreadful picture which presented itself to his imagination.

" Why, to be sure," said the servant to himself, whilst leaving the room, " Mynheer Isaac Boxtel must be very sick not to have jumped from his bed on hearing such good news."

And, in reality, Isaac Boxtel was very sick, like a man who has murdered another.

But he had murdered his man with a double object; the first was attained, the second was still to be attained.

Night closed in. It was the night which Boxtel had looked forward to.

As soon as it was dark he got up.

He then climbed into his sycamore.

He had correctly calculated, no one thought of keeping watch over the garden; the house and the servants were all in the utmost confusion.

He heard the clock strike ten, eleven, twelve.

At midnight, with a beating heart, trembling hands and a livid countenance, he descended from the tree, took a ladder, leaned it against the wall, mounted it to the last step but one, and listened.

All was perfectly quiet, not a sound broke the silence of the night; one solitary light, that of the housekeeper, was burning in the house.

This silence and this darkness emboldened Boxtel; he got astride on the wall, stopped for an instant, and, after having ascertained that there was nothing to fear, he put his ladder from his own garden into that of Cornelius, and descended.

After this, knowing to an inch where the bulbs which were to produce the black tulip were planted, he ran towards the spot, following, however, the crisp gravelled walks in order not to be betrayed by his footprints, and on arriving at the precise spot, he rushed, with the eagerness of a tiger, to plunge his hand into the soft ground.

He found nothing, and thought he was mistaken.

In the meanwhile the cold sweat stood on his brow.

He rummaged close by it—Nothing.

He rummaged on the right, and on the left—Nothing.

He rummaged in front, and at the back—Nothing.

He was nearly mad, when at last he satisfied himself that on that very morning the earth had been turned.

In fact, whilst Boxtel was lying in bed, Cornelius had gone down to his garden, had taken up the mother-bulb, and, as we have seen, divided it into three.

Boxtel could not bring himself to leave the place. He dug with his hands more than ten square feet of ground.

At last no doubt remained of his misfortune.

Mad with rage, he returned to his ladder, mounted the wall, drew up the ladder, flung it into his own garden, and jumped after it.

All at once, a last ray of hope presented itself to his mind: the seedling bulbs might be in the dry-room; it was therefore only requisite to make his entry there as he had done into the garden.

There he would find them; and, moreover, it was not at all difficult, as the sashes of the dry-room might be raised like those of a greenhouse. Cornelius had opened them on that morning, and no one had thought of closing them again.

Everything, therefore, depended upon whether he could procure a ladder of sufficient length—one of twenty-five feet, instead of ten.

Boxtel had noticed in the street where he lived a house, which was being repaired, and against which a very tall ladder was placed.

This ladder would do admirably, unless the workmen had taken it away.

He ran to the house, the ladder was there. Boxtel took it, carried it with great exertion to his garden, and with even greater difficulty raised it against the wall of Van Baerle's house, where it just reached to the window.

Boxtel put a lighted dark lantern into his pocket, mounted the ladder, and slipped into the dry-room.

On reaching this sanctuary of the florist, he stopped, supporting himself against the table; his legs failed him, his heart beat as if it would choke him. Here it was even worse than in the garden: there Boxtel was only a trespasser, here he was a thief.

However, he took courage again; he had not gone so far to turn back with empty hands.

But it was of no use to search the whole room, to open and shut all the drawers, even that privileged one where the parcel which had been so fatal to Cornelius had been deposited; he found ticketed, as in a botanical garden, the " Jane ", the " John De Witte ", the hazel-nut, and the roasted coffee-coloured tulip; but of the black tulip, or rather of the seedling bulbs within which it was still sleeping, not a trace was to be found. And yet, on looking over the register of seeds and bulbs, which Van Baerle kept, if possible, even with greater exactitude and care than the first commercial houses of Amsterdam their ledgers, Boxtel read the following entry :—

" To-day, 20th of August, 1672, I have taken up the mother-bulb of the grand black tulip, which I have divided into three perfect suckers."

" Oh, these suckers, these suckers! " howled Boxtel, turning over everything in the dry-room, " Where could he have concealed them? "

Then, suddenly striking his forehead in his frenzy, he called out, " Oh, wretch that I am! Would anyone be separated from his suckers? Would one leave them at Dort, when one goes to the Hague? Could one live far from one's bulbs, when they inclose the grand black tulip? He had time to get hold of them, the scoundrel, he has them about him, he has taken them to the Hague!"

It was like a flash of lightning which showed to Boxtel the abyss of a uselessly-committed crime.

Boxtel sank quite paralysed on that very table, and on that very spot where, some hours before, the unfortunate Van Baerle had so leisurely, and with such intense delight, contemplated his darling bulbs.

" Well, then, after all," said the envious Boxtel—raising his livid face from his hands in which it had been buried—" if he has them, he can keep them only as long as he lives, and——"

The rest of this detestable thought merged in a hideous smile.

" The suckers are at the Hague," he said, " therefore, I can no longer live at Dort: away, then, for them, to the Hague! to the Hague!"

And Boxtel, without taking any notice of the treasures about him—so entirely were his thoughts absorbed by another inestimable treasure—let himself out by the window, glided down the ladder, carried it back to the place whence he had taken it, and, like a beast of prey, returned growling to his house.

CHAPTER IX

THE FAMILY CELL

It was about midnight when poor Van Baerle was locked up in the prison of the Buitenhof.

What Rosa foresaw had come to pass. On finding the cell of Cornelius De Witte empty, the wrath of the people ran very high, and had Gryphus fallen into the hands of those madmen, he would certainly have had to pay with his life for the prisoner.

But this fury had vented itself most amply on the two brothers when they were overtaken by the murderers, thanks to the precaution which William—the man of precautions—had taken in having the gates of the city closed.

A momentary lull had therefore set in, whilst the prison was empty, and Rosa availed herself of this favourable moment to come forth from her hiding-place, which she also induced her father to leave.

The prison was, therefore, completely deserted. Why should people remain in the jail, whilst murder was going on at the Tol-Hek?

Gryphus came forth trembling behind the courageous Rosa. They went to close the great gate, at least as well as it would close, considering that it was half demolished. It was easy to see that a hurricane of mighty fury had passed here.

About four o'clock a return of the noise was heard, but of no threatening character to Gryphus and his daughter. The people were only dragging in the two corpses, which they came back to gibbet at the usual place of execution.

Rosa hid herself this time also, but only that she might not see the ghastly spectacle.

At midnight, people again knocked at the gate of the jail, or rather at the barricade which served in its stead: it was Cornelius Van Baerle whom they were bringing.

When the jailer received this new inmate, and saw from the warrant the name and station of his prisoner, he muttered with his turnkey smile:

"Godson of Cornelius De Witte! Well, young man, we have just here the family cell, and we shall give it to you."

And quite enchanted with his joke, the ferocious Orangeman took his cresset and his keys to conduct Cornelius to the cell, which, on that very morning, Cornelius De Witte had left to go into exile, or what, in revolutionary times, is meant instead by those sublime philosophers who lay it down as an axiom of high policy: "It is the dead only who do not return."

On the way which the despairing florist had to traverse to reach that cell, he heard nothing but the barking of a dog, and saw nothing but the face of a young girl.

The dog rushed forth from a niche in the wall, shaking his heavy chain, and sniffing all round Cornelius in order so much the better to recognise him, in case he should be ordered to pounce upon him.

The young girl, whilst the prisoner was mounting the stair-case, appeared at the narrow door of her chamber, which opened on that very flight of steps; and, holding the lamp in her right hand, she at the same time lit up her pretty bloom-ing face, surrounded by a profusion of rich wavy golden locks, whilst with her left she held her white night-dress closely over her breast, having been roused from her first slumber by the unexpected arrival of Van Baerle.

It would have made a fine picture, worthy of Rembrandt,

the gloomy winding stairs illuminated by the reddish glare of
the cresset of Gryphus, with his scowling jailer's countenance
at the top, the melancholy figure of Cornelius bending over
the banister, to look down upon the sweet face of Rosa, standing as it were, in the bright frame of the door of her chamber,
with flurried mien at being thus seen by a stranger.

And at the bottom, quite in the shade, where the details
are absorbed in the obscurity, the mastiff, with his eyes
glistening like carbuncles, and shaking his chain, on which
the double light from the lamp of Rosa and cresset of
Gryphus threw a brilliant glitter.

The sublime master would, however, have been altogether
unable to render the sorrow expressd in the face of Rosa,
when she saw this pale, handsome young man, slowly climbing
the stairs, and thought of the full import of the words, which
her father had just spoken: " You will have the family cell."
This vision lasted but a moment—much less time than we
have taken to describe it—Gryphus then proceeded on his
way, Cornelius was forced to follow him and five minutes
after he entered his prison, of which it is unnecessary to say
more, as the reader is already acquainted with it.

Gryphus pointed with his finger to the bed on which the
martyr had suffered so much, who on that day had rendered
his soul to God. Then taking up his cresset, he quitted the
cell.

Thus left alone, Cornelius threw himself on his bed, but he
slept not; he kept his eye fixed on the narrow window, barred
with iron, which looked on the Buitenhof; and in this way saw
from behind the trees that first pale beam of light which
morning sheds on the earth, as a white mantle.

Now and then during the night, horses had galloped at a
smart pace over the Buitenhof, the heavy tramp of the patrols
had resounded from the pavement, and the slow matches of
the arquebuses, flaring in the east wind, had thrown up at
intervals a sudden glare as far as to the panes of his window.

But when the rising sun began to gild the coping stones at
the gable ends of the houses, Cornelius, eager to know
whether there was any living creature about him, approached
the window and cast a sad look round the circular yard before
him.

At the end of the yard a dark mass, tinted with a dingy
blue by the morning dawn, rose before him, its dark outlines
standing out in contrast to the houses already illuminated by
the pale light of early morning.

Cornelius recognised the gibbet.

On it were suspended two shapeless trunks, which indeed were no more than bleeding skeletons.

The good people of the Hague had chopped off the flesh of its victims, but faithfully carried the remainder to the gibbet, to have a pretext for a double inscription, written on a huge placard, on which Cornelius, with the keen sight of a young man of twenty-eight, was able to read the following lines, daubed by the coarse brush of a sign-painter:—

"Here are hanging the great rogue of the name of John De Witte, and the little rogue Cornelius De Witte, his brother, two enemies of the people, but great friends of the King of France."

Cornelius uttered a cry of horror, and in the agony of his frantic terror, knocked with his hands and feet at his door so violently and continuously, that Gryphus, with his huge bunch of keys in his hand, ran furiously up to him.

The jailer opened the door, with terrible imprecations against the prisoner who disturbed him at an hour at which master Gryphus was not accustomed to be aroused.

"Well, now, I declare, he is mad, this new De Witte," he cried; "but all those De Wittes have the devil in them."

"Master, master," cried Cornelius, seizing the jailer by the arm and dragging him towards the window; "master what have I read down there?"

"Where, down there?"

"On that placard."

And trembling, pale, and gasping for breath, he pointed to the gibbet at the other side of the yard, with the cynic inscription surmounting it.

Gryphus broke out in a laugh.

"Eh! Eh!" he answered, "so, you have read it. Well, my good sir, that's what people will get for corresponding with the enemies of His Highness the Prince of Orange."

"The brothers De Witte are murdered!" Cornelius muttered, with the cold sweat on his brow, and sank on his bed, his arms hanging by his side, and his eyes closed.

"The brothers De Witte have been judged by the people," said Gryphus; "you call that murdered, do you? well, I call it executed."

And, seeing that the prisoner was not only quiet, but entirely prostrate and senseless, he rushed from the cell, violently slamming the door, and noisily drawing the bolts.

Recovering his consciousness, Cornelius found himself alone, and recognised the room where he was—"the family cell" as Gryphus had called it—as the passage leading to ignominious death. And as he was a philosopher, and, more than that, as he was a Christian, he began to pray for the soul of his godfather, then for that of the Grand Pensionary, and at last submitted with resignation to the sufferings which God might ordain for him.

Then, turning again to the concerns of earth, and having satisfied himself that he was alone in his dungeon, he drew from his breast the three bulbs of the black tulip, and concealed them behind a block of stone, on which the traditional water-jug of the prison was standing, in the darkest corner of his cell.

Useless labour of so many years! such sweet hopes crushed; his discovery was, after all, to lead to naught, just as his own career was to be cut short. Here, in his prison there was not a trace of vegetation, not an atom of soil, not a ray of sunshine.

At this thought Cornelius fell into a gloomy despair, from which he was only roused by an extraordinary circumstance.

What was this circumstance?

We shall inform the reader in the next chapter.

CHAPTER X

THE JAILER'S DAUGHTER

On the same evening Gryphus, as he brought the prisoner his mess, slipped on the damp flags whilst opening the door of the cell, and fell in the attempt to steady himself on his hand, but as it was turned the wrong way he broke his arm just above the wrist.

Cornelius rushed forward toward the jailer, but Gryphus, who was not yet aware of the serious nature of his injury, called out to him:

"It is nothing, don't you stir."

He then tried to support himself on his arm, but the bone gave way; then only he felt the pain, and uttered a cry.

When he became aware that his arm was broken, this man so harsh to others, fell swooning on the threshold, where he remained motionless and cold as if dead.

During all this time the door of the cell stood open, and Cornelius found himself almost free. But the thought never entered his mind of profiting by this accident; he had seen from the manner in which the arm was bent, and from the noise it made in bending, that the bone was fractured, and that the patient must be in great pain; and now he thought of nothing else but of administering relief to the sufferer, however little benevolent the man had shown himself during their short interview.

At the noise of Gryphus's fall, and at the cry which escaped him, a hasty step was heard on the staircase, and immediately after a lovely apparition presented itself to the eyes of Cornelius.

It was the beautiful young Frisian, who, seeing her father stretched on the ground, and the prisoner bending over him, uttered a faint cry, as, in the first fright, she thought Gryphus, whose brutality she well knew, had fallen in consequence of a struggle between him and the prisoner.

Cornelius understood what was passing in the mind of the girl, at the very moment when the suspicion arose in her heart.

But one moment told her the true state of the case, and, ashamed of her first thoughts, she cast her beautiful eyes, wet with tears, on the young man, and said to him:

"I beg your pardon, and thank you, sir; the first for what I have thought, and the second for what you are doing."

Cornelius blushed, and said: "I am but doing my duty as a Christian, in helping my neighbour."

"Yes, and affording him your help this evening, you have forgotten the abuse which he heaped on you this morning. Oh, sir! this is more than humanity—this is indeed Christian charity."

Cornelius cast his eyes on the beautiful girl, quite astonished to hear from the mouth of one so humble such a noble and feeling speech.

But he had no time to express his surprise. Gryphus recovered from his swoon, opened his eyes, and as his brutality was returning with his senses, he growled: "That's it, a fellow is in a hurry to bring a prisoner his supper, and falls and breaks his arm, and is left lying on the ground."

"Hush, my father," said Rosa, "you are unjust to this gentleman, whom I found endeavouring to give you his aid."

"His aid?" Gryphus replied, with a doubtful air.

"It is quite true, master; I am quite ready to help you still more."

"You!" said Gryphus, "are you a medical man?"

"It was formerly my profession."

"And so you would be able to set my arm?"

"Perfectly."

"And what would you need to do it, let us hear?"

"Two splinters of wood, and some linen for a bandage."

"Do you hear, Rosa?" said Gryphus, "the prisoner is

going to set my arm, that's a saving; come, assist me to get up, I feel as heavy as lead."

Rosa lent the sufferer her shoulder; he put his unhurt arm round her neck, and, making an effort, got on his legs, whilst Cornelius, to save him a walk, pushed a chair towards him.

Gryphus sat down; then turning towards his daughter, he said:

"Well, didn't you hear? Go and fetch what is wanted."

Rosa went down, and immediately after returned with two staves of a small barrel and a large roll of linen bandage.

Cornelius had made use of the intervening moments to take off the man's coat, and to tuck up his shirt sleeve.

"Is this what you require, sir?" asked Rosa.

"Yes, miss," answered Cornelius, looking at the things which she had brought, "yes, that's right. Now push this table, whilst I support the arm of your father."

Rosa pushed the table, Cornelius placed the broken arm on it, so as to make it flat, and with perfect skill set the bone, adjusted the splinters, and fastened the bandages.

At the last touch, the jailer fainted a second time.

"Go and fetch vinegar, miss," said Cornelius; "we will bathe his temples, and he will recover."

But, instead of acting up to the doctor's prescription, Rosa, after having assured herself that her father was still unconscious, approached Cornelius and said:

"Service for service, sir."

"What do you mean, my dear?" said Cornelius.

"I mean to say, sir, that the judge who is to examine you to-morrow has inquired to-day for the room in which you are confined, and, on being told that you were occupying the cell of Mynheer Cornelius de Witt, laughed in a very strange and disagreeable manner, which makes me fear that no good awaits you."

"But," asked Cornelius, "what harm can they do to me?"

"Look at that gibbet!"

"But I am not guilty," said Cornelius.

"Were they guilty whom you see down there? gibbeted, mangled, and torn to pieces?"

"That's true," said Cornelius gravely.

"And besides," continued Rosa, "the people want to find you guilty. But whether innocent or guilty, your trial begins to-morrow, and the day after you will be condemned. Matters are settled very quickly in these times."

"Well, and what do you conclude from all this?"

"I conclude that I am alone, that I am weak, that my father is lying in a swoon, that the dog is muzzled, and that consequently there is nothing to prevent you making your escape. Fly, then; that's what I mean."

"I will not; they would accuse you."

"Never mind," said Rosa, blushing, "never mind that."

"You are very good, my dear child," replied Cornelius, "but I stay."

"You stay, oh, sir! oh, sir! don't you understand that you will be condemned to death, executed on the scaffold, perhaps assassinated and torn to pieces, just like Mynheer John and Mynheer Cornelius. For heaven's sake don't think of me, but fly from this place. Take care, it bears ill luck to the De Wittes!"

"Halloa!" cried the jailer, recovering his senses, "who is talking of those rogues, those wretches, those villains, the De Wittes?"

"Don't be angry, my good man," said Cornelius, with his good-tempered smile, "the worst thing for a fracture is excitement, by which the blood is heated."

Thereupon, he said in an undertone to Rosa: "My child, I am innocent, and I shall await my trial with tranquillity and an easy mind."

"Hush," said Rosa.

"Why hush?"

"My father must not suppose that we have been talking to each other."

"What harm would that do?"

"What harm? He would never allow me to come here any more," said Rosa.

Cornelius received this innocent confidence with a smile; he felt as if a ray of good fortune was shining on his path.

"Now, then, what are you chattering there together about?" said Gryphus, rising and supporting his right arm with his left.

"Nothing," said Rosa: "the doctor is explaining to me what diet you are to keep."

"Diet, diet, for me? Well, my fine girl, I shall put you on diet, too."

"On what diet, my father?"

"Never to go to the cells of the prisoners, and if ever you should happen to go, to leave them as soon as possible. Come, off with me, lead the way, and be quick."

Rosa and Cornelius exchanged glances.

That of Rosa tried to express:

"There, you see?"

That of Cornelius said:

"Let it be as the Lord will."

CHAPTER XI

CORNELIUS VAN BAERLE'S WILL

Rosa had not been mistaken; the judges came on the following day to the Buitenhof, and proceeded with the trial of Cornelius Van Baerle. The examination, however, did not last long, it having appeared on evidence, that Cornelius had kept at his house that fatal correspondence of the brothers De Witte with France.

He did not deny it.

The only point about which there seemed any difficulty was, whether this correspondence had been intrusted to him by his godfather, Cornelius De Witte.

But as, since the death of those two martyrs, Van Baerle had no longer any reason for withholding the truth, he not only did not deny that the parcel had been delivered to him by Cornelius De Witte himself, but he also stated all the circumstances under which it was done.

This confession involved the godson in the crime of the godfather; manifest complicity being considered to exist between Cornelius De Witte and Cornelius Van Baerle.

The honest doctor did not confine himself to this avowal, but told the whole truth with regard to his own tastes, habit and daily life. He described his indifference to politics, his love of study, of the fine arts, of science, and of flowers. He explained that, since the day when Cornelius De Witte handed him the parcel at Dort, he himself had never touched, nor even noticed it.

To this it was objected, that in this respect he could not possibly be speaking the truth, since the papers had been deposited in a press, in which both his hands and his eyes must have been engaged every day.

Cornelius answered that it was indeed so; that, however, he never put his hand into the press, but to ascertain whether his bulbs were dry, and that he never looked into it, but to see if they were beginning to sprout.

To this again it was objected, that his pretended indifference respecting this deposit was not to be reasonably entertained, as he could not have received such papers from the hand of his godfather without being made acquainted with their important character

He replied that his godfather Cornelius loved him too well, and, above all, that he was too considerate a man to have communicated to him anything of the contents of the parcel, well knowing that such a confidence would only have caused anxiety to him who received it.

To this it was objected, that if De Witte had wished to act in such a way, he would have added to the parcel in case of accidents, a certificate, setting forth that his godson was an entire stranger to the nature of this correspondence, or at least he would, during his trial, have written a letter to him, which might be produced as his justification.

Cornelius replied that undoubtedly his godfather could not have thought that there was any risk for the safety of his deposit, hidden as it was in a press, which was looked upon as sacred as the tabernacle by the whole household of Van Baerle: and that, consequently, he had considered the certificate as useless. As to a letter, he certainly had some remembrance that some moments previous to his arrest, whilst he was absorbed in the contemplation of one of the rarest of his bulbs, John De Witte's servant entered his dry room, and handed to him a paper, but the whole was to him only like a vague dream; the servant had disappeared; and as to the paper, perhaps it might be found, if a proper search was made.

As far as Craeke was concerned, it was impossible to find him, as he had left Holland.

The paper also was not very likely to be found, and no one gave himself the trouble to look for it.

Cornelius himself did not much press this point, since, even supposing that the paper should turn up, it could not have any direct connection with the correspondence which constituted the crime.

The judges wished to make it appear as though they wanted to urge Cornelius to make a better defence; they displayed that benevolent patience, which is generally a sign of the magistrates being interested for the prisoner; or of a man's having so completely got the better of his adversary, that he needs no longer any oppressive means to ruin him.

Cornelius did not accept of this hypocritical protection, and in a last answer, which he set forth with the noble bearing of a martyr, and the calm serenity of a righteous man, he said:

"You ask me things, gentlemen, to which I can answer only the exact truth. Hear it. The parcel was put into my hands in the way I have described; I vow before God, that I was, and am still, ignorant of its contents, and that it was not until my arrest that I learned that this deposit was the correspondence of the Grand Pensionary with the Marquis de Louvois. And, lastly, I vow and protest that I do not understand how anyone should have known that this parcel was in my house, and, above all, how I can be deemed criminal for having received what my illustrious and unfortunate godfather brought to my house."

This was Van Baerle's whole defence, after which the judges began to deliberate on the verdict. They considered that every offshoot of civil discord is mischievous, because it revives the contest which it is the interest of all to put down.

One of them, who bore the character of a profound observer, laid down as his opinion that this young man, so phlegmatic in appearance, must in reality be very dangerous, as, under this icy exterior, he was sure to conceal an ardent desire to revenge his friends the De Wittes.

Another observed that the love of tulips agreed perfectly well with that of politics, and that it was proved in history that many very dangerous men were engaged in gardening, just as if it had been their profession, whilst really they occupied themselves with perfectly different concerns; witness Tarquin the Elder, who grew poppies at Gabii, and the Great Condé, who watered his carnations at the dungeon of Vincennes, at the very moment when the former meditated his return to Rome, and the latter his escape from prison.

The judge summed up with the following dilemma: —

"Either Cornelius Van Baerle is a great lover of tulips, or a great lover of politics; in either case he has told us a falsehood, first, because his having occupied himself with politics is proved by the letters which were found at his house; and, secondly, because his having occupied himself with tulips is proved by the bulbs, which leave no doubt of the fact; and herein lies the enormity of the case. As Cornelius Van Baerle was concerned in the growing of tulips, and in the pursuit of politics at one and the same time, the prisoner is of a hybrid character, of an amphibious organisation, working with equal ardour at politics and at tulips, which proves him to belong to the class of men most dangerous to public tranquillity, and shows a certain or rather a complete analogy between his character, and that of these master minds, of which just now Tarquin the Elder and the Great Condé have been felicitously quoted as examples."

The upshot of all these reasonings was, that his Highness, the Prince Stadtholder of Holland, would feel infinitely obliged to the magistracy of the Hague, if they simplified for him the government of the Seven Provinces, by destroying even the least germ of conspiracy against his authority.

This argument capped all the others, and in order so much the more effectually to destroy the germ of conspiracy, sentence of death was unanimously pronounced against Cornelius Van Baerle, as being arraigned and convicted, for having, under the innocent appearance of a tulip-fancier, participated in the detestable intrigues and abominable plots of the brothers De Witte against Dutch nationality, and in their secret relations with their French enemy.

A supplementary clause was tacked to the sentence to the effect that " the aforesaid Cornelius Van Baerle should be led from the prison of the Buitenhof to the scaffold in the yard of the same name, where the public executioner would cut off his head."

As this deliberation was a most serious affair, it lasted a full half-hour, during which the prisoner was remanded to his cell.

There the Recorder of the States came to read the sentence to him.

Master Gryphus was detained in bed by the fever caused by the fracture of his arm. His keys had passed into the hands of one of his assistants. Behind, his turnkey, who introduced the Recorder, Rosa, the fair Frisian maid, had slipped into the recess of the door, with a handkerchief to her mouth to stifle her sobs.

Cornelius listened to the sentence with an expression rather of surprise than sadness.

After the sentence was read, the Recorder asked him whether he had anything to answer.

" Indeed, I have not," he replied. " Only I confess that among all the causes of death, against which a cautious man may guard, I should never have supposed this to be comprised."

On this answer, the Recorder saluted Van Baerle, with all that consideration which such functionaries generally bestow upon great criminals of every sort.

But whilst he was about to withdraw, Cornelius asked, " By-the-bye, Mr. Recorder, what day is the thing—you know what I mean—to take place?"

" Well, to-day," answered the Recorder, a little surprised by the self-possession of the condemned man.

A sob was heard behind the door, and Cornelius turned round to look from whom it came; but Rosa, who had foreseen this movement, had fallen back.

" And," continued Cornelius, " What hour is appointed?"

" Twelve o'clock, sir."

"Indeed," said Cornelius. "I think I heard the clock strike ten about twenty minutes ago: I have not much time to spare."

"Indeed, you have not, if you wish to make your peace with God," said the Recorder, bowing to the ground. "You may ask for any clergyman you please."

Saying these words he went out backwards, and the assistant turnkey was going to follow him, and to lock the door of Cornelius's cell, when a white and trembling arm interposed between him and the heavy door.

Cornelius saw nothing but the golden brocade cap, tipped with lace, such as the Frisian girls wore; he heard nothing but someone whispering into the ear of the turnkey. But the latter put his heavy keys into the white hand which was stretched out to receive them, and, descending some steps, sat down on the staircase, which thus was guarded above by himself, and below by the dog. The head-dress turned round, and Cornelius beheld the face of Rosa, blanched with grief, and her beautiful eyes streaming with tears.

She went up to Cornelius, crossing her arms on her heaving breast.

"Oh, sir, sir!" she said, but sobs choked her utterance.

"My good girl," Cornelius replied with emotion, "what do you wish? I may tell you that my time on earth is short."

"I come to ask a favour of you," said Rosa, extending her arms partly towards him and partly towards heaven.

"Don't weep so, Rosa," said the prisoner, "for your tears go much more to my heart than my approaching fate, and you know, the less guilty a prisoner is, the more it is his duty to die calmly, and even joyfully, as he dies a martyr. Come, there's a dear, don't cry any more, and tell me what you want, my pretty Rosa."

She fell on her knees. "Forgive my father," she said.

"Your father, your father!" said Cornelius, astonished.

"Yes, he has been so harsh to you, but it is his nature, he is so to everyone, and you are not the only one whom he has bullied."

"He is punished, my dear Rosa, more than punished by the accident that has befallen him, and I forgive him."

"I thank you, sir," said Rosa. "And now tell me—oh, tell me—can I do anything for you?"

"You can dry your beautiful eyes, my dear child," answered Cornelius, with a good-tempered smile.

"But what can I do for you, for you I mean?"

"A man who has only one hour longer to live must be a great Sybarite, still to want anything, my dear Rosa."

"The clergyman whom they have proposed to you?"

"I have worshipped God all my life, I have worshipped Him in His works, and praised Him in His decrees. I am at peace with Him, and do not wish for a clergyman. The last thought which occupies my mind, however, has reference to the glory of the Almighty, and indeed, my dear, I should ask you to help me in carrying out this last thought."

"Oh, Mynheer Cornelius, speak, speak!" exclaimed Rosa, still bathed in tears.

"Give me your hand, and promise me not to laugh, my dear child."

"Laugh," exclaimed Rosa, frantic with grief, "laugh, at this moment! but do you not see my tears?"

"Rosa, you are no stranger to me. I have not seen much of you, but that little is enough to make me appreciate your character. I have never seen a woman more fair or more pure than you are, and, if from this moment I take no more notice of you, forgive me; it is only because, on leaving this world, I do not wish to have any further regret."

Rosa felt a shudder creeping over her frame, for, whilst the prisoner pronounced these words, the belfry clock of the Buitenhof struck eleven.

Cornelius understood her. "Yes, yes, let us make haste," he said, "you are right, Rosa."

Then, taking the paper with the three suckers from his breast, where he had again put it, since he had no longer any fear of being searched, he said: "My dear girl, I have been very fond of flowers. That was at a time when I did not know that there was anything else to be loved. Don't blush, Rosa, nor turn away; and even if I were making you a declaration of love, alas! poor dear, it would be of no more consequence. Down there in the yard, there is an instrument of steel, which in sixty minutes will put an end to my boldness. Well, Rosa, I loved flowers dearly, and I have found, or at least I believe so, the secret of the grand black tulip, which it has been considered impossible to grow, and for which, as you know or may not know, a prize of a hundred thousand guilders has been offered by the Horticultural Society of Haarlem. These hundred thousand guilders—and heaven knows, I do not regret them—these hundred thousand guilders I have here in this paper; for they are won by the three bulbs wrapped up in it, which you may take, Rosa, as I make you a present of them."

"Mynheer Cornelius!"

"Yes, yes, Rosa, you may take them, you are not wrong-
ing anyone, my child. I am alone in this world; my parents
are dead; I never had a sister or a brother. I have never
had a thought of loving anyone with what is called love, and
if anyone has loved me, I have not known it. However, you
see well, Rosa, that I am abandoned by everybody, and in
this sad hour you alone are with me in my prison, consoling
and assisting me."

"But, sir, a hundred thousand guilders!"

"Well, let us talk seriously, my dear child: those hundred
thousand guilders will be a nice marriage-portion, with your
pretty face; you shall have them, for I am quite sure of my
bulb. You shall have them, Rosa, dear Rosa, and I ask
nothing in return but your promise that you will marry a fine
young man, whom you love, and who will love you, as dearly
as I love my flowers. Don't interrupt me, Rosa, dear, I have
only a few minutes more."

The poor girl was nearly choking with her sobs.

Cornelius took her by the hand.

"Listen to me," he continued: "I'll teach you how to
manage it. Go to Dort and ask Butruysheim, my gardener,
for soil from my border number six, fill a deep box with it,
and plant in it these three bulbs. They will flower next May,
that is to say, in seven months; and, when you see the flower
forming on the stem, be careful at night to protect them from
the wind, and by day to screen them from the sun. They
will flower black; I am quite sure of it. You are then to
apprise the President of the Haarlem Society. He will cause
the colour of the flower to be proved before the committee,
and those hundred thousand guilders will be paid to you."

Rosa heaved a deep sigh. "And now," continued Cornelius, wiping away a tear which was glistening in his eye, and
which was shed much more for that marvellous black tulip
which he was not to see, than for the life which he was about
to lose, "I have no wish left, except that the tulip should be
called 'Rosa Barlæensis', that is to say, that its name should
combine yours and mine; and as, of course, you do not
understand Latin, and might therefore forget this name, try
to get for me pencil and paper, that I may write it down
for you."

Rosa sobbed afresh, and handed to him a book, bound in
shagreen, which bore the initials C. W.

"What is this?" asked the prisoner.

"Alas!" replied Rosa, "it is the Bible of your poor godfather, Cornelius De Witte. From it he derived strength to endure the torture, and to hear his sentence without flinching. I found it in this cell, after the death of the martyr, and have preserved it as a relic. To-day I brought it to you, for it seemed to me that this book must possess in itself a power which is quite heavenly. Write in it what you have to write, Mynheer Cornelius; and though, unfortunately, I am not able to read, I will take care that what you write shall be accomplished." Cornelius took the Bible, and kissed it reverently.

"With what shall I write?" asked Cornelius.

"There is a pencil in the Bible," said Rosa.

This was the pencil which John De Witte had lent to his brother, and which he had forgotten to take away with him.

Cornelius took it, and, on the last fly-leaf (for it will be remembered that the first was torn out), drawing near his end like his godfather, he wrote, with a no less firm hand:

"On this day, the 23rd August, 1672, being on the point of rendering, although innocent, my soul to God on the scaffold, I bequeath to Rosa Gryphus the only worldly good which has remained to me of all that I have possessed in this world, the rest having been confiscated; I bequeath, I say, to Rosa Gryphus three bulbs, which I am convinced must produce, in May next, the Grand Black Tulip, for which a prize of a hundred thousand guilders has been offered by the Haarlem Society, requesting that she may be paid the same sum in my stead, as my sole heiress, under the only condition of her marrying a respectable young man of about my age, who loves her, and whom she loves, and of her giving the grand black tulip, which will constitute a new species, the name of 'Rosa Barlæensis,' that is to say, hers and mine combined.

"So may God grant me mercy! and to her health and long life!

"CORNELIUS VAN BAERLE."

The prisoner, then giving the Bible to Rosa, said:
"Read."

"Alas!" she answered, "I have already told you I cannot read."

Cornelius then read to Rosa the testament that he had just made.

The agony of the poor girl almost overpowered her.

"Do you accept my conditions?" asked the prisoner, with a melancholy smile, kissing the trembling hands of the afflicted girl.

" Oh, I don't know, sir," she stammered.

" You don't know, child, and why not?"

" Because there is one condition which I am afraid I cannot keep."

" Which? I should have thought that all was settled between us."

" You give me the hundred thousand guilders as a marriage-portion, don't you?"

" Yes."

" And under the condition of my marrying a man whom I love?"

" Certainly."

" Well, then, sir, this money cannot belong to me. I shall never love anyone; neither shall I marry."

And, after having with difficulty uttered these words, Rosa swooned away in the violence of her grief.

Cornelius, frightened at seeing her so pale and sinking, was going to take her in his arms, when a heavy step, followed by other dismal sounds, was heard on the staircase, amidst the continued barking of the dog.

" They are coming to fetch you. Oh, God! Oh, God!" cried Rosa, wringing her hands. " And have you nothing more to tell me?"

She fell on her knees, with her face buried in her hands, and became almost senseless.

" I have only to say, that I wish you to preserve these bulbs as the most precious treasure, and carefully treat them according to the directions I have given you! Do it for my sake; and now farewell, Rosa."

" Yes, yes," she said, without raising her head, " I will do anything you bid me, except marrying," she added, in a low voice " for that, oh! that is impossible for me."

She then put that cherished treasure next her beating heart.

The noise on the staircase which Cornelius and Rosa had heard was caused by the Recorder, who was coming for the prisoner. He was followed by the executioner, by the soldiers who were to form the guard round the scaffold, and by some curious hangers-on of the prison.

Cornelius, without showing any weakness, but likewise without any bravado, received them rather as friends than as persecutors, and quietly submitted to all those preparations which these men were obliged to make in performance of their duty.

Then, casting a glance into the yard through the narrow iron-barred window of his cell, he perceived the scaffold, and, at twenty paces from it, the gibbet, from which, by order of

the Stadtholder, the outraged remains of the two brothers
De Witte had been taken down.

When the moment came to descend, in order to follow the
guards, Cornelius sought with his eyes the angelic look of
Rosa; but he saw, behind the sword and halberts, only a
form lying outstretched near a wooden bench, and a death-
like face, half-covered with long golden locks.

But, whilst falling down senseless, Rosa, still obeying her
friend, had pressed her hand on her velvet bodice, and, forgetting everything in the world besides, instinctively grasped
the precious deposit which Cornelius had entrusted to her
care.

Leaving the cell the young man could still see, in the con-
vulsively-clenched fingers of Rosa, the yellowish leaf from
that Bible on which Cornelius de Witte had with such difficulty and pain written those few lines, which, if Van Baerle
had read them, would undoubtedly have been the saving of
a man and a tulip.

CHAPTER XII

THE EXECUTION

Cornelius had not three hundred paces to walk outside the
prison to reach the foot of the scaffold. At the bottom of
the staircase, the dog quietly looked at him whilst he was
passing. Cornelius even fancied he saw in the eyes of the
monster a certain expression, as it were, of compassion.

The dog, perhaps, knew the condemned prisoners, and only
bit those who left as free men.

The shorter the way from the door of the prison to the
foot of the scaffold, the more fully, of course, it was crowded
with curious people.

These were the same who, not satisfied with the blood which
they had shed three days before, were now craving for a third
victim.

And scarcely had Cornelius made his appearance than a
fierce groan ran through the whole street, spreading all over
the yard, and re-echoing from the streets which led to the
scaffold, and which were likewise crowded with spectators.

The scaffold indeed looked like an islet at the confluence
of several rivers.

In the midst of these threats, groans and yells, Cornelius,
very likely in order not to hear them, had buried himself in
his own thoughts.

And what did he think of, in his last melancholy journey?

Neither of his enemies, nor of his judges, nor of his executioners.

He thought of the beautiful tulips which he would see from heaven above, at Ceylon, or Bengal, or elsewhere, when he would be able to look with pity upon this earth, where John and Cornelius de Witte had been murdered, for having thought too much of politics, and where Cornelius Van Baerle was about to be murdered for having thought too much of tulips.

"It is only one stroke of the axe," said the philosopher to himself, "and my beautiful dream will begin to be realised."

Only there was still a chance, just as it had happened before to M. De Chalais, to M. de Thou, and other slovenly-executed people, that the headsman might inflict more than one stroke, that is to say, more than one martyrdom, on the poor tulip-fancier.

Yet, notwithstanding all this, Van Baerle mounted the scaffold none the less resolutely, proud of having been the friend of that illustrious John, and godson of that noble Cornelius de Witte, whom the ruffians, who were now crowding to witness his own doom, had torn to pieces and burnt three days before.

He knelt down, said his prayers, and observed, not without a feeling of sincere joy, that laying his head on the block, and keeping his eyes open, he would be able, to his last moment, to see the grated window of the Buitenhof.

At length the fatal moment arrived, and Cornelius placed his chin on the cold, damp block. But in this moment, his eyes closed involuntarily, to receive more resolutely the terrible avalanche which was about to fall on his head, and to engulf his life.

A gleam, like that of lightning, passed across the scaffold: it was the executioner raising his sword.

Van Baerle bade farewell to the grand black tulip, certain of awaking in another world full of light and glorious tints.

Three times he felt, with a shudder, the cold stream of air coming from the knife near his neck, but, what a surprise! he felt neither pain nor shock.

He saw no change in the colour of the sky, and of the world around him.

Then, suddenly, Van Baerle felt gentle hands raising him, and soon stood on his feet again, although trembling a little.

He looked around him. There was someone by his side, reading a large parchment, sealed with a huge seal of red wax.

And the same sun, yellow and pale, as it behoves a Dutch sun to be, was shining in the skies; and the same grated window looked down upon him, from the Buitenhof.

And the same rabble, no longer yelling, but completely thunderstruck, was staring at him from the streets below.

Van Baerle began to be sensible of what was going on around him.

His Highness, William, Prince of Orange, very likely afraid that Van Baerle's blood would turn the scale of judgment against him, had compassionately taken into consideration his good character, and the apparent proofs of his innocence.

His Highness, accordingly, had granted him his life.

Cornelius at first hoped that the pardon would be complete, and that he would be restored to his full liberty and to his flower-borders at Dort.

But Cornelius was mistaken. To use an expression of Madame de Sevigné, who wrote about the same time, " there was a postscript to the letter;" and the most important point of the letter was contained in the postscript.

In this postscript, William of Orange, Stadtholder of Holland, condemned Cornelius Van Baerle to imprisonment for life. He was not sufficiently guilty to suffer death, but he was too much so to be set at liberty.

Cornelius heard this clause, but, the first feeling of vexation and disappointment over, he said to himself,—

" Never mind, all is not lost yet, there is some good in this perpetual imprisonment; Rosa will be there, and also my three bulbs of the black tulip are there."

But Cornelius forgot that the Seven Provinces had seven prisons, one for each; and that the board of the prisoner is anywhere else less expensive than at the Hague, which is a capital.

His Highness, who, as it seems, did not possess the means to feed Van Baerle at the Hague, sent him to undergo his perpetual imprisonment at the fortress of Lœvestein, very near Dort, but, alas! also very far from it; for Lœvestein, as the geographers tell us, is situated at the point of the islet which is formed by the confluence of the Waal and the Meuse, opposite Gorcum.

Van Baerle was sufficiently versed in the history of his country to know that the celebrated Grotius was confined in that castle, after the death of Barneveldt; and that the States, in their generosity to the illustrious publicist, jurist, historian, poet, and divine, had granted to him for his daily maintenance the sum of twenty-four stivers.

" I," said Baerle to himself, " I am worth much less than

Grotius, they will hardly give me twelve stivers, and I shall
live miserably; but, never mind, at all events, I shall live."

Then suddenly, a terrible thought struck him.

"Ah!" he exclaimed, "how damp and misty that part
of the country is; and the soil so bad for the tulips, and
then Rosa will not be at Lœvestein!"

CHAPTER XIII

WHAT WAS GOING ON ALL THIS TIME IN THE MIND OF ONE OF THE SPECTATORS

Whilst Cornelius was engaged in his own thoughts, a coach
had driven up to the scaffold. This vehicle was for the
prisoner. He was invited to enter it, and he obeyed.

His last look was towards the Buitenhof. He hoped to see
at the window the face of Rosa, brightening up again. But
the coach was drawn by good horses, who soon carried Van
Baerle away from among the shouts, which the rabble roared
in honour of the most magnanimous Stadtholder, mixing with
it a spice of abuse against the brothers De Witte and the
godson of Cornelius, who had just now been saved from
death.

This reprieve suggested to the worthy spectators remarks
such as the following:

"It's very fortunate that we used such speed in having
justice done to that great villain John, and to that little
rogue Cornelius, otherwise his Highness might have snatched
them from us, just as he has done this fellow."

Among all the spectators whom Van Baerle's execution
had attracted to the Buitenhof, and whom the sudden turn
of affairs had disagreeably surprised, undoubtedly the one
most disappointed was a certain respectably-dressed burgher,
who, from early morning, had made such good use of his
feet and elbows, that he at last was separated from the
scaffold only by the file of soldiers which surrounded it.

And when the executioner had brought the prisoner to the
scaffold, the burgher who had mounted on the stone of the
pump, the better to see and be seen, made to the executioner
a sign, which meant,—

"It's a bargain, isn't it?"

The executioner answered by another sign which was
meant to say,—

"Be quiet, it's all right."

This burgher was no other than Mynheer Isaac Boxtel,

who, since the arrest of Cornelius, had come to the Hague, to try if he could not get hold of the three suckers of the black tulip.

Boxtel had at first tried to bring over Gryphus to his interest, but the jailer had not only the snarling fierceness, but likewise the fidelity, of a dog. He had therefore bristled up at Boxtel's hatred, whom he suspected to be a warm friend of the prisoner, making trifling inquiries, to contrive, with the more certainty, some means of escape for him.

Thus to the very first proposals which Boxtel made to Gryphus to steal the bulbs, which Cornelius Van Baerle must be supposed to conceal, if not in his breast, at least in some corner of his cell, the surly jailer had only answered by kicking Mynheer Isaac out and setting the dog at him.

The piece which the mastiff had torn from his hose did not discourage Boxtel. He came back to the charge, but this time Gryphus was in his bed, feverish, with a broken arm. He, therefore, was not able to admit the petitioner, who then addressed himself to Rosa, offering to buy for her a head-dress of pure gold, if she would but get the bulbs for him. On this, the generous girl, although not yet knowing the value of the object of the robbery, which was to be so well remunerated, had directed the tempter to the executioner, as the heir of the prisoner.

In the meanwhile the sentence had been pronounced. Thus Isaac had no more time to bribe anyone. He, therefore, clung to the idea which Rosa had suggested: he went to the executioner.

Isaac had not the least doubt but that Cornelius would die with his bulbs on his heart.

But there were two things which Boxtel did not calculate upon.

Rosa, that is to say—love.

William of Orange, that is to say—clemency.

But for Rosa and William, the calculations of the envious neighbour would have been correct.

But for William, Cornelius would have died.

But for Rosa, Cornelius would have died with his bulbs on his heart.

Mynheer Boxtel went to the headsman, to whom he gave himself out as a great friend of the condemned man, and from whom he bought all the clothes of the dead man that was to be, for one hundred guilders, rather an exorbitant sum, as he engaged to leave all the trinkets of gold and silver to the executioner.

But what was the sum of a hundred guilders to a man who

was all but sure to buy with it the prize of the Haarlem Society?

It was money lent at a thousand per cent., which, as nobody will deny, was a very handsome investment.

The headsman, on the other hand, had scarcely anything to do to earn his hundred guilders. He needed only, as soon as the execution was over, to allow Mynheer Boxtel to ascend the scaffold with his servants, to remove the inanimate remains of his friend.

The thing was, moreover, quite customary among the "faithful brethren", when one of their masters died a public death in the yard of the Buitenhof.

A fanatic like Cornelius might very easily have found another fanatic to give a hundred guilders for his remains.

The executioner also readily acquiesced in the proposal, making only one condition—that of being paid in advance.

Boxtel, like the people who enter a show at a fair, might not be pleased, and refuse to pay on going out.

Boxtel paid in advance, and waited.

After this the reader may imagine how excited Boxtel was; with what anxiety he watched the guards, the Recorder, and the executioner; and with what intense interest he surveyed the movements of Van Baerle. How would he place himself on the block? how would he fall? and would he not, in falling, crush those inestimable bulbs?

But when he saw the Recorder take the hand of the condemned, and raise him, whilst drawing forth the parchment from his pocket; when he heard the pardon of the Stadtholder publicly read out—then Boxtel was no more like a human being; the rage and malice of the tiger, of the hyena, and of the serpent glistened in his eyes, and vented itself in his yell and his movements. Had he been able to get at Van Baerle, he would have pounced upon him and strangled him.

And so, then, Cornelius was to live, and was to go to Lœvestein, and thither to his prison he would take with him his bulbs; and perhaps he would even find a garden where the black tulip would flower for him.

Boxtel, quite overcome by his frenzy, fell from the stone on some Orangemen, who, like him, were sorely vexed at the turn which affairs had taken. They, mistaking the frantic cries of Mynheer Isaac for demonstrations of joy, began to belabour him with kicks and cuffs, such as could not have been administered in better style by any prize-fighter on the other side of the Channel.

Blows were, however, nothing to him. He wanted to run after the coach which was carrying away Cornelius with his bulbs. But in his hurry he overlooked a paving-stone in his way, stumbled, lost his centre of gravity, rolled over to a distance of some yards, and only rose again, bruised and begrimed, after the whole rabble of the Hague, with their muddy feet, had passed over him.

One would think that this was enough for one day, but Mynheer Boxtel did not seem to think so, as in addition to having his clothes torn, his back bruised, and his hands scratched, he inflicted upon himself the further punishment of tearing out his hair by handfuls, as an offering to that goddess of envy, who, as mythology teaches us, has for head-dress only a set of serpents.

CHAPTER XIV

THE PIGEONS OF DORT

It was, indeed, in itself a great honour for Cornelius Van Baerle to be confined in the same prison which had once received the learned master Grotius.

But, on arriving at the prison, he met with an honour even greater. As chance would have it, the cell formerly inhabited by the illustrious Barneveldt happened to be vacant, when the clemency of the Prince of Orange sent the tulip-fancier Van Baerle there.

The cell had a very bad character at the castle, since the time when Grotius, by means of the device of his wife, made escape thence in that famous book-chest, which the jailers forgot to examine.

On the other hand, it seemed to Van Baerle an auspicious omen that this very cell was assigned to him; for, according to his ideas, a jailer ought never to have given to a second pigeon the cage from which the first had so easily flown.

The cell has an historical character. We will only state here that, with the exception of an alcove, which was contrived there for the use of Madame Grotius, it differed in no respect from the other cells of the prison; only, perhaps, it was a little higher, and had a splendid view from the grated window.

One morning, whilst at his window, inhaling the fresh air which came from the river, and casting a longing look to the windmills of his dear old city Dort, which were looming in the distance behind a forest of chimneys, he saw flocks of pigeons coming from that quarter, to perch fluttering on the pointed gable ends of Lœvestein.

These pigeons, Van Baerle said to himself, are coming from Dort, and consequently may return there. By fastening a little note to the wing of one of these pigeons, one might have a chance to send a message there. Then, after a few moments' consideration, he exclaimed,—

" I will do it."

A man grows very patient who is twenty-eight years of age, and condemned to a prison for life, that is to say, to something like twenty-two or twenty-three thousand days of captivity.

Van Baerle, from whose thoughts the three bulbs were never absent, made a snare for catching the pigeons, baiting the birds with all the resources of his kitchen, such as it was, for eight stivers (sixpence English) a day; and, after a month of unsuccessful attempts, he at last caught a female bird.

It cost him two more months to catch a male bird; he then shut them up together, and having, about the beginning of the year 1673, obtained some eggs from them, he released the female, which, leaving the male behind to hatch the eggs in her stead, flew joyously to Dort, with the note under her wing.

She returned in the evening. She had preserved the note.

Thus it went on for fifteen days, at first to the disappointment, and then to the great grief of Van Baerle.

On the sixteenth day, at last, she came back without it.

Van Baerle had addressed it to his nurse, the old Frisian woman; and implored any charitable soul who might find it, to convey it to her as safely and speedily as possible.

In this letter there was a little note enclosed for Rosa.

Van Baerle's nurse had received the letter in the following way.

Leaving Dort, Mynheer Isaac Boxtel had abandoned not only his house, his servant, his observatory, and his telescope, but also his pigeons.

The servant having being left without wages, first lived on his little savings, and then on his master's pigeons.

Seeing this, the pigeons emigrated from the roof of Isaac Boxtel to that of Cornelius Van Baerle.

The nurse was a kind-hearted woman, who could not live without having something to love. She conceived an affection for the pigeons which had thrown themselves on her hospitality; and when Boxtel's servant reclaimed them with culinary intentions, having eaten the first fifteen already, and now wishing to eat the other fifteen, she offered to buy them from him, for a consideration of six stivers per head.

This being just double their value, the man was very glad to close the bargain, and the nurse found herself in undisputed possession of the pigeons of her master's envious neighbour.

The note as we have said, had reached Van Baerle's nurse.

And also, it came to pass, that one evening in the beginning of February, just when the stars were beginning to twinkle, Cornelius heard on the staircase of the little turret a voice, which thrilled through him.

He put his hand on his heart and listened.

It was the sweet and harmonious voice of Rosa.

Let us confess it, Cornelius was not so stupefied with surprise, or so beside himself with joy, as he would have been, but for the pigeon, which, in answer to his letter, had brought back hope to him, under her empty wing; and, knowing Rosa, he expected, if the note had ever reached her, to hear of her whom he loved, and also of his three darling bulbs.

He rose, listened once more, and bent forward towards the door.

Yes, they were indeed the accents which had fallen so sweetly on his heart at the Hague.

The question now was, whether Rosa, who had made the journey from the Hague to Lœvestein, and who—Cornelius did not understand how—had succeeded even in penetrating the prison, would also be fortunate enough in penetrating to the prisoner himself.

Whilst Cornelius, debating this point within himself, was building all sorts of castles in the air, and was struggling between hope and fear, the shutter of the grating in the door opened, and Rosa, beaming with joy, and beautiful in her pretty national costume—but still more beautiful from the grief which for the last five months had blanched her cheeks—pressed her little face against the wire grating of the window, saying to him:

" Oh! Sir, sir, here I am!"

Cornelius stretched out his arms, and, looking to heaven, uttered a cry of joy:

" Oh, Rosa, Rosa!"

" Hush! let us speak low; my father follows on my heels," said the girl.

" Your father?"

" Yes, he is in the courtyard at the bottom of the staircase, receiving the instructions of the Governor; he will presently come up."

"The instructions of the Governor?"

"Listen to me, I'll try to tell you all in a few words. The Stadtholder has a country-house, one league distant from Leyden, properly speaking a kind of large dairy, and my aunt, who was his nurse, has the management of it. As soon as I received your letter, which, alas! I could not read myself, but which your housekeeper read to me, I hastened to my aunt; there I remained until the Prince should come to the dairy; and when he came, I asked him as a favour, to allow my father to exchange his post at the prison of the Hague with the jailer at the fortress of Lœvestein. The Prince could not have suspected my object; had he known it, he would have refused my request, but, as it is, he granted it."

"And so you are here?"

"As you see."

"And thus I shall see you every day?"

"As often as I can manage it."

"Oh, Rosa, my beautiful Rosa, do you love me a little?"

"A little?" she said; "you make no great pretensions, Mynheer Cornelius."

Cornelius tenderly stretched out his hands towards her, but they were only able to touch each other with the tips of their fingers through the wire grating.

"Here is my father," said she.

Rosa then abruptly drew back from the door, and ran to meet old Gryphus, who made his appearance at the top of the staircase.

CHAPTER XV

THE LITTLE GRATED WINDOW

Gryphus was followed by the mastiff.

The turnkey took the animal round the jail, so that if need be, he might recognise the prisoners.

"Father," said Rosa, "here is the famous prison from which Mynheer Grotius escaped. You know Mynheer Grotius?"

"Oh, yes, that rogue Grotius; a friend of that villain Barneveldt, whom I saw executed when I was a child. Ah! so Grotius; and that's the chamber from which he escaped. Well, I'll answer for it that no one shall escape after him in my time."

And thus opening the door, he began in the dark to talk to the prisoner.

The dog, on his part, went up to the prisoner, and growling, smelled about his legs, just as though to ask him what right he had still to be alive, after having left the prison in the company of the Recorder and the executioner.

But the fair Rosa called him to her side.

"Well, my master," said Gryphus, holding up his lantern to throw a little light around, you see in me your new jailer. I am head turnkey, and have all the cells under my care. I'm not vicious, but I'm not to be trifled with, as far as discipline goes."

"My good Master Gryphus, I know you perfectly well," said the prisoner, approaching to within the circle of light cast around by the lantern.

"Holloa! that's you, Mynheer Van Baerle," said Gryphus. "That's you; well I declare, it's astonishing how people do meet."

"Oh, yes, and it's really a great pleasure to me, good Master Gryphus, to see that your arm is doing well, as you are able to hold your lantern with it."

Gryphus knitted his brow. "Now, that's just it," he said; "people always make blunders in politics. His Highness has granted you your life; I'm sure I should never have done so."

"Don't say so," replied Cornelius: "why not?"

"Because you are the very man to conspire again. You learned people have dealings with the devil."

"Nonsense, Master Gryphus. Are you dissatisfied with the manner in which I have set your arm, or with the price that I asked you?" said Cornelius, laughing.

"On the contrary," growled the jailer, "you have set it only too well. There is some witchcraft in this. After six weeks, I was able to use it as if nothing had happened; so much so, that the doctor of the Buitenhof, who knows his trade well, wanted to break it again, to set it in the regular way, and promised me that I should have my blessed three months for my money, before I should be able to move it."

"And you did not want that?"

"I said: 'Nay, as long as I can make the sign of the cross with that arm I laugh at the devil.'"

"But if you laugh at the devil, Master Gryphus, you ought with so much more reason to laugh at learned people."

"Ah, learned people, learned people. Why I would rather have to guard ten soldiers than one scholar. The soldiers smoke, guzzle, and get drunk; they are as gentle as lambs, if you only give them brandy or Moselle; but scholars drink, smoke and fuddle—ah, yes, that's altogether different. They

keep sober, spend nothing, and have their heads always clear
to make conspiracies. But I tell you, at the very outset, it
won't be such an easy matter for you to conspire. First of
all, you will have no books, no paper, and no conjuring book.
It's books that helped Mynheer Grotius to get off."

"I assure you, Master Gryphus," replied Van Baerle, "that
if I have entertained the idea of escaping, I most decidedly
have it no longer."

"Well, well," said Gryphus, "just look sharp; that's what
I shall do also. But, for all that, I say His Highness has
made a great mistake."

"Not to have cut off my head? thank you, Master
Gryphus."

"Just so, look whether the Mynheers de Witte don't keep
very quiet now."

"That's very shocking what you say now, Master Gryphus,"
cried Van Baerle, turning away his head to conceal his dis-
gust. "You forget that one of those unfortunate gentlemen
was my friend and the other my second father."

"Yes, but I also remembered that the one, as well as the
other, is a conspirator. And, moreover, I am speaking from
Christian charity."

"Oh, indeed, explain that a little to me, my good Master
Gryphus. I do not quite understand it."

"Well, then, if you had remained on the block of Master
Harbruck——"

"What?"

"You would not suffer any longer; whereas, I will not
disguise it from you, I shall lead you a sad life."

"Thank you for the promise, Master Gryphus."

And whilst the prisoner smiled ironically at the old jailer,
Rosa, from the outside, answered by a bright smile, which
carried sweet consolation to the heart of Van Baerle.

Gryphus stepped towards the window.

It was still light enough to see, although indistinctly,
through the grey haze of the evening, the vast expanse of
the horizon.

"What view has one from here?" asked Gryphus.

"Why, a very fine and pleasant one," said Cornelius, looking at Rosa.

"Yes, yes, too much of a view, too much."

And at this moment the two pigeons, scared by the sight,
and especially by the voice of the stranger, left their nest, and
disappeared, quite frightened, in the evening mist.

"Halloa! what's this?" cried Gryphus.

"My pigeons," answered Cornelius."

"Your pigeons," cried the jailer, "your pigeons! has a prisoner anything of his own?"

"Why, then," said Cornelius, "the pigeons which a merciful Father in Heaven has lent to me."

"So, here we have a breach of the rules already," replied Gryphus. "Pigeons! ah, young man, young man; I'll tell you one thing, that before to-morrow is over your pigeons will boil in my pot."

"First of all you should catch them, Master Gryphus. You won't allow these pigeons to be mine. Well, I vow they are even less yours than mine."

"Omission is no acquittance," growled the jailer, "and I shall certainly wring their necks before twenty-four hours are over; you may be sure of that."

Whilst giving utterance to this ill-natured promise, Gryphus put his head out of the window to examine the nest. This gave Van Baerle time to run to the door, and squeeze the hand of Rosa, who whispered to him,—

"At nine o'clock this evening."

Gryphus, quite taken up with the desire of catching the pigeons next day, as he had promised he would do, saw and heard nothing of this short interlude; and, after having closed the window, he took the arm of his daughter, left the cell, turned the key twice, drew the bolts and went off to make the same kind promises to the other prisoners.

He had scarcely withdrawn, when Cornelius went to the door to listen to the sound of his footsteps, and, as soon as they had died away; he ran to the window, and completely demolished the nest of the pigeons.

Rather than expose them to the tender mercies of his bullying jailer, he drove away for ever those gentle messengers, to whom he owed the happiness of having seen Rosa again.

This visit of the jailer, his brutal threats, and the gloomy prospect of the harshness with which, as he had before experienced, Gryphus watched his prisoners,—all this was unable to extinguish in Cornelius the sweet thoughts, and especially the sweet hope, which the presence of Rosa had re-awakened in his heart.

He waited eagerly to hear the clock of the tower of Lœvestein strike nine.

The last chime was still vibrating through the air, when

Cornelius heard on the staircase the light step and the rustle of the flowing dress of the fair Frisian maid, and, soon after, a light appeared at the little grated window in the door, on which the prisoner fixed his earnest gaze.

The shutter opened on the outside.

"Here I am," said Rosa, out of breath from running up the stairs; "here I am."

"Oh, my good Rosa!"

"You are then glad to see me?"

"Can you ask? But how did you contrive to get here? tell me."

"Now, listen to me. My father falls asleep every evening, almost immediately after his supper; I then make him lie down, a little stupefied with his gin. Don't say anything about it, because, thanks to this nap, I shall be able to come every evening and chat for an hour with you."

"Oh, I thank you, Rosa, dear Rosa."

Saying these words, Cornelius put his face so near the little window, that Rosa withdrew hers.

"I have brought back to you your bulbs."

Cornelius' heart leaped for joy. He had not yet dared to ask Rosa what she had done with the precious treasure which he had entrusted to her.

"Oh! you have preserved them, then?"

"Did you not give them to me as a thing which was dear to you?"

"Yes, but as I have given them to you, it seems to me that they belong to you."

"They would have belonged to me after your death, but, fortunately, you are alive now. Oh, how I blessed His Highness in my heart. If God grants to him all the happiness that I have wished him, certainly Prince William will be the happiest man on earth. When I looked at the Bible of your godfather Cornelius, I was resolved to bring back to you your bulbs, only I did not know how to accomplish it. I had, however, already formed the plan of going to the Stadtholder, to ask from him, for my father, the appointment of jailer at Lœvestein, when your housekeeper brought me your letter. Oh, how we wept together. But your letter only confirmed me the more in my resolution. I then left for Leyden, and the rest you know."

"What! my dear Rosa, you thought, even before receiving my letter, of coming to meet me again?"

"Thought of it?" said Rosa, allowing her love to get the better of her bashfulness, "I thought of nothing else."

And, saying these words, Rosa looked so exceedingly pretty, that for the second time Cornelius placed his forehead and lips against the wire grating; of course, we must presume with the laudable desire to thank the young lady.

Rosa, however, drew back as before.

" In truth," she said, with that coquetry which somehow or other is in the heart of every young girl, " I have often been sorry that I am not able to read, but never so much so, as when your housekeeper brought me your letter. I kept the paper in my hands, which spoke to other people, and which was dumb to poor stupid me."

" So, you have often regretted not being able to read," said Cornelius. " I should just like to know on what occasions."

" Troth," said she, laughing, " to read all the letters which were written to me."

" Oh, you received letters, Rosa?"

" By hundreds!"

" But who wrote to you?"

" Who! why, in the first place, all the students who passed over the Buitenhof, all the officers who went to parade, all the clerks, and even the merchants who saw me at my little window."

" And what did you do with all these notes, my dear Rosa?"

" Formerly," she answered, " I got some friend to read them to me, which was capital fun; but since a certain time— well, what use is it to attend to all this nonsense? since a certain time I have burnt them."

" Since a certain time!" exclaimed Cornelius, with a look beaming with love and joy.

Rosa cast down her eyes, blushing. In her sweet confusion she did not observe the lips of Cornelius, which, alas! only met the cold wire grating. Yet in spite of this obstacle, they communicated to the lips of the young girl the glowing breath of the most tender kiss.

At this sudden outburst of tenderness, Rosa grew as pale, and perhaps paler than she had been on the day of the execution. She uttered a plaintive sob, closed her fine eyes, and fled, trying in vain to still the beating of her heart.

And thus Cornelius was again alone.

Rosa had fled so precipitately, that she completely forgot to return to Cornelius the three bulbs of the Black Tulip.

CHAPTER XVI

MASTER AND PUPIL

The worthy Master Gryphus, as the reader may have seen, was far from sharing the kindly feelings of his daughter for the godson of Cornelius de Witte.

There being only five prisoners at Lœvestein, the post of turnkey was not a very onerous one, but rather a sort of sinecure, given after a long period of service.

But the worthy jailer, in his zeal, had magnified, with all the power of his imagination, the importance of his office.

To him Cornelius had swelled to the gigantic proportions of a criminal of the first order. He looked upon him, therefore, as the most dangerous of all his prisoners. He watched all his steps, and always spoke to him with an angry countenance; punishing him for what he called his dreadful rebellion against such a clement prince as the Stadtholder.

Three times a day he entered Van Baerle's cell, expecting to find him trespassing; but Cornelius had ceased to correspond, since his correspondent was at hand. It is even probable that if Cornelius had obtained his full liberty, with permission to go wherever he liked, the prison, with Rosa and his bulbs, would have appeared to him preferable to any other habitation in the world without Rosa and his bulbs.

Rosa, in fact, had promised to come and see him every evening, and from the first evening she had kept her word.

On the following evening she went up as before, with the same mysteriousness and the same precaution. Only she had this time resolved within herself not to approach too near the grating. In order, however, to engage Van Baerle in a conversation from the very first, which would seriously occupy his attention, she tendered to him through the grating the three bulbs, which were still wrapped up in the same paper.

But to the great astonishment of Rosa, Van Baerle pushed back her white hand with the tips of his fingers.

The young man had been considering about the matter.

"Listen to me," he said. "I think we should risk too much by embarking our whole fortune in one ship. Only think, my dear Rosa, that the question is to carry out an enterprise, which, until now, has been considered impossible, namely, that of making the grand Black Tulip flower. Let us, therefore, take every possible precaution, so that in case of a failure, we may not have anything to reproach ourselves with. I will now tell you the way I have traced out for us."

Rosa was all attention to what he would say, much more on account of the importance which the unfortunate tulip-fancier attached to it, than that she felt interested in the matter herself.

"I will explain to you, Rosa," he said. "I dare say you will have in this fortress a small garden, or some courtyard, or, if not that, at least some terrace."

"We have a very fine garden," said Rosa; "it runs along the edge of the Waal, and is full of fine old trees."

"Could you bring me some soil from the garden, that I may judge?"

"I will do so to-morrow."

"Take some from a sunny spot, and some from a shady, so that I may judge of its properties in a dry and in a moist state."

"Be assured I shall."

"After having chosen the soil, and if it be necessary, modified it, we will divide our three suckers; you will take one and plant it, on the day that I will tell you, in the soil chosen by me. It is sure to flower, if you tend it according to my directions."

"I will not lose sight of it for a minute."

"You will give me another, which I will try to grow here in my cell, and which will help me to beguile those long weary hours when I cannot see you. I confess to you I have very little hope for the latter one, and I look beforehand on this unfortunate bulb as sacrificed to my selfishness. However, the sun sometimes visits me. I will, besides, try to convert everything into an artificial help, even the heat and the ashes of my pipe; and lastly we, or rather you, will keep in reserve the third sucker as our last resource, in case our first two experiments should prove a failure. In this manner, my dear Rosa, it is impossible that we should not succeed in gaining the hundred thousand guilders for your marriage-portion; and how dearly shall we enjoy that supreme happiness of seeing our work brought to a successful issue!"

"I know it all now," said Rosa. "I will bring you the soil to-morrow, and you will choose it for your bulb and for mine. As to that in which yours is to grow, I shall have several journeys to convey it to you, as I cannot bring much at a time."

"There is no hurry for it, dear Rosa; our tulips need not be put into the ground for a month at least. So you see we have plenty of time before us. Only I hope that, in planting your bulb, you will strictly follow all my instructions."

" I promise you I will."

" And when you have once planted it, you will communicate to me all the circumstances which may interest our nursling; such as change of weather, footprints on the walks, or footprints in the borders. You will listen at night whether our garden is not resorted to by cats. A couple of those untoward animals laid waste two of my borders at Dort."

" I will listen."

" On moonlight nights have you ever looked at your garden, my dear child?"

" The window of my sleeping-room overlooks it."

" Well, on moonlight nights you will observe whether any rats come out from the holes in the wall. The rats are most mischievous by their gnawing everything; and I have heard unfortunate tulip-growers complain most bitterly of Noah for having put a couple of rats in the ark."

" I will observe, and if there are cats or rats——"

" You will apprise me of it—that's right. And moreover," Van Baerle having become mistrustful in his captivity, continued, " there is an animal much more to be feared than even the cat or the rat."

" What animal?"

" Man. You comprehend, my dear Rosa, a man may steal a guilder, and risk the prison for such a trifle, and, consequently, it is much more likely that some one might steal a hundred thousand guilders."

" No one ever enters the garden but myself."

" Thank you, thank you, my dear Rosa. All the joy of my life has still to come from you."

And as the lips of Van Baerle approached the grating with the same ardour as the day before, and as, moreover, the hour for retiring had struck, Rosa drew back her head, and stretched out her hand.

In this pretty little hand, of which the coquettish damsel was particularly proud, was the bulb.

Cornelius kissed most tenderly the tips of her fingers. Did he do so because her hand kept one of the bulbs of the Grand Black Tulip, or because this hand was Rosa's? We shall leave this point to the decision of wiser heads than ours.

Rosa withdrew with the two other suckers, pressing them to her heart.

Did she press them to her heart because they were the bulbs of the Grand Black Tulip, or because she had them from Cornelius?

This point, we believe, might be more readily decided than the other.

However that may have been, from that moment life became sweet, and again full of interest to the prisoner.

Rosa, as we have seen, had returned to him one of the suckers.

Every evening she brought to him, handful by handful, a quantity of soil from that part of the garden which he had found to be the best, and which, indeed, was excellent.

A large jug, which Cornelius had skilfully broken, did service as a flower-pot. He half filled it, and mixed the earth of the garden with a small portion of dried river-mud; a mixture which formed an excellent soil.

Then, at the beginning of April, he planted his first sucker in that jug.

Not a day passed on which Rosa did not come to have a chat with Cornelius.

The tulips, concerning whose cultivation Rosa was taught all the mysteries of the art, formed the principal topic of the conversation; but, interesting as the subject was, people cannot always talk about tulips.

They, therefore, began to chat also about other things, and the tulip-fancier found out, to his great astonishment, what a vast range of subjects a conversation may comprise.

Only Rosa had made it a habit to keep her pretty face invariably six inches distant from the grating, having, perhaps, become mistrustful of herself.

There was one thing especially which gave Cornelius almost as much anxiety as his bulbs—a subject to which he always returned—the dependance of Rosa on her father.

Indeed, Van Baerle's happiness depended on the whim of this man. He might one day find Lœvestein dull, and leave the fortress, and take his daughter with him, when Cornelius and Rosa would again be separated.

"Of what use would the carrier-pigeons then be?" said Cornelius to Rosa, "as you, my dear girl, would not be able to read what I should write to you, nor to write to me your thoughts in return."

"Well," answered Rosa, who, in her heart was as much afraid of a separation as Cornelius himself, "we have one hour every evening, let us make a good use of it."

"I don't think we make such a bad use of it as it is."

"Let us employ it even better," said Rosa, smiling. "Teach me to read and to write. I shall make the best of your lessons, believe me; and, in this way, we shall never be separated any more, except by our own will."

"Oh, then, we have eternity before us," said Cornelius.

Rosa smiled, and quietly shrugged her shoulders.

"Will you remain for ever in prison?" she said, "and, after having granted you your life, will not His Highness also grant you your liberty? And will you not then recover your fortune, and be a rich man; and then, when you are driving in your own coach, riding your own horse, will you still look at poor Rosa, the daughter of a jailer, scarcely better than a hangman?"

Cornelius tried to contradict her, and certainly he would have done so with all his heart, and with all the sincerity of a soul full of love.

She, however, smilingly interrupted him, saying, "How is your tulip going on?"

To speak to Cornelius of his tulip was an expedient resorted to by her to make him forget everything, even Rosa herself.

"Pretty well, indeed," he said, "the coat is growing black; the sprouting has commenced; the veins of the bulb are swelling; in eight days hence, and perhaps sooner, we may distinguish the first buds of the leaves protruding—and yours, Rosa?"

"Oh, I have done things on a large scale, and, according to your directions."

"Now, let me hear, Rosa, what you have done," said Cornelius, with as tender an anxiety as he had lately shown to herself.

"Well," she said, smiling, for in her own heart she could not help studying this double love of the prisoner for herself and the black tulip, "I have done things on a large scale; I have prepared a bed as you described it to me, on a clear spot, far from trees and walls, in a soil slightly mixed with sand, rather moist than dry, without a fragment of stone or pebble."

"Well done, Rosa, well done!"

"I am now only waiting for your further orders to put in the bulb; you know that I must be behind-hand with you, as I have in my favour all the chances of good air, of the sun, and abundance of moisture."

"All true, all true," exclaimed Cornelius, clapping his hands with joy, "you are a good pupil, Rosa, and you are sure to gain your hundred thousand guilders."

"Don't forget," said Rosa, smiling, "that your pupil, as

you call me, has still other things to learn besides the cultivation of tulips."

"Yes, yes, and I am as anxious as you are, Rosa, that you should learn to read."

"When shall we begin?"

"At once."

"No, to-morrow."

"Why to-morrow?"

"Because, to-day our hour is expired, and I must go."

"Already? but what shall we read?"

"Oh!" said Rosa, "I have a book, a book which I hope will bring us luck."

"To-morrow, then."

"Yes, to-morrow."

On the following evening, as we have said, Rosa returned with the Bible of Cornelius De Witte.

CHAPTER XVII

THE FIRST SUCKER

On the following evening, as we have said, Rosa returned with the Bible of Cornelius De Witte.

Then began between the master and the pupil one of those charming scenes, which are the delight of the novelist who has to describe them.

The grated window, the only opening through which the two lovers were able to communicate, was too high for conveniently reading a book, although it had been quite sufficient for them to read each other's faces.

Rosa, therefore, had to press the open book against the grating edgeways, holding above it, in her right hand, the lamp, but Cornelius hit upon the lucky idea of fixing it to the bars, so as to afford her a little rest. Rosa was then enabled to follow with her finger the letters and syllables, which she was to spell for Cornelius, who with a straw pointed out the letters to his attentive pupil through the holes of the grating.

The light of the lamp illuminated the rich complexion of Rosa, her blue liquid eyes, and her golden hair under her head-dress of gold brocade; with her fingers held up, and showing in the blood, as it flowed downwards in the veins, that pale pink hue which shines before the light, owing to the living transparency of the flesh tint.

Rosa's intellect rapidly developed itself under the animating influence of the mind of Cornelius, and when the difficulties seemed too arduous, the sympathy of the two loving hearts seemed to smooth them away.

And Rosa, after having returned to her room, repeated in her solitude the reading lessons, but, at the same time, recalled all the delight which she had felt whilst receiving them.

One evening she came half an hour later than usual. This was too extraordinary an incident not to call forth, at once, Cornelius' inquiries after its cause.

"Oh! do not be angry with me," she said, "it is not my fault. My father has renewed an acquaintance with an old crony who used to visit him at the Hague, and to ask him to let him see the prison. He is a good sort of fellow, fond of his bottle, tells funny stories, and, moreover, is very free with his money, so is always ready to stand a treat."

"You don't know anything further of him?" asked Cornelius, surprised.

"No," she answered, "it's only for about a fortnight that my father has taken such a fancy to this friend who is so assiduous in visiting him."

"Ah, so," said Cornelius, shaking his head uneasily, as every new incident seemed to him to forebode some catastrophe, "very likely some spy, one of those who are sent into jails to watch both prisoners and their keepers."

"I don't believe that," said Rosa, smiling, "if that worthy person is spying after any one, it is certainly not after my father."

"After whom, then?"

"Me, for instance?"

"You?"

"Why not?" said Rosa, smiling.

"Ah, that's true," Cornelius observed with a sigh. "You will not always have suitors in vain, this man may become your husband."

"I don't say anything to the contrary."

"What cause have you to entertain such a happy prospect?"

"Rather say, this fear, Mynheer Cornelius."

"Thank you, Rosa, you are right; well, I will say then, this fear?"

"I have only this reason——"

"Tell me, I am anxious to hear."

"This man, came several times before to the Buitenhof, at the Hague. I remember now, it was just about the time when you were confined there.

"When I left, he left too, when I came here, he came after me. At the Hague his pretext was that he wanted to see you."

"See me?"

"Yes, it must have undoubtedly been only a pretext; for now, when he could plead the same reason, as you are my father's prisoner again, he does not care any longer for you; quite the contrary, I heard him say to my father only yesterday that he did not know you."

"Go on, Rosa, pray do, that I may guess who that man is, and what he wants."

"Are you quite sure, Mynheer Cornelius, that none of your friends can interest himself for you?"

"I have no friends, Rosa, I have only my old nurse, whom you know, and who knows you. Alas! poor Sue, she would come herself, and use no roundabout ways. She would at once say to your father or to you, 'My good sir, or my good miss, my child is here, see how grieved I am, let me see him only for one hour and I'll pray for you as long as I live.' No, no," continued Cornelius, "with the exception of my poor old Sue, I have no friends in this world."

"Then I come back to what I thought before; and the more so as last evening at sunset, whilst I was arranging the border where I am to plant your bulb, I saw a shadow gliding between the elder trees, and the aspens. I did not appear to see him, but it was this man. He concealed himself and saw me digging the ground, and certainly it was me, whom he followed, and me, whom he was spying after. I could not move my rake, or touch one atom of soil, without his noticing it."

"Oh! yes, yes, he is in love with you," said Cornelius. "Is he young? Is he handsome?"

Saying this, he looked anxiously at Rosa, eagerly waiting for her answer.

"Young? handsome?" cried Rosa, bursting into a laugh. "He is hideous to look at; crooked, nearly fifty years of age, and never dares to look me in the face, or to speak, except in an undertone."

"And his name?"

"Jacob Gisels."

"I don't know him."

"Then you see that, at all events, he does not come after you."

"At any rate, if he loves you, Rosa, which is very likely, as to see you is to love you, at least you don't love him."

"To be sure I don't."

"Then you wish me to keep my mind easy?"

"I should certainly ask you to do so."

"Well, then, now as you begin to know how to read, you will read all that I write to you of the pangs of jealousy and of absence, won't you, Rosa?"

"I shall read it, if you write with good big letters."

Then, as the turn which the conversation took began to make Rosa uneasy, she asked,—

"By-the-bye, how is your tulip going on?"

"Oh, Rosa, only imagine my joy; this morning I looked at it in the sun, and after having moved the soil aside which covers the bulb, I saw the first sprouting of the leaves. This small germ has caused me a much greater emotion than the order of His Highness, which turned aside the sword, already raised, at the Buitenhof."

"You hope, then?" said Rosa, smiling.

"Yes, yes, I hope."

"And I, in my turn, when shall I plant my bulb?"

"Oh, the first favourable day I will tell you, but whatever you do, let nobody help you, and don't confide your secret to any one in the world; do you see, a connoisseur, by merely looking at the bulb, would be able to distinguish its value; and so, my dearest Rosa, be careful in locking up the third sucker which remains to you."

"It is still wrapped up in the same paper in which you put it, and just as you gave it me. I have laid it at the bottom of my chest under my point lace, which keeps it dry, without pressing upon it. But good night, my poor captive gentleman."

"What? already?"

"It must be, it must be."

"Coming so late, and going so soon."

"My father might grow impatient at not seeing me return, and that precious lover might suspect a rival."

Here she listened uneasily.

"What is it?" asked Van Baerle.

"I thought I heard something."

"What, then?"

"Something like a step, creaking on the staircase."

"Surely," said the prisoner, "that cannot be master Gryphus, he is always heard at a distance."

"No, it is not my father, I am quite sure, but——"

"But?"

"But it might be Mynheer Jacob."

Rosa rushed towards the staircase, and a door was really heard rapidly to close, before the young damsel had got down the first ten steps.

Cornelius was very uneasy about it, but it was, after all, only a prelude to greater anxieties.

The following day passed without any remarkable incident. Gryphus made his three visits, and discovered nothing. He never came at the same hours, as he hoped thus to discover the secrets of the prisoner. Van Baerle, therefore, had devised a contrivance, a sort of pulley, by means of which he was able to lower or to raise his jug below the ledge of tiles and stone before his window. The strings by which this was effected, he had found means to cover with that moss which generally grows on tiles, or in the crannies of the walls.

Gryphus suspected nothing, and the device succeeded for eight days. One morning, however, when Cornelius, absorbed in the contemplation of his bulb, from which a germ of vegetation was already peeping forth, had not heard old Gryphus coming up stairs, as a gale of wind was blowing which shook the whole tower, the door suddenly opened.

Gryphus, perceiving an unknown and, consequently, a forbidden object in the hands of his prisoner, pounced upon it with the same rapidity as the hawk on its prey.

As ill luck would have it, his coarse, hard hand, the same which he had broken, and which Cornelius Van Baerle had set so well, grasped at once in the midst of the jug the spot where the bulb was lying in the soil.

"What have you got here?" he roared. "Ah! have I caught you?" and with this he grubbed in the soil.

"I? nothing, nothing," cried Cornelius, trembling.

"Ah! have I caught you? a jug, and earth in it; there is some criminal secret at the bottom of all this."

"Oh, my good master Gryphus," said Van Baerle imploringly, and anxious, like the partridge robbed of her young by the reaper.

In fact, Gryphus was beginning to dig the soil with his crooked fingers.

"Take care, sir, take care," said Cornelius, growing quite pale.

"Care of what! zounds! of what?" roared the jailer.

"Take care, I say you will crush it, Master Gryphus."

And with a rapid and almost frantic movement he snatched the jug from the hands of Gryphus, and hid it like a treasure under his arms.

But Gryphus, obstinate, like an old man, and more and more convinced that he was discovering here a conspiracy against the Prince of Orange, rushed up to his prisoner, raising his stick; seeing, however, the impassible resolution of the captive to protect his flower-pot, he was convinced that Cornelius trembled much less for his head than for his jug.

He, therefore tried to wrest it from him by force.

"Halloa!" said the jailer, furious, "here you see, you are rebelling."

"Leave me my tulip," cried Van Baerle.

"Ah, yes, tulip," replied the old man, "we know well the shifts of prisoners."

"But I vow to you——"

"Let go," repeated Gryphus, stamping his foot, "let go, or I shall call the guard."

"Call whoever you like, but you shall not have this flower except with my life."

Gryphus, exasperated, plunged his finger a second time into the soil, and now he drew out the bulb; which certainly looked quite black; and whilst Van Baerle, quite happy to have saved the vessel, did not suspect that the adversary had possessed himself of its precious contents, Gryphus hurled the softened bulb with all his force on the flags, where, almost immediately after, it was crushed to atoms under his heavy shoe.

Van Baerle saw the work of destruction, got a glimpse of the juicy remains of his darling bulb, and, guessing the cause of the ferocious joy of Gryphus, uttered a cry of agony, which would have melted the heart even of that ruthless jailer who some years before killed Pellisson's spider.

The idea of striking down this spiteful bully passed like lightning through the brain of the tulip-fancier. The blood rushed to his brow, and seemed like fire in his eyes, which blinded him; and he raised in his two hands the heavy jug with all the now useless earth which remained in it. One instant more, and he would have flung it on the bald head of old Gryphus.

But a cry stopped him; a cry of agony, uttered by poor Rosa, who, trembling and pale, with her arms raised to heaven made her appearance behind the grated window, and thus interposed between her father and her friend.

Gryphus then understood the danger with which he had been threatened, and he broke out in a volley of the most terrible abuse.

"Indeed," said Cornelius to him, "you must be a very mean and spiteful fellow, to rob a poor prisoner of his only consolation, a tulip bulb."

"For shame, my father," Rosa chimed in, "it is indeed a crime you have committed here."

"Ah, is that you, my little chatterbox?" the old man cried, boiling with rage and turning towards her; "don't you meddle with what don't concern you, but go down as quickly as possible."

"Unfortunate me," continued Cornelius, overwhelmed with grief.

"After all, it is but a tulip," Gryphus resumed, as he began to be a little ashamed of himself. "You may have as many tulips as you like. I have three hundred of them in my loft."

"To the devil with your tulips!" cried Cornelius; "you are worthy of each other: had I a hundred thousand millions of them, I would gladly give them for the one which you have just destroyed!"

"Ah, so," Gryphus said, in a tone of triumph; "now there we have it. It was not your tulip you cared for. There was in that false bulb some witchcraft, perhaps some means of correspondence with conspirators against His Highness, who has granted you your life. I always said they were wrong in not cutting your head off."

"Father, father!" cried Rosa.

"Yes, yes; it is better as it is now," repeated Gryphus, growing warm; "I have destroyed it, and I'll do the same again, as often as you repeat the trick. Didn't I tell you, my fine fellow, that I would make your life a hard one?"

"A curse on you!" Cornelius exclaimed, quite beyond himself with despair, as he gathered, with his trembling fingers, the remnants of that bulb on which he had rested so many joys and so many hopes.

"We shall plant the other to-morrow, my dear Mynheer Cornelius," said Rosa, in a low voice, who understood the intense grief of the unfortunate tulip-fancier, and who, with the pure sacred love of her innocent heart, poured these kind words, like a drop of balm, on the bleeding wounds of Cornelius.

CHAPTER XVIII

ROSA'S LOVER

Rosa had scarcely pronounced these consolatory words when a voice was heard from the staircase, asking Gryphus how matters were going on.

"Do you hear, father?" said Rosa.

"What?"

"Master Jacob calls you, he is uneasy."

"There was such a noise," said Gryphus; "wouldn't you have thought he would murder me, this doctor? They are always very troublesome fellows, these scholars."

Then, pointing with his finger towards the staircase, he said to Rosa, "Just lead the way, Miss."

After this, he locked the door and called out "I shall be with you directly, friend Jacob."

Poor Cornelius, thus left alone with his bitter grief, muttered to himself,—

"Ah! you old hangman, it is I you have trodden under foot; you have murdered me, I shall not survive it!"

And certainly the unfortunate prisoner would have fallen ill, but for the counterpoise which Providence had granted to his grief, and which was called Rosa.

In the evening she came back. Her first words announced to Cornelius, that henceforth her father would no longer make any objection to his cultivating flowers.

"And how do you know that?" the prisoner asked, with a doleful look.

"I know it, because he has said so."

"To deceive me, perhaps."

"No, he repents."

"Ah! yes, but too late."

"This repentance is not of himself."

"And who put it into him?"

"If you only knew how his friend scolded him."

"Ah, Master Jacob; he does not leave you, then, that Master Jacob?"

"At any rate, he leaves us as little as he can help."

Saying this, she smiled in such a way, that the little cloud of jealousy which had darkened the brow of Cornelius speedily vanished.

"How was it?" asked the prisoner.

"Well, being asked by his friend, my father told at supper

the whole story of the tulip, or rather of the bulb, and of his own fine exploit of crushing it."

Cornelius heaved a sigh, which might have been called a groan.

"Had you only seen Master Jacob at that moment!" continued Rosa. "I really thought he would set fire to the castle; his eyes were like two flaming torches, his hair stood on end, and he clenched his fist for a moment: I thought he would have strangled my father."

"'You have done that,' he cried 'you have crushed the bulb?'

"'Indeed I have.'

"'It is infamous,' said Master Jacob, 'it is odious! You have committed a great crime!'

"My father was quite dumbfounded.

"'Are you mad, too?' he asked his friend."

"Oh! what a worthy man is this Master Jacob," muttered Cornelius, "an honest soul, an excellent heart, that he is."

"The truth is, that it is impossible to treat a man more rudely than he did my father; he was really quite in despair, repeating, over and over again—

"'Crushed, crushed the bulb! my God, my God! crushed!'

"Then, turning towards me he asked, 'But it was not the only one that he had?'"

"Did he ask that?" inquired Cornelius, with some anxiety.

"'You think it was not the only one?' said my father. 'Very well, we shall search for the others.'

"'You will search for the others?' cried Jacob, taking my father by the collar; but he immediately loosed him. Then, turning towards me, he continued asking—'And what did that poor young man say?'

"I did not know what to answer, as you had so strictly enjoined me never to allow any one to guess the interest which you are taking in the bulb. Fortunately, my father saved me from the difficulty by chiming in,—

"'What did he say? Didn't he fume and fret?'

"I interrupted him, saying, 'Was it not natural that he should be furious, you were so unjust and brutal, father?'

"'Well, now! are you mad?' cried my father; 'what immense misfortune is it to crush a tulip-bulb? You may buy a hundred of them in the market of Gorcum.'

"'Perhaps some less precious one than that was!' I incautiously replied."

"And what did Jacob say or do at these words?" asked Cornelius.

" At these words, if I must say it, his eyes seemed to flash like lightning "

" But," said Cornelius, " that was not all; I am sure he said something in his turn."

" ' So then, my pretty Rosa,' he said, with a voice as sweet as honey, ' so you think that bulb to have been a precious one?'

" I saw that I had made a blunder.

" ' What do I know?' I said negligently; ' do I understand anything of tulips? I only know—as unfortunately it is our lot to live with prisoners—that for them any pastime is of value. This poor Mynheer Van Baerle amused himself with this bulb. Well, I think it very cruel to take from him the only thing that he could have amused himself with.'

" ' But, first of all,' said my father, ' we ought to know how he has contrived to procure this bulb.'

" I turned my eyes away to avoid my father's look; but I met those of Jacob.

" It was as if he had tried to read my thoughts at the bottom of my heart.

" Some little show of anger sometimes saves an answer. I shrugged my shoulders, turned my back, and advanced towards the door.

" But I was kept by something which I heard, although it was uttered in a very low voice only.

" Jacob said to my father,—

" ' It would not be so difficult to ascertain that.'

" How so?'

" ' You need only search his person; and if he has the other bulbs, we shall find them, as there usually are three suckers!' "

" Three suckers!" cried Cornelius. " Did he say that I have three?"

" The word certainly struck me just as much as it does you. I turned round. They were both of them so deeply engaged in their conversation, that they did not observe my movement.

" ' But,' said my father, ' perhaps he has not got his bulbs about him?'

" ' Then take him down, under some pretext or other, and I will search his cell in the meanwhile.' "

" Halloa, halloa!" said Cornelius. " But this Mr. Jacob of yours is a villain, it seems."

" I am afraid he is."

" Tell me, Rosa," continued Cornelius, with a pensive air.

" What?"

"Did not you tell me, that on the day when you prepared your border this man followed you?"

"So he did,"

"That he glided like a shadow behind the elder-trees?"

"Certainly."

"That not one of your movements escaped him?"

"Not one, indeed."

"Rosa," said Cornelius, growing quite pale.

"Well?"

"It was not you he was after."

"Who else then?"

"It is not you that he is in love with!"

"But with whom else?"

"He was after my bulb, and is in love with my tulip!"

"You don't say so!—and yet it is very possible, said Rosa.

"Will you make sure of it?"

"In what manner?"

"Oh! It would be very easy."

"Tell me."

"Go to-morrow into the garden; manage matters so that Jacob may know, as he did the first time, that you are going there, and that he may follow you. Feign to put the bulb in the ground; leave the garden; but look through the keyhole of the door and watch him."

"Well, and what then?"

"What then? We shall do as he does."

"Oh!" said Rosa with a sigh, "you are very fond of your bulbs."

"To tell the truth," said the prisoner, sighing likewise, "since your father crushed that unfortunate bulb, I feel as if part of my own self had been paralysed."

"Now just hear me," said Rosa; "will you try something else?"

"What?"

"Will you accept the proposition of my father?"

"Which proposition?"

"Did not he offer to you tulip-bulbs by hundreds?"

"Indeed he did."

"Accept two or three and, along with them, you may grow the third sucker."

"Yes, that would do very well," said Cornelius, knitting his brow, "if your father were alone; but there is that Master Jacob, who watches all our actions."

"Well, that is true; but only think! you are depriving yourself, as I can easily see, of a very great pleasure."

She pronounced these words with a smile, which was not altogether without a tinge of irony.

Cornelius reflected for a moment; he evidently was struggling against some vehement desire.

" No!" he cried at last, with the stoicism of a Roman of old, " no, it would be a weakness, it would be a folly, it would be a meanness! If I thus gave up the only and last resource which we possess, to the uncertain chances of the bad passions of anger and envy, I should never hope to be forgiven. No, Rosa, no; to-morrow we shall come to a conclusion as to the spot to be chosen for your tulip; you will plant it according to my instructions; and as to the third sucker "—Cornelius here heaved a deep sigh—" watch over it, as a miser over his first or last piece of gold; as the mother over her child; as the wounded over the last drop of blood in his veins—watch over it, Rosa! Some voice within me tells me that it will be our saving, that it will be a source of good to us."

" Be easy, Mynheer Cornelius," said Rosa, with a sweet mixture of melancholy and gravity; " be easy, your wishes are commands to me."

" And even," continued Van Baerle, warming more and more with his subject, " if you should perceive that your steps are watched, and that your speech has excited the suspicion of your father and of that detestable Master Jacob; well, Rosa, don't hesitate for one moment to sacrifice me, who only still living through you; me, who have no one in the world but you; sacrifice me, don't come to see me any more."

Rosa felt her heart sing within her, and her eyes were filling with tears.

" Alas!" she said.

" What is it?" asked Cornelius.

" I see one thing."

" What do you see?"

" I see," she said, bursting out in sobs, " I see, that you love your tulips with such love, as to have no more room in your heart left for other affections."

Saying this, she fled.

Cornelius, after this, passed one of the worst nights he had ever had in his life.

Rosa was vexed with him, and with good reason. Perhaps she would never return to see the prisoner, and then he would have no more news either of Rosa or of his tulips.

We have to confess, to the disgrace of our hero and of floriculture, that of his two affections he felt most strongly inclined to regret the loss of Rosa; and when, at about three in the morning, he fell asleep, overcome with fatigue, and harassed with remorse, the grand black tulip yielded precedence in his dreams to the sweet blue eyes of the fair maid of Friesland.

CHAPTER XIX

THE MAID AND THE FLOWER

But poor Rosa, in her secluded chamber, could not have known of whom or of what Cornelius was dreaming.

From what he had said she was more ready to believe that he dreamed of the black tulip than of her; and yet Rosa was mistaken.

But as there was no one to tell her so, and as the words of Cornelius' thoughtless speech had fallen upon her heart like drops of poison, she did not dream, but she wept.

During the whole of this terrible night the poor girl did not close an eye, and before she rose in the morning, she had come to the resolution of making her appearance at the grated window no more.

But as she knew with what ardent desire Cornelius looked forward to the news about his tulip; and as, notwithstanding her determination not to see any more a man for whose fate her pity was fast growing into love, she did not, on the other hand, wish to drive him to despair: she resolved to continue by herself the reading and writing lessons; and, fortunately, she had made sufficient progress to dispense with the help of a master, when the master was not to be Cornelius.

Rosa, therefore, applied herself most diligently to reading poor Cornelius De Witte's Bible, on the second fly-leaf of which the last will of Cornelius Van Baerle was written.

"Alas!" she muttered, when perusing again this document which she never finished without a tear, the pearl of love, rolling from her limpid eyes on her blanched cheeks; "alas! at that time, I thought for one moment he loved me."

Poor Rosa! she was mistaken. Never had the love of the prisoner been more sincere than at the time at which we are now arrived, when in the contest between the black tulip and Rosa, the tulip had had to yield to her the first and foremost place in Cornelius' heart.

But Rosa was not aware of it.

Having finished reading, she took her pen, and began with as laudable diligence the by far more difficult task of writing.

As, however, Rosa was already able to write a legible hand, when Cornelius so uncautiously opened his heart, she did not despair of progressing quickly enough, to write, after eight days at the latest, to the prisoner an account of his tulip.

She had not forgotten one word of the directions given to her by Cornelius, whose speeches she treasured in her heart, even when they did not take the shape of directions.

He, on his part, awoke deeper in love than ever. The tulip, indeed, was still a luminous and prominent object in his mind; but he no longer looked upon it as a treasure to which he ought to sacrifice everything, and even Rosa; but as a marvellous combination of nature and art, with which he would have been happy to adorn the bosom of his beloved one.

Yet during the whole of that day he was haunted with a vague uneasiness, at the bottom of which was the fear lest Rosa should not come in the evening to pay him her usual visit. This thought took more and more hold of him, until at the approach of evening his whole mind was absorbed in it.

In Cornelius' cell one heard the chimes of the clock of the fortress. It struck seven, it struck eight, it struck nine. Never did the metal voice vibrate more forcibly through the heart of any man than did the last stroke, marking the ninth hour, through the heart of Cornelius.

All was then silent again. Cornelius put his hand on his heart, to repress, as it were, its violent palpitation, and listened.

The noise of her footstep, the rustling of her gown on the staircase, were so familiar to his ear, that she had no sooner mounted one step, than he used to say to himself:—

" Here comes Rosa."

This evening none of those little noises broke the silence of the lobby; the clock struck nine, a quarter past; the half hour; then a quarter to ten; at last its deep tone announced, not only to the inmates of the fortress, but also to all the inhabitants of Lœvestein, that it was ten.

This was the hour at which Rosa generally used to leave Cornelius. The hour had struck, but Rosa had not come.

Thus, then, his foreboding had not deceived him. Rosa, being vexed, shut herself up in her room and left him to himself.

" Alas!" he thought, " I have deserved all this. She will come no more, and she is right in staying away; in her place I should do just the same."

Yet, notwithstanding all this, Cornelius listened, waited and hoped, until midnight; then he threw himself, in his clothes, on his bed.

It was a long and sad night for him; and the day brought no hope to the prisoner.

At eight in the morning, the door of his cell opened; but Cornelius did not even turn his head; he had heard the heavy step of Gryphus in the lobby, but his step had perfectly satisfied the prisoner that his jailer was coming alone.

Thus Cornelius did not even look at Gryphus.

And yet he would have been so glad to draw him out, and to inquire about Rosa. He even very nearly made this inquiry, strange as it would needs have appeared to her father. To tell the truth, there was in all this some selfish hope, to hear from Gryphus that his daughter was ill.

Except on extraordinary occasions, Rosa never came during the day. Cornelius, therefore, did not really expect her, as long as the day lasted. Yet his sudden starts, his listening at the door, his rapid glances, at every little noise, towards the grated window, showed clearly that the prisoner entertained some latent hope that Rosa would, somehow or other, break her rule.

At the second visit of Gryphus, Cornelius, contrary to all his former habits, asked the old jailer, with the most winning voice, about her health; but Gryphus contented himself with giving the laconical answer:—

" All's well."

At the third visit of the day, Cornelius changed his former inquiry.

" I hope nobody is ill at Lœvestein?"

" Nobody," replied, even more laconically, the jailer, shutting the door before the nose of the prisoner.

Gryphus, being little used to this sort of civility on the part of Cornelius, began to suspect that his prisoner was about to try and bribe him.

Cornelius now was alone once more; it was seven o'clock in the evening, and the anxiety of yesterday returned with increased intensity.

But once more the hours passed away without bringing the sweet vision, which lighted up through the grated window the cell of poor Cornelius; and which, in retiring, left light enough in his heart to last until it came back again.

Van Baerle passed the night in an agony of despair. On the following day, Gryphus appeared to him even more hideous, brutal, and hateful than usual: in his mind, or rather in his heart, there had been some hope that it was the old man who prevented his daughter from coming.

In his wrath he would have strangled Gryphus, but would not this have separated him for ever from Rosa?

The evening closing in, his despair changed into melancholy, which was the more gloomy as, involuntarily, Van Baerle mixed up with it the thought of his poor tulip. It was now just that week in April, which the most experienced gardeners point out as the precise time when tulips ought to be planted. He had said to Rosa:—

"I shall tell you the day when you are to put the bulb in the ground."

He had intended to fix, at the vainly-hoped-for interview, the following day as the time for that momentous operation. The weather was propitious; the air, although still damp, began to be tempered by those pale rays of the April sun which, being the first, appear so congenial, although so pale. What if Rosa allowed the right moment for planting the bulb to pass by? If, in addition to the grief of seeing her no more, he should have to deplore the misfortune of seeing his tulip fail on account of its having been planted too late, or of its not having been planted at all!

These two vexations, combined, might well make him leave off eating and drinking.

This was the case on the fourth day.

It was pitiful to see Cornelius, dumb with grief, and pale from utter prostration, stretch out his head through the iron bars of his window, at the risk of not being able to draw it back again, to try and get a glimpse of the garden on the left, spoken of by Rosa, who had told him that its parapet overlooked the river. He hoped that perhaps he might see, in the light of the April sun, Rosa, or the tulip, the two lost objects of his love.

In the evening, Gryphus took away the breakfast and dinner of Cornelius who had scarcely touched them.

On the following day, he did not touch them at all, and Gryphus carried the dishes away just as he had brought them.

Cornelius had remained in bed the whole day.

"Well," said Gryphus, coming down from the last visit; "I think we shall soon get rid of our scholar."

Rosa was startled.

"Nonsense," said Jacob, "what do you mean?"

"He doesn't drink, he doesn't eat, he doesn't leave his bed. He will get out of it, like Mynheer Grotius in a chest; only the chest will be a coffin."

Rosa grew as pale as death.

"Ah!" she said to herself, "he is uneasy about his tulip."

And rising with a heavy heart, she returned to her chamber,

where she took a pen and paper, and, during the whole of that night, busied herself with tracing letters.

On the following morning, when Cornelius got up to drag himself to the window, he perceived a paper which had been slipped under the door.

He pounced upon it, opened it, and read the following words—in a handwriting which he could scarcely have recognised as that of Rosa, so much had she improved during her short absence of seven days:—

" Be easy, your tulip is going on well."

Although these few words of Rosa's somewhat soothed the grief of Cornelius, yet he felt not the less the irony which was at the bottom of them. Rosa, then, was not ill, she was offended; she had not been forcibly prevented from coming, but had voluntarily stayed away. Thus Rosa, being at liberty, found in her own will the force not to come and see him, who was dying with grief at not having seen her.

Cornelius had paper and a pencil which Rosa had brought to him. He guessed that she expected an answer, but that she would not come before the evening to fetch it. He therefore wrote on a piece of paper, similar to that which he had received:—

" It was not my anxiety about the tulip that has made me ill, but grief at not seeing you."

After Gryphus had made his last visit of the day, and darkness had set in, he slipped the paper under the door, and listened with the most intense attention; but he neither heard Rosa's footsteps nor the rustling of her gown.

He only heard a voice as feeble as a breath, and gentle like a caress, which whispered through the grated little window in the door, the word:—

" To-morrow."

Now to-morrow was the eighth day. For eight days Cornelius and Rosa had not seen each other.

CHAPTER XX

THE EVENTS WHICH TOOK PLACE DURING THOSE EIGHT DAYS

On the following evening, at the usual hour, Van Baerle heard someone scratch at the grated little window, just as Rosa had been in the habit of doing in the hey-day of their friendship.

Cornelius being, as may easily be imagined, not far off from the door, perceived Rosa, who at last was waiting again for him with her lamp in her hand.

Seeing him so sad and pale she was startled, and said:—

"You are ill, Mynheer Cornelius?"

"Yes, I am," he answered, as indeed he was suffering in mind and in body.

"I saw that you did not eat," said Rosa; "my father told me that you remained in bed all day. I then wrote to you to calm your uneasiness concerning the fate of the most precious object of your anxiety"

"And I," said Cornelius, "I have answered. Seeing you return, my dear Rosa, I thought you had received my letter."

"It is true I have received it."

"You cannot this time excuse yourself with not being able to read. Not only do you read very fluently, but also you have made marvellous progress in writing."

"Indeed, I have not only received, but also read your note. Accordingly I am come to see whether there might not be some remedy to restore you to health."

"Restore me to health?" cried Cornelius; "but have you any good news to communicate to me?"

Saying this, the poor prisoner looked at Rosa, his eyes sparkling with hope.

Whether she did not, or would not, understand this look, Rosa answered gravely:—

"I have only to speak to you about your tulip, which, as I well know, is the object uppermost in your mind."

Rosa pronounced these few words in a freezing tone, which cut deeply into the heart of Cornelius. He did not suspect what lay hidden under this appearance of indifference, with which the poor girl affected to speak of her rival, the black tulip.

"Oh!" muttered Cornelius, "again! again! Have I not told you, Rosa, that I thought but of you; that it was you alone whom I regretted, you whom I missed, you whose absence I felt more than the loss of liberty and of life itself?"

Rosa smiled with a melancholy air.

"Ah!" she said, "your tulip has been in such danger."

Cornelius trembled involuntarily, and allowed himself to be caught in the trap, if ever the remark was meant as such.

"Danger!" he cried, quite alarmed, "what danger?"

Rosa looked at him with gentle compassion; she felt that what she wished was beyond the power of this man, and that he must be taken, as he was, with his little foible.

"Yes," she said, "you have guessed the truth, that suitor and amorous swain, Jacob, did not come on my account."

"And what did he come for?" Cornelius anxiously asked.

" He came for the sake of the tulip."

" Alas!" said Cornelius, growing even paler at this piece of information than he had been when Rosa, a fortnight before, had told him that Jacob was coming for her sake.

Rosa saw this alarm, and Cornelius guessed, from the expression of her face, in what direction her thoughts were running.

" Oh! pardon me, Rosa," he said, " I know you and I am well aware of the kindness and sincerity of your heart. To you God has given the thought and strength for defending yourself, but to my poor tulip, when it is in danger, God has given nothing of the sort."

Rosa, without replying to this excuse of the prisoner, continued:—

" From the moment when I first knew that you were uneasy on account of the man who followed me, and in whom I had recognised Jacob, I was even more uneasy myself. On the day, therefore, after that on which I saw you last, and on which you said——"

Cornelius interrupted her.

" Once more, pardon me, Rosa!" he cried. " I was wrong in saying to you what I said. I have asked your pardon for that unfortunate speech before. I ask it again: shall I always ask it in vain?"

" On the following day," Rosa continued, " remembering what you had told me about the stratagem which I was to employ to ascertain whether that odious man was after the tulip, or after me——"

" Yes, yes, odious. Tell me," he said, " do you hate that man?"

" I do hate him," said Rosa, " as he is the cause of all the unhappiness I have suffered these eight days."

" You, too, have been unhappy, Rosa? I thank you a thousand times for this kind confession."

" Well, on the day after that unfortunate one, I went down into the garden, and proceeded towards the border, where I was to plant your tulip, looking round all the while to see whether I was again followed as I was last time."

" And then?" Cornelius asked.

" And then the same shadow glided between the gate and the wall, and once more disappeared behind the elder-trees."

" You feigned not to see him, didn't you?" Cornelius asked, remembering all the details of the advice which he had given to Rosa.

"Yes, and I stooped over the border, in which I dug with a spade, as if I was going to put the bulb in."

"And he—what did he do during all this time?"

"I saw his eyes glisten through the branches of the tree, like those of a tiger."

"There you see, there you see!" cried Cornelius.

"Then, after having finished my make-believe work, I retired."

"But only behind the garden-door, I daresay, so that you might see through the keyhole what he was going to do when you had left?"

"He waited for a moment, very likely to make sure of my not coming back; after which he sneaked forth from his hiding-place, and approached the border by a long round-about; at last, having reached his goal, that is to say, the spot where the ground was newly turned, he stopped with a careless air, looking about in all directions, and scanning every corner of the garden, every window of the neighbour-ing houses, and even the sky; after which, thinking himself quite alone, quite isolated, and out of everybody's sight, he pounced upon the border, plunged both his hands into the soft soil, took a handful of the mould, which he gently frittered between his fingers to see whether the bulb was in it, and repeated the same thing twice or three times, until at last he perceived that he was outwitted. Then, keeping down the agitation which was raging in his breast, he took up the rake, smoothed the ground, so as to leave it, on his retiring, in the same state as he had found it; and, quite abashed and rueful walked back to the door, affecting the unconcerned air of an ordinary visitor of the garden."

"Oh! the wretch," muttered Cornelius, wiping the cold sweat from his brow. "Oh! the wretch. I guessed his intentions. But the sucker, Rosa; what have you done with it? It is already rather late to plant it."

"The sucker? It has been in the ground for these six days."

"Where? and how?" cried Cornelius. "Good Heaven! what imprudence. Where is it? In what sort of soil is it? In what aspect? Good or bad? Is there no risk of having it stolen by that detestable Jacob?"

"There is no danger of its being stolen," said Rosa, "unless Jacob will force the door of my chamber."

"Oh! then it is with you in your bedroom?" said Cornelius, somewhat relieved. "But in what soil? in what vessel? You don't let it grow, I hope, in water, like those good ladies of Haarlem and Dort, who imagine that water could replace the earth?"

"You may make yourself comfortable on that score," said Rosa, smiling; "your sucker is not growing in water."

"I breathe again."

"It is in a good sound stone-pot, just about the size of the jug in which you had planted yours. The soil is composed of three parts of common mould, taken from the best spot of the garden, and one of the sweepings of the road. I have heard you and that detestable Jacob, as you call him, so often talk about what is the soil best fitted for growing tulips, that I know it as well as the first gardener of Haarlem."

"And now, what is the aspect, Rosa?"

"At present, it has the sun all day long, that is to say, when the sun shines. But when it once peeps out of the ground, I shall do, as you have done here, dear Mynheer Cornelius, I shall put it out in my window, on the eastern side, from eight in the morning until eleven, and in my window, towards the west, from three to five in the after-noon."

"That's it, that's it," cried Cornelius; "and you are a perfect gardener, my pretty Rosa. But I am afraid the nursing of my tulip will take up all your time."

"Yes, it will," said Rosa, "but never mind. Your tulip is my daughter. I shall devote to it the same time as I should to a child of mine, if I were a mother. Only by becoming its mother," Rosa added, smilingly, "can I cease to be its rival."

"My kind and pretty Rosa!" muttered Cornelius, casting on her a glance, in which there was much more of the lover than of the gardener, and which afforded Rosa some consolation.

"Then, after a silence of some moments, during which Cornelius had reached through the openings of the grating for the receding hand of Rosa, he said:—

"Do you mean to say that the bulb has now been in the ground for six days?"

"Yes, six days, Mynheer Cornelius," she answered.

"And it does not yet show leaf?"

"No; but I think it will to-morrow."

"Well then, to-morrow you will bring me news about it, and about yourself, won't you, Rosa? I care very much for the daughter, as you called it just now, but I care even much more for the mother."

"To-morrow?" said Rosa, looking at Cornelius askance, "I don't know whether I shall be able to-morrow."

"Good Heavens!" said Cornelius, "why can't you come to-morrow?"

"Mynheer Cornelius, I have lots of things to do."

"And I have only one," muttered Cornelius.

"Yes," said Rosa, "to love your tulip."

"To love you, Rosa."

Rosa shook her head, after which followed a pause.

"Well"—Cornelius at last broke the silence—"well, Rosa, everything changes in the realm of nature; the flowers of spring are succeeded by other flowers; and the bees, which so tenderly caressed the violets and the wallflowers, will flutter with just as much love about the honeysuckles, the rose, the jessamine, and the carnation."

"What does all this mean?" asked Rosa.

"You have abandoned me, Miss Rosa, to seek your pleasure elsewhere. You have done well, and I will not complain. What claim have I to your fidelity?"

"My fidelity!" Rosa exclaimed, with her eyes full of tears, and without caring any longer to hide from Cornelius this dew of pearls dropping on her cheeks, "my fidelity! have I not been faithful to you?"

"Do you call it faithful to desert me, and to leave me here to die?"

"But, Mynheer Cornelius," said Rosa, "am I not doing everything for you that could give you pleasure? have I not devoted myself to your tulip?"

"You are bitter, Rosa; you reproach me with the only unalloyed pleasure which I have had in this world."

"I reproach you with nothing, Mynheer Cornelius, except, perhaps, with the intense grief which I felt when people came to tell me at the Buitenhof that you were about to be put to death."

"You are displeased, Rosa, my sweet girl, with my loving flowers."

"I am not displeased at your loving them, Mynheer Cornelius, only it makes me sad to think that you love them better than you do me."

"Oh! my dear, dear Rosa, look how my hands tremble; look at my pale cheek, hear how my heart beats. It is for you, my love, not for the black tulip. Destroy the bulb, destroy the germ of that flower, extinguish the gentle light of that innocent and delightful dream, to which I have accustomed myself; but love me; Rosa, love me; for I feel deeply that I love but you."

"Yes, after the black tulip," sighed Rosa, who at last no

longer coyly withdrew her warm hands from the grating, as Cornelius most affectionately kissed them.

"Above and before everything in this world, Rosa."

"May I believe you?"

"As you believe in your own existence."

"Well, then, be it so; but loving me does not bind you to much."

"Unfortunately it does not bind me more than I am bound, but it binds you, Rosa, you."

"To what?"

"First of all, not to marry."

She smiled.

"That's your way," she said; "you are tyrants, all of you. You worship a certain beauty; you think of nothing but her. Then you are condemned to death and, whilst walking to the scaffold, you devote to her your last sigh; and now you expect poor me to sacrifice to you all my dreams and my happiness."

"But who is the beauty you are talking of, Rosa?" said Cornelius, trying in vain to remember a woman to whom Rosa might possibly be alluding.

"The dark beauty, with a slender waist, small feet, and a noble head; in short, I am speaking of your flower."

Cornelius smiled.

"That is an imaginary lady-love, at all events; whereas, without counting that amorous Master Jacob—you, by your own account, are surrounded with all sorts of swains eager to make love to you. Do you remember, Rosa, what you told me of the students, officers, and clerks of the Hague? Are there no clerks, officers, or students at Lœvestein?"

"Indeed there are, and lots of them."

"Who write letters?"

"They do write."

"And now, as you know how to read?"

Here Cornelius heaved a sigh at the thought, that, poor captive as he was, to him alone Rosa owed the faculty of reading the love-letters which she received.

"As to that," said Rosa, "I think that in reading the notes addressed to me, and passing the different swains in review, who send them to me, I am only following your instructions."

"How so? My instructions?"

"Indeed, your instruction, sir," said Rosa, sighing in her turn; "have you forgotten the will written by your hand on the Bible of Cornelius De Witte? I have not forgotten it; for now, as I know how to read, I read it every day over and over again. In that will, you bid me to love and marry a handsome young man of twenty-six or eight years. I am on the look-out for that young man, and as the whole of my day is taken up with your tulip, you must needs leave me the evenings to find him."

"But Rosa, the will was made in the expectation of death, and, thanks to Heaven, I am still alive."

"Well, then, I shall not be after the handsome young man, and I shall come and see you."

"That's it, Rosa, come! come!"

"On one condition."

"Granted beforehand!"

"That the black tulip shall not be mentioned for the next three days."

"It shall never be mentioned any more, if you wish it, Rosa."

"No, no," the damsel said, laughing, "I will not ask for impossibilities."

And, saying this, she brought her fresh cheek, as if unconsciously, so near the iron grating, that Cornelius was able to touch it with his lips.

Rosa uttered a little scream, which, however, was full of love, and disappeared.

CHAPTER XXI

THE SECOND SUCKER

The night was a happy one, and the whole of the next day happier still.

During the last few days, the prison had been heavy, dark, and lowering, as it were, with all its weight on the unfortunate captive. Its walls were black, its air chilling, the iron bars seemed to exclude every ray of light.

But when Cornelius awoke next morning, a beam of the morning sun was playing about those iron bars; pigeons were hovering about with outspread wings, whilst others were lovingly cooing on the roof or near the still closed window.

Cornelius ran to that window and opened it; it seemed to him as if new life, and joy, and liberty itself were entering, with this sunbeam, into his cell, which, so dreary of late, was now cheered and irradiated by the light of love.

When Gryphus, therefore, came to see his prisoner in the morning, he no longer found him morose and lying in bed, but standing at the window, and singing a little ditty.

"Halloa!" exclaimed the jailer.

"How are you this morning?" asked Cornelius.

Gryphus looked at him with a scowl.

"And how is the dog, and Master Jacob, and our pretty Rosa?"

Gryphus ground his teeth, saying,—

"Here is your breakfast."

"Thank you, friend Cerberus," said the prisoner; "you are just in time, I am very hungry."

"Oh! you are hungry, are you?" said Gryphus.

"And why not?" asked Van Baerle.

"The conspiracy seemed to thrive," remarked Gryphus.

"What conspiracy?"

"Very well, I know what I know, Master Scholar: just be quiet, we shall be on our guard."

"Be on your guard, friend Gryphus; be on your guard as long as you please; my conspiracy as well as my person is entirely at your service."

"We'll see that at noon."

Saying this, Gryphus went out.

"At noon?" repeated Cornelius; "what does that mean? Well, let us wait until the clock strikes twelve, and we shall see."

It was very easy for Cornelius to wait for twelve at midday, as he was already waiting for nine at night.

It struck twelve, and there were heard on the staircase, not only the steps of Gryphus, but also those of three or four soldiers who were coming up with him.

The door opened, Gryphus entered, led his men in, and shut the door after them.

"There, now search!"

They searched not only the pockets of Cornelius, but even his person; yet they found nothing.

They then searched the sheets, the mattress, and the straw-mattress of his bed; and again they found nothing.

Now, Cornelius rejoiced that he had not taken the third sucker under his own care. Gryphus would have been sure to ferret it out in the search, and would then have treated it as he did the first.

And, certainly, never did prisoner look with greater complacency at a search made in his cell than Cornelius.

Gryphus retired with the pencil and the two or three leaves of white paper which Rosa had given to Van Baerle; this was the only trophy brought back from the expedition.

At six Gryphus came again, but alone; Cornelius tried to

propitiate him, but Gryphus growled, showed a large tooth like a tusk, which he had in the corner of his mouth, and went out backwards like a man who is afraid of being attacked from behind.

Cornelius burst out laughing, to which Gryphus answered through the grating:

" Let him laugh that wins."

The winner that day was Cornelius—Rosa came at nine.

She was without a lantern. She needed no longer a light as she could now read. Moreover, the light might betray her, as Jacob was dodging her steps more than ever. And, lastly, the light would have shown her blushes.

Of what did the young people speak that evening? Of those matters of which lovers speak at the house-doors in France, or from a balcony into the street in Spain; or down from a terrace into a garden in the East.

They spoke of those things which gave wings to the hours; they spoke of everything except the black tulip.

At last, when the clock struck ten, they parted as usual.

Cornelius was happy, as thoroughly happy as a tulip-fancier could be, to whom one has not spoken about his tulip.

He found Rosa pretty, good, graceful and charming.

But why did Rosa object to the tulip being spoken of?

This was indeed a great defect in Rosa.

Cornelius confessed to himself, sighing, that woman was not perfect.

Part of the night he thought of this imperfection; that is to say, as long as he was awake he thought of Rosa.

After having fallen asleep he dreamed of her.

But the Rosa of his dreams was more perfect by far than the Rosa of real life. Not only did the Rosa of his dreams speak of the tulip, but also brought to him a black one in a china vase.

Cornelius then awoke, trembling with joy and muttering:

" Rosa, Rosa, I love you."

And as it was already day he thought it right not to fall asleep again, and he continued following up the line of thought in which his mind was engaged when he awoke."

Ah! if Rosa had only conversed about the tulip, Cornelius would have preferred her to Queen Semiramis, to Queen Cleopatra, to Queen Elizabeth, to Queen Anne of Austria; that is to say, to the greatest or most beautiful queens whom the world has seen.

There was one consolation—of the seventy-two hours, during which Rosa would not allow the tulip to be mentioned, thirty-six had passed already; and the remaining thirty-six would pass quickly enough, eighteen with waiting for the evening's interview, and eighteen with rejoicing in its remembrance.

Rosa came at the same hour, and Cornelius submitted most heroically to the pangs which the compulsory silence concerning the tulip gave him.

His fair visitor, however, was well aware, that to command on the one hand people must yield on another; she, therefore, no longer drew back her hands from the grating, and even allowed Cornelius tenderly to kiss her beautiful golden tresses.

Poor girl! she had no idea that these playful little lovers' tricks were much more dangerous than speaking of the tulip was; but she became aware of the fact as she returned with a beating heart, with glowing cheeks, dry lips, and moist eyes.

And on the following evening, after the first exchange of salutations, she retired a step, looking at him with a glance, the expression of which would have rejoiced his heart could he but have seen it.

"Well," she said, "she is up."

"She is up! Who? What?" asked Cornelius, who did not venture on a belief that Rosa would, of her own accord, have abridged the term of his probation.

"She? Well! my daughter, the tulip," said Rosa.

"What?" cried Cornelius, "you give me permission, then?"

"I do," said Rosa, with the tone of an affectionate mother who grants a pleasure to her child.

"Ah, Rosa!" said Cornelius, putting his lips to the grating, with the hope of touching a cheek, a hand, a forehead—anything, in short.

He touched something much better—two warm and half-open lips.

Rosa uttered a slight scream.

Cornelius understood that he must make haste to continue the conversation. He guessed that this unexpected kiss had frightened Rosa.

"Is it growing up straight?" he asked.

"Straight as a rocket," said Rosa.

"How high?"

"At least two inches."

"Oh, Rosa, take good care of it, and we shall soon see it grow quickly."

"Can I take more care of it?" said she; "indeed I think of nothing else but the tulip."

"Of nothing else, Rosa? Why now, I shall grow jealous in my turn."

"Oh, you know that to think of the tulip is to think of you: I never lose sight of it. I see it from my bed; on my awaking, it is the first object that meets my eyes; and on falling asleep the last on which they rest. During the day I sit and work by its side, for I have never left my chamber since I put it there."

"You are right, Rosa, it is your dowry, you know."

"Yes, and with it I may marry a young man of twenty-six or twenty-eight years, whom I shall be in love with."

"Don't talk in that way, you naughty girl."

That evening Cornelius was one of the happiest of men. Rosa allowed him to press her hand in his, and to keep it as long as he would, besides which he might talk of his tulip as much as he liked.

From that hour, every day marked some progress in the growth of the tulip and in the affection of the two young people.

At one time it was that the leaves had expanded, and at another that the flower itself had formed.

Great was the joy of Cornelius at this news, and his questions succeeded each other with a rapidity which gave proof of their importance.

"Formed!" exclaimed Cornelius, "it is really formed?"

"It is," repeated Rosa.

Cornelius trembled with joy, so much so that he was obliged to hold by the grating.

"Good Heavens!" he exclaimed.

Then turning again to Rosa, he continued his questions.

"Is the oval regular? the cylinder full? and are the points very green?"

"The oval is almost one inch long, and tapers like a needle, the cylinder swells at the sides, and the points are ready to open."

Two days after, Rosa announced that they were open.

"Open, Rosa!" cried Cornelius. "Is the involucrum open? but then one may see, and already distinguish——"

Here the prisoner paused, anxiously taking breath.

"Yes," answered Rosa, "one may already distinguish a thread of different colour, as thin as a hair."

"And its colour?" asked Cornelius, trembling.

"Oh," answered Rosa, "it is very dark."

"Brown?"

"Darker than that."

"Darker, my good Rosa, darker? thank you.   Dark like——"

"Dark, like the ink with which I wrote to you."

Cornelius uttered a cry of mad joy.

Then suddenly stopping, and clasping his hands, he said:

"Oh, there is not an angel in heaven that may be compared to you, Rosa!"

"Indeed!" said Rosa, smiling at his enthusiasm.

"Rosa, you have worked with such ardour; you have done so much for me. Rosa, my tulip is about to flower, and it will flower black. Rosa! Rosa! you are the most perfect being on earth."

"After the tulip, though."

"Ah! be quiet, you malicious little creature, be quiet; for shame, do not spoil my pleasure! But tell me, Rosa; as the tulip is so far advanced, it will flower in two or three days at the latest?"

"To-morrow, or the day after."

"Ah! and I shall not see it," cried Cornelius, starting back, "I shall not kiss it as a wonderful work of the Almighty, as I kiss your hand and your cheek, Rosa, when by chance they are near the grating."

Rosa drew near, not by accident, but intentionally, and Cornelius kissed her tenderly.

"Faith, I shall cull it, if you wish it."

"Oh, no, no, Rosa, when it is open, place it carefully in the shade and immediately send a message to Haarlem, to the President of the Horticultural Society, that the grand black tulip is in flower. I know well it is far to Haarlem, but with money you will find a messenger; have you any money, Rosa?"

Rosa smiled.

"Oh! yes," she said.

"Enough?" asked Cornelius.

"I have three hundred guilders."

"Oh! if you have three hundred guilders, you must not send a messenger, Rosa, but you must go to Haarlem yourself."

"But what, in the meanwhile, is to become of the flower?"

"Oh, the flower, you must take it with you. You understand that you must not separate from it for an instant."

"But whilst I am not separating from it, I am separating from you, Mynheer Cornelius."

"Ah! that's true, my sweet Rosa. Oh! good Heavens! how wicked men are! What have I done to offend them,

and why have they deprived me of my liberty? You are
right, Rosa, I cannot live without you. Well, you will send
someone to Haarlem—that's settled; really, the matter is
wonderful enough for the President to put himself to some
trouble. He will come himself to Lœvestein to see the tulip."

Then, suddenly checking himself, he said with a faltering
voice:

"Rosa, Rosa, if after all it should not flower black!"

"Oh, surely, surely you will know to-morrow, or the day
after."

"And to wait until evening to know it, Rosa! I shall die
with impatience. Could we not agree about a signal?"

"I shall do better than that."

"What will you do?"

"If it opens at night, I shall come and tell you myself. If
it is day, I shall pass your door, and slip you a note either
under the door, or through the grating, during the time
between my father's first and second inspection."

"Yes, Rosa, let it be so. One word of yours, announcing
this news to me, will be a double happiness."

"There, ten o'clock strikes," said Rosa, "I must now
leave you."

"Yes, yes," said Cornelius, "go, Rosa, go."

Rosa withdrew, almost melancholy, for Cornelius had all
but sent her away.

It is true that he did so, in order that she might watch
over his black tulip.

CHAPTER XXII

JOY

The night passed away very sweetly for Cornelius, although
in great agitation. Every instant he fancied he heard the
gentle voice of Rosa calling him. He then started up, went
to the door, and looked through the grating, but no one was
behind it, and the lobby was empty.

Day came, without any news; the tulip was not yet in
flower.

The day passed as the night. Night came, and with it Rosa,
joyous and cheerful as a bird.

"Well?" asked Cornelius.

"Well, all is going on prosperously. This night, without
any doubt, our tulip will be in flower."

"And will it flower black?"

"Black as jet."

"Without a speck of any other colour?"

"Without one speck."

"Good Heavens! my dear Rosa, I have been dreaming all night, in the first place of you" (Rosa made a sign of incredulity), "and then of what we must do."

"Well?"

"Well, and I will tell you now what I have decided on. The tulip once being in flower, and it being quite certain that it is perfectly black, you must find a messenger."

"If it is no more than that, I have a messenger quite ready."

"Is he safe?

"One for whom I will answer—he is one of my lovers."

"I hope not Jacob."

"No, be quiet; it is the ferryman of Lœvestein, a smart young man of twenty-five."

"By Jove!"

"Be quiet," said Rosa, smiling, "he is still under age, as you have yourself fixed it as from twenty-six to twenty-eight."

"In fine, do you think you may rely on this young man?"

"As on myself; he would throw himself into the Waal or the Meuse if I bade him."

"Well, Rosa, this lad may be at Haarlem in ten hours, you will give me paper and pencil, and, perhaps better still, pen and ink, and I will write, or rather, on second thoughts, you will, for if I did it, being a poor prisoner, people might, like your father, see a conspiracy in it. You will write to the President of the Horticultural Society, and I am sure he will come."

"But if he tarries?"

"Well, let us suppose that he tarries one day, or even two; but it is impossible. A tulip-fancier like him will not tarry one hour, not one minute, not one second, to set out to see the eighth wonder of the world. But, as I said, if he tarried one or even two days, the tulip will still be in its full splendour. The flower once being seen by the President, and the protocol being drawn up, all is in order; you will only keep a duplicate of the protocol, and intrust the tulip to him. Ah, if we had been able to carry it ourselves, Rosa, it would never have left my hands but to pass into yours; but this is a dream, which we must not entertain," continued Cornelius, with a sigh, "the eyes of strangers will see it flower to the last. And above all, Rosa, before the President has seen it, let it not be seen by anyone. Alas! if anyone saw the black tulip, it would be stolen."

"Oh!"

"Did you not tell me yourself what you apprehend from your lover, Jacob? people will steal one guilder, why not a hundred thousand?"

"I shall watch; be quiet."

"But if it opened whilst you are here?"

"The whimsical little thing would indeed be quite capable of playing such a trick," said Rosa.

"And if on your return you find it open?"

"Well?"

"Oh, Rosa, whenever it opens, remember that not a moment must be lost in apprising the President."

"And in apprising you. Yes, I understand."

Rosa sighed, yet without any bitter feeling, but rather like a woman who begins to understand a foible, and to accustom herself to it.

"I return to your tulip, Mynheer Van Baerle, and as soon as it opens, I will give you news, which being done, the messenger will set out immediately."

"Rosa, Rosa, I don't know to what wonder under the sun I shall compare you."

"Compare me to the black tulip, and I promise you I shall feel very much flattered. Good-night, then, till we meet again, Mynheer Cornelius."

"Oh, say good-night, my friend."

"Good-night, my friend," said Rosa, a little consoled.

"Say my very dear friend."

"Oh, my friend."

"Very dear friend, I entreat you, say, very dear, Rosa, very dear."

"Very dear, yes, very dear," said Rosa, with a beating heart, beside herself with happiness.

During part of the night, Cornelius, with his heart full of joy and delight, remained at his window, gazing at the stars, and listening for every sound.

Then casting a glance from time to time towards the lobby:

"Down there," he said, "is Rosa, watching like myself, and waiting from minute to minute; down there, under Rosa's eyes, is the mysterious flower, which lives, which expands, which opens; perhaps Rosa holds in this moment the stem of the tulip between her delicate fingers. Touch it gently, Rosa. Perhaps she touches with her lips its expanding chalice. Touch it cautiously, Rosa, your lips are burning. Yes, perhaps at this moment, the two objects of my dearest love caress each other under the eye of Heaven."

At this moment a star blazed in the southern sky, and shot through the whole horizon, falling down, as it were, on the fortress of Lœvestein.

Cornelius felt a thrill run through his frame.

"Ah!" he said, "here is Heaven sending a soul to my flower."

And as if he had guessed correctly, nearly at that very moment the prisoner heard in the lobby a step light as that of a sylph, and the rustling of a gown, and a well-known voice, which said to him:

"Cornelius, my friend, my very dear friend, and very happy friend, come, come quickly."

Cornelius darted with one spring from the window to the door, his lips met those of Rosa, who told him, with a kiss:

"It is open, it is black, here it is."

"How, here it is!" exclaimed Cornelius.

"Yes, yes, we ought, indeed, to run some little risk, to give a great joy; here it is, take it."

And with one hand she raised to the level of the grating a dark lantern, which she had lit in the meanwhile, whilst with the other she held to the same height the miraculous tulip.

Cornelius uttered a cry, and was nearly fainting.

"Oh!" muttered he, "my God, my God, Thou dost reward me for my innocence and my captivity, as Thou hast allowed two such flowers to grow at the grated window of my prison."

The tulip was beautiful, splendid, magnificent; its stem was more than eighteen inches high, it rose from out of four green leaves, which were as smooth and straight as iron lance heads; the whole of the flower was as black and shining as jet.

"Rosa," said Cornelius, almost gasping, "Rosa, there is not one moment to lose in writing the letter."

"It is written, my dearest Cornelius," said Rosa.

"Is it, indeed?"

"Whilst the tulip opened I wrote it myself, for I did not wish to lose a moment. Here is the letter, and tell me whether you approve of it."

Cornelius took the letter, and read, in a hand which was much improved even since the last little note he had received from Rosa, as follows:—

" MYNHEER PRESIDENT,

"The black tulip is about to open, perhaps in ten minutes.

As soon as it is open I shall send a messenger to you, with the request that you will come and fetch it in person from the fortress at Lœvestein. I am the daughter of the jailer, Gryphus, almost as much a captive as the prisoners of my father. I cannot, therefore, bring to you this wonderful flower. This is the reason why I beg you to come and fetch it yourself.

"It is my wish that it should be called *Rosa Barlænsis*.

"It has opened; it is perfectly black; come, Mynheer President, come.

"I have the honour to be, your humble servant,
                                        "ROSA GRYPHUS."

"That's it, dear Rosa, that's it. Your letter is admirable! I could not have written it with such beautiful simplicity. You will give to the committee all the information that will be asked of you. They will then know how the tulip has been grown, how much care and anxiety, and how many sleepless nights it has cost. But, for the present, not a minute must be lost, for the messenger, the messenger."

"What's the name of the President?"

"Give me the letter, I will direct it. Oh, he is very well known, it is Mynheer Van Herysen, the burgomaster of Haarlem; give it me, Rosa, give it me."

And with a trembling hand Cornelius wrote the address.

"To Mynheer Peter Van Herysen, Burgomaster, and President of the Horticultural Society of Haarlem."

"And now, Rosa, go, go," said Cornelius, "and let us implore the protection of God who has so kindly watched over us until now."

CHAPTER XXIII

THE RIVAL

And in fact the poor young people were in great need of protection.

They had never been so near the destruction of their hopes as at this moment, when they thought themselves certain of their fulfilment.

The reader cannot but have recognised in Jacob our old friend, or rather enemy, Isaac Boxtel, and has guessed, no doubt, that this worthy had followed, from the Buitenhof to Lœvestein, the object of his love and the object of his hatred—the black tulip and Cornelius Van Baerle.

What no one but a tulip-fancier, and an envious tulip-fancier could have discovered—the existence of the suckers and the endeavours of the prisoner—jealousy had enabled Boxtel if not to discover, at least to guess.

We have seen him, more successful under the name of Jacob than under that of Isaac, gain the friendship of Gryphus, which for several months he cultivated by means of the best *genièvre* ever distilled from the Texel to Antwerp, and he lulled the suspicion of the jealous turnkey by holding out to him the flattering prospect of his designing to marry Rosa.

Besides thus offering a bait to the ambition of the father, he managed, at the same time, to interest his zeal as a jailer, picturing to him in the blackest colours the learned prisoner whom Gryphus had in his keeping, and who, as the sham Jacob had it, was in league with Satan, to the detriment of His Highness the Prince of Orange.

At first he had also made some way with Rosa; not, indeed, in her affections, but inasmuch as, by talking to her of marriage and of love, he had evaded all suspicions which he might otherwise have excited.

We have seen how his prudence in following Rosa into the garden had unmasked him in the eyes of the young damsel, and how the instinctive fears of Cornelius had put the two lovers on their guard against him.

The reader will remember that the first cause for uneasiness was given to the prisoner by the rage of Jacob when Gryphus crushed the first sucker. In that moment Boxtel's exasperation was the more fierce, as, though suspecting that Cornelius possessed a second sucker, he by no means felt sure of it.

From that moment he began to dodge the steps of Rosa, not only following her to the garden, but also to the lobbies.

Only at this time he followed her in the night, and bare-footed, he was neither seen nor heard, except once, when Rosa thought she saw something like a shadow on the staircase.

Her discovery, however, was made too late, as Boxtel had heard from the mouth of the prisoner himself that a second sucker existed.

Taken in by the stratagem of Rosa, who had feigned to put it in the ground, and entertaining no doubt but that this little farce had been played in order to force him to betray himself, he redoubled his precaution, and employed every means suggested by his crafty nature to watch the others without being watched himself.

He saw Rosa conveying a large flower-pot of white

earthenware from her father's kitchen to her bedroom. He saw Rosa washing in pails of water her pretty little hands, begrimed as they were with the mould which she had handled, to give her tulip the best soil possible.

And at last he hired, just opposite Rosa's window, a little attic, distant enough not to allow him to be recognised with the naked eye, but sufficiently near to enable him, with the help of his telescope, to watch everything that was going on at Lœvestein in Rosa's room, just as at Dort he had watched the dry-room of Cornelius.

He had not been installed more than three days in his attic before all his doubts were removed.

From morning to sunset the flower-pot was in the window, and like those charming female figures of Mieris and Metzys, Rosa appeared at that window as in a frame, formed by the first budding sprays of the wild vine and the honeysuckle encircling her window.

Rosa watched the flower-pot with an interest which betrayed to Boxtel the real value of the object inclosed in it.

This object could not be anything else but the second sucker, that is to say, the quintessence of all the hopes of the prisoner.

When the nights threatened to be too cold, Rosa took in the flower-pot.

Well, it was then quite evident she was following the instructions of Cornelius, who was afraid of the bulb being killed by frost.

When the sun became too hot, Rosa likewise took in the pot from eleven in the morning until two in the afternoon.

Another proof: Cornelius was afraid lest the soil should become too dry.

But when the first leaves peeped out of the earth Boxtel was fully convinced, and his telescope left him no longer in any uncertainty before they had grown one inch in height.

Cornelius possessed two suckers, and the second was intrusted to the love and care of Rosa.

For it may well be imagined that the tender secret of the two lovers had not escaped the prying curiosity of Boxtel.

The question, therefore, was how to wrest the second sucker from the care of Rosa.

Certainly this was no easy task.

Rosa watched over her tulip as a mother over her child, or a dove over her eggs.

Rosa never left her room during the day, and, more than that, strange to say she never left it in the evening.

For seven days, Boxtel in vain watched Rosa; she was always at her post.

This happened during those seven days which made Cornelius so unhappy, depriving him at the same time of all news of Rosa and of his tulip.

Would the coolness between Rosa and Cornelius last for ever?

This would have made the theft much more difficult than Mynheer Isaac had at first expected.

We say the theft, for Isaac had simply made up his mind to steal the tulip; and as it grew in the most profound secrecy, and as, moreover, his word, being that of a renowned tulip-grower, would any day be taken against that of an unknown girl, without any knowledge of horticulture, or against that of a prisoner convicted of high treason, he confidently hoped that, having once got possession of the bulb, he would be certain to obtain the prize; and then the tulip, instead of being called *Tulipa nigra Barlæensis,* would go down to posterity under the name of *Tulipa nigra Boxtellensis* or *Boxtellea.*

Mynheer Isaac had not yet quite decided which of these two names he would give to the tulip, but as both meant the same thing, this was, after all, not the question.

The question was, to steal the tulip. But in order that Boxtel might steal the tulip, it was necessary that Rosa should leave her room.

Great, therefore, was his joy when he saw the usual evening meetings of the lovers resumed.

He, first of all, took advantage of Rosa's absence to make himself fully acquainted with all peculiarities of the door of her chamber. The lock was a double one, and in good order, but Rosa always took the key with her.

Boxtel, at first, entertained an idea of stealing the key, but it soon occurred to him that not only would it be exceedingly difficult to abstract it from her pocket, but also that, when she perceived her loss, she would not leave her room until the lock was changed, and then Boxtel's first theft would be useless.

He thought it, therefore, better to employ a different expedient. He collected as many keys as he could, and tried all of them during one of those delightful hours which Rosa and Cornelius passed together at the grating of the cell.

Two of the keys entered the lock, and one of them turned round once, but not the second time.

There was therefore only a little to be done to this key.

Boxtel covered it with a slight coat of wax, and when he thus renewed the experiment, the obstacle which prevented the key from being turned a second time, left its impression on the wax.

It cost Boxtel two days more to bring his key to perfection, with the aid of a small file.

Rosa's door thus opened without noise and without difficulty, and Boxtel found himself in her room alone with the tulip.

The first guilty act of Boxtel had been to climb over a wall in order to dig up the tulip; the second, to introduce himself into the dry-room of Cornelius, through an open window; and the third, to enter Rosa's room by means of a false key.

Thus envy urged Boxtel on with rapid steps in the career of crime.

Boxtel, as we have said, was alone with the tulip.

A common thief would have taken the pot under his arm, and carried it off.

But Boxtel was not a common thief, and he reflected.

It was not yet certain, although very probable, that the tulip would flower black; if, therefore, he stole it now, he not only might be committing a useless crime, but also the theft might be discovered in the time which must elapse until the flower should open.

He, therefore—as, being in possession of the key, he might enter Rosa's chamber whenever he liked—thought it better to wait and to take it either an hour before or after opening, and to start on the instant to Haarlem, where the tulip would be before the judges of the committee before anyone else could put in a reclamation.

Should any one then reclaim it, Boxtel would, in his turn, charge him or her with theft.

This was a deep-laid scheme, and quite worthy of its author.

Thus, every evening during that delightful hour which the two lovers passed together at the grated window, Boxtel entered Rosa's chamber to watch the progress which the black tulip had made towards flowering.

On the evening at which we have arrived, he was going to enter according to custom; but the two lovers, as we have seen, only exchanged a few words before Cornelius sent Rosa back to watch over the tulip.

Seeing Rosa enter her room ten minutes after she had left it, Boxtel guessed that the tulip had opened, or was about to open.

During that night, therefore, the great blow was to be struck. Boxtel presented himself before Gryphus with a double supply of genièvre, that is to say, with a bottle in each pocket.

Gryphus being once fuddled, Boxtel was very nearly master of the house.

At eleven o'clock Gryphus was dead drunk. At two in the morning Boxtel saw Rosa leaving the chamber; but evidently she held in her arms something which she carried with great care.

He did not doubt but that this was the black tulip which was in flower.

But what was she going to do with it? would she set out that instant to Haarlem with it?

It was not possible that a young girl should undertake such a journey alone during the night.

Was she only going to show the tulip to Cornelius? This was more likely.

He followed Rosa, in his stockinged feeet, walking on tip-toe.

He saw her approach the grated window. He heard her calling Cornelius. By the light of the dark-lantern he saw the tulip, open, and black as the night in which he was hidden.

He heard the plan concerted between Cornelius and Rosa to send a messenger to Haarlem. He saw the lips of the lovers meet, and then heard Cornelius send Rosa away.

He saw Rosa extinguish the light, and return to her chamber. Ten minutes after, he saw her leave the room again, and lock it twice.

Boxtel, who saw all this whilst hiding himself on the landing-place of the staircase above, descended step by step from his story, as Rosa descended from hers; so that when she touched with her light foot the lowest step of the stair-case, Boxtel touched, with a still lighter hand, the lock of Rosa's chamber.

And in that hand, it must be understood, he held the false key which opened Rosa's door as easily as did the real one.

And this is why, in the beginning of the chapter, we said that the poor young people were in great need of the pro-tection of God.

CHAPTER XXIV

THE BLACK TULIP CHANGES MASTERS

Cornelius remained standing on the spot where Rosa had left him. He was quite overpowered with the weight of his twofold happiness.

Half-an-hour passed away Already did the first rays of the sun enter through the iron grating of the prison, when Cornelius was suddenly startled at the noise of steps which came up the staircase, and of cries which approached nearer and nearer.

Almost at the same instant he saw before him the pale and distracted face of Rosa.

He started, and turned pale with fright.

"Cornelius, Cornelius!" she screamed, gasping for breath.

"Good Heavens! what is it?" asked the prisoner.

"Cornelius, the tulip."

"Well?"

"How shall I tell you?"

"Speak, speak, Rosa!"

"Someone has taken—stolen it from us."

"Stolen—taken," said Cornelius.

"Yes," said Rosa, leaning against the door to support herself; "yes, taken, stolen."

And saying this, she felt her limbs failing her, and she fell on her knees.

"But how? tell me, explain to me."

"Oh, it is not my fault, my friend."

Poor Rosa! she no longer dared to call him "My beloved one."

"You have then left it alone," said Cornelius ruefully.

"One minute only, to instruct our messenger, who lives scarcely fifty yards off, on the banks of the Waal."

"And during that time, notwithstanding all my injunctions, you left the key behind—unfortunate child!"

"No, no, no! that is what I cannot understand. The key was never out of my hands; I clenched it as if I were afraid it would take wings."

"But how did it happen, then?"

"That's what I cannot make out. I had given the letter to my messenger; he started before I left his house; I came home, and my door was locked; everything in my room was as I had left it, except the tulip—that was gone. Someone must have had a key for my room, or have got a false one made on purpose."

She was nearly choking with sobs, and was unable to continue.

Cornelius, immovable and full of consternation, heard almost without understanding, and only muttered:—

"Stolen, stolen, stolen, I am lost!"

"Oh, Cornelius, forgive me, forgive me, it will kill me."

Seeing Rosa's distress, Cornelius seized the iron bars of the grating and furiously shaking them, called out:—

"Rosa, Rosa, we have been robbed, it is true, but shall we allow ourselves to be dejected for all that? No, no; the misfortune is great, but it may perhaps be remedied; Rosa, we know the thief!"

"Alas! what can I say about it?"

"But I say, that it is no one else but that infamous Jacob. Shall we allow him to carry to Haarlem the fruit of our labour, the fruit of our sleepless nights, the child of our love? Rosa, we must pursue, we must overtake him!"

"But how can we do all this, my friend, without letting my father know that we were in communication with each other? How should I, a poor girl with so little knowledge of the world and its ways, be able to attain this end, which, perhaps, you could not attain yourself?"

"Rosa Rosa, open this door to me, and you will see whether I will not find the thief—whether I will not make him confess his crime and beg for mercy."

"Alas!" cried Rosa, sobbing, "can I open the door for you? have I the keys? If I had had them, would not you have been free long ago?"

"Your father has them—your wicked father who has already crushed the first sucker of my tulip. Oh, the wretch, the wretch, he is an accomplice of Jacob!"

"Don't speak so loud, for Heaven's sake."

"Oh, Rosa, if you don't open the door to me," Cornelius cried, in his rage, "I shall force these bars and kill everything I find in the prison!"

"Be merciful, be merciful, my friend."

"I tell you, Rosa, that I shall demolish this prison, stone for stone;" and the unfortunate man, whose strength was increased tenfold by his rage, began to shake the door with a great noise, little heeding that the thunder of his voice was re-echoing through the spiral staircase.

Rosa, in her fright, made vain attempts to check this furious outbreak.

"I tell you that I shall kill that infamous Gryphus!"

roared Cornelius, " I tell you I shall shed his blood, as he did
that of my black tulip!"

The wretched prisoner began really to rave.

" Well, then, yes;" said Rosa, all in a tremble. " Yes,
yes, only be quiet. Yes, I will take his keys, I will open the
door for you—yes, only be quiet, my own dear Cornelius."

She did not finish her speech, as a growl by her side
interrupted her.

" My father!" cried Rosa.

" Gryphus!" roared Van Baerle. " Oh, you villain."

Old Gryphus, in the midst of all the noise, had ascended
the staircase without being heard.

He rudely seized his daughter by the wrist.

" So you will take my keys?" he said, in a voice choking
with rage; " Ah! this dastardly fellow, this monster, this
gallows-bird of a conspirator is your own dear Cornelius, is
he? Ah!   Missy has communications with prisoners of
State. Ah! won't I teach you, won't I?"

Rosa clasped her hands in despair.

" Ah!" Gryphus continued, passing from the madness of
anger to the cool irony of a man who has got the better of
his enemy, " Ah! you innocent tulip-fancier, you gentle
scholar; you will kill me, and drink my blood! Very well!
Very well! And you have my daughter for an accomplice.
Am I, forsooth, in a den of thieves—in a cave of brigands?
Yes; but the Governor shall know all to-morrow, and His
Highness the Stadtholder the day after. We know the law;
we shall give a second edition of the Buitenhof, Master
Scholar, and a good one this time. Yes, yes; just gnaw your
paws like a bear in his cage, and you, my fine little lady,
devour your dear Cornelius with your eyes. I tell you, my
lambkins, you shall not much longer have the felicity of
conspiring together. Away with you! unnatural daughter!
And as to you, Master Scholar, we shall see each other again.
Just be quiet—we shall."

Rosa, beside herself with terror and despair, kissed her
hands to her friend; then, suddenly struck with a bright
thought, she rushed towards the staircase, saying:—

" All is not yet lost, Cornelius.   Rely on me, my
Cornelius"

Her father followed her, growling.

As to poor Cornelius, he gradually loosened his hold of
the bars, which his fingers still grasped convulsively. His
head was heavy, his eyes had almost started from their
sockets, and he fell heavily on the floor of his cell,
muttering:—

" Stolen; it has been stolen from me!"

During this time Boxtel had left the fortress, by the door which Rosa herself had opened. He carried the black tulip wrapped up in a cloak, and, throwing himself into a coach, which was waiting for him at Gorcum, he drove off, without, as may well be imagined, having informed his friend Gryphus of his sudden departure.

And now, as we have seen him enter his coach, we shall, with the consent of the reader, follow him to the end of his journey.

He proceeded but slowly, as a black tulip could not bear travelling post haste.

But Boxtel, fearing that he might not arrive early enough, procured at Delft a box, lined all round with fresh moss, in which he packed the tulip. The flower was so lightly pressed upon all sides, with a supply of air from above, that the coach could now travel full speed without any possibility of injury to the tulip.

He arrived next morning at Haarlem, fatigued but triumphant; and, to do away with every trace of the theft, he transplanted the tulip, and, breaking the original flower-pot, threw the pieces into the canal. After which he wrote the President of the Horticultural Society a letter, in which he announced to him, that he had just arrived at Haarlem with a perfectly black tulip; and, with his flower all safe, took up his quarters at a good hotel in the town and there he waited.

CHAPTER XXV

THE PRESIDENT VAN HERYSEN

Rosa, on leaving Cornelius, had fixed on her plan, which was no other than to restore to Cornelius the stolen tulip, or never to see him again.

She had seen the despair of the prisoner, and she knew that it was derived from a double source, and that it was incurable.

On the one hand, separation became inevitable; Gryphus having, at the same time, surprised the secret of their love, and of their secret meetings.

On the other hand, all the hopes, on the fulfilment of which Cornelius Van Baerle had rested his ambition for the last seven years, were now crushed.

Rosa was one of those women who are dejected by trifles;

but who, in great emergencies, are supplied by the misfortune itself with the energy for combating, or with the resources for remedying it.

She went to her room, and cast a last glance about her, to see whether she had not been mistaken, and whether the tulip was not stowed away in some corner, where it had escaped her notice. But she sought in vain; the tulip was still wanting; the tulip was indeed stolen.

Rosa made up a little parcel of things indispensable for a journey; took her three hundred guilders, that is to say, all her fortune; fetched the third sucker from among her lace, where she had laid it up, and carefully hid it in her bosom; after which she locked her door twice, to disguise her flight as long as possible! and, leaving the prison by the same door which an hour before had let out Boxtel, she went to a stable-keeper to hire a carriage.

The man had only a two-wheel chaise, and this was the vehicle which Boxtel had hired since last evening, and in which he was now driving along the road to Delft; for the road from Lœvestein to Haarlem, owing to the many canals, rivers, and rivulets intersecting the country, is exceedingly circuitous.

Not being able to procure a vehicle, Rosa was obliged to take a horse with which the stable-keeper readily intrusted her, knowing her to be the daughter of the jailer of the fortress.

Rosa hoped to overtake her messenger, a kind-hearted and honest lad, whom she would take with her, and who might, at the same time, serve her as a guide and a protector.

And, in fact, she had not proceeded more than a league before she saw him hastening along one of the side paths of a very pretty road by the river.

Setting her horse off at a canter, she soon came up with him.

The honest lad was not aware of the important character of his message; nevertheless, he used as much speed as if he had known it; and in less than an hour, he had already gone a league and a half.

Rosa took from him the note, which had now become useless, and explained to him what she wanted him to do for her. The boatman placed himself entirely at her disposal, promising to keep pace with the horse, if Rosa would allow him to take hold of either the crupper, or the bridle of her horse. The two travellers had been on their way for five hours, and made more than eight leagues, and yet Gryphus had not the least suspicion of his daughter having left the fortress.

The jailer, who was of a very spiteful and cruel disposition, chuckled within himself at the idea of having struck such terror into his daughter's heart.

But while he was congratulating himself on having such a nice story to tell to his boon companion, Jacob, that worthy was on his road to Delft; and, thanks to the swiftness of the horse, had already the start of Rosa and her companion by four leagues.

And whilst the affectionate father was rejoicing at the thought of his daughter weeping in her room, Rosa was making the best of her way towards Haarlem.

Thus, the prisoner alone was where Gryphus thought him to be.

Rosa was so little with her father since she took care of the tulip, that at his dinner hour, that is to say, at twelve o'clock, he was reminded, for the first time, by his appetite, that his daughter was fretting rather too long.

He sent one of the under-turnkeys to call her; and, when the man came back to tell him that he had called and sought her in vain, he resolved to go and call her himself.

He first went to her room, but loud as he knocked, Rosa answered not.

The locksmith of the fortress was sent for; he opened the door, but Gryphus no more found Rosa, than she had found the tulip.

At that very moment she entered Rotterdam.

Gryphus, therefore, had just as little chance of finding her in the kitchen as in her room, and just as little in the garden as in the kitchen.

The reader may imagine the anger of the jailer when, after having made inquiries about the neighbourhood, he heard that his daughter had hired a horse, and like an adventuress, set out on a journey, without saying where she was going.

Gryphus again went up in his fury to Van Baerle, abused him, threatened him, knocked all the miserable furniture of his cell about, and promised him all sorts of misery, even starvation and flogging.

Cornelius, without even hearing what his jailer said, allowed himself to be ill-treated, abused, and threatened, remaining all the while sullen, immovable, dead to every emotion and fear.

After having sought for Rosa in every direction, Gryphus looked out for Jacob, and, as he could not find him either, he began to suspect from that moment that Jacob had run away with her.

The damsel, in the meanwhile, after having stopped for two hours at Rotterdam, had started again on her journey. On that evening she slept at Delft; and, on the following morning, she reached Haarlem, four hours after Boxtel had arrived there.

Rosa, first of all, caused herself to be led before Mynheer Van Herysen, the President of the Horticultural Society of Haarlem.

She found that worthy gentleman in a situation which, to do justice to our story, we must not pass over in our description.

The President was drawing up a report to the Committee of the Society.

This report was written on large-sized paper, in the finest handwriting of the President.

Rosa was announced simply as Rosa Gryphus; but, as her name, well as it might sound, was unknown to the President, she was refused admittance.

Rosa, however, was by no means abashed, having vowed in her heart, in pursuing her cause, not to allow herself to be put down either by refusal or abuse, or even brutality.

" Announce to the President," she said to the servant, " that I want to speak to him about the black tulip."

These words seemed to be an " Open Sesame," for she soon found herself in the office of the President, Van Herysen, who gallantly rose from his chair to meet her.

He was a spare little man, resembling the stem of a flower, his head forming its chalice, and his two limp arms representing the double leaf of the tulip; the resemblance was rendered complete by his waddling gait, which made him even more like that flower, when it bends under a breeze.

" Well, miss," he said, " you have come, I am told, about the affair of the black tulip."

To the President of the Horticultural Society the *Tulipa nigra* was a first-rate power, which, in its character as queen of the tulips, might send ambassadors.

" Yes, sir," answered Rosa, " I come, at least to speak of it."

" It is doing well, then?" asked Van Herysen, with a smile of tender veneration.

" Alas! sir, I don't know," said Rosa.

"How is that?" could any misfortune have happened to it?"

"A great one, sir; yet not to it, but to me."

"What?"

"It has been stolen from me."

"Stolen! the black tulip!"

"Yes, sir."

"Do you know the thief?"

"I have my suspicions, but I must not yet accuse anyone."

"But the matter may very easily be ascertained."

"How is that?"

"As it has been stolen from you, the thief cannot be far off."

"Why not?"

"Because I have seen the black tulip only two hours ago."

"You have seen the black tulip!" cried Rosa, rushing up to Mynheer Van Herysen.

"As I see you, miss."

"But where?"

"Well, with your master, of course."

"With my master?"

"Yes, are you not in the service of Master Isaac Boxtel?"

"I?"

"Yes, you."

"But for whom do you take me, sir?"

"And for whom do you take me?"

"I hope, sir, I take you for what you are, that is to say, for the honourable Mynheer Van Herysen, burgomaster of Haarlem, and President of the Horticultural Society."

"And what is it you told me just now?"

"I told you, sir, that my tulip has been stolen."

"Then your tulip is that of Mynheer Boxtel. Well, my child, you express yourself very badly. The tulip has been stolen not from you, but from Mynheer Boxtel."

"I repeat to you, sir, that I do not know who this Mynheer Boxtel is, and that I have now heard his name pronounced for the first time."

"You do not know who Mynheer Boxtel is; and you also had a black tulip?"

"But is there any other besides mine?" asked Rosa, trembling.

"Yes—that of Mynheer Boxtel."

"What is it like?"

"Black, of course."

"Without speck?"

" Without a single speck, or even point."

" And you have this tulip, you have it deposited here?"

" No, but it will be, as it has to be exhibited before the Committee, previous to the prize being awarded."

" Oh, sir!" cried Rosa, " this Boxtel, this Isaac Boxtel, who calls himself the owner of the black tulip——"

" And who is its owner——"

" Is he not a very thin man?"

" Yes."

"Bald?"

" Yes."

" With sunken eyes?"

" I think he has."

" Restless, stooping, and bow-legged."

" In truth you draw Master Boxtel's portrait, feature by feature."

" And the tulip, sir? Is it not in a pot of white and blue earthenware, with yellowish flowers in a basket on three sides?"

" Oh, as to that, I am not quite sure; I looked more at the flower than at the pot."

" Oh, sir! that's my tulip, which has been stolen from me. I come here to reclaim it before you and from you."

" Oh! oh!" said Van Herysen, looking at Rosa. " What! you are here to claim the tulip of Master Boxtel? Well, I must say, you are pretty cool."

" Honoured sir," said Rosa, a little put out by this apostrophe, " I do not say that I am coming to claim the tulip of Master Boxtel, but to reclaim my own."

" Yours?"

" Yes, the one which I have myself planted and nursed."

" Well, then, go, and find out Master Boxtel, at the White Swan Inn, and you can then settle matters with him; as for me, considering that the cause seems to me as difficult to judge as that which was brought before King Solomon, and that I do not pretend to be as wise as he was, I shall content myself with making my report, establishing the existence of the black tulip, and ordering the hundred thousand guilders to be paid to its grower. Good-bye, my child."

" Oh, sir, sir," said Rosa, imploringly.

" Only, my child," continued Van Herysen, " as you are young and pretty and as there may be still some good in you, I'll give you good advice. Be prudent in this matter, for we have a court of justice, and a prison here at Haarlem; and, moreover, we are exceedingly ticklish, as far as the honour of our tulips is concerned—go, my child, go, remember, Master Isaac Boxtel at the White Swan Inn."

And Mynheer Van Herysen taking up his fine pen, resumed his report, which had been interrupted by Rosa's visit.

CHAPTER XXVI

A MEMBER OF THE HORTICULTURAL SOCIETY

Rosa, beside herself, and nearly mad with joy and fear at the idea of the black tulip being found again, started for the White Swan, followed by the boatman, a stout lad from Frisia, who was strong enough to knock down a dozen Boxtels single-handed.

He had been made acquainted in the course of the journey with the state of affairs, and was not afraid of any encounter; only he had orders, in such a case, to spare the tulip.

But on arriving in the great market-place, Rosa at once stopped; a sudden thought had struck her, just as Homer's Minerva seizes Achilles by the hair at the moment when he is about to be carried away by his anger.

" Good Heavens!" she muttered to herself, " I have made a grievous blunder; maybe I have ruined Cornelius, the tulip, and myself. I have given the alarm, and perhaps awakened suspicion. I am but a woman; these men may league themselves against me, and then I shall be lost. If I am lost, that matters nothing—but Cornelius and the tulip!"

She reflected for a moment.

" If I go to that Boxtel and do not know him; if that Boxtel is not my Jacob, but another fancier, who has also discovered the black tulip; or if any tulip has been stolen by someone else, or has already passed into the hands of a third person; if I do not recognise the man, only the tulip, how shall I prove that it belongs to me? On the other hand, if I recognise this Boxtel as Jacob, who knows what will come out of it? whilst we are contesting with each other, the tulip will die."

In the meanwhile, a great noise was heard, like the distant roar of the sea, at the other extremity of the market-place. People were running about, doors opening and shutting; Rosa alone was unconscious of all this hubbub among the multitude.

" We must return to the president," she muttered.

" Well, then, let us return," said the boatman.

They took a small street, which led them straight to the

mansion of Mynheer Van Herysen, who, with his best pen, in his finest hand, continued to draw up his report.

Everywhere on her way, Rosa heard people speaking only of the black tulip, and the prize of a hundred thousand guilders. The news had spread like wildfire through the town.

Rosa had not a little difficulty in penetrating a second time into the office of Mynheer Van Herysen, who, however, was again moved by the magic name of the black tulip.

But when he recognised Rosa, whom in his own mind he had set down as mad, or even worse, he grew angry, and wanted to send her away.

Rosa, however, clasped her hands, and said with that tone of honest truth, which generally finds its way to the hearts of men:

" For Heaven's sake, sir, do not turn me away, listen to what I have to tell you, and if it be not possible for you to do me justice, at least you will not one day have to reproach yourself before God for having made yourself the accomplice of a bad action."

Van Herysen stamped his foot with impatience; it was the second time that Rosa interrupted him in the midst of a composition, which stimulated his vanity, both as a burgo-master and as the President of the Horticultural Society.

" But my report! " he cried, " my report on the black tulip!"

" Mynheer Van Herysen," Rosa continued, with the firm-ness of innocence and truth, " your report on the black tulip will, if you don't hear me, be based on crime or on false-hood. I implore you, sir, let this Master Boxtel, whom I assert to be Master Jacob, be brought here before you and me, and I swear that I will leave him in undisturbed possession of the tulip if I do not recognise the flower and its holder."

" Well, I declare, here is a proposal," said Van Herysen.

" What do you mean?"

" I ask you what can be proved by your recognising them?"

" After all," said Rosa, in her despair, " you are an honest man, sir; how would you feel if one day you had found out that you had given the prize to a man for something which he not only had not produced, but which he had even stolen?"

Rosa's speech seemed to have brought a certain conviction into the heart of Van Herysen, and he was going to answer her in a gentler tone, when at once a great noise was heard in the street, and loud cheers shook the house.

" What is this?" cried the burgomaster; " what is this? Is it possible? have I heard right?"

And he rushed towards the ante-room, without any longer heeding Rosa, whom he left in his cabinet.

Scarcely had he reached his ante-room, when he cried out aloud, on seeing his staircase invaded up to the very landing-place by the multitude, which was accompanying, or rather following, a young man, simply clad in a coat of violet-coloured velvet, embroidered with silver; who, with a certain aristocratic slowness, ascended the shining white stone steps of the house.

In his wake followed two officers, one of the navy, and the other of the cavalry.

Van Herysen, having found his way through the frightened domestics, began to bow, almost to prostrate himself before his visitor, who had been the cause of all this stir.

"Monseigneur!" he called out, "Monseigneur! What distinguished honour is Your Highness bestowing for ever on my humble house by your visit!"

"Dear Mynheer Van Herysen," said William of Orange, with a serenity which, with him, took the place of a smile, "I am a true Hollander; I am fond of the water, of beer, and of flowers, sometimes even of that cheese, the flavour of which seems so grateful to the French; the flower which I prefer to all others is, of course, the tulip. I heard at Leyden that the city of Haarlem at last possessed the black tulip; and, after having satisfied myself of the truth of news which seemed so incredible, I have come to know all about it from the President of the Horticultural Society."

"Oh! Monseigneur, Monseigneur," said Van Herysen, "what glory to the Society, if its endeavours are pleasing to Your Highness!"

"Have you got the flower here?" said the Prince, who, very likely, already regretted having made such a long speech.

"I am sorry to say we have not."

"And where is it?"

"With its owner."

"Who is he?"

"An honest tulip-grower of Dort."

"His name?"

"Boxtel."

"His quarters?"

"At the White Swan; I shall send for him, and if, in the meanwhile, Your Highness will do me the honour of stepping into my drawing-room, he will be sure—know   that Your Highness is here—to lose no time in bringing his tulip."

"Very well, send for him."

"Yes, Your Highness, but——"

" What is it?"

" Oh! nothing of any consequence, Monseigneur."

" Everything is of consequence, Mynheer Van Herysen."

" Well, then, Monseigneur, if it must be said, a little difficulty has presented itself."

" What difficulty?"

" This tulip has already been claimed by usurpers. It's true that it is worth a hundred thousand guilders."

" Indeed!"

" Yes, Monseigneur, by usurpers, by forgers."

" This is a crime, Mynheer Van Herysen."

" So it is, Your Highness."

" And have you any proofs of their guilt?"

" No, Monseigneur, the guilty woman——"

" The guilty woman, sir?"

" I ought to say, the woman who claims the tulip, Monseigneur, is here in the room close by."

" And what do you think of her?"

" I think, Monseigneur, that the bait of a hundred thousand guilders may have tempted her."

" And so she claims the tulip?"

" Yes, Monseigneur."

" And what proof does she offer?"

" I was just going to question her, when Your Highness came in."

" Question her, Mynheer Van Herysen, question her; I am the first magistrate of the country, I will hear the case, and administer justice."

" I have found my King Solomon," said Van Herysen, bowing, and showing the way to the Prince.

His Highness was just going to walk ahead, but, suddenly recollecting himself, he said:

" Go before me, and call me plain Mynheer."

The two then entered the cabinet.

Rosa was still standing at the same place, leaning on the window, and looking through the panes into the garden.

" Ah! a Frisian girl," said the Prince, as he observed Rosa's gold brocade head-dress and red petticoat.

At the noise of their footsteps she turned round, but scarcely saw the Prince, who seated himself in the darkest corner of the apartment.

All her attention, as may easily be imagined, was fixed on that important person who was called Van Herysen, so that she had no time to notice the humble stranger, who was following the master of the house, and who, for aught that she knew, might be somebody or nobody.

The humble stranger took a book down from the shelf, and made Van Herysen a sign to commence the examination forthwith.

Van Herysen, likewise at the invitation of the young man in the violet coat, sat down in his turn, and, quite happy and proud of the importance thus cast upon him, began:

"My child, you promise to tell me the truth, and the entire truth, concerning this tulip?"

"I promise."

"Well, then, speak before this gentleman; this gentleman is one of the members of the Horticultural Society."

"What am I to tell you, sir," said Rosa, "besides that which I have told you already?"

"Well, then, what is it?"

"I repeat the request which I have addressed to you before."

"Which?"

"That you will order Mynheer Boxtel to come here, with his tulip; if I do not recognise it as mine I will frankly tell it; but if I do recognise it I will reclaim it, even if I must go before His Highness, the Stadtholder himself, with my proofs in my hands."

"You have, then, some proofs, my child?"

"God, who knows my good right, will assist me to some."

Van Herysen exchanged a look with the Prince, who, since the first words of Rosa, seemed to try to remember her, as if it was not for the first time that this sweet voice rang in his ears.

An officer went off to fetch Boxtel, and Van Herysen, in the meanwhile, continued his examination.

"And with what do you support your assertion that you are the real owner of the black tulip?"

"With the very simple fact of my having planted it and grown it in my own chamber."

"In your chamber? Where was your chamber?"

"At Lœvestein."

"You are from Lœvestein?"

"I am the daughter of the jailer of the fortress."

The Prince made a little movement, as much as to say: "Well, that's it, I remember now."

And, all the while feigning to be engaged with his book, he watched Rosa with even more attention than he had done before.

"And you are fond of flowers?" continued Mynheer Van Herysen.

"Yes, sir."

"Then you are an experienced florist, I dare say?"

Rosa hesitated a moment; then with a tone which came from the depth of her heart, she said:

"Gentlemen, I am speaking to men of honour?"

There was such an expression of truth in the tone of her voice, that Van Herysen and the Prince answered simultaneously by an affirmative movement of their heads.

"Well, then, I am not an experienced florist; I am only a poor girl, one of the people, who, three months ago, knew neither how to read nor write. No, the black tulip has not been found by myself."

"But by whom else?"

"By a poor prisoner of Lœvestein."

"By a prisoner of Lœvesten?" repeated the Prince.

The tone of this voice startled Rosa, who was sure she had heard it before.

"By a prisoner of state, then," continued the Prince, "as there are none else there."

Having said this, he began to read again, at least in appearance.

"Yes," said Rosa with a faltering voice, "yes, by a prisoner of state."

Van Herysen trembled as he heard such a confession made in the presence of such a witness.

"Continue," said William drily, to the President of the Horticultural Society.

"Ah, sir," said Rosa, addressing the person whom she thought to be her real judge, "I am going to incriminate myself very seriously."

"Certainly," said Van Herysen, "the prisoners of state ought to be kept in close confinement at Lœvestein."

"Alas! sir."

"And from what you tell me you took advantage of your position, as daughter of the jailer, to communicate with a prisoner of state about the cultivation of flowers."

"So it is, sir," Rosa murmured in dismay; "yes, I am bound to confess, I saw him every day."

"Unfortunate girl!" exclaimed Van Herysen.

The Prince, observing the fright of Rosa, and the pallor of the President, raised his head, and said, in his clear and decided tone:

"This cannot signify anything to the members of the Horticultural Society; they have to judge on the black tulip, and have no cognizance to take of political offences. Go on, young woman; go on."

Van Herysen, by means of an eloquent glance, offered, in

the name of the tulip, his thanks to the new member of the Horticultural Society.

Rosa, reassured by this sort of encouragement which the stranger was giving her, related all that had happened for the last three months, all that she had done, all that she had suffered. She described the cruelty of Gryphus: the destruction of the first sucker; the grief of the prisoner; the precautions taken to insure the success of the second sucker; the patience of the prisoner; and his anxiety during their separation: how he was about to starve himself, because he had no longer any news of his tulip; his joy when she went to see him again; and lastly, their despair when they found that the tulip, which had come into flower, was stolen just one hour after it had opened.

All this was detailed with an accent of truth, which, although producing no change in the impassible mien of the Prince, did not fail to take effect on Van Herysen.

" But," said the Prince, " it cannot be long since you knew the prisoner."

Rosa opened her large eyes and looked at the stranger, who drew back into the dark corner, as if he wished to escape her observation.

" Why, sir?" she asked him.

" Because it is not yet four months since the jailer Gryphus and his daughter were removed from Lœvestein."

" That is true, sir."

" Otherwise, you must have solicited the transfer of your father, in order to be able to follow some prisoner who may have been transported from the Hague to Lœvestein."

" Sir," said Rosa, blushing.

" Finish what you have to say," said William.

" I confess, I knew the prisoner at the Hague."

" Happy prisoner!" said William, smiling.

At this moment, the officer who had been sent for Boxtel returned and announced to the Prince that the person whom he had been to fetch was following on his heels with his tulip.

CHAPTER XXVII

THE THIRD SUCKER

Boxtel's return was scarcely announced, when he entered in person the drawing-room of Mynheer Van Herysen, followed by two men, who carried in a box their precious burden, and deposited it on a table.

The Prince, on being informed, left the cabinet, passed into the drawing-room, admired the flower and silently resumed his seat in the dark corner where he had himself placed his chair.

Rosa, trembling, pale, and terrified, expected to be invited in her turn to see the tulip.

She now heard the voice of Boxtel.

" It is he!" she exclaimed.

The Prince made her a sign to go and look through the open door into the drawing-room.

" It is my tulip," cried Rosa, " I recognise it. Oh, my poor Cornelius!"

And saying this she burst into tears.

The Prince rose from his seat, went to the door, where he stood for some time with the full light falling upon his figure.

As Rosa's eyes now rested upon him, she felt more than ever convinced that this was not the first time she had seen the stranger.

" Master Boxtel," said the Prince, " come in here, if you please."

Boxtel eagerly approached, and finding himself face to face with William of Orange, started back.

" His Highness!" he called out.

" His Highness!" Rosa repeated in dismay.

Hearing this exclamation on his left, Boxtel turned round, and perceived Rosa.

At this sight the whole frame of the thief shook as if under the influence of a galvanic shock.

" Ah!" muttered the Prince to himself, " he is confused."

But Boxtel, making a violent effort to control his feelings, was already himself again.

" Master Boxtel," said William, " you seem to have discovered the secret of growing the black tulip?"

" Yes, Your Highness," answered Boxtel, in a voice which still betrayed some confusion.

It is true his agitation might have been attributable to the emotion which the man must have felt on suddenly recognising the Prince.

" But," continued the Stadtholder, " here is a young damsel who also pretends to have found it."

Boxtel, with a disdainful smile, shrugged his shoulders.

William watched all his movements with evident interest and curiosity.

" Then you don't know this young girl?" said the Prince.

" No, Your Highness!"

" And you, child, do you know Master Boxtel?"

"No; I don't know Master Boxtel, but I know Master Jacob."

"What do you mean?"

"I mean to say that at Lœvestein the man who here calls himself Isaac Boxtel went by the name of Master Jacob."

"What do you say to that, Master Boxtel?"

"I say, that this damsel lies, Your Highness."

"You deny, therefore, having ever been at Lœvestein?"

Boxtel hesitated; the fixed and searching glance of the proud eye of the Prince prevented him from lying.

"I cannot deny having been at Lœvestein, Your Highness, but I deny having stolen the tulip."

"You have stolen it, and that from my room," cried Rosa, with indignation.

"I deny it."

"Now listen to me. Do you deny having followed me into the garden, on the day when I prepared the border where I was to plant it? Do you deny having followed me into the garden, when I pretended to plant it? Do you deny that, on that evening, you rushed, after my departure, to the spot where you hoped to find the bulb? Do you deny having dug in the ground with your hands—but, thank God! in vain; as it was but a stratagem to discover your intentions. Say, do you deny all this?"

Boxtel did not deem it fit to answer these several charges, but, turning to the Prince, continued:—

"I have now for twenty years grown tulips at Dort. I have even acquired some reputation in this art; one of my hybrids is entered in the catalogue under the name of an illustrious personage. I have dedicated it to the King of Portugal. The truth in the matter is as I shall now tell Your Highness. This damsel knew that I had produced the Black Tulip, and, in concert with a lover of hers, in the fortress of Lœvestein, she formed the plan of ruining me, by appropriating to herself the prize of a hundred thousand guilders, which, with the help of Your Highness's justice, I hope to gain."

"Yah!" cried Rosa, beyond herself with anger.

"Silence!" said the Prince.

Then, turning to Boxtel, he said:

"And who is that prisoner to whom you allude as the lover of this young woman?"

Rosa nearly swooned, for Cornelius was designated as a dangerous prisoner, and recommended, by the Prince, to the especial surveillance of the jailer.

Nothing could have been more agreeable to Boxtel than this question.

" This prisoner," he said, " is a man, whose name in itself will prove to Your Highness what trust you may place in his probity. He is a prisoner of state, who was once condemned to death."

" And his name?"

Rosa hid her face with a movement of despair.

" His name is Cornelius Van Baerle," said Boxtel, " and he is godson of that villain, Cornelius De Witte."

The Prince gave a start! his generally quiet eye flashed, and a death-like paleness spread over his impassible features.

He went up to Rosa, and, with his finger, gave her a sign to remove her hands from her face.

Rosa obeyed, as if under mesmeric influence, without having seen the sign.

" It was then to follow this man, that you came to me at Leyden to solicit for the transfer of your father?"

Rosa hung down her head, and, nearly choking, said:

" Yes, Your Highness."

" Go on," said the Prince to Boxtel.

" I have nothing more to say," Isaac, however, continued. " Your Highness knows all. But there is one thing which I did not intend to say, because I did not wish to make this girl blush for her ingratitude. I came to Lœvestein, because I had business there. On this occasion I made the acquaintance of old Gryphus, and, falling in love with his daughter, made an offer of marriage to her, and, not being rich, I committed the imprudence of mentioning to them my prospect of gaining a hundred thousand guilders, in proof of which I showed to them the black tulip. Her lover having himself made a show at Dort of cultivating tulips, to hide his political intrigues, they now plotted together for my ruin. On the eve of the day when the flower was expected to open, the tulip was taken away by this young woman. She carried it to her room, from whence I had the good luck to recover it, at the very moment when she had the impudence to despatch a messenger to announce to the members of the Horticultural Society that she had produced the Grand Black Tulip. But she did not stop there. There is no doubt but that, during the few hours which she kept the flower in her room, she showed it to some persons, whom she may now call as witnesses. But, fortunately, Your Highness has now been warned against this imposter and her witnesses."

" Oh, my God! my God! what infamous falsehoods," said

Rosa, bursting into tears, and throwing herself at the feet of the Stadtholder, who, although thinking her guilty, felt pity for her dreadful agony.

"You have done very wrong, my child," he said, "and your lover shall be punished for having thus badly advised you. For you are so young, and have such an honest look, that I am inclined to believe the mischief to have been his doing, and not yours."

"Monseigneur! Monseigneur!" cried Rosa, "Cornelius is not guilty."

William started.

"Not guilty of having advised you; that's what you want to say, is it not?"

"What I wish to say, Your Highness, is, that Cornelius, is as little guilty of the second crime imputed to him, as he was of the first."

"Of the first? And do you know what was his first crime? Do you know of what he was accused and convicted? Of having, as an accomplice of Cornelius De Witte, concealed the correspondence of the Grand Pensionary and the Marquis De Louvois."

"Well, sir, he was ignorant of the correspondence being deposited with him; completely ignorant. I am as certain, as of my life, that if it were not so, he would have told me; for how could that pure mind have harboured a secret without revealing it to me? No, no, Your Highness, I repeat it, and even at the risk of incurring your displeasure, Cornelius is no more guilty of the first crime than of the second; and of the second, no more than of the first. Oh, would to Heaven, that you knew my Cornelius, Monseigneur!"

"He is a De Witte!" cried Boxtel. "His Highness knows only too much of him, having once granted him his life."

"Silence!" said the Prince; "all these affairs of state, as I have already said, are completely out of the province of the Horticultural Society of Haarlem."

Then knitting his brow,, he added:

"As to the tulip, make yourself easy, Master Boxtel, you shall have justice done to you."

Boxtel bowed with a heart full of joy, and received the congratulations of the President.

"You, my child," William of Orange continued, "you were going to commit a crime. I shall not punish you; but the real evil-doer will pay the penalty for both. A man of his name, may be a conspirator, and even a traitor, but he ought not to be a thief."

"A thief!" cried Rosa. "Cornelius a thief! Pray, Your Highness, do not say such a word; it would kill him, if he knew it. If theft there has been, I swear to you, sir, no one else but this man has committed it."

"Prove it," Boxtel coolly remarked.

"I shall prove it. With God's help I shall."

Then turning towards Boxtel, she asked:

"The tulip is yours?"

"It is."

"How many suckers were there of it?"

Boxtel hesitated for a moment, but, after a short consideration, he came to the conclusion that she would not ask this question, if there were none besides the two bulbs of which he had known already. He, therefore, answered:

"Three."

"What has become of these suckers?"

"Oh! what has become of them? Well, one has failed; the second has produced the black tulip."

"And the third?"

"The third!"

"The third—where is it?"

"I have it at home," said Boxtel, quite confused.

"At home? Where? At Lœvestein, or at Dort?"

"At Dort," said Boxtel.

"You lie!" cried Rosa. "Monseigneur," she continued, whilst turning round to the Prince, "I will tell you the true story of those three suckers. The first was crushed by my father in the prisoner's cell, and this man is quite aware of it, for he himself wanted to get hold of it, and being baulked in his hope, he very nearly fell out with my father, who had been the cause of his disappointment. The second sucker, planted by me, has produced the Black tulip; and the third and last"—saying this, she drew it from her bosom—"here it is, in the very same paper in which it was wrapped up together with the two others. When about to be led to the scaffold, Cornelius Van Baerle gave me all the three. Take it, Monseigneur, take it."

And Rosa, unfolding the paper, offered the bulb to the Prince, who took it from her hands and examined it.

"But, Monseigneur, this young woman may have stolen the bulb, as she did the tulip," Boxtel said, with a faltering voice, and evidently alarmed at the attention with which the Prince examined the bulb; and even more at the movements of Rosa, who was reading some lines written on the paper which remained in her hands.

Her eyes suddenly lighted up; she read, with breathless

anxiety, the mysterious paper over and over again; and at last, uttering a cry, held it out to the Prince and said:

"Read, Monseigneur, for Heaven's sake, read!"

William handed the third sucker to Van Herysen, took the paper and read.

No sooner had he looked at it than he began to stagger; his hand trembled, and very nearly let the paper fall to the ground; and the expression of pain and compassion in his features was really frightful to see.

It was that fly-leaf, taken from the Bible, which Cornelius De Witte had sent to Dort by Craeke, the servant of his brother John, to request Van Baerle to burn the correspondence of the Grand Pensionary with the Marquis de Louvois.

This request, as the reader may remember, was couched in the following terms:—

"MY DEAR GODSON,

"Burn the parcel which I have entrusted to you. Burn it, without looking at it and without opening it, so that its contents may remain unknown to yourself. Secrets of this description are death to those with whom they are deposited. Burn it, and you will have saved John and Cornelius De Witte.

"Farewell, and love me.
"CORNELIUS DE WITTE."

"20th of August, 1672."

This slip of paper offered the proofs both of Van Baerle's innocence and of his claim to the property of the tulip.

Rosa and the Stadtholder exchanged one look only.

That of Rosa was meant to express: "Here, you see yourself."

That of the Stadtholder signified: "Be quiet, and wait."

The Prince wiped the cold sweat from his forehead, and slowly folded up the paper, whilst his thoughts were wandering in that labyrinth without a goal and without a guide, which is called remorse and shame of the past.

Soon, however, raising his head with an effort, he said, in his usual voice:

"Go, Mr. Boxtel, justice shall be done, I promise you."

Then, turning to the President, he added:

"You, my dear Mynheer Van Herysen, take charge of this young woman and of the tulip. Good-bye."

All bowed, and the Prince left, amid the deafening cheers of the crowd outside.

Boxtel returned to his inn, rather puzzled and uneasy, tormented by misgivings about that paper which William had received from the hand of Rosa, and which His Highness had read, folded up, and so carefully put in his pocket. What was the meaning of all this?

Rosa went up to the tulip, tenderly kissed its leaves, and, with a heart full of happiness and confidence in the ways of God, broke out in the words:

" Thou knowest best for what end thou madest my good Cornelius teach me to read."

CHAPTER XXVIII

THE HYMN OF THE FLOWERS

Whilst the events we have described in our last chapters were taking place, the unfortunate Van Baerle, forgotten in his cell in the fortress of Lœvestein, suffered, at the hands of Gryphus, all that a prisoner can suffer when his jailer has formed the determination of playing the part of hangman.

Gryphus, not having received any tidings of Rosa, nor of Jacob, persuaded himself that all that had happened was the devil's work, and that Doctor Cornelius Van Baerle had been sent on earth by Satan.

The result of it was, that one fine morning, the third after the disappearance of Jacob and Rosa, he went up to the cell of Cornelius in even a greater rage than usual.

The latter, leaning with his elbows on the window-sill, and supporting his head with his two hands, whilst his eyes wandered over the distant hazy horizon, where the windmills of Dort were turning their sails, was breathing the fresh air, in order to be able to keep down his tears, and to fortify himself in his philosophy.

The pigeons were still there, but hope was not; there was no future to look forward to.

Alas! Rosa, being watched, was no longer able to come. Could she not write? and if so, could she convey her letters to him?

No, no. He had seen, during the two preceding days, too much fury and malignity in the eyes of old Gryphus to expect that his vigilance would relax, even for one moment. Moreover, had not she to suffer even worse torments than those of seclusion and separation? Did this brutal, blaspheming, drunken bully take revenge on his daughter, like the ruthless fathers of the Greek drama? and when the *genièvre* had cheated his brain, would it not give to his arm which had been only too well set by Cornelius, even double force?

The idea that Rosa might, perhaps, be ill-treated, nearly drove Cornelius mad.

He then felt his own powerlessness. He asked himself whether God was just in inflicting so much tribulation on two innocent creatures. And certainly in these moments he began to doubt the wisdom of Providence. It is one of the curses of misfortune that it begets doubt.

Van Baerle had proposed to write to Rosa, but where was she?

He also would have wished to write to the Hague to be beforehand with Gryphus, who, he had no doubt, would, by denouncing him, do his best to bring new storms on his head.

But how should he write? Gryphus had taken the paper and pencil from him; and even if he had both, he could hardly expect Gryphus to despatch his letter.

Then Cornelius revolved in his mind all those stratagems resorted to by unfortunate prisoners.

He had thought of an attempt to escape, a thing which never entered his head whilst he could see Rosa every day; but the more he thought of it, the more clearly he saw the impracticability of such an attempt. He was one of those choice spirits who abhor everything that is common, and who often lose a good chance through not taking the way of the vulgar, that high road of mediocrity which leads to everything.

"How is it possible," said Cornelius to himself, "that I should escape from Lœvestein, as Grotius has done the same thing before me? Has not every precaution been taken since? Are not the windows barred? Are not the doors of double and even treble strength? and the sentinels ten times more watchful? And have not I, besides all this, an Argus so much the more dangerous, as he has the keen eyes of hatred? I am losing my patience, since I have lost the joy and company of Rosa, and especially since I have lost my tulip. Undoubtedly, one day or other, Gryphus will attack me in a manner painful to my self-respect, or to my love, or even threaten my personal safety. I don't know how it is, but since my imprisonment I feel a strange and almost irresistible pugnacity. Well, I shall get at the throat of that old villain, and strangle him."

Cornelius, at these words, stopped for a moment, biting his lips, and staring out before him; then, eagerly returning to an idea which seemed to possess a strange fascination for him, he continued:—

"Well, and once having strangled him, why should I not take his keys from him; why not go down the stairs as if I had done the most virtuous action; why not go and fetch Rosa from her room; why not tell her all, and jump from her window into the Waal? I am expert enough as a swimmer to save both of us. Rosa! but, oh, Heavens, Gryphus is her father. Whatever may be her affection for me, she will never approve of my having strangled her father, brutal and malicious as he has been. It will not do, Cornelius, my fine fellow—it is a bad plan. But, then, what is to become of me, and how shall I find Rosa again?"

Such were the cogitations of Cornelius three days after the sad scene of separation from Rosa, at the moment when we find him standing at the window.

And at that very moment Gryphus entered.

He held in his hand a huge stick; his eyes glistening with spiteful thoughts, a malignant smile played round his lips, and the whole of his carriage, and even all his movements, betokened bad and malicious intentions.

Cornelius heard him enter, and guessed that it was he, but did not turn round, as he knew well that Rosa was not coming after him.

There is nothing more galling to angry people than the coolness of those on whom they wish to vent their spleen.

The expense being once incurred, one does not like to lose it; one's passion is roused, and one's blood boiling, so it would be labour lost not to have at least a nice little row.

Gryphus, therefore, on seeing that Cornelius did not stir, tried to attract his attention by a loud—

"Umph, umph."

Cornelius was humming beween his teeth the "Hymn of Flowers," a sad but very charming song:

"We are the daughters of the secret fire,
Of the fire which circulates through the veins of the earth;
We are the daughters of Aurora, and of the morning dew;
We are the daughters of the air:
We are the daughters of the water;
But we are, above all, the daughters of heaven."

This song, the placid melancholy of which was still heightened by its calm and sweet melody, exasperated Gryphus.

He struck his stick on the stone pavement of the cell, and called out:—

"Halloa! my warbling gentleman, don't you hear me?"
Cornelius turned round, merely saying:—
"Good morning," and then began his song again:

"Men defile us, and kill us while loving us,
    We hang to the earth by a thread;
  This thread is our root, that is to say, our life,
    But we raise on high our arms towards heaven."

"Ah, you accursed sorcerer! you are making game of me, I believe," roared Gryphus.
Cornelius continued:—

"For heaven is our home.
Our true home, as from thence comes our soul,
    As thither our soul returns,
    Our soul, that is to say, our perfume."

Gryphus went up to the prisoner and said:
"But you don't see that I have taken means to get you under, and to force you to confess your crimes."
"Are you mad, my dear Master Gryphus?" asked Cornelius.
And as he now for the first time observed the frenzied features, the flashing eyes, and foaming mouth of the old jailer, he said:
"Bless the man, he is more than mad, it seems, he is furious."
Gryphus flourished his stick above his head, but Van Baerle moved not, and remained standing with his arms akimbo.
"It seems your intention to threaten me, Master Gryphus."
"Yes, indeed, I threaten you," cried the jailer.
"And with what?"
"First of all, look what I have in my hand."
"I think that's a stick," said Cornelius calmly, "but I don't suppose you will threaten me with that."
"Oh, you don't suppose—oh! why not?"
"Because any jailer who strikes a prisoner is liable to two penalties; the first laid down in Article 9 of the regulations at Lœvestein:—
"'Any jailer, inspector, or turnkey, who lays hand upon a prisoner of State, will be dismissed.'"
"Yes, who lays hands," said Gryphus, mad with rage, "but there is not a word about a stick in the regulation."
"And the second," continued Cornelius, which is not

written in the regulation, but which is to be found elsewhere:

"'Whosoever takes up the stick will be thrashed by the stick.'"

Gryphus, growing more and more exasperated by the calm and sententious tone of Cornelius, brandished his cudgel, but, at the moment he raised it, Cornelius rushed at him, snatched it from his hands and put it under his own arm.

Gryphus fairly bellowed with rage.

"Hush, hush, my good man," said Cornelius, "don't do anything to lose your place."

"Ah! you sorcerer, I'll pinch you worse," roared Gryphus.

"I wish you may."

"Don't you see that my hand is empty?"

"Yes, I see it, and I am glad of it."

"You know that it is not generally so, when I come up stairs in the morning."

"It's true, you generally bring me the worst soup, and the most miserable rations one can imagine. But that's not a punishment to me; I eat only bread, and the worse the bread is to your taste, Gryphus, the better it is to mine."

"How so?"

"Oh, it's a very simple thing."

"Well, tell it me," said Gryphus.

"Very willingly. I know that in giving me bad bread, you know you do me harm."

"Certainly, I don't give it you to please you, you brigand."

"Well, then, I, who am a sorcerer, as you know, change your bad into excellent bread, which I relish more than the best cake; and then I have the double pleasure of eating something that gratifies my palate, and of doing something that puts you in a rage."

Gryphus answered with a growl.

"Oh! you confess, then, that you are a sorcerer."

"Indeed, I am one, I don't say it before all the world, because they might burn me for it, but as we are alone, I don't mind telling you."

"Well, well, well," answered Gryphus, "but if a sorcerer can change black bread into white, won't he die of hunger if he has no bread at all?"

"What's that?" said Cornelius.

"Consequently, I shall not bring you any bread at all, and we shall see how it will be after eight days."

Cornelius grew pale.

"And," continued Gryphus, "we'll begin this very day! As you are such a clever sorcerer, why, you had better change the furniture of your room into bread; as to myself, I shall pocket the eighteen sous which are paid to me for your board."

"But that's murder," cried Cornelius, carried away by the first impulse of the very natural terror with which this horrible mode of death inspired him.

"Well," Gryphus went on in his jeering way, "as you are a sorcerer, you will live notwithstanding."

Cornelius put on a smiling face, and said:

"Have not you seen me make the pigeons come here from Dort?"

"Well?" said Gryphus.

"Well, a pigeon is a very dainty morsel, and a man, who eats one every day would not starve, I think."

"And how about the fire?" said Gryphus.

"Fire! but you know that I'm in league with the devil. Do you think the devil will leave me without fire? why, fire is his proper element."

"A man, however healthy his appetite may be, would not eat a pigeon every day. Wagers have been laid to do so, and those who made them gave them up."

"Well, but when I am tired of pigeons, I shall make the fish of the Waal and of the Meuse come up to me."

Gryphus opened his large eyes, quite bewildered.

"I am rather fond of fish," continued Cornelius; "you never let me have any. Well, I shall turn your starving me to advantage, and regale myself with fish."

Gryphus nearly fainted with anger and with fright, but he soon rallied, and said, putting his hand in his pocket:

"Well, as you force me to it," and with these words, he drew forth a clasp-knife and opened it.

"Halloa, a knife!" said Cornelius, preparing to defend himself with his stick.

CHAPTER XXIX

IN WHICH VAN BAERLE, BEFORE LEAVING LŒVESTEIN, SETTLES
ACCOUNTS WITH GRYPHUS

The two remained silent for some minutes, Gryphus on the offensive, and Van Baerle on the defensive.

Then, as the situation might be prolonged to an indefinite length, Cornelius, anxious to know something more of the causes which had so fiercely exasperated his jailer, spoke first, by putting the question:

" Well, what do you want, after all?"

" I'll tell you what I want," answered Gryphus, " I want you to restore to me my daughter Rosa."

" Your daughter?" cried Van Baerle.

" Yes, my daughter Rosa, whom you have taken from me by your devilish magic. Now, will you tell me where she is?"

And the attitude of Gryphus became more and more threatening.

" Rosa is not at Lœvestein?" cried Cornelius.

" You know well she is not. Once more, will you restore her to me?"

" I see," said Cornelius, " this is a trap you are laying for me."

" Now, for the last time, will you tell me where my daughter is?"

" Guess it, you rogue, if you don't know it."

" Only wait, only wait," growled Gryphus, white with rage, and with quivering lips, as his brain began to turn. " Ah, you will not tell me anything? Well, I'll unlock your teeth!"

He advanced a step towards Cornelius, and said, showing him the weapon which he held in his hand:

" Do you see this knife? Well, I have killed more than fifty black cocks with it, and I vow I'll kill their master the devil, as well as them."

" But, you blockhead," said Cornelius, " will you really kill me?"

" I shall open your heart, to see in it the place where you hide my daughter."

Saying this, Gryphus, in his frenzy, rushed towards Cornelius, who had barely time to retreat behind his table to avoid the first thrust; but as Gryphus continued, with horrid threats, to brandish his huge knife, and as, although out of the reach of his weapon, yet, as long as it remained in the madman's hand, the ruffian might fling it at him—Cornelius lost no time, and, availing himself of the stick, which he held tight under his arm, dealt the jailer a vigorous blow on the wrist of that hand which held the knife.

The knife fell to the ground, and Cornelius put his foot on it.

Then, as Gryphus seemed bent upon engaging in a struggle which the pain in his wrist, and shame for having allowed himself to be disarmed, would have made desperate, Cornelius took a decisive step, belabouring his jailer with the

most heroic self-possession, and deliberately aiming his blows
at him.

It was not long before Gryphus begged for mercy. But,
before begging for mercy, he had justly roared for help, and
his cries had roused all the functionaries of the prison. Two
turnkeys, an inspector, and three or four guards, made their
appearance all at once, and found Cornelius still using the
stick, with the knife under his foot.

At the sight of these witnesses, who could not know all the
circumstances which had provoked and might justify his
offence, Cornelius felt that he was irretrievably lost.

In fact, appearances were sadly against him.

In one moment Cornelius was disarmed, and Gryphus
raised and supported; and, bellowing with rage and pain,
he was able to count on his back and shoulders the bruises
which were beginning to swell like the hills dotting the slopes
of a mountain-ridge.

A report of the violence practised by the prisoner against
his jailer was immediately drawn up, and as it was made on
the depositions of Gryphus, it certainly could not be said
to be too tame; the prisoner being charged with neither more
nor less than with an attempt to murder, for a long time
premeditated, with open rebellion.

Whilst the charge was made out against Cornelius,
Gryphus, whose presence was no longer necessary after
having made his depositions, was taken down by his turnkeys to his lodge, groaning, and covered with bruises.

During this time, the guards who had seized Cornelius
busied themselves in charitably informing their prisoner of
the usages and customs of Lœvestein, which, however, he
knew as well as they did. The regulations had been read to
him, at the moment of his entering the prison, and certain
articles in them remained fixed in his memory.

Among other things, they told him, that this regulation
had been carried out to its full extent in the case of a
prisoner named Mathias, who in 1668, that is to say, five
years before, had committed a much less violent act of
rebellion than that of which Cornelius was guilty. He had
found his soup too hot, and thrown it at the head of the
chief turnkey, who, in consequence of this ablution, had
been put to the inconvenience of having his skin come off as
he wiped his face.

Mathias was taken within twelve hours from his cell, then
led to the jailer's lodge, where he was registered as leaving
Lœvestein, then taken to the Esplanade, from which there is

a very fine prospect over a wide expanse of country. There they fettered his hands, bandaged his eyes, and let him say his prayers.

Hereupon he was invited to go down on his knees, and the guards of Lœvestein, twelve in number, at a sign from a sergeant, very cleverly lodged a musket ball each in his body.

In consequence of this proceeding, Mathias incontinently did then and there die.

Cornelius listened with the greatest attention to this delightful recital, and then said:

"Ah! ah! within twelve hours, you say?"

"Yes, the twelfth hour had not even struck, if I remember right," said the guard, who had told him the story.

"Thank you," said Cornelius.

The guard still had the smile on his face, with which he accompanied, and, as it were, accentuated his tale, when footsteps and a jingling of spurs were heard ascending the staircase.

The guards fell back to allow an officer to pass, who entered the cell of Cornelius, at the moment when the clerk of Lœvestein was still making out his report.

"Is this No. 11?" he asked.

"Yes, Captain," answered a non-commissioned officer.

"Then this is the cell of the prisoner Cornelius Van Baerle?"

"Exactly, Captain."

"Where is the prisoner?"

"Here I am, sir," answered Cornelius, growing rather pale, notwithstanding all his courage.

"You are Doctor Cornelius Van Baerle?" asked he, this time addressing the prisoner himself.

"Yes, sir."

"Then follow me."

"Oh! oh!" said Cornelius, whose heart felt oppressed by the first dread of death. "What quick work they make here in the fortress of Lœvestein. And the rascal talked to me of twelve hours!"

"Ah! what did I tell you?" whispered the communicative guard into the ear of the culprit.

"A lie."

"How so?"

"You promised me twelve hours."

"Ah, yes, but here comes to you an aide-de-camp of His Highness, even one of his most intimate companions, Van Decken. Zounds! they did not grant such an honour to poor Mathias."

"Come, come!" said Cornelius, drawing a long breath. "Come, I'll show to these people that an honest burgher godson of Cornelius De Witt, can, without flinching, receive as many musket-balls as that Mathias."

Saying this, he passed proudly before the clerk, who, being interrupted in his work, ventured to say to the officer:

"But, Captain Van Decken, the report is not yet finished."

"It is not worth while finishing it," answered the officer.

"All right," replied the clerk, philosophically putting up his paper and pen into a greasy and well-worn writing case.

"It was written," thought poor Cornelius, "that I should not, in this world, give my name either to a child, to a flower, or to a book, the three things by which a man's memory is perpetuated."

But repressing his melancholy thoughts, he followed the officer with a resolute heart, and carrying his head erect.

Cornelius counted the steps which led to the Esplanade, regretting that he had not asked the guard how many there were of them, which the man in his officious complaisance would not have failed to tell him.

What the poor prisoner was most afraid of during this walk, which he considered as leading him to the end of the journey of life, was to see Gryphus and not to see Rosa. What savage satisfaction would glisten in the eyes of the father, and what sorrow dim those of the daughter!

Indeed, the poor tulip-fancier needed all his courage and resolution, not to burst into tears at the thought of the latter, and of her foster-daughter the black tulip.

Although he looked to the right and to the left, he saw neither Rosa nor Gryphus.

On reaching the Esplanade, he bravely looked about for the guards who were to be his executioners, and in reality saw a dozen soldiers assembled. But they were not standing in line, or carrying muskets, but talking together so gaily, that Cornelius felt almost shocked.

All at once, Gryphus, limping, staggering, and supporting himself on a crooked stick, came forth from the jailer's lodge; his old eyes, grey as those of a cat, were lit up by a gleam in which all his hatred was concentrated. He then began to pour forth such a torrent of disgusting imprecations against Cornelius, that the latter, addressing the officer, said:

"I do not think it very becoming, sir, that I should be thus insulted by this man, especially at a moment like this."

"Well! hear me," said the officer, laughing, "it is quite natural that this worthy fellow should bear you a grudge—you seem to have given it him very soundly."

" But, sir, it was only in self-defence."

" Never mind," said the captain, shrugging his shoulders like a true philosopher, " let him talk; what does it matter to you now?"

The cold sweat stood on the brow of Cornelius at this answer, which he looked upon somewhat in the light of brutal irony, especially as coming from an officer of whom he had heard it said that he was attached to the person of the Prince.

The unfortunate tulip-fancier then felt that he had no more resources, and no more friends, and resigned himself to his fate.

" God's will be done," he muttered bowing his head; then, turning towards the officer who seemed complacently to wait until he had finished his meditations, he asked:

" Please, sir, tell me now, where am I to go?"

The officer pointed to a carriage drawn by four horses, which reminded him · very strongly of that which, under similar circumstances, had before attracted his attention at the Buitenhof.

" Enter," said the officer.

" Ah!" muttered Cornelius to himself, " it seems they are not going to treat me to the honours of the Esplanade."

He uttered these words loud enough for the chatty guard, who was at his heels, to overhear him.

That kind soul very likely thought it his duty to give Cornelius some new information; for, approaching the door of the carriage, whilst the officer, with one foot on the step, was still giving some orders, he whispered to Van Baerle:

" Condemned prisoners have sometimes been taken to their own town, to be made an example of, and they have then been executed before the door of their own house. It's all according to circumstances."

Cornelius thanked him by signs, and then said to himself:

" Well, here is a fellow, who never misses giving consolation whenever an opportunity presents itself. In truth, my friend, I'm very much obliged to you. Good-bye."

The carriage drove away.

" Ah! you villain, you brigand," roared Gryphus, clenching his fists at the victim who was escaping from his clutches; " is it not a shame that this fellow gets off, without having restored my daughter to me?"

" If they take me to Dort," thought Cornelius, " I shall see, in passing my house, whether my poor borders have been much spoiled."

CHAPTER XXX

WHEREIN THE READER BEGINS TO GUESS THE KIND OF EXECUTION THAT WAS AWAITING CORNELIUS VAN BAERLE

The carriage rolled on during the whole day; it passed on the right of Dort, went through Rotterdam, and reached Delft. At five o'clock in the evening, at least twenty leagues had been travelled.

Cornelius addressed some questions to the officer, who was at the same time his guard and his companion; but, cautious as were his inquiries, he had the disappointment of receiving no answer.

Cornelius regretted that he had no longer by his side that chatty soldier, who would talk without being questioned.

That obliging person would, undoubtedly, have given him as pleasant details, and exact explanations, concerning this third strange part of his adventures, as he had done concerning the two first.

The travellers passed the night in the carriage. On the following morning, Cornelius found himself beyond Leyden, having the North Sea on his left, and the Zuyder Zee on his right.

Three hours after, he entered Haarlem.

Cornelius was not aware of what had passed at Haarlem, and we shall leave him in ignorance of it until the course of events enlightens him.

But the reader has a right to know all about it, even before our hero, and, therefore, we shall not make him wait.

We have seen that Rosa and the tulip, like two orphan sisters, had been left, by the Prince William of Orange, at the house of the President Van Herysen.

Rosa did not hear again from the Stadtholder until the evening of that day on which she had seen him face to face.

Towards evening, an officer called at Van Herysen's house. He came from His Highness, with a request for Rosa to appear at the Town-hall.

There, in the large Council Room, into which she was ushered, she found the Prince writing.

He was alone, with a large Frisian greyhound at his feet, which looked at him with a steady glance, as if the faithful animal were wishing to do what no man could do—read the thoughts of his master in his face.

William continued his writing for a moment; then, raising

his eyes, and seeing Rosa standing near the door, he said,
without laying down his pen:

"Come here, my child."

Rosa advanced a few steps towards the table.

"Sit down," he said.

Rosa obeyed, for the Prince was fixing his eyes upon her;
but he had scarcely turned them again to his paper, when she
bashfully retired to the door.

The Prince finished his letter.

During this time, the greyhound went up to Rosa, surveyed
her, and began to caress her.

"Ah! ah!" said William to his dog, "it's easy to see that
she is a countrywoman of yours, and that you recognise her."

Then, turning towards Rosa, and fixing on her his scruti-
nising, and, at the same time, impenetrable glance, he said:

"Now, my child."

The Prince was scarcely twenty-three, and Rosa, eighteen
or twenty. He might, therefore, perhaps, better have said, my
sister.

"My child," he said, with that strangely-commanding
accent, which chilled all those who approached him. "We
are alone; let us speak together."

Rosa began to tremble; and yet there was nothing but kindness in the expression of the Prince's face.

"Monseigneur," she stammered.

"You have a father at Lœvestein?"

"Yes, Your Highness."

"You do not love him?"

"I do not—at least, not as a daughter ought to do,
Monseigneur."

"It is not right not to love one's father, but it is right not
to tell a falsehood."

Rosa cast her eyes to the ground.

"What is the reason of your not loving your father?"

"He is wicked."

"In what way does he show his wickedness?"

"He illtreats the prisoners."

"All of them?"

"All."

"But don't you bear him a grudge for illtreating someone
in particular?"

"My father illtreats in particular Mynheer Van Baerle,
who——"

"Who is your lover?"

Rosa started back a step.

"Whom I love, Monseigneur," she answered, proudly.

"Since when?" asked the Prince.

"Since the day when I first saw him."

"And when was that?"

"The day after that on which the Grand Pensionary John and his brother Cornelius met with such an awful death."

The Prince compressed his lips and knit his brow, and his eyelids dropped so as to hide his eyes for an instant. After a momentary silence he resumed the conversation.

"But to what can it lead to love a man who is doomed to live and die in prison?"

"It will lead, if he lives and dies in prison, to my aiding him in life and in death."

"And would you accept the lot of being the wife of a prisoner?"

"As the wife of Mynheer Van Baerle, I should, under any circumstances, be the proudest and happiest woman in the world; but——"

"But, what?"

"I dare not say, Monseigneur."

"There is something like hope in your tone—what do you hope?"

She raised her moist and beautiful eyes, and looked at William with a glance full of meaning, which was calculated to stir up in the recesses of his heart the clemency which was slumbering there.

"Ah! I understand you," he said.

Rosa, with a smile, clasped her hands.

"You hope in me?" said the Prince.

"Yes, Monseigneur."

"Umph!"

The Prince sealed the letter which he had just written, and summoned one of his officers, to whom he said:

"Captain Van Decken, carry this despatch to Lœvestein; you will read the orders which I give to the Governor, and execute them as far as they regard you."

The officer bowed, and, a few minutes afterwards, the gallop of a horse was heard resounding in the vaulted archway.

"My child," continued the Prince, "the feast of the tulip will be on Sunday next, that is to say, the day after to-morrow. Make yourself smart with these five hundred guilders, as I wish that day to be a great day for you."

"How does Your Highness wish me to be dressed?" faltered Rosa.

"Take the costume of a Frisian bride," said William, "it will suit you very well indeed."

CHAPTER XXXI

HAARLEM

The fifteenth of May, 1673, was a great day for the good city of Haarlem. It had to celebrate a three-fold festival. In the first place, the black tulip had been produced; secondly, the Prince William of Orange, as a true Hollander, had promised to be present at the ceremony of its inauguration; and, thirdly, it was a point of honour with the States to show to the French, at the conclusion of such a disastrous war as that of 1672, that the flooring of the Batavian Republic was solid enough for its people to dance on it, with the accompaniment of the cannon of their fleets.

The Horticultural Society of Haarlem had shown itself worthy of its fame, by giving a hundred thousand guilders for the bulb of a tulip. The town, which did not wish to remain behindhand, voted a like sum, which was placed in the hands of that notable body to solemnise the auspicious event.

And, indeed, on the Sunday fixed for this ceremony, there was such a stir among the people, and such an enthusiasm among the townsfolk, that even a Frenchman, who laughs at everything at all times, could not have helped admiring the character of those honest Hollanders, who were equally ready to spend their money for the construction of a man-of-war, that is to say, for the support of national honour, as they were to reward the grower of a new flower, destined to bloom for one day, and to serve during that day to divert the ladies, the learned, and the curious.

At the head of the Notables and of the Horticultural Committee shone Mynheer Van Herysen, dressed in his richest habiliments.

The worthy man had done his best to resemble his favourite flower, in the sombre and stern elegance of his garments; and we are bound to record, to his honour, that he had perfectly succeeded in his object.

Dark crimson velvet, dark purple silk, and jet-black cloth, with linen of dazzling whiteness, composed the festive dress of the President, who marched at the head of his Committee, carrying an enormous nosegay, like that which, a hundred and twenty-one years later, Monsieur de Robespierre displayed at the festival of "The Supreme Being."

There was, however, a little difference between the two:

very different from the French tribune, whose heart was so full of hatred and ambitious vindictiveness, the honest President carried in his bosom a heart as innocent as the flowers which he held in his hand.

Behind the Committee, who were as gay as a meadow, and as fragrant as a garden in spring, marched the learned societies of the town, the magistrates, the military, the nobles, and the boors.

The people, even among the respected republicans of the Seven Provinces, had no place assigned to them in the procession: they merely lined the streets.

Haarlem had no other triumphers, except its gardeners. Worshipping flowers, Haarlem idolised the florist.

In the centre of this pacific and fragrant cortège the black tulip was seen, carried on a litter which was covered with white velvet and fringed with gold.

It was arranged that the Prince Stadtholder himself should give the prize of a hundred thousand guilders, which interested the people at large, and it was thought that, perhaps, he would make a speech, which interested more particularly his friends and enemies.

The whole population of Haarlem, swelled by that of the neighbourhood, had arranged itself along the beautiful avenues of trees, with the fixed resolution, this time, to applaud neither the heroes of war, nor those of science, but merely to conqueror of nature, who had forced her to produce the black tulip.

Nothing, however, is more fickle than such a resolution of the people. When a crowd is once in the humour to cheer, it is just the same as when it begins to hiss. It never knows when to stop.

All eyes were on the look-out for the hero of the day—of course we mean the grower of the tulip.

This hero made his appearance at the conclusion of the reading of the report, which we have seen Van Herysen drawing up with such conscientiousness; and he produced almost a greater sensation than the Stadtholder himself.

There he walked, covered with flowers down to his girdle; well-combed and brushed and entirely dressed in scarlet, a colour which contrasted strongly with his black hair and yellow complexion.

This hero, radiant with rapturous joy, who had the distinguished honour of making the people forget the speech of Van Herysen, and even the presence of the Stadtholder, was

Isaac Boxtel, who saw, carried on his right before him, the black tulip, his pretended daughter; and on his left, in a large purse, the hundred thousand guilders in glittering gold pieces, towards which he was constantly squinting, fearful of losing sight of them for one moment.

Another quarter of an hour and the Prince will arrive, and the procession will halt for the last time; after the tulip is placed on its throne, the Prince, yielding precedence to this rival for the popular adoration, will take a magnificently-emblazoned parchment, on which is written the name of the grower; and His Highness, in a loud and audible tone, will proclaim him to be the discoverer of a wonder: that Holland, by the instrumentality of him, Boxtel, has forced nature to produce a black flower, which shall henceforth be called *Tulipa nigra Boxtellea.*

From time to time, however, Boxtel withdrew his eyes for a moment from the tulip and the purse, timidly looking among the crowd, for, more than anything, he dreaded to descry there the pale face of the pretty Frisian girl.

She would have been a spectre spoiling the joy of the festival for him, just as Banquo's ghost did that of Macbeth.

And yet, if the truth must be told, this wretch, who had stolen what was the boast of a man, and the dowry of a woman, did not consider himself as a thief. He had so intently watched this tulip, followed it so eagerly from the drawer in Cornelius's dry-room to the scaffold of the Buiten-hof, and from the scaffold to the fortress of Lœvestein; he had seen it bud and grow in Rosa's window, and so often warmed the air round it with his breath, that he felt as if no one had a better right to call himself its producer than he had; and anyone who would now take the black tulip from him, would have appeared to him as a thief.

Yet he did not perceive Rosa; his joy, therefore, was not spoiled.

In the centre of a circle of magnificent trees, which were decorated with garlands and inscriptions, the procession halted, amidst the sounds of lively music; and the young damsels of Haarlem made their appearance to escort the tulip to the raised seat which it was to occupy on the platform, by the side of the gilded chair of His Highness the Stadtholder.

And the proud tulip, raised on its pedestal, soon over-looked the assembled crowd of people, who clapped their hands, and made the old town of Haarlem re-echo with their tremendous cheers.

CHAPTER XXXII

A LAST BEQUEST

In this solemn moment, and whilst the cheers still resounded, a carriage was driving along the road on the outskirts of the green on which the scene occurred; it pursued its way slowly, on account of the flocks of children who were pushed out of the avenue by the crowd of men and women.

This carriage, covered with dust, and creaking on its axles, the result of a long journey, contained the unfortunate Van Baerle, who was quite dazzled and bewildered by this festive splendour and bustle.

Notwithstanding the little readiness which his companion had shown in answering his questions concerning his fate, he ventured once more to ask what all this meant.

" As you may see, sir," replied the officer, " it is a feast."

" Ah, a feast," said Cornelius, in the sad tone of indifference of a man to whom no joy remains in this world.

Then, after some moments' silence, during which the carriage had proceeded a few yards, he asked once more:

" The feast of the patron saint of Haarlem? as I see so many flowers."

" It is indeed a feast in which flowers play a principal part."

" Oh, the sweet scents! oh, the beautiful colours!" cried Cornelius.

" Stop, that the gentleman may see," said the officer, with that frank kindliness which is peculiar to military men, to the soldier who was acting as postillion.

" Oh, thank you, sir, for your kindness," replied Van Baerle, in a melancholy tone; " the joys of others pain me, please spare me this pang."

" Just as you wish. Drive on! I ordered the driver to stop because I thought it would please you, as you are said to love flowers, and especially that, the feast of which is celebrated to-day."

" And what flower is that?"

" The tulip."

" The tulip!" cried Van Baerle; " is to-day the feast of the tulip?"

" Yes, sir, but as this spectacle displeases you, let us drive on."

The officer was about to give the order to proceed, but

Cornelius stopped him, a painful thought having struck him. He asked, with faltering voice:

" Is the prize given to-day, sir?"

" Yes, the prize for the black tulip."

Cornelius' cheek flushed, his whole frame trembled, and the cold sweat stood on his brow.

" Alas! sir," he said, " all these good people will be as unfortunate as myself, for they will not see the solemnity which they have come to witness, or at least they will see it incompletely."

" What is it you mean to say?"

" I mean to say," replied Cornelius, throwing himself back in the carriage, " that the black tulip will not be found, except by one whom I know."

" In that case," said the officer, " the person whom you know has found it, for the thing which the whole of Haarlem is looking at this moment is neither more nor less than the black tulip."

" The black tulip ! " cried Van Baerle, thrusting half of his body out of the carriage window. " Where is it? where is it"

" Down there, near the throne, don't you see?"

" I do see it."

" Come along, sir," said the officer. " Now we must drive off."

" Oh! have pity, have mercy, sir," said Van Baerle, " don't take me away. Let me look once more. Is what I see down there the black tulip? Quite black? Is it possible? Oh, sir, have you seen it? It must have specks, it must be imperfect, it must only be dyed black; ah, if I were there! I should see it at once. Let me alight, let me see it close, I beg of you."

" Are you mad, sir? How could I allow such a thing?"

" I implore you."

" But you forget that you are a prisoner."

" It is true I am a prisoner, but I am a man of honour, and I promise you on my word that I will not run away, I will not attempt to escape—only let me see the flower."

" But my orders, sir, my orders." And the officer again made the driver a sign to proceed.

Cornelius stopped him once more.

" Oh, be forbearing, be generous, my whole life depends upon your pity. Alas! perhaps it will not be much longer. You don't know, sir, what I suffer. You don't know the struggle going on in my heart and mind; for after all," Cornelius cried in despair, " if this were my tulip, if it were the one which has been stolen from Rosa! Oh! I must alight, sir! I must see the flower, you may kill me afterwards if you like, but I will see it, I must see it."

"Be quiet, unfortunate man, and come quickly back into the carriage, for here is the escort of His Highness the Stadtholder, and if the Prince observed any disturbance, or heard any noise, it would be ruin to me, as well as to you."

Van Baerle, more afraid for his companion than himself, threw himself back into the carriage, but he could only keep quiet for half a minute, and the first twenty horsemen had scarcely passed when he again leaned out of the carriage window, gesticulating imploringly towards the Stadtholder at the very moment when he passed.

William, impassible and quiet as usual, was proceeding to the green to fulfil his duty as chairman. He held in his hand the roll of parchment, which, on this festive day, had become his *bâton*.

Seeing the man gesticulate with imploring mien and perhaps also recognising the officer who accompanied him, His Highness ordered his carriage to stop.

In one instant his snorting steeds stood still, at a distance of about six yards from the carriage in which Van Baerle was caged.

"What is this?" the Prince asked the officer, who at the first order of the Stadtholder had jumped out of the carriage, and was respectfully approaching him.

"Monseigneur," he cried, "this is the prisoner of State whom I have fetched from Lœvestein, and whom I have brought to Haarlem according to Your Highness's command."

"What does he want?"

"He entreats for permission to stop here for a moment."

"To see the black tulip, Monseigneur," said Van Baerle, clasping his hands, "and when I have seen it—when I have seen what I desire to know, I am quite ready to die, if die I must; but in dying I shall bless Your Highness's mercy for having allowed me to witness the glorification of my work."

It was, indeed, a curious spectacle to see these two men, at the windows of their several carriages; the one, surrounded by his guards, and all-powerful, the other a prisoner and miserable; the one going to mount a throne, the other believing himself to be on his way to the scaffold.

William, looking with his cold glance on Cornelius, listened to his anxious and urgent request.

Then, addressing himself to the officer, he said:

" Is this person the mutinous prisoner who has attempted to kill his jailer at Lœvestein?"

Cornelius heaved a sigh and hung his head. His good-tempered, honest face turned pale and red at the same instant. These words of the all-powerful Prince, who, by some secret messenger, unavailable to other mortals, had already been apprised of his crime, seemed to him to forebode not only his doom, but also the refusal of his last request.

He did not try to make a struggle, or to defend himself; and he presented to the Prince the affecting spectacle of despairing innocence, like that of a child; a spectacle which was fully understood and felt by the great mind and the great heart of him who observed it.

" Allow the prisoner to alight, and let him see the black tulip; it is well worth being seen once."

" Thank you, Monseigneur, thank you," said Cornelius, nearly swooning with joy, and staggering on the steps of his carriage; had not the officer supported him, our poor friend would have made his thanks to His Highness prostrate on his knees with his forehead in the dust.

After having granted this permission, the Prince proceeded on his way over the green amidst the most enthusiastic acclamations.

He soon arrived at the platform, and the thunder of cannon shook the air.

CHAPTER XXXIII

CONCLUSION

Van Baerle, led by four guards, who pushed their way through the crowd, sidled up to the black tulip, towards which his gaze was attracted with increasing interest, the nearer he approached to it.

He saw it; that unique flower, which he was to see once, and no more. He saw it at the distance of six paces, and was delighted with its perfection and gracefulness; he saw it surrounded by young and beautiful girls, who formed, as it were, a guard of honour for this queen of excellence and purity. And yet, the more he ascertained with his own eyes the perfection of the flower, the more wretched and miserable he felt. He looked all around for someone to whom he might address only one question; but his eyes everywhere met strange faces, and the attention of all was directed towards the chair of state, on which the Stadtholder had seated himself.

William arose, casting a tranquil glance over the enthusiastic crowd, and his keen eye rested by turns on the three extremities of a triangle, formed opposite to him by three persons of very different interests and feelings.

At one of the angles, Boxtel, trembling with impatience, and quite absorbed in watching the Prince, the guilders, the black tulip, and the crowd.

At the other, Cornelius, panting for breath, silent, and his attention, his eyes, his life, his heart, his love, quite concentrated on the black tulip.

And, thirdly, standing on a raised step among the maidens of Haarlem, a beautiful Frisian girl, dressed in fine scarlet, woollen cloth, embroidered with silver, and covered with a lace veil which fell in rich folds from her head-dress of gold brocade; in one word, Rosa, who, faint, and with swimming eyes, was leaning on the arm of one of the officers of William.

The Prince then slowly unfolded the parchment, and said, with a calm, clear voice, which, although low, made itself perfectly heard amidst the respectful silence, which all at once arrested the breath of fifty thousand spectators:

" You know what has brought us here.

" A prize of one hundred thousand guilders has been promised to whosoever should grow the black tulip.

" The black tulip has been grown; here it is before your eyes, fulfilling all the conditions required by the programme of the Horticultural Society of Haarlem.

" The history of its production, and the name of its grower, will be inscribed in the book of honour of the city.

" Let the person approach to whom the black tulip belongs."

In pronouncing these words, the Prince, to judge of the effect they produced, surveyed with his eagle eye the three extremities of the triangle.

He saw Boxtel rushing forward. He saw Cornelius make an involuntary movement; and, lastly, he saw the officer, who was taking care of Rosa, lead or, rather, push her forwards towards him.

At the sight of Rosa, a double cry arose on the right and left of the Prince.

Boxtel, thunderstruck, and Cornelius, in joyful amazement, both exclaimed:

"Rosa! Rosa!"

" This tulip is yours, is it not, my child?" said the Prince.

"Yes, Monseigneur," stammered Rosa, whose striking beauty excited a general murmur of applause.

"Oh!" muttered Cornelius, "she has then lied to me, when she said this flower was stolen from her. Oh! that is why she left Lœvestein. Alas! am I then forgotten, betrayed by her whom I thought my best friend on earth?"

"Oh!" sighed Boxtel, "I am lost."

"This tulip," continued the Prince, "will, therefore, bear the name of its producer, and figure in the catalogue under the title *Tulipa nigra Rosa Barlœensis*, which will henceforth be the name of this damsel."

At the same time William took Rosa's hand, and placed it in that of a young man, who rushed forth, pale and beyond himself with joy, to the foot of the throne, greeting alternately the Prince and his bride; and who with a graceful look to Heaven, returned his thanks to the Giver of all this happiness.

At the same moment, there fell at the feet of the President Van Herysen, another man, struck down by a very different emotion.

Boxtel, crushed by the failure of his hopes, lay senseless on the ground.

When they raised him, and examined his pulse and his heart, he was quite dead.

This incident did not much disturb the festival, as neither the Prince nor the President seemed to mind it much.

Cornelius started back in dismay when, in the thief, in the pretended Jacob, he recognised his neighbour, Isaac Boxtel, whom, in the innocence of his heart, he had not for one instant suspected of such a wicked action.

Then, to the sound of trumpets, the procession marched back without any change in its order, except that Boxtel was now dead, and that Cornelius and Rosa were walking triumphantly side by side, and hand in hand.

On their arriving at the Hôtel de Ville, the Prince, pointing with his finger to the purse with the hundred thousand guilders, said to Cornelius:

"It is difficult to say by whom this money is gained, by you or by Rosa; for if you have found the black tulip, she has nursed it, and brought it into flower. It would, therefore, be unjust to consider it as her dowry: it is the gift of the town of Haarlem to the tulip."

Cornelius wondered what the Prince was driving at. The latter continued:

"I give to Rosa the sum of a hundred thousand guilders, which she had fairly earned, and which she can offer to you. They are the reward of her love, her courage, and her honesty. As to you, sir,—thanks to Rosa again, who has furnished the proofs of your innocence—"

And, saying these words, the Prince handed to Cornelius that fly-leaf of the Bible, on which was written the letter of Cornelius de Witte, and in which the third sucker had been wrapped—

"As to you, it has come to light that you were imprisoned for a crime which you had not committed. This means, that you are not only free, but that your property will be restored to you, as the property of an innocent man cannot be confiscated. Cornelius Van Baerle, you are the god-son of Cornelius de Witte, and the friend of his brother John. Remain worthy of the name you have received from one of them, and of the friendship you have enjoyed with the other. The two De Wittes, wrongly judged, and wrongly punished in a moment of popular error, were two great citizens, of whom Holland is now proud."

The Prince, after these last words, which, contrary to his custom, he pronounced with a voice full of emotion, gave his hands to the lovers to kiss, whilst they were kneeling before him.

Then, heaving a sigh, he said:

"Alas! you are happy, who, dreaming only of what perhaps is the true glory of Holland, and forms especially her true happiness, do not attempt to acquire for her anything beyond the true colours of a tulip."

And, casting a glance towards that point of the compass where France lay, as if he saw new clouds gathering there, he entered his carriage, and drove off.

Cornelius, on his part, started on the same day to Dort with Rosa, who sent her lover's old housekeeper as a messenger to her father, to apprise him of all that had taken place.

Old Gryphus was by no means ready to be reconciled to his son-in-law. He had not yet forgotten the blows which he had received in that famous encounter. To judge from the weals which he counted, their number, he said, amounted to forty-one; but, at last, in order, as he declared, not to be less generous than His Highness the Stadtholder, he consented to make his peace.

Appointed to watch over the tulips, the old man made the rudest keeper of flowers in the whole of the Seven Provinces.

It was indeed a sight to see him watching the obnoxious moths and butterflies, killing slugs and driving away the hungry bees.

As he had heard Boxtel's story, and was furious at having

been the dupe of the pretended Jacob, he destroyed the sycamore behind which the envious Isaac had spied into the garden; for the plot of ground belonging to him had been bought by Cornelius, and taken into his own garden.

Rosa, growing not only in beauty but in wisdom also, after two years of her married life could read and write so well, that she was able to undertake by herself the education of two beautiful children which she had borne in 1674 and 1675, both in May, the month of flowers.

As a matter of course, one was a boy, the other a girl, the former being called Cornelius, the other Rosa.

Van Baerle remained faithfully attached to Rosa, and to his tulips. The whole of his life was devoted to the happiness of his wife, and the culture of flowers, in the latter of which occupations he was so successful, that a great number of his varieties found a place in the catalogue of Holland.

The two principal ornaments of his drawing-room were those two leaves from the Bible of Cornelius De Witte, in large golden frames; one of them containing the letter in which his godfather enjoined him to burn the correspondence of the Marquis de Louvois, and the other, his own will, in which he bequeathed to Rosa his suckers on condition that she should marry a young man of from twenty-six to twenty-eight years, who loved her, and whom she loved, a condition which was scrupulously fulfilled, although, or rather because, Cornelius did not die.

And to ward off any envious attempts of another Isaac Boxtel, he wrote over his door the lines which Grotius had, on the day of his flight, engraved on the wall of his prison:

"One has sometimes suffered enough to have a right ever afterwards to say, I am too happy."

THE END.

THE CORSICAN BROTHERS

CHAPTER I

Early in the month of March, in the year 1841, I was travelling through Corsica. Nothing could be more picturesque or more pleasant than a tour through Corsica; one takes ship at Toulon; in twenty hours one reaches Ajaccio; or, in twenty-four hours, Bastia.

There, one can buy or hire a horse; if one hires, the cost is five francs a day; if one purchases, a hundred francs is the usual amount. Don't smile at the modest cost; the horse, whether hired or bought, like the famous Gascon's steed, which leapt from the Pont Neuf into the Seine, will perform as great feats as those of Prospero and Nautilus, heroes of Chantilly and the *Champs de Mars*. He will take you along tracks where Balmat himself would have worn climbing irons, and across bridges where Auriol would have needed a balancing pole.

As for the traveller, all he has to do is to shut his eyes and give the animal its head; danger does not worry the beast.

And, let us add, the horse can do any journey, travelling fifteen leagues a day without water or fodder.

As to one's night's lodging, that is simpler still; a traveller having reached a village goes down the main street, chooses a house that takes his fancy and knocks at the door. In a moment the master or mistress appears in the doorway, asks the wayfarer to dismount, offers him half his supper, the whole of his bed—if he has only one—and the next morning, as he escorts him out, he thanks him for the honour he has bestowed on him in selecting his house.

As to any payment, such a thing is never mentioned; the master would consider it an insult if the slightest allusion were made to the subject. If the servant is a young girl one may offer her a coloured silk handkerchief, which she will turn into a picturesque head-dress when she goes to Calvi or Corte fête. If it is a man, he will willingly accept a nice pointed knife with which he can kill his enemy, if he happens to meet him.

As for robbers, one never hears them spoken of; bandits in plenty, yes; but don't confuse the one with the other.

183

You can go without fear from Ajaccio to Bastia with a purse full of gold slung at your saddle-bow, and you can travel right across the island without the slightest danger; but do not go from Occana to Levaco, if you have an enemy who has declared a vendetta against you; because I would not be responsible for your safety even on that six-mile journey.

I was in Corsica then, as I have said, at the beginning of March.

I had come from the isle of Elba; I had landed at Bastia; I had bought a horse at the above-named price.

I had visited Corte and Ajaccio and I was, at that time, passing through the province of Sartène.

On that particular day I was going from Sartène to Sullacaro.

The stage was a short one—thirty miles, perhaps—with its winding road and the spur of the chief range of mountains, the backbone of the island, that one has to cross; and I had, for that reason, taken a guide with me for fear of losing myself in the Maquis. About five o'clock we reached the top of the hill which overlooks Olmeto and Sullacaro.

Here we halted for a while.

"Where would your honour like to put up?" asked the guide.

Looking down at the village I was able to see into the streets which seemed almost deserted; only a few women were in them, and they hurried along casting cautious looks as they went.

In accordance with the established laws of hospitality, about which I have spoken, I had the choice of about a hundred or a hundred and twenty houses which formed the village. I looked for a dwelling that seemed to hold out the greatest chance of comfort, and I paused at a square house, built like a fortress, with battlements and loop-holes in front of the windows and above the doors.

It was the first time I had seen fortified private houses; but one must remember that the province of Sartène is the classic land of the vendetta.

"Ah! good," said the guide, his eyes turned to where I was pointing. "We will go to Madame Savilia de Franchi's house. Well, your honour has not made a bad choice, and one can tell you don't lack experience."

One must not forget to say that in this eighty-sixth French Department Italian is the ordinary language.

"But," I inquired, "is there any objection to my asking

hospitality from a woman? For I understand that this house belongs to a woman."

"Oh, no," he answered, looking surprised. "What objection can there be?"

"How old is Madame Savilia?" I asked.

"About forty."

"Oh!" I answered, and, expressing my thoughts, "that's all right; and she has children, I suppose?"

"Two sons; two fine young fellows."

"Shall I see them?"

"You will see one—the one who lives with her."

"And the other?"

"The other lives in Paris."

"And how old are they?"

"Twenty-one."

"Both of them?"

"Yes; they are twins."

"And what profession are they adopting?"

"The one in Paris is a lawyer."

"And the other?"

"The other will be a good Corsican."

"Ah! ah!" said I, thinking the answer truly characteristic, and spoken in the most matter-of-fact way. "Very well, let us make for Madame Savilia de Franchi's house."

And away we went.

Ten minutes later we reached the village. Then I noticed something that I had not seen from the top of the mountain. Each house was fortified like Madame Savilia's, not with battlements and loopholes, the poverty of the owners did not allow such luxurious fortifications, but simply with beams of timber fixed behind the windows, leaving loopholes for rifles. Other windows were fortified with red bricks.

I asked my guide what they called these loopholes. He told me that they were *archères,* an answer that explained to me that Corsican vendettas existed before the invention of firearms.

We reached the house that I had pointed out to my guide; it was by far the most important in the village.

Only one thing struck me: it was that the fortifications, battlements and loopholes that I had noticed were sham; that is to say, the windows had neither beams, nor bricks, nor *archères,* but just glass diamond panels that were protected at night by shutters. It is true that these shutters bore traces that an observant eye could not fail to see were bullet holes, at least ten years old.

Scarcely had my guide knocked when the door opened, not timidly, hesitatingly, half open, but wide open, and a butler appeared. . . .

When I said butler, I made a mistake; I ought to have said a man.

The livery makes the butler, and the person who opened the door was dressed quite simply in a velvet jacket, breeches of the same material and leather gaiters.

The breeches were held at the waist by a striped silk sash, from which the handle of a Spanish knife protruded.

" My friend," I said, " is it indiscreet of a stranger who knows no one in Sullacaro to come and beg hospitality from your mistress?"

" No, certainly not, your honour," he replied; " the stranger honours the house at which he stops. Maria," he continued, turning to a servant who had appeared behind him, " tell Madame Savilia a French traveller seeks hospitality."

At the same moment he came down the flight of eight steps, steep as the rungs of a ladder, which led up to the front door and took my horse's bridle.

I dismounted.

" Will your honour please not trouble," said he; " all your luggage will be taken to your room."

I thoroughly enjoyed this invitation to laziness—one of the most pleasant offers that can be made to a traveller.

CHAPTER II

I slowly mounted the aforesaid ladder-like steps and went into the house.

At the end of the corridor I found myself face to face with a tall woman, dressed in black.

I gathered that this lady, thirty-eight or forty years old, still handsome, was the mistress of the house, and I stopped.

" Madame," I said, bowing, " you may consider me somewhat indiscreet, but the custom of the country and the invitation of your serving-man are my excuses."

" I am happy to welcome you," Madame de Franchi replied, " and my son will be glad to welcome you, also. From this moment the house is at your disposal; treat it as though it were your own."

" I come to ask hospitality for one night only, madame. To-morrow at dawn I must take my departure."

" You are at liberty to do what is most convenient to you.

However, I hope that you will change your mind and honour us with a long visit."

I bowed again.

"Maria" said Madame de Franchi, "show monsieur to Louis's room. Light the fire immediately and take up some hot water. Forgive me," she continued, turning to me, as the servant prepared to carry out her instructions, "I know that the tired traveller's first needs are water and fire. Will you follow that maid, monsieur? Ask her for anything you may want. We sup in an hour's time, and my son, who will be back by then, would like to see you."

"You will excuse my travelling dress, madame?"

"Yes, monsieur," she answered with a smile; "but only on condition that you, on your part, will excuse our countrified ways."

The servant went upstairs. I bowed once more and followed her.

The room was on the first floor and looked out on to the back. I knew at once that they had given me this room, her absent son's room, because it was the most comfortable in the house.

The furniture was modern; in this part of the island, where civilisation had not penetrated, this fact alone was a sign of a considerable and unusual affluence. There was an iron bedstead with three mattresses and a pillow, a divan, four arm-chairs, six ordinary chairs, and a bookcase and writing- table combined—all of mahogany, bought, obviously, from the leading furniture dealer in Ajaccio.

The divan, the arm-chairs and the chairs were covered with flowered chintz, window-curtains and bed-curtains being of the same materials.

The keys were in the drawers of the bureau. I opened one of them. I found in it scraps of a history of Corsica, a treatise on the way to abolish the vendetta, a few French verses, some Italian sonnets, all in manuscript. It was as much as I needed, and I had the presumption to think that I had no necessity to push my researches further in order to form an opinion of M. Louis de Franchi.

He must be a pleasant, studious young fellow and an upholder of French reforms. I understood now why he had gone to Paris to qualify as a lawyer. He had undoubtedly the welfare of civilisation at heart. Such were my thoughts as I dressed.

I had just finished dressing when the door opened and the same man who had received me appeared.

He came to tell me that his young master, M. Lucien de Franchi, had just returned and asked if it was convenient for him to come and bid me welcome.

A moment later I heard the noise of a hurried step and I found myself almost immediately face to face with my host.

CHAPTER III

He was, as my guide had said, a young man of about twenty or twenty-one, black hair and eyes, complexion tanned by the sun, short, rather than tall, but very well built. In his anxiety to welcome me he had come up as he was; that is to say, in riding kit consisting of a green cloth waistcoat, whilst a cartridge belt round his waist gave him a military appearance, grey cloth breeches, leather seated, and boots and spurs. A cap like our African chasseurs completed his costume.

From his cartridge belt were hung, on one side a drinking flask, on the other a pistol. He also carried an English carbine.

"Please forgive me, if I disturb you, monsieur," said he to me, " but I do it with the best intention, namely, to know if you want anything. I am not without a little misgiving when I see a man arrive at our house from the Continent; for we are still savages, we Corsicans, and it is only with fear and trembling that we offer, particularly to Frenchmen, that ancient hospitality which will very soon be the only tradition left to us by our fathers."

"You are wrong to be alarmed, monsieur," I replied. "It would be indeed difficult to anticipate all the needs of a traveller better than Madame de Franchi has done. "Besides," I added "in glancing round the room here one can't complain of the savagery that you playfully mention, and if I did not see from my window this beautiful country I should imagine myself in a room in the Chaussée d'Antin."

"Yes," replied the young man, "it is a mania with my poor brother Louis. He loves to live in French fashion; but I very much doubt whether, when he returns from Paris, this poor parody of civilisation that he left behind him will satisfy him as it satisfied him before he went away."

"And your brother has he been away from Corsica a long time?" I asked.

"Ten months, monsieur."

"You expect him soon?"

"Oh, not for three or four years."

"It is a long separation for two brothers who, doubtless, have never been parted."

"Yes, and above all, who are as fond of one another as we are."

"I suppose he will come and see you before he finishes his studies?"

"Probably; he has promised to, anyway."

"Well, that would not prevent you, on your part, from paying him a visit?"

"No—me—I never leave Corsica."

There was in the tone of his reply that love of country which looks upon the rest of the world with pitiful contempt. I smiled.

"It appears strange to you," he answered, smiling also, "that one does not want to leave a wretched country like ours. What can you expect? I am a product of the soil, like the holm oak and the oleander, I must needs have my sea-borne air, my mountain mists; I must needs have my torrents to cross, my crags to climb, and forests to explore. I must needs have space and freedom. If I was taken to a town I think I should die."

"But how is it that there is so great a difference in temperament between you and your brother?"

"With so great a physical resemblance you would add, if you knew him."

"You are much alike?"

"So much that when we were children my father and mother were forced to put a mark on our clothes to tell one from the other."

"And as you grew up?"

"As we grew up our manner showed a slight difference in our complexions, that was all. Always indoors, bending over his books and drawings, my brother became paler, whilst I, on the other hand, always wandering over mountain or plain, have become tanned."

"I hope," I said to him, "that you will give me the opportunity to judge of this difference by giving me some message for M. Louis de Franchi."

"Yes, certainly, with great pleasure, if you will be so kind. But forgive me. I see that you are more forward with your toilet than I am, and in a quarter of an hour we sit down to supper."

"Is it on my account that you trouble to change?"

"If it is, you have only yourself to blame, for you have

set me the example; but anyway I am in riding kit and I must put on mountaineering things. I have, after supper, to make a journey in which my boots and spurs would be in the way."

"You are going out after supper?" I asked.

"Yes, I have an appointment."

I smiled.

"Oh, not the sort you suggest; it is a business appointment."

"Do you think I am presumptuous enough to think that I have a right to your confidence?"

"Why not? One should live in such a way that one can speak freely of all that one does. I have never had a mistress, and I never shall. If my brother marries and has children it is probable that I myself shall never marry. If, on the other hand, he does not find a wife, it will then be necessary for me to find one so that our line does not die out. I have told you," he added, laughing, "I am a regular savage and I came into the world a century too late. But if I go on chattering here like a crow I shall not be ready for supper."

"But can't we continue the conversation?" I asked; "doesn't your room face this one? Leave the door open and we can talk."

"Better still, come to mine; I can dress in my dressing-room in the meanwhile. You are a lover of weapons, I think; if so, look at mine; there are some which have a certain value—historical, I mean."

CHAPTER IV

The invitation coincided too well with my wish to compare the rooms of the two brothers for me not to accept. I hastened therefore to follow my host, who, opening the door of his room, went in front of me to show me the way. This time I thought I had entered a regular arsenal.

All the furniture was of the XVth or XVIth century. The bed, with its carved canopy supported by great twisted posts, was hung in green damask with golden flowers; the window curtains were of the same material. The walls were covered with Spanish leather, and in all vacant spaces were pieces of furniture covered with trophies of modern and Gothic arms.

There was no mistaking the tastes of the man who occupied this room: they were as warlike as his brother's were peace-loving.

"See," he said, as he went into his dressing-room, "here

you are in the midst of three centuries: have a look. In the meantime I will put on my mountaineering clothes, as I told you; for, as soon as supper is over, I must go out."

"And which, among these swords, arquebuses and daggers, are the historic arms you spoke about?"

"There are three; we will take them in order. Look, by the head of my bed there is a dagger by itself with a large handle, the pommel acting as a seal."

"I have it. Well?"

"It is Sampiètro's dagger."

"The notorious Sampiètro, Vanina's assassin!"

"Assassin? No; avenger."

"The same thing, it seems to me."

"In the rest of the world, perhaps; not in Corsica."

"And is the dagger authentic?"

"Look! It bears Sampiètro's arms; but the *fleur de lis* of France is not yet there; you remember, Sampiètro was not authorised to add the lily to his escutcheon until after the siege of Perpignan."

"No. I did not know that fact. And how did this dagger come into your possession?"

"Oh! It has been in the family for three hundred years. It was given to Napoleon de Franchi by Sampiètro himself."

"Do you know on what occasion?"

"Yes. Sampiètro and my ancestor fell into a Genoese ambuscade and defended themselves like lions. Sampiètro's helmet fell off, and a Genoese on horseback was just going to strike him down with his club when my ancestor drove his dagger through a joint in his cuirass; the cavalier, feeling himself wounded, put spurs to his horse and fled away with Napoleon's dagger so deeply embedded in the wound that he could not pull it out. Well, my ancestor it seems set great store by the dagger and as he was greatly distressed at its loss Sampiètro gave him his. Napoleon took great care of it, for it was made in Spain, as you can see, and will go through two five franc pieces put one upon the other."

"May I try?"

"Certainly."

I put two five franc pieces on the floor and gave them a sharp, powerful blow. Lucien had not deceived me. When I took up the dagger the two pieces were fixed to the point, pierced right through.

"Well," said I, "it's Sampiètro's dagger right enough. The only thing that surprises me is, that having such a weapon, he used a cord to kill his wife."

"He hadn't it then," said Lucien, "because he'd given it to my ancestor."

"Quite true."

"Sampiètro was over sixty years of age when he hurried from Constantinople to Aix to teach the world a great lesson: that women should not mix themselves up in affairs of State."

I bowed assent and put back the dagger.

"And now," said I to Lucien, who was still dressing, "there is Sampiètro's dagger on its hook. Let us take another."

"Do you see two portraits by the side of one another?"

"Yes, Paoli and Napoleon."

"Well, near the portrait of Paoli is a sword."

"Yes."

"It is his."

"Paoli's sword? And it is as authentic as Sampiètro's?"

"Quite; because, like it, it was given, not to one of my ancestors, but to one of my ancestresses."

"To one of your ancestresses?"

"Yes. Mayhap you have heard tell of the lady who, during the War of Independence, presented herself at the tower of Sullacaro, accompanied by a young man?"

"I'm all attention."

"Well, this lady and this young man went to Sullacaro tower and asked to speak to Paoli. But, as Paoli was busy writing, they were refused admission and as the lady was insistent, two sentries pulled her back. Paoli, however, who heard the disturbance, opened the door and asked what it was all about.

"'It is I,' said the woman, 'I want to speak to you.'

"'And what do you want to say to me?'

"'I want to say that I have two sons. I heard yesterday that my elder had been killed in defending his country, so I have walked twenty leagues to bring you the younger.'"

"It is quite a Spartan story you are telling."

"Yes; rather like one."

"And who was this woman?"

"It was my grandmother. Paoli took off his sword and gave it to her."

"My word! I like his way of apologising to a woman."

"She was worthy of it, don't you think?"

"And now, what about this sabre?"

"That? Oh, Bonaparte wore that at the Battle of the Pyramids."

"No doubt it came to your family in the same way as the dagger and the sword?"

"Exactly. After the battle, Bonaparte gave my grandfather, an officer in the Guides, orders to charge, with fifty men, a group of Mamelukes who still rallied round a wounded chief. My grandfather obeyed, scattered the Mamelukes and brought back the chief to the First Consul. But when he wanted to sheath his sword, the blade was so hacked about by the Mamelukes' Damascan weapons that it would not go into the scabbard. My grandfather then threw away his sabre and scabbard as useless; when Bonaparte saw this he gave him his own."

"But," said I, "in your place, I would much rather have my grandfather's sabre, hacked about as it was, than the Commander-in-Chief's in good condition, that you have kept."

"Then look opposite and you will see it. The First Consul picked it up, had a diamond, as you see, set in the hilt, and sent it back to my family with the inscription that you can read on the blade."

There, sure enough, between two windows, sheathed as far as it would go, hung the sabre, hacked and twisted, with this simple inscription:

"Battle of the Pyramids, 21 July, 1798."

At this moment, the manservant, who had opened the door to me and who had come up to announce the return of his young master appeared.

"Excellency," said he, addressing Lucien, "Madame de Franchi wishes you to know that supper is ready."

"Very well, Griffo," replied the young man, "tell my mother that we will come down."

Just then he came out of his dressing-room wearing, as he said, mountaineering clothes; that is to say, a short velvet jacket, breeches and gaiters. Of his other garb he had only kept the cartridge belt round his waist. He found me busy looking at two carbines hung opposite one another, both bearing this date engraved on the butt:

"21 September, 1819—eleven o'clock in the morning."

"And the carbines, are they also arms of historical interest?"

"Yes; at least to us. One belonged to my father."

He stopped.

" And the other?" I asked.

" And the other," he said with a laugh, " belongs to my mother. But we must go down; they are waiting for us."

And, going in front to show the way, he made a sign to me to follow him.

CHAPTER V

I admit that I went downstairs thinking over Lucien's last phrase: " That is my mother's carbine." That made me scrutinise Madame de Franchi more closely than I had done at our first meeting. Her son,, when he entered the dining-room, respectfully kissed her hand, and she received this homage with the dignity of a queen.

" Forgive me, mother, but I am afraid I have kept you waiting."

" Anyhow, it is my fault," I said, bowing. " M. Lucien has told me and shown me such interesting things that my endless questions have made him late."

" Rest contented," she said to me. " I only came down just now. But," she continued, speaking to her son, " I am anxious to see you to have news of Louis."

" Is your son ill?" I asked Madame de Franchi

" Lucien is afraid so," she said.

" You have had a letter from your son?" I asked.

" No," said Lucien; " that is why I am troubled about him."

" But what makes you think he is ill?"

" Because, for several days, I have not been well myself."

" Forgive my continuous questions, but that does not explain to me . . ."

" Don't you know that we are twins?"

" Yes; I do. My guide told me."

" Don't you know that when we were born our sides were united?"

" No; I did not know that."

" Well, it needed the surgeon's knife to separate us; the consequence is, that far apart as we are now, we still have the same body; and whatever impression, be it physical or mental, one of us receives, is felt also by the other. Well, for these last few days, without any reason, I have been sad morose, dull. I have felt a sinking in the heart. It is obvious that my brother is suffering under some great sorrow."

I looked at this young man with astonishment, for he had made this strange statement without showing any signs of doubt; his mother also seemed to have the same conviction. Madame de Franchi smiled sadly and said:

"The absent are in God's hands. The great thing is that you are sure he is alive."

"If he were dead," said Lucien quietly, "I should have seen him."

"And you would have told me, wouldn't you, my son?"

"Of course, at once. I swear to you, mother."

"That is well. Forgive me, monsieur," she added, turning to me, "for not being able to conceal my motherly anxieties. It is not only that Louis and Lucien are my sons, but they are the last of our name. . . . Will you be seated on my right? Lucien, sit there." She pointed to the empty seat on her left.

The table was plentifully spread; but I admit that, although at the time I was almost dying with hunger, I merely satisfied my material needs, for my preoccupied mind prevented me from enjoying to the full the delicacies of the table.

The mother and son saw immediately that I wished to continue the conversation.

"And so," said Lucien, as if he were continuing an interrupted conversation, "you thereupon decided to come to Corsica?"

"Yes, as you see. For a long time I have had this idea and I have at last made it a reality."

"Upon my word, you have acted wisely in not putting it off; for in a few years, with the continued inroads of French taste and customs people who come here to seek Corsica will not find it."

"However," I replied, "if the old national spirit gives way to civilisation and takes shelter in some corner of the island, it will certainly be in the province of Sartène in the valley of Tavaro."

"You think so?" said the young man, smiling.

"For it seems to me that I have before me a fine and noble picture of old Corsican manners."

"Quite so; but, nevertheless, in spite of my mother and myself, in spite of traditions four hundred years old, in this same house with its battlements and loopholes, the French spirit came, sought out my brother, took him and transported him to Paris, whence he will return a qualified lawyer. He will live at Ajaccio, instead of residing in the home of his fathers; he will practise; if he shows talent, he will, perhaps, be appointed *procureur du roi*; then he will prosecute the poor devils who have brought down their man, *fait une peau*, as we say in the country; he will mix up the assassin with the murderer, as you did just now; he will demand, in the name of the law, those who have done what their fathers would have considered it dishonourable not to do; he will substitute the judgment of men for the judgment of God, and in the evening, when he has claimed a head for the scaffold, he will think he has served his country and 'laid another stone in the temple of civilisation' . . . as our Prefect said. Ah, my God! my God!" And the young man raised his eyes to heaven, as Hannibal is said to have done after the battle of Zama.

"However," I replied, "you will admit that God has wished to balance things; for, while he made your brother a follower of new ideas, he has made you an adherent to the old customs."

"Yes; but who can say that my brother will not follow his uncle's example instead of mine? As for me, well, do I not do things unworthy of a Franchi?"

"You?" I exclaimed, with astonishment.

"Ah! My God, yes—me. Would you like me to tell you what you have come to see in the province of Sartène?"

"Tell me."

"Man of the world, artist, or poet, you have come out of curiosity. I do not know which you are, I do not ask; you can tell me if you like before you go; if not, remain silent; you are perfectly free. . . . Well, you have come in the hope of seeing some village vendetta, of meeting a real bandit, the type that M. Merimee describes in 'Colomba'."

"Well, it seems to me that I have not done so badly," I answered. "If I am not mistaken your house is the only one in the village that is not fortified."

"That is in itself a proof that I have degenerated; my father, my grandfather, my grandsires for generations past would have taken one side or the other of the two factions that have divided the village for the last ten years. Well, do you know what part I take in all this shooting and stabbing with knives? I am the umpire. You came to the province of Sartène to see bandits, didn't you? Very well, come with me this evening and I will show you one."

"What! You will let me go with you?"

"Why, good heavens, yes, if it will interest you. That is for you to say."

"Then I accept with pleasure."

"Monsieur is tired," said Madame de Franchi, glancing at

her son as though she had shared his shame in seeing Corsica becoming so degenerate.

"No, mother, no, far from it; he had better come; and when he is back in some Paris drawing-room and people talk of the terrible vendettas and cruel Corsican bandits who terrify the children of Bastia and Ajaccio he will at least be able to shrug his shoulders and tell the truth."

"But what was the beginning of this long quarrel which, so far as I judge from what you tell me, is about to be settled."

"Oh," said Lucien, "in a quarrel it is not the cause, but the result which is important. If a fly, flying in front of a man, causes his death, the man is none the less dead."

I saw that he hesitated to tell me himself the cause of this terrible strife which, for the last ten years, had decimated the village of Sullacaro. But, as you can understand, the more reticent he was, the more curious I became.

"Anyway," I said, "there must have been a reason for the quarrel. Is the reason a secret?"

"Heavens, no! It started between the Orlandi and the Colona."

"How did it happen?"

"Well, a fowl escaped from the Orlandi's back yard and flew into Colona's. The Orlandis went to get their fowl back; the Colonas maintained that it was theirs; the Orlandis threatened to bring the Colonas before the justice of the peace and to swear it was theirs. Then an old woman who caught the fowl wrung its neck and threw it in her neighbour's face, saying: 'Very well, if it is yours, eat it.' Then one of the Orlandi picked up the fowl by its legs, and wanted to belabour the woman who had thrown it in his sister's face. But, just as he was raising his hand, a Colona, who unluckily had his rifle loaded, fired point blank and killed him."

"And how many people have been killed in this dispute?"

"Nine have been killed."

"And all for a paltry fowl worth about a dozen sous."

"Quite so; but as I told you just now, it is not the cause, it is the result that matters."

"And because nine have been killed, must there be a tenth?"

"As you will see," replied Lucien, "why, no, since I am the umpire."

"Doubtless at the request of one of the two families."

"Heavens, no! At the instance of my brother, who was spoken to about it at the Chancellor's house. Why, I ask you

—why the devil do they go bothering in Paris about what happens in a little village in Corsica? It is the Prefect who has played us this trick, by writing to Paris saying that if I liked I had only to say one word and the whole thing would end like a comic opera, with a wedding and a dance; then someone communicated with my brother, who, without losing a moment, wrote to me saying that he had promised that I would do it. Well, there you are," added the young man, with a toss of the head. " One could not let it be said that a Franchi had given his brother's word, and his brother had not honoured the pledge."

" And we are going to meet the chief of one of the two parties this evening, I suppose?"

" Exactly. Last night I saw the other."

" Is it an Orlandi or a Colona that we are going to see?"

" An Orlandi."

" Is the meeting far from here?"

" In the ruins of the Château di Vincentello d'Istria."

" Ah, just so! They told me the ruins were in the neighbourhood."

" About a league away."

" So in three quarters of an hour we shall be there."

" Three quarters of an hour at the very most."

" Lucien," said Madame de Franchi, " remember that you are speaking for yourself—for you who are mountain bred, it takes barely three quarters of an hour, but monsieur will not be able to go the same way that you do."

" Quite true; it will take us an hour and a half, at least."

" You have no time to waste," said Madame de Franchi, looking at the clock.

" Mother," said Lucien, " will you excuse us if we start?"

She put out her hand and the young man kissed it with the same respect that he had done before.

" If, on the other hand," said Lucien, " you would rather finish your supper in peace, go to your room, warm your toes, and smoke your cigar. . . ."

" No! not at all!" I exclaimed. " Hang it, you have promised me a bandit and a bandit I will have."

" Very well, we'll get our rifles and start."

I bowed respectfully to Madame de Franchi and we left the room, preceded by Griffo who lighted us.

We were not long getting ready. I put on a travelling belt that I had had made before I left Paris, to which was attached a kind of hunting knife, and which carried on one side my powder and on the other my bullets. Lucien had his cartridge bag, a double-barrelled Manton, a peak cap, beautifully embroidered, the handiwork of some Sullacaro Penelope.

" Shall I come, your Excellency?" asked Griffo.

" No, you need not," replied Lucien, " but let Diamante loose, and he might perhaps put up a pheasant, and by the light of the moon we can shoot as well as in broad daylight."

An instant later, a large spaniel came bounding along, barking with joy at our heels.

We had gone about ten yards from the house.

" By the way," said Lucien, turning round, " warn the villagers if they hear gun shots on the mountain that it is we who are shooting."

" I will see to that, Excellency."

" Without this precaution," continued Lucien, " they might perhaps think that hostilities had broken out again if they heard the echo of our shots in the streets of Sullacaro."

After going a few yards we turned to the right along a little path which led straight up the mountain.

CHAPTER VI

As we mounted the eye sought in vain to penetrate the deep night shadows where the Tavaro lay hid, but we could see the calm Mediterranean, like a huge polished steel mirror stretching away to the horizon.

When we reached a little fork where the path divides into two, Lucien stopped. There was one path which appeared to go round the mountain; and another, hardly visible, which went straight up it.

" Look here," said he, " have you a mountaineer's sure foot?"

" Yes, but not a mountaineer's head."

" You mean you turn giddy."

" Yes, a sheer drop draws me towards it."

" Then we'd better take this path, where there are no precipices, only rough country."

Lucien led the way through a little coppice of holly trees and I followed him. Diamante was about fifty or sixty yards away, drawing the wood right and left, every now and then returning to the path, wagging his tail gaily to show us that we could without danger, trusting to his instinct, go peacefully on our way. One could see that—like horses which are used for two purposes by semi-fashionable people who are in High Finance in the morning and in High Society in the evening, and like to have a horse which is useful for two purposes, to ride and to drive—so it was easy to see that Diamante was trained to hunt the biped, the quadruped, the bandit and the boar. Not wanting to appear ignorant of Corsican ways, I told Lucien what I had noticed.

"You are mistaken," said he; "Diamante hunts equally well man or animal; but the man he hunts is not the bandit, it is that triple breed, the gendarme, the mounted police and the volunteer."

"Then," I inquired, "is Diamante a bandit's dog?"

"Yes. Diamante belonged to an Orlandi to whom sometimes I used to send—into the country—bread, powder and bullets, and various things in short that a bandit requires. He was killed by a Colona, and the next day I received his dog which, being in the habit of coming to the house, has easily made friends with me."

"But I fancy," I said, "that from my room, or rather your brother's, I have seen another dog besides Diamante?"

"Yes; that's Brusco; he has the same traits as this one, only he came to me from a Colona who was killed by an Orlandi. Consequently, when I go to pay a visit to a Colona I take Brusco; when, on the other hand, I have any business with an Orlandi I let loose Diamante. If one had the misfortune to let the two loose at the same time they would kill each other. There," continued Lucien, with a bitter smile, "men will make it up with one another, live in peace, take the sacrament together, but their dogs will never eat out of the same basin."

"Very good," I replied, laughing; "here are two true Corsican dogs."

CHAPTER VII

We continued our journey, and as Lucien had warned me, the path became steeper and steeper.

I slung my gun over my shoulder, for I saw that very soon I should need both my hands. As for my guide, he walked on as unconcernedly as ever and did not appear to notice the difference in the path. After climbing for a few minutes over rocks, with the help of creepers and roots, we reached a sort of platform surmounted by some ruined walls. They were those of the Château di Vicentello d'Istria, which was our destination.

After another five minutes' climb, still more difficult and

steeper than the first, Lucien, on reaching the last terrace, stretched out his hand and drew me up to him.

"Here we are. Four centuries ago my ancestors would have opened their doors and would have said: 'Welcome to our château.' To-day their descendant shows you this tumbled-down building and says: 'Welcome to our ruins.'"

"Has this chateau, then, belonged to your family since the death of Vicentello d'Istria?" I asked.

"No; but before his birth it was the dwelling of the common ancestress of us all, the famous Savilia, widow of Lucien de Franchi."

"Isn't there a terrible story in Filippini about this woman?"

"Yes. . . . If it were daylight you would be able to see the ruins of the Château de Valle. It is there that Seigneur de Guidice lived, who was hated as deeply as she was loved, who was as ugly as she was beautiful. He fell in love with her, and as she was in no hurry to return his affection according to his wishes, he warned her that if she did not agree to accept him as a husband in a stated time he would abduct her by force. Savilia appeared to yield and invited Guidice to come to dinner with her. Guidice, elated with joy and forgetting that he had only arrived at this flattering position by threats, accepted the invitation, accompanied by one or two servants only. The door was shut behind them, and five minutes afterwards Guidice found himself a prisoner, and was locked up in a dungeon."

I continued along the way indicated and I found myself in a kind of square courtyard. Through the gaps, littered with rubbish, that time had caused, the moon cast great patches of light. All the rest of the ground was in the shadow cast by the walls that were still standing.

Lucien took out his watch.

"Ah!" said he, "we are twenty minutes too soon. Let us sit down; you must be tired."

We sat down, or rather lay down, on the grassy slope in front of a large gap.

"But it seems to me," said I to my companion, "that you have not told me the whole story."

"No," added Lucien; "because, every morning and evening, Savilia went down to the dungeon adjoining the one in which Guidice was confined and there, separated from him only by a grating, she used to torment him. 'Guidice,' she used to say to him, 'how could a man so ugly as you are ever imagine that I should be your wife?'

"This torture lasted three months and was gone through

twice a day. But at the end of three months, thanks to the help of a chambermaid, Guidice escaped. Then he came back with all his vassals, far more numerous than Savilia's, took the château by storm, seized Savilia and imprisoned her in a large cage at the cross-roads in the forest of Rocca di Cilaccia. After three days of this public outrage Savilia died."

"Ah, well," I remarked, "it seems to me that your ancestors understood, to some purpose, how to avenge themselves; and that in merely killing with gun-shot and dagger-thrust their descendants have somewhat degenerated."

"Not to mention the fact that soon they won't kill one another at all. But, at any rate," replied the young man, "it has not yet reached that pitch in our family. The two sons of Savilia, who were at Ajaccio under the guardianship of their uncle, were brought up to be true Corsicans and continued to make war upon Guidice's sons. That war lasted four centuries and ended only, as you saw engraved on my father's and mother's carbines, September 21st, 1819, at eleven o'clock in the morning."

"Oh, yes, I remember the inscription, but I had not time to ask you to explain it, because I read it just as we were going down to supper."

"Well, this is it. Of the Guidice family in 1819 there were only two brothers left; of the Franchi family there was only my father, who had married his cousin. Three months after this marriage the Guidices determined to wipe us out at a single stroke. One of the brothers hid himself on the Olmedo road and waited for my father, who was coming from Sartène; whilst the other, taking advantage of his absence, determined to attack our house. The affair was carried out according to plan, but turned out very differently from what the assailants anticipated. My father, who had been warned, was on his guard; my mother, who had been informed, called together the shepherds, so that when the double attack was launched, each of them was on the watch: my father on the mountain, my mother in my room. Well, after five minutes' fighting the two brothers Guidice fell, one cut down by my father, the other laid low by my mother. When my father saw his enemy fall he took out his watch: It was eleven o'clock! When my mother saw her adversary laid low she looked at the clock: It was eleven o'clock! It all happened at the same instant, the Guidices ceased to exist, the family had been destroyed. The victorious Franchi family was in future left in peace, and having honourably carried on this warfare for four centuries, the trouble was at an end. So my father had the date and the hour of this strange coincidence engraved on the butts of the carbines which had fired the shots, and hung them on each side of the clock, in the self-same place that you have seen them. Seven months later my mother bore twins, one of whom is your servant, Lucien the Corsican, and the other his brother, Louis the philosopher."

At that instant, on one of the patches of ground lit by the moon, I saw the shadow of a man and a dog—the shadows of the bandit and Diamante. At the self-same moment we heard the chimes of Sullacaro clock; it struck nine.

Master Orlandi was, it seemed, of the same opinion as Louis XV, who held that punctuality is the politeness of princes. It was impossible to be more punctual than this king of the mountain with whom Lucien had made an appointment at the stroke of nine.

When we saw him we both got up.

CHAPTER VIII

"You are not alone, Monsieur Lucien?" said the bandit.

"Do not trouble about that, Orlandi; Monsieur is a friend of mine who has heard speak of you and who wishes to pay you a visit. I did not think I ought to deny him this pleasure."

"Monsieur is welcome to the country," said the bandit, bowing and coming towards us.

I returned his salute with studied politeness.

"Haven't we something to say Monsieur Lucien?" the bandit inquired.

"Yes, and if you will follow me——"

"At your service."

Lucien turned to me.

"You will excuse me, won't you?" he said.

"Why, certainly."

The two went away, and climbing over the gap where Orlandi had come they stood there silhouetted in the moonlight, which seemed to bathe the outline of their figures with liquid silver.

Then, for the first time I was able to take stock of Orlandi more closely.

He was a tall fellow, wearing a full length beard, and dressed exactly like young Franchi, the only difference being that his clothes showed signs of constant contact with the brushwood which he lived amongst, with the brambles through which more than once he had been compelled to flee, and with the hard ground on which he lay every night.

I was not able to hear what they said, first of all because they were twenty yards away, and secondly because they spoke a Corsican dialect.

But I could tell by their gestures that the bandit was refuting, with considerable heat, a series of arguments that the young man was bringing forward with perfect restraint which showed the absolute impartiality he was exercising in the affair.

At length Orlandi's gestures became less frequent and less wild; the tone of his voice also seemed more subdued. After a last remark he bent his head; and at length, after a moment's pause, he held out his hand to the young man.

The conference was, in all probability at an end; for they both came towards me.

"My dear guest," said the young man to me, "this is Orlandi, who wishes to shake your hand to thank you."

"For what?" I asked.

"For agreeing to be one of his sureties. I have given my word that you will."

"If you have given your word for me you were sure that I should accept without even knowing what it is about."

I offered my hand to the bandit, who honoured me by touching it with the end of his fingers.

"And so now," Lucien went on, "you will be able to say to my brother that all is settled according to his wishes, and that you yourself have signed the contract."

"Is it a marriage then?"

"No, not yet; but perhaps it will come to that."

A contemptuous smile spread over the bandit's lips.

"Peace," said he, "since you wish it so much, Monsieur Lucien, but not an alliance; that is not included in the bond."

"No," said Lucien, "that is only written, in all probability, in the future. But let us talk of other things. You did not hear anything whilst I was talking with Orlandi?"

"You mean what you were saying?"

"No but what a pheasant close by was saying."

"As a matter of fact for a moment I fancied I did hear the kor-ork of one, but I thought I was mistaken."

"You were not mistaken; there is a cock bird perched in that large chestnut tree you saw, a hundred yards back. I heard him just now when I passed. Ah, well, we must eat it to-morrow," said Lucien gaily.

"I should have brought it down already," said Orlandi, "if I had not been afraid that they would think in the village that I was firing on something that wasn't a pheasant."

"I have provided against that contingency," said Lucien. "By the way," he added, turning to me and slinging his gun that he had just loaded over his shoulder, "the first shot is yours."

"Wait a moment, I am not sure that I am such a good shot as you, but I can do my share in eating the bird; so you shoot."

"Very well," said Lucien. "You are not accustomed as we are, to night shooting, so you would be sure to aim too low; anyway, if you have nothing to do to-morrow during the day you shall have your revenge."

CHAPTER IX

We left the ruins by the opposite side to which we had entered, Lucien walking first.

The instant we got into the undergrowth the pheasant, giving himself away, began kor-orking again.

He was about eighty yards from us, perhaps a little less, hidden in the branches of the chestnut tree surrounded on all sides by thick brushwood.

"How will you get to him without his hearing you?" I asked Lucien. "It does not seem to me to be very easy."

"No," he answered; "if I could only see him I would fire from here."

"What, from here? You have a gun that kills pheasants at eighty yards."

"With shot, no; with a bullet, yes."

"Ah, a bullet; I'm not talking of that, that is quite another matter and you were right to take the shot."

"Would you like to see the pheasant?" Orlandi asked.

"Yes," said Lucien, "I admit I should very much."

"Wait a moment then."

And Orlandi began to imitate the half-clucking, half-whistling sound of a hen pheasant.

Immediately, without seeing the pheasant, we noticed a movement in the leaves of the chestnut tree; the pheasant hopped from branch to branch kor-orking all the time in reply to the advances that Orlandi was making.

At last he appeared on the top of the tree, perfectly visible, standing out clearly against the dull grey of the sky. Orlandi ceased calling and the pheasant remained perfectly still. At that very instant Lucien put up his gun and, after aiming for a moment, fired. The pheasant fell like a stone.

" Go and seek," said Lucien to Diamante.

The dog dived into the undergrowth and five minutes later came back with the pheasant in his mouth.

The bullet had gone right through its body.

" That was a splendid shot, especially with a double-barrelled gun," said I, " and I offer you my congratulations."

" Oh," said Lucien, " there is less merit in what I have done than you think; one of the barrels is rifled and fires a bullet like a carbine."

" No matter! Even with a carbine the shot deserves praise."

" Bah!" said Orlandi. " With a carbine Monsieur Lucien hits a five franc piece at three hundred yards."

" And do you fire a revolver as well as you do a carbine?"

" Very nearly," said Lucien. " At twenty-five yards I can split six bullets out of twelve on the blade of a knife."

I raised my hat and saluted Lucien.

" And is your brother as good a shot?"

" My brother," he replied. " Poor Louis! He has never handled either a pistol or a gun in his life. I am therefore in constant dread that he will get mixed up in some nasty affair in Paris; because a brave man such as he is, to uphold the honour of his country would risk being killed."

And Lucien put the pheasant in the large pocket of his velvet coat.

" Well," said he, " my dear Orlandi, until to-morrow."

" Till to-morrow, Monsieur Lucien."

" I know your punctuality. At ten o'clock, you, your friends and relations, will be at the end of the street, see? From the mountain side at the opposite end of the street, Colona will be with his relations and friends. We shall be on the steps of the church."

" Very well, Monsieur Lucien; thank you for your trouble. And you, Monsieur," added Orlandi, turning to me and bowing, " thank you for the honour."

And after the exchange of compliments we parted, Orlandi going into the brushwood and we making our way to the village. As for Diamante, he stood for a moment uncertain between Orlandi and ourselves, looking alternatively right and left. After five minutes' hesitation he did us the honour of giving us the preference.

I admit I was not without misgivings, as I scaled the thick

stone wall that I spoke of, as to how I was going to descend; the descent, as one knows, is often considerably more difficult than the ascent.

I noted with a good deal of satisfaction that Lucien had, doubtlessly reading my thoughts, chosen another way back from that which we came.

This way had another advantage as regards conversation that the steep spurs naturally interrupted.

Well, as the slope was gentle and the path easy I had not gone fifty yards before I began my usual questions.

" So," I said, " peace is made?"

" Yes, and as you saw, not without some difficulty. In the end I persuaded him that all the advances were made by the Colonas. To begin with, they had had five men killed; while the Orlandis had had only four. The Colonas had consented yesterday to a reconciliation, whilst the Orlandis consented to it only to-day. And, as well, the Colonas agreed to offer a live fowl publicly to the Orlandis—a concession which showed that they admitted they were in the wrong. This last point settled it."

" And it is to-morrow that this touching reconciliation takes place?"

" To-morrow at ten o'clock. So you are by no means unlucky. You wanted to see a vendetta," the young man replied with a bitter laugh. " Bah! A vendetta is a beautiful thing. For four hundred years in Corsica one has talked of nothing else. You will see a reconciliation. That, indeed, is much rarer than the vendetta itself."

I began to laugh.

" There you go," said he, " you laugh at us, and you are right; we are truly funny folk."

" No," said I to him, " I am laughing at a very unique thing: it is seeing you furious with yourself for having succeeded."

" Really? Ah, if you could have understood you would have admired my eloquence. But come in ten years time; rest assured, everybody will speak French."

" You are an excellent pleader."

" Not I; maybe I am an arbitrator. What do you expect? The duty of an arbitrator is conciliation. They ought to make me an arbitrator between God and the Devil. Although I should try and settle their differences, at the bottom of my heart I should be quite convinced that in listening to my pleading the good Lord would be behaving foolishly."

As I saw that the course of the conversation was only

irritating my companion I dropped the subject; and as on his part he did nothing to pursue it we reached the house without speaking another word.

CHAPTER X

Griffo was waiting for us.

Before his master had said a word he had foraged into his coat pocket and had pulled out the pheasant. He had heard the gunshot. Madame de Franchi had not yet gone to bed; but she had retired to her room telling Griffo to beg her son to go to her before he went to bed.

The young man asked if I wanted anything, and when I said " No," he begged leave to carry out his mother's wishes.

I gave it very willingly and went up to my room.

I surveyed it once more with a certain feeling of self-satisfaction. My studies in analogies had not misled me, and I was proud of having divined Louis's character as correctly as I had divined Lucien's.

I undressed leisurely, and after taking the "Orientals" of Victor Hugo from the future lawyer's bookcase, I began to read, well pleased with myself. I had just re-read for the hundredth time "Le Feu du Ciel" when I heard footsteps coming up the staircase which stopped outside my room; I imagined it was my host who had come, intending to wish me good-night but who, fearing doubtlessly that I was already asleep, hesitated to open the door.

" Come in," I said, putting my book on the table by my bed.

Thereupon the door opened and Lucien appeared.

" Forgive me," said he, " but I am afraid, on thinking it over, that I have been disagreeable this evening and I could not go to bed without begging your pardon. I have come to apologise, and as you still have evidently a number of questions to ask me, to put myself at your disposal."

" Thank you very much," I said. " Thanks to your kindness, on the contrary, I have been pretty well informed about all that I wanted to know, and there is only one thing left—that, I have promised not to ask you."

" Why?"

" Because it would certainly be very indiscreet. However, I warn you, don't press me; I will not answer for myself."

" Very well then—come, out with it. There is nothing worse than unsatisfied curiosity; it naturally arouses suspicions, and out of three suspicions two are always more to the disadvantage of the person concerned than the truth would be."

"You may rest easy on that score: my worst suspicions with regard to you lead me simply to the conclusion that you are a wizard."

The young man laughed heartily.

"Devil take it!" said he, "you have now made me as curious as yourself; tell me why, I pray you."

"Well, you have made clear everything that was obscure except on one point: when Madame de Franchi spoke of the sadness that you felt, which made you believe that some untoward event was happening to your brother, and asked you if you were sure that he was not dead, you said to her: ' No; if he were dead, I should have seen him.' "

"Yes, quite true, I did say that."

"Very well, if the explanation of those words may be allowed to a profane ear, explain them to me, I beg you."

The young man's face had assumed, as I spoke, such a serious expression that I uttered the last words hesitatingly.

And, indeed, after I had finished speaking both of us were silent.

"There," I said, "I see that I have been indiscreet; take no notice of what I have said."

"No," he said; "only being a man of the world you are consequently a little sceptical. I am sorry to see you treat with suspicion an ancient family tradition that has existed for four centuries."

"Listen," I said, "one thing I swear to you: it is that no one is more credulous than I am as regards legends and traditions; and there are, in fact, some things which I specially believe in: impossible things."

"So you believe in ghosts?"

"Do you have visions of your departed relatives?"

"Whenever some great event is about to happen or has happened."

"To what reason do you attribute this privilege, that is accorded to your family?"

"I can only say that it is an old tradition; I told you that Savilia died leaving two sons."

"Yes, I remember."

"These two sons grew up, and they showered upon each other the love that they would have bestowed upon their parents if they had lived. They took an oath that nothing, not even death, should separate them; and then, under some secret spell, they wrote in their blood on pieces of parchment that they exchanged a mutual oath that the one who died first would appear to the other at his death and then afterwards at every critical moment of his life. Three months later one of the brothers was killed in an ambush, at the very moment that his brother was sealing a letter to him; as he was just impressing the burning wax with his signet ring he heard a sigh behind him and, turning round, he saw his brother standing there with his hand on his shoulder, although he did not feel that hand. Then, quite mechanically, he gave him the letter which he had addressed to him; his brother took it and disappeared. On the eve of his own death he saw him again. Doubtless, the two brothers signed the compact not only for themselves but also for their descendants; because, since that time, the appearances have been repeated not only at the passing away but on the eve of all important happenings."

"Have you never seen a spirit?"

"No; but, as my father, on the night before his death, was warned by his father that he was about to die, I suppose my brother and I will enjoy the same privilege as our ancestors, having done nothing to forfeit this favour."

In Paris I should have taken this young man for a humbug; but in the heart of Corsica, in a little out-of-the-way village one must look upon him either as a fool who honestly is deceiving himself, or as a privileged being who is more happy or less happy than the ordinary mortal.

"And now," he said, after a long silence, "have you found out all you want to know?"

"Yes, thank you," I replied; "I much appreciate your confidence in me and I promise to keep your secret."

"Why, in Heaven's name," said he, smiling, "there's no secret in that; the first villager you happened to meet would have told you these facts, just as I have. I only hope that in Paris my brother will not boast of this privilege, which would in all likelihood simply draw supercilious smiles from the men and hysterics from the women."

Whereupon he rose, and bidding me good night he went to his room.

Although very tired I found it difficult to get to sleep; and when I did, it was not until dawn that I had any restful sleep.

Lucien had said that at half-past nine he would come into my room. When he appeared he was dressed in French fashion, in fact as a French dandy. He was wearing a black coat, a fancy waistcoat and white trousers: because at the beginning of March one has usually been wearing white trousers for some time in Corsica. He noticed that I seemed astonished.

"You admire my get-up," he said; "it is another proof that I am civilised."

"Yes, indeed," I replied; "and I admit that I am considerably astonished that you have such a good tailor in Ajaccio. Why, with my velvet coat I look like a *Jean de Paris* by the side of you."

"Well, my suit comes straight from Humann's, that is the explanation, my dear friend. As my brother and myself are exactly the same size my brother, for fun, has sent me a complete wardrobe and I don it on great occasions. When the Prefect comes, when the General commanding the eighty-sixth Department makes his inspection, or when I receive a guest like yourself, and when that pleasure coincides with an event as solemn as the one that is going to take place."

This young man possessed bitter irony, kept in control by his good breeding, which, though it might put one off one's balance, never went beyond the limits of good taste. So I merely bowed in acquiescence whilst he, with the usual precautions, put on a pair of yellow gloves made either by Boisin or Rousseau. In this garb he had the appearance of a really smart Parisian.

In the meantime I got dressed.

"Come along," said Lucien, "if you want to see the show."

CHAPTER XI

From the top of a flight of eight steps leading to the door of the château where Madame de Franchi and her son lived one could overlook the square.

This square, so different from the previous night, was full of people; the crowd, however, was composed entirely of women and children under twelve years of age: not a man amongst them.

On the lowest step up to the church stood a man wearing a tri-coloured sash: it was the mayor.

Under the porch there was another man, dressed in black, seated at a table; he had a paper with some writing on it in his hand. This man was the lawyer; the paper with writing on it was the deed of reconciliation.

I took my place on one side of the table with the sponsor

of the Orlandi. On the opposite side were the sponsors of the Colona; behind the lawyer stood Lucien, who represented both sides equally. Further back in the chancel of the church, one could see the priests ready to say the Mass.

The clock struck ten.

As it did so, a thrill ran through the crowd and all eyes turned towards the ends of the street, if one can call an irregular opening left by the fifty houses built according to the sweet will of their owners, a street.

Immediately we saw coming from the mountain side Orlandi; from the river, Colona, each followed by his adherents: but, according to the arrangements that had been made, none of them carried arms; and if their faces had been a little less surly one might have taken them for respectable churchwardens taking part in a procession.

The chiefs of the two parties presented a very sharp contrast as regards physique. Orlandi, as I have said, was tall, slight, dark and active.

Colona was short, stout and sturdy; his hair and beard were reddish, cropped and curly.

They both carried an olive branch in their hands, emblem of the peace they were about to sign. This was a poetic touch by the mayor.

Colona, in addition, carried a white fowl by its legs— which was to replace, in lieu of damages, the fowl which, ten years before, had started the quarrel.

The fowl was alive.

This point had been discussed at great length and had very nearly put an end to the whole proceedings; Colona looking upon it as a double humiliation to have to replace with a live fowl the dead one that his aunt had flung in Orlandi's cousin's face. However, by logical argument Lucien had persuaded Colona to give the fowl and Orlandi to accept it.

The instant the two enemies appeared, the bells, which up to that moment had been silent, rang out a merry peal.

When Orlandi and Colona caught sight of one another they both made the same gesture, showing quite plainly their mutual abhorrence; however, they marched on.

In front of the church door they halted about four yards from each other.

If, three days before, these two men had come within a hundred yards of one another, one of the two would have certainly been left on the ground.

For five minutes there was dead silence, not only in the two groups but also in the whole crowd—a silence which, notwithstanding the conciliatory purpose of the ceremony had nothing very peaceful about it.

Then the mayor spoke.

"Come, Colona," he said, "don't you know that it is your place to speak first?"

Colona, pulling himself together with a great effort, muttered some words in Corsican dialect.

As far as I could gather he expressed his regret that he had been ten years in vendetta with his good neighbour, Orlandi, and that he offered, in reparation, the white fowl which he carried in his hand.

Orlandi waited till his adversary had quite finished speaking and then replied also in Corsican dialect, saying that on his part he promised to remember only this present and solemn reconciliation held under the auspices of the mayor and the arbitration of Monsieur Lucien, drawn up by the lawyer.

Then there was a fresh silence on the part of the two men.

"Well, gentlemen," said the mayor, "it was agreed, I think, that you should shake hands."

Instinctively the two enemies put their hands behind their backs.

The mayor came down from the top of the steps where he was standing, took Colona's hand from behind his back and Orlandi's from behind his; then, after some difficulty—which he tried to cover up with a smile—he joined their two hands.

The lawyer, seizing the moment, stood up, whilst the mayor, holding the two hands together, which at first they tried to unclasp, but by degrees becoming resigned remained one in the other, read as follows:

"In the presence of us, Guiseppe-Antonio Sarrola, Notary Royal at Sullacaro in the province of Sartène.

"In the great square of the village, in front of the church, in the presence of the Mayor, the sponsors and the whole population.

"Between Gaetano-Orso Orlandi, called Orlandi;

"And Marco-Vincenzio Colona, called Schioppone;

"It has been solemnly agreed as follows:

"From this day, the 4th of March, 1841, the Vendetta declared ten years ago between them shall cease.

"From this same day they will live as good neighbours and friends, as their relations did before this unfortunate business brought discord between their families and friends.

" In witness whereof they have signed these presents in the village church porch with M. Polo Arbori, Mayor of the parish, M. Lucien de Franchi, arbitrator, the sponsors of each of the two contracting parties and the notary.

" Sullacaro, this 4th day of March, 1841."

I noted with admiration that, showing great prudence, the lawyer had not said a word about the fowl, which put Colona in such an invidious position with Orlandi.

The more Colona's face beamed the more Orlandi's grew dark and sullen. The latter looked at the fowl which he held in his hand, and was obviously almost tempted to throw it in Colona's face. But a glance from Lucien de Franchi nipped the intention in the bud.

The mayor saw that there was no time to lose; he mounted the steps backwards, carefully holding the two hands, keeping his eyes closely fixed on the newly reconciled parties. Then, in order to prevent a fresh argument—which was bound to take place at the moment of signing, because each would look upon it as a concession to sign first—he took the pen and signed himself, and, by that means turning the humiliation into an honour, he handed the pen to Orlandi who took it, signed and handed it to Lucien who, adopting the same pacifying ruse, handed it in turn to Colona, who made the sign of the Cross.

At that moment the chanting of the *Te Deum* was heard as if in celebration of a victory.

Everybody signed then, regardless of rank or title, just as the nobility of France had signed, one hundred and twenty-three years previously, the protest against the Duke of Maine.

Then the two heroes of the day entered the church and knelt on either side of the choir at the place set apart for them. I noticed that from this moment Lucien was quite at ease; it was over, the reconciliation was sworn, not only before men but before God.

The rest of the service passed off without any incident worth recording. When the Mass was over, Orlandi and Colona went out with the same ceremonial.

At the door, prompted by the Mayor, they once more shook hands; then each of them, accompanied by his party of friends, went to his house which neither one nor the other had entered for three years.

Lucien and I went back to Madame de Franchi's house when dinner was ready. It was easy to see, by his special attentiveness to me, that Lucien had read my name over my shoulder when I signed the deed, and that the name was not altogether unknown to him.

That morning I had told Lucien of my intention to leave after dinner; I was forcibly recalled to Paris for the rehearsals of *A Marriage under Louis XV,* so, in spite of the pleadings of the mother and the son, I adhered to my first decision. Lucien asked leave to avail himself of my offer by writing to his brother, and Madame de Franchi—whose outward austerity hid a mother's heart—made me promise that I would myself deliver this letter to her son. The trouble was not great: Louis de Franchi, like the true Parisian that he was, lived in the rue du Helder No. 7.

I asked to have a last look at Lucien's room. He took me to it himself and, pointing with his hand to all its contents:

" You know," said he, " if there is anything that appeals to you please take it, it is yours."

I unhooked a little dagger, hanging in a dark corner, which made me think that it had no special value, and as I had noticed Lucien cast a look of curiosity at my hunting belt and praise the arrangement of it, I begged him to accept it. He had the good taste to accept it without forcing me to repeat my request a second time.

At that moment Griffo appeared at the door. He came to say that my horse was saddled and that my guide was waiting for me. I had put aside the present that I meant to give Griffo: a sort of hunting knife with two pistols attached to the side of the blade with locks hidden in the hilt. I have never seen anyone express delight as he did.

I went down and found Madame de Franchi at the bottom of the staircase; she was waiting to wish me a comfortable journey at the self-same place where she had welcomed me. I kissed her hand; I had a great regard for this lady, who was so unaffected in her manner and yet so dignified. Lucien accompanied me to the door.

" On any other day," said he, " I would saddle my horse and come with you up the mountain; but to-day I dare not leave Sullacaro for fear that one or other of our new-made friends commits some act of folly."

We embraced.

" Shan't I see you one of these days?" I asked him.

" Yes, if you come to Corsica."

" No, but when you come to Paris."

" I shall never go there," replied Lucien.

" Anyway, you will find some of my cards on the mantelpiece in your brother's room. Don't forget the address."

"I promise you, if any event whatever should take me to the Continent, I shall pay a visit to you first."

"Good, that is understood."

He gave me his hand once more and we parted; but as long as he was able to see me going down the street which led to the river his eyes followed me.

Everything was quiet in the village, although one could note that sort of restlessness which follows in the trail of great happenings, and I scrutinised each door as I passed it, expecting to see my god-child Orlandi who, as a matter of fact, had never thanked me for what I had done. But I passed by the last house in the village and got into the open country without having caught a glimpse of him.

I thought I had been quite forgotten, and I must say that in the midst of the serious business that Orlandi had had to face on such a day I forgave him his forgetfulness, when, all of a sudden, on reaching Bicchisano Heath I saw, coming out of the brushwood, a man who stood in the middle of the road and whom I realised at the same time, with my French impetuosity and my ideas of Parisian manners, I had deemed ungrateful.

I noticed that he had already had time to put on the same clothes which he wore when he arrived at the ruins of Vicentello; that is to say, he wore his cartridge belt to which the usual pistol was attached and he carried a rifle. When I was twenty yards away, he put his hat in his hand whilst I, on my part, spurred my horse so as not to make him wait.

"Monsieur," he said, "I could not let you leave Sullacaro without thanking you for the honour you have conferred upon a poor peasant like myself by acting as surety; and, as down there, my mind was uneasy and I could find no words, I have come to wait for you here."

"I thank you," I said, "but you need not have put yourself to all this trouble on that account; all the honour has been mine."

"But," added the bandit, "what do you expect, monsieur! One cannot get rid of a habit of four years' standing in an instant. The mountain air is life to me: when once you have breathed it you stifle everywhere else. Just now, in those miserable houses, I kept thinking that every minute the roof was going to fall on my head."

"But now," I replied, "you will take up your ordinary life. You have a house, they tell me, a paddock and vineyard."

" Yes, quite true; but my sister took care of the house, the Lucquois cultivated and harvested my grapes. We Corsicans don't work."

" What do you do then?"

" We inspect the workers, we go out with our rifles, we shoot."

" Ah, well, my dear Monsieur Orlandi," I said to him, holding out my hand, " good luck! but remember that my honour as well as yours is pledged that you only fire at mountain sheep, deer, wild boar, pheasants and partridges and never at Marco-Vicenzio Colona nor any of his family."

" Ah, Excellency," he answered, with an expression on his face that I have noticed only on Norman litigants, " the fowl that he gave me back was very skinny."

And without uttering another word he dived into the brush-wood and vanished.

Eight days later I was in Paris.

CHAPTER XII

The day I arrived I called upon M. Louis de Franchi; he was out.

I left my card with a word or two saying that I had come straight from Sullacaro and that I had a letter for him from his brother Lucien. I asked when he would be in, adding that I had undertaken to hand it to him myself.

In showing me to his master's study, the servant took me through the dining-room and the drawing-room. I observed everything with curiosity, as you can understand, and I recognised the same taste that I had already noted at Sullacaro; only the ensemble was enhanced by Parisian refinement. M. Louis de Franchi seemed to me to have a very charming suite of apartments for a bachelor.

The next day, as I was getting dressed about eleven in the morning, my servant told me that M. Louis de Franchi had called. I told him to show him into the drawing-room, give him the newspapers and say that I would be with him directly.

As I entered, M. de Franchi, who from courtesy no doubt had begun to read a serial of mine which was then coming out in " The Press ", raised his head.

I was amazed at the likeness to his brother. He rose.

" Monsieur," he said, " I could hardly believe my good luck when I read this little note that my servant gave me when I got home. I made him describe you twenty times in order to be sure that it was in keeping with your portraits;

at last, this morning, in my eagerness to thank you and to have news of my family I have called at your house without regard to the hour; I am afraid I have come a little too early."

"Forgive me," I answered, "if I do not reply at once to your gracious compliment; but I assure you, monsieur, I look at you and I ask myself, is it M. Louis or M. Lucien de Franchi to whom I have the honour of speaking."

"Yes, the likeness is very great; and when I was at Sulla-caro nobody but my brother and myself could avoid making a mistake. However, if he has not, since my departure, given up his Corsican ways, you will have seen him generally dressed in clothes that mark the great difference between us."

"Quite so," I replied. "By chance, when I left he was, except for the white trousers which are not yet worn in Paris, dressed exactly as you are; consequently to distinguish you from one another there is not even the difference of costume of which you speak. But," I added, taking out the letter from my case, "I am sure you are eager to have news of your family; take this letter that I should have left yesterday if I had not promised Madame de Franchi to give it to you myself."

"And you left them all well?"

"Yes, but rather anxious."

"About me?"

"About you. But read the letter, I pray you."

"If you will excuse me?"

"Of course."

M. de Franchi opened the letter whilst I rolled some cigarettes.

I watched his face while he glanced rapidly over his brother's epistle; every now and then he smiled and murmured:

"My dear Lucien! My good mother! . . . Why yes . . . yes . . . I understand. . . ."

I had not yet got over the strange likeness; however, as Lucien had said, I noticed that his complexion was whiter, that his pronunciation of the French language was much clearer.

"Ah, well," I said, when he had finished, offering him a cigarette that he lighted from mine, "you see, as I told you, your family have been anxious, but I am glad to see their alarm was needless."

"No," he said sorrowfully, "not altogether. I have been ill, it is true; but I have had a disappointment, a serious one, which I admit has been made worse by the idea that in suffering here I have made my brother suffer over there."

"M. Lucien has already told me what you are speaking of, monsieur, but really, to believe such an extraordinary thing is true and not the imagination of his brain, only such a proof as I have just had would convince me. So you are yourself quite sure, monsieur, that the uneasiness that your brother has been suffering over there is the result of your suffering over here."

"Yes, monsieur, absolutely."

"Then," I continued, "your answer in the affirmative doubles my interest in what has happened to you. May I ask out of interest, not out of curiosity, if the disappointment of which you spoke just now is passed and if you are getting over it."

"Oh! my God! you know, monsieur," he said, "that the most bitter grief heals with time, and if nothing happens to poison the wound in my heart it will bleed for a time and then it will heal. Meanwhile, let me thank you once more, and may I, even now and again, come and see you and talk about Sullacaro?"

"With the greatest pleasure," I said; "but why not now continue a conversation which is as pleasant to me as to you? Sir, here is my servant coming to say that lunch is ready. Do me the honour of eating a cutlet with me, then we can talk as we like."

"Impossible, I am sorry to say. Yesterday I received a letter from the Chancellor, who asked me to come at twelve o'clock to-day at the Ministry of Justice, and you can understand that I, a poor little lawyer in the making, cannot keep so great a personage waiting."

"Ah! It is probably about the Orlandi and Colona affair that he wants you to call."

"I imagine so, and, as my brother tells me, the quarrel is at an end . . ."

"Before the notary; I can give you fresh details; I signed the deed as surety for Orlandi."

"As a matter of fact my brother said something about that. Listen," said he, taking out his watch, "it is five minutes to twelve; I will go and tell the Chancellor that my brother has fulfilled my promise."

"Most religiously, I'll answer for it."

"Dear Lucien! I knew very well that although it went against his wishes he would do it."

"Yes, and one must thank him, because, I will answer for it, it cost him dear."

"We will talk of that later; for you know quite well what great pleasure it is for me to see in my mind's eye, conjured up by you, the picture of my mother, my brother, my country! So, if you will tell me what time . . ."

"It is rather difficult now. During the first days of my return I shall be a little uncertain. But tell me, where can I find you?"

"Listen," he said. "To-morrow is *Mi-Carême,* isn't it?"

"Well?"

"Are you going to the ball at the Opera?"

"Yes and no. Yes, if you ask me to meet you there; no if I have no interest in going."

"I must go; I am obliged to go."

"Ah," I said, smiling, "I see quite well, as you said just now, that time heals the bitterest griefs and that the wound in your heart will heal itself."

"You are mistaken because I am going probably to find fresh trouble."

"Then don't go."

"Ah! My God, can anyone do what they want in this world? I am dragged there in spite of myself. I go where Fate leads me. It would be better if I did not go, I know that quite well. However, I shall go."

"What time?"

"Half-past twelve, if you like."

"Where?"

"In the foyer. At one o'clock I have a meeting under the clock."

"That's settled."

We shook hands and he went out quickly. It was almost twelve o'clock.

Next evening, at half-past twelve, I kept the appointment. Louis arrived a little late; he had been following through the corridors a mask that he thought he recognised, but the mask got lost in the crowd and he could not find it.

I wanted to talk about Corsica, but Louis was too distrait to follow so serious a subject of conversation; his eyes were constantly turning to the clock, and all of a sudden he left me, exclaiming:

"Ah! There is my 'bouquet' of violets."

He pushed his way through the crowd in order to catch up the lady who carried an enormous bouquet of violets in her hand.

Luckily for the dancers, there were " bouquets " of all sorts in the foyer. I was soon spoken to by a " bouquet " of camellias, who wished to offer me her congratulations on my happy return to Paris. After the camellias came wild roses. After the wild roses a " bouquet " of heliotrope. At last I was with my fifth " bouquet " when I met D——

" Ah! it is you, my good friend," said he. " Welcome. You have come just in the nick of time; we are supping this evening at my house with so-and-so "—he mentioned three or four mutual friends—" and we shall look for you."

" Many thanks, dear friend," I replied, " but in spite of the pleasure it would give me to accept your invitation, I cannot, as I am already engaged."

" That's of no consequence, everybody will bring a ' bouquet '; we have arranged to have six jugs of water on the table solely for the purpose of keeping the ' bouquets ' fresh."

" Ah! my friend, there you are wrong. I haven't a ' bouquet ' to put in your jugs. I am with a man friend."

" Well, you know the old saw: ' Your friends are our friends ' . . ."

" It's a young man that you don't know."

" Well, let us make his acquaintance."

" I will tell him of your kind offer."

" Yes. If he refuses, bring him by force."

" I will do what I can, I promise you. And what time do you sit down?"

" At three o'clock; but, as supper will last until six, you've plenty of time."

" Very well."

A " bouquet " of myosotis, who had overheard the last part of our conversation, took D——'s arm and went off with him. A few minutes later I came across Louis who, apparently, had got rid of his " bouquet " of violets. As the domino who accompanied me just then was rather dull, I handed her over to one of my friends and took Louis's arm.

" Well," I said, " have you found out what you wanted to know?"

" Oh, my God, yes; you know, as a rule, at a *bal masqué* people discuss the very things they ought to avoid."

" My poor old friend," I said, " forgive me speaking like this; but I feel that I know you since I know your brother. . . . Well, you are out of luck, aren't you? . . . What's the matter?"

I saw that he wished to keep his secret, so I said no more.

We took two or three turns up and down in silence; it made no difference to me as I was not expecting anybody; but he scrutinised every domino that came near him.

"Look here," I said, "do you know what you ought to do?"

He started, like a man suddenly aroused.

"I? . . . No! . . . What did you say? I beg your pardon?"

"Come to supper with a friend of mine."

"Oh, no; I should be such a mournful guest."

"Bah! they will talk nonsense, and that will cheer you up."

"Besides, I am not invited."

"There you are wrong; you are."

"It is very kind of your host; but, truth and honour, I don't feel up to it. . . ."

At that moment we passed D——. He seemed very interested in his "bouquet" of myosotis. However, he caught sight of me.

"Well, it is settled," said he, "isn't it? At three o'clock."

"Far from it, my friend; I cannot join you."

"Oh, then go to the devil."

He passed on.

"Who is that gentleman?" asked Louis, obviously for the sake of saying something.

"Why it is D——, one of our friends, a lively fellow. He is the manager of one of our leading newspapers."

"Monsieur D——!" exclaimed Louis, "Monsieur D——! You know him?"

"Certainly; for the last two or three years I have had business dealings with him and we are also friends."

"Is it at his house you were going to have supper this evening?"

"That is so."

"In that case I accept. Oh! I accept with great pleasure."

"Good! But don't do so merely to please me."

"Perhaps I ought not to go," said Louis, smiling sadly; "but you know what I told you yesterday; one does not go where one ought to go, one goes where destiny compels us to go; and the fact is that I should have been wiser if I had not come here this evening."

Just then we met D—— again.

"My dear friend," I said to him, "I have changed my mind."

"Ah! Bravo! However, I ought to warn you of one thing."

"What is that?"

"That whoever sups with us this evening must sup with us again the day after to-morrow."

"Why so?"

"Because of a bet with Château-Renaud."

I felt Louis grip my arm. I looked at him; although he was a little paler than before, his face betrayed no sign of emotion.

"And what is the bet?" I asked D——.

"Oh! it would take too long to tell you here. Besides, there is someone concerned in this bet who could make him lose if she heard me talking about it."

"Quite right! At three o'clock."

We parted again. As we passed the clock I looked up and saw that it was two thirty-five.

"Do you know this M. de Château-Renaud?" Louis asked, trying in vain to hide his emotion.

"Only by sight; I have met him once or twice in society."

"Then he is not one of your friends?"

"He is not even an ordinary acquaintance."

"Ah! So much the better," said Louis.

"Why?"

"For no particular reason."

"Do you know him yourself?"

"In a sort of way."

In spite of his evasive answer, it was easy to see that, between M. de Franchi and M. de Château-Renaud there was some mysterious relationship in which a woman was the link. I had an instinctive feeling that it would be best for my friend if both of us went quietly home.

"Look here," I said to him, "M. de Franchi, will you take my advice?"

"What is it?"

"Don't go to supper at D——'s."

"For what reason? Doesn't he expect us, or rather, have you not told him that you were bringing a guest?"

"Yes, but that's not the reason."

"Then what is it?"

"Simply because I think it would be better if we didn't go."

"But, surely, you must have some reason for changing your opinion; just now you insisted on taking me, almost in spite of myself."

"We shall be sure to meet M. Château-Renaud."

"So much the better! They say he is a very pleasant person, and I should be glad to know him better."

"Very well, so be it," I replied. "Then we will go, as you wish it."

We went down and put on our coats. D—— lived quite close to the Opera; it was fine; I thought the fresh air would have a soothing effect on my friend's mind. I suggested that we should walk: he agreed.

CHAPTER XIII

We found a good many of my friends in the drawing room, habitués of the foyer at the Opera, tenants of the stage boxes, de B——, L——, V——, A——. Also, as I had expected, two or three unmasked dominoes who held their bouquets till they were able to put them in the water jugs.

I introduced Louis de Franchi to several people; I need hardly say that he was warmly welcomed by them.

Ten minutes later D—— returned bringing with him his myosotis "bouquet", who unmasked with a freedom and ease that suggests a pretty woman, and also one who is accustomed to parties of this kind.

I introduced M. de Franchi to D——.

"Now," said de B——, "if everybody has been introduced, I propose that we sit down to table."

"Everybody has been introduced; but all the guests have not arrived," answered D——.

"And who is there to come?"

"Château-Renaud has not come yet."

"No more he has. Hasn't he some bet?" asked V——.

"Yes, a bet of a supper for twelve people that he does not bring a certain lady here whom he has undertaken to bring."

"And who is the lady," asked the "bouquet" of myosotis, "who is so retiring that such bets can be made on her account?"

I looked at de Franchi; he was outwardly quite calm, but pale as death.

"On my honour," replied D——, "I don't think it would be very indiscreet to put a name to the mask, more particularly as in all probability you don't know her. It is Madame ——."

Louis put his hand on D——'s arm.

"Monsieur," he said, "in honour of our new acquaintance, will you do me a favour?"

"What is that, monsieur?"

"Don't mention the name of the person who is to come

with M. Château-Renaud: you know that she is a married woman."

"Yes, but then her husband is in Smyrna, India, Mexico, or somewhere. When a woman has a husband so far away it is as though she hadn't one at all."

"Her husband comes home in a few days; I know him; a brave fellow, and I should like, if possible, to spare him the mortification of learning on his return that his wife has behaved so foolishly."

"Then, monsieur, forgive me," said D——. "I did not know you were acquainted with this lady; I was not even sure that she was married; but since you know her and you know her husband . . ."

"Yes, I know them."

"We will exercise the greatest discretion. Ladies and gentlemen, whether Château-Renaud comes or does not come, alone or accompanied, wins or loses his bet, I ask you not to say a word about this adventure."

Secrecy was promised unanimously, probably not from a deep regard for social conventions, but because everyone was hungry and therefore eager to sit down to table.

"Thank you, monsieur," said de Franchi to D——, shaking his hand; "I assure you, you have acted like a gallant gentleman."

We went into the dining-room and everyone took their seats. There were two empty places; those for Château-Renaud and the lady that he was to bring.

The servant was just going to take them away.

"No," said the master of the house, "leave them; Château-Renaud has till four o'clock. At four o'clock you can remove them; when four strikes he will have lost."

I kept my eyes on M. de Franchi; I saw him glance at the clock; it said twenty minutes to four.

"Is your time correct?" asked Louis quietly.

"That does not concern me," said D—— laughing; "that's Château-Renaud's business. I set my clock by his watch so that he cannot have any cause of complaint."

"Ah, messieurs," said the "bouquet" of myosotis, "since we must not talk of Château-Renaud and his unknown lady let us dismiss the subject; because we shall drop into symbols. allegories and riddles; and that is deadly dull."

"You are right Est——," replied V——, "there are so many women that one can speak about, and who love you to do so, that one can't do better than talk about them."

"Let us drink their health, then," said D——.

And they began to fill their glasses with iced champagne. Each guest had his bottle near him.

I noticed that Louis hardly put his glass to his lips.

"Come, drink," I said to him; "you see that he is not coming."

"It is still a quarter to four," he said. "At four o'clock, however behindhand I may be, I promise to catch up the leader."

"Very well."

Whilst we were talking like this in low tones the conversation became general and noisy; at times D—— and Louis glanced at the clock which moved on steadily regardless of the two impatient people who were watching its hands. At five minutes to four I looked at Louis.

"Your health!" I said to him.

He took up his glass and, smiling, put it to his lips.

He had drunk nearly half when there was a loud ring at the bell.

I did not think it possible that he could become more pale, but I was mistaken.

"This is he," he said.

The ring at the bell had attracted everybody's attention, and a deep silence had followed the noisy conversation which ran round the table and which occasionally rose to a shout.

We heard a sort of argument going on in the vestibule.

D——got up immediately and went and opened the door.

"I recognise his voice," said Louis to me, seizing my wrist and gripping it with force.

"Come, come, don't give way, be a man," I replied. "It is obvious that if she comes to supper at the house of a man she does not know and with people that she did not know either, she is a light o' love, and a light o' love is not worthy of the love of an honest man."

"But I pray you, madame," said D—— in the vestibule, "come in, I beg; I can assure you it is quite a friendly party."

"Pray come in, my dear Emily," said M. de Château-Renaud. "You need not unmask if you do not wish."

"The blackguard!" murmured Louis de Franchi.

At that moment a lady entered, dragged, rather than escorted, by Château-Renaud and D——, who thought he was doing the honours of the house.

"Three minutes to four," Château-Renaud said quietly to D——:

"Quite right, my friend; you have won."

"Not yet, monsieur," said the unknown lady addressing Château-Renaud and pulling herself up to her full height.

"Now I understand your insistence . . . you have bet that you would bring me to supper here; isn't that so?"

Château-Renaud did not reply, so she turned to D—•—.

"Since this gentleman does not answer, monsieur," she said, "hasn't M. de Château-Renaud bet that he would bring me to supper at your house?"

"I cannot hide from you, madame, that M. de Château-Renaud has flattered me by leading me to hope."

"Well, M. de Château-Renaud has lost; because I did not know where he was taking me. I thought we were going to supper at one of my friends; so, as I have not come of my own free will, M. de Château-Renaud ought, it seems to me, to lose his wager."

"But now you are here, dear Emily," said M. de Château-Renaud, "won't you stay? See, there is a goodly company as regards the men, and a charming bevy of ladies."

"Since I am here," said the unknown lady, "I thank the gentleman who appears to be the master of the house for the kind courtesy he has shown me; but as, unfortunately, I cannot accept his gracious invitation, may I ask M. Louis de Franchi to give me his arm and escort me home."

Louis de Franchi rushed forward and in an instant stood between M. de Château-Renaud and the unknown lady.

"I must remind you, madame," the latter said, biting his lips with rage, "it is I who have escorted you here and consequently it is I who ought to take you away."

"Messieurs," said the unknown lady, "there are five gentlemen here. I place myself in your honourable keeping; you will, I think, prevent M. de Château-Renaud from insulting me."

Château-Renaud made a move: we all sprang to our feet.

"Very well, madame," he said, "you are free; I know with whom I have to deal."

"If you mean me, monsieur," said Louis de Franchi with a dignified air that no words can describe, "you can find me all day to-morrow at rue de Helder No. 7."

"Very good, monsieur: I shall not have the honour of calling at your house myself: but I trust that in my place you will receive two of my friends."

"You forget yourself, monsieur," said Louis de Franchi shrugging his shoulders, "to make such an appointment before a lady. Come, madame," he added, taking the unknown lady's arm, "and believe me, I thank you from the bottom of my heart for the honour you have paid me."

As the two left the room there was dead silence.

CHAPTER XIV

The next day, or rather the same day, at ten o'clock in the morning I was at Louis de Franchi's door. As I went up the stairs I met two people who were coming down: one was obviously a man about town; the other, who wore the Legion of Honour appeared, although dressed in civilian clothes, to be a soldier. I felt sure that these two men had come from M. Louis de Franchi's and I watched them to the bottom of the staircase, then I went on and rang.

The servant opened the door; his master was in his study.

When he went in to announce me, Louis, who was busy writing a letter, turned his head.

"Ah, good," said he, crumpling up the note that he had begun to write and throwing it in the fire, "that letter was for you. I was just going to send it to your house. All right, Joseph, I am at home to nobody."

The servant went out.

"Did you meet two gentlemen on the stairs?" asked Louis, as he offered me a chair.

"Yes; one was wearing a decoration."

"Those are they."

"Did they come on behalf of M. de Château-Renaud?"

"They are his seconds."

"Ah! Devil take it, he has treated the matter seriously, it seems."

"He could hardly do otherwise, you'll admit," replied Louis de Franchi.

"And they came. . .?"

"To ask me to send two of my friends to discuss matters with them; it was then I thought of you."

"I feel highly honoured, but I cannot go to them alone."

"I have asked one of my friends, Baron Giordano Martelli, to come and lunch with me. At eleven o'clock he will be here. We will lunch together and, at noon, perhaps you will be good enough to go and call on these gentlemen, who have promised to be at home until three o'clock. Here are their names and addresses." Louis gave me two cards.

One was called Viscount René de Châteaugrand, and the other M. Adrien de Boissy.

I kept turning over the cards in my fingers.

"Well, what are you bothering over?" asked Louis.

"I want to know if you really look on this matter as a serious affair. You see, that will guide us in settling it."

"What do you mean? It is very serious! Besides, as you heard, I put myself at M. de Château-Renaud's disposal; he has sent his seconds to me; it is no longer in my hands."

"But then one must know why you fight. One can't watch two men cut one another's throats without, at any rate, knowing the cause of the quarrel. As you know, the position of the seconds is more responsible than that of the combatants."

"Well, I will tell you as briefly as I can the cause of this quarrel. This is it:

"On my arrival in Paris, one of my friends, the captain of a frigate, introduced me to his wife. She was both beautiful and young; her appearance made a great impression on me, and being afraid of falling in love with her, I did not often take advantage of the invitation to come when I liked to the house.

"My friend grumbled at me for coming so rarely, so then I told him the truth, which was that his wife was far too attractive for me to dare to go and see him very often. He smiled, shook hands with me and insisted that I should dine with him that very day.

"'My dear Louis,' he said at dessert, 'I start in three weeks for Mexico; I may be away three months, perhaps longer. We sailormen sometimes know the time we have to start, but never when we shall return. I leave Emily in your charge during my absence. Emily, I ask you to treat Louis de Franchi as a brother.'

"The young wife replied by shaking my hand.

"I was astonished: I did not know what to answer. I must have looked rather silly to my future sister.

"Three weeks later, as a matter of fact, my friend went away.

"During those three weeks he had insisted that I dined at his house at least once a week.

"Emily lived with her mother; and when her husband set off he insisted that she should continue to entertain their friends. There was nothing my friend dreaded more than getting the reputation for being a jealous man; the truth was, he adored Emily and had implicit faith in her.

"Emily continued to entertain. Her parties were small, and her mother's presence prevented any breath of scandal; so no one dared say a word against her reputation.

"Three months ago, or very nearly, M. de Château-Renaud came on to the scene.

" You believe in presentiments, don't you? At his appearance I felt uneasy; he never spoke a word to me; he was everything that a man of the world should be in a drawing-room, and yet when he went away I hated him.

" Why I did so I can't say.

" Probably I saw that he had experienced the same impression that I had had when I saw Emily for the first time.

" In addition to that, it seemed to me that Emily received him with a good deal of coquetry that was unusual to her. Doubtless I was wrong; but I confess to you that at the bottom of my heart I had loved Emily unceasingly and I was jealous.

" So, on the next evening I kept my eye on M. de Château-Renaud : perhaps he noticed that my eyes followed him and I fancied that, as he talked in undertones to Emily, he tried to make fun of me.

" If I had followed the inclinations of my heart I should have picked a quarrel with him that very evening under some pretext or another and have fought a duel with him; but I held myself in check by repeating to myself that such conduct would be absurd.

" What was the result? Every Friday in future was torture to me.

" M. de Château-Renaud is a regular man of the world, a dandy, a celebrity; I realised his superiority over me in many ways; but it seemed to me that Emily put a higher value on him than he deserved.

" Soon I discovered that I was not the only person who noticed the preference that Emily showed to M. de Château-Renaud, and this preference grew to such a pitch that at last it was so obvious that one day Giordano, who also was a regular visitor at the house, spoke to me about it. From that moment I made up my mind what to do; I determined to speak straightway to Emily, as I felt sure it was only thoughtlessness on her part, and that I had merely to open her eyes to her behaviour and then she would at once cease doing anything which could be construed indiscreet.

" But, to my great astonishment, Emily took my remarks as a joke, pretending that I was absurd and those who shared my ideas were equally absurd.

" However, I insisted.

" Emily replied that she could not agree with me and that a man in love is necessarily a biassed judge.

" I was amazed; her husband had told her everything.

" From that moment, you see, my position, looked at

from the standpoint of an unfortunate and jealous lover, became ridiculous and almost hateful; I ceased going to Emily's house.

"Although I ceased going to Emily's ' at homes ' I nevertheless knew all about her doings, and I was still very unhappy about her; for people began to notice M. de Château-Renaud's attentions to Emily and to speak quite openly about them

"I determined to write to her. I did so with all the diplomacy at my command, begging her in honour's sake not to compromise herself; for the sake of her absent husband, who had such confidence in her, to be strictly careful as to what she did. She did not reply.

"What can you expect? Love is not guided by the will; the poor thing was in love, and consequently was blind, or rather deliberately would not see.

"Some little time after, I heard it publicly stated that she was M. de Château-Renaud's mistress.

"What I suffered no one knows.

"It was at that time that my poor brother felt the effect of my grief.

"However, a fortnight elapsed and meanwhile you came back.

"The very day you called at my house I had received an anonymous letter. This letter was from an unknown lady who made an appointment with me at the Opera Ball.

"This lady told me that she had certain information to give me about the wife of one of my friends, whom she would for the time being, only call by her Christian name.

"That name was *Emily*.

"I should know her by her bouquet of violets.

"I told you at the time I ought not to have gone to the ball; but I repeat to you that I was driven there by fate.

"I went to it; I found my domino at the time and place mentioned. Her information left no doubt about the truth of what I had already heard: that M. de Château-Renaud was Emily's lover, and, as I doubted her, or rather pretended to doubt her, she proved it by saying that M. de Château-Renaud had bet that he would take his new mistress to supper with M. D——.

"Chance willed it that you knew M. D——; that you were invited to the supper; that you had the right to take a friend with you; that you offered to take me and that I accepted.

"You know the rest.

"After that, how can I do otherwise than accept the proposals that will be made to me?"

I had no answer to give; I bowed my head.

"But," I inquired a moment later, with a feeling of dread, "I thought I remembered—I am mistaken, I hope—that your brother told me that you had never handled a pistol or a sword."

"Quite true."

"Why, then, you are at the mercy of your adversary."

"Do not worry; I am in God's hands."

CHAPTER XV

At this moment the manservant announced Baron Giordano Martelli.

He was, like Louis de Franchi, a young Corsican from the province of Sartène; he was serving in the 14th regiment, and several fine feats of arms had won him promotion to captain's rank at twenty-three years of age. I need hardly say that he was in civilian dress.

"Well," he said, after bowing to me, "the affair then is settled at last. When is it to come off, for, judging from your letter, in all probability M. Château-Renaud's seconds will call on you to-day."

"They have been," said Louis.

"Good! Your man told me that lunch is ready; shall we have it and then go and see them?"

We went into the dining-room, and dismissed the affair from our minds. Then, for the first time, Louis asked me about my trip to Corsica, and I took the opportunity of telling him about it, which the reader knows already.

The clock struck twelve.

"I think, if I am not hurrying you at all, messieurs," said Louis "it is time to go and call on these gentlemen; if we delay at all they might think that we were deliberately impolite."

"Oh, as regards that, you need not worry," I said; "they only left here about two hours ago and you need some time to let us know."

"All the same," said Baron Giordano, "Louis is right."

"Now," I said to Louis, "we must know what weapons you prefer—swords or pistols?"

"Oh, good heavens! As I told you, it's all the same to me, as I know nothing about either one or the other.

Besides, M. de Château-Renaud will save me the trouble of choosing. He considers himself, doubtless, the offended party, and on that ground will have the right to choose what weapons he likes."

"But as to who is the offending party is a matter of opinion. You only offered your arm as you were requested to do."

"Listen," said Louis. "Any discussion, to my mind, would look like trying to smooth it over. I am a peaceful person, as you know. I am anything but a duellist, and it is the first affair I have ever had; but for that very reason I wish to do the correct thing."

"It is all very easy to say that, my good friend; you are simply risking your life and you leave us to face the responsibility for what may happen with your family."

"Oh, for that matter, don't worry! I know my mother and my brother. They will ask you: 'Did Louis act like a gentleman?' And if you reply 'Yes,' they will say: 'Good.'"

"But for all that we must know what weapon you prefer."

"Well, if they suggest pistols, accept straightway."

"That's my opinion, too," said the Baron.

"Let it be pistols," I replied, "as it is the opinion of both of you. But the pistol is a nasty weapon."

"Have I time to learn to use the sword between now and to-morrow?"

"No. However, with one good lesson from Grisier, you might perhaps learn to defend yourself."

Louis smiled.

"Believe me," he said, "whatever happens to me to-morrow is already in the Great Book and all we can do will not alter it."

After that we shook hands and went down. Our first call was naturally to his adversary's seconds, who were not far away. We called on Viscount René de Châteaugrand, who lived at No. 12 Rue de la Paix. He was only at home to anyone who called on behalf of M. Louis de Franchi. We explained the object of our visit, handed in our cards, and were immediately shown in.

We found Viscount de Châteaugrand a polished man of the world. He did not want to bother us to go to M. de Boissy's, saying that they had arranged that at whose house we called first would send for the other. He at once sent his servant to tell M. Adrien de Boissy that we were waiting for him here.

Whilst we waited we never touched upon the business that brought us there. We talked of racing, hunting and the opera.

M. de Boissy came in about ten minutes later. These gentle-men did not put forward any particular choice of weapons; M. de Château-Renaud being equally at home with sword or pistol, they left the choice to M. de Franchi himself or to chance. We tossed with a louis, "heads" for the sword, "tails" for the pistol; it came "tails".

It was then settled that the duel should take place at nine o'clock next morning in the Bois de Vincennes; that the opponents should stand twenty paces apart; that there should be three claps of the hand, and at the third clap they should fire.

CHAPTER XVI

At eight o'clock that evening I went to M. de Franchi's flat to ask him if he had any instructions to give me; but he begged me to wait until next day, speaking to me in a strange manner:

"Night brings counsel."

The next day, therefore, instead of calling for him at eight o'clock, which would have given us plenty of time to be at the meeting place by nine, I was at Louis de Franchi's at half-past seven.

He was already in his study, writing.

"Excuse me," he said; "I am just finishing a letter to my mother; sit down; take a newspaper if they have come; stop, there is *La Presse*; there is a charming serial in it by M. Merey."

I took the newspaper he pointed out and sat down, noticing with astonishment the contrast of the young man's paleness, that was almost ashy, with his quiet calm manner and his soft voice.

I tried to read. Although my eyes followed the print it conveyed no meaning to my mind.

Five minutes later:

"I have finished," he said.

And, ringing at once for his man-servant:

"Joseph, I cannot see anyone, not even Giordano; show him into the sitting-room; I wish to be alone with this gentle-man for ten minutes without any interruption."

The servant shut the door.

"You see," he said, "my dear Alexandre, Giordano is a Corsican, he has Corsican ideas; I cannot therefore give him the confidence I should like to do; I shall ask him to be silent, that is all; in your case, you must promise me that you will carry out to the letter my instructions."

"Of course! Isn't that a second's duty?"

"A serious duty, because you can perhaps save our family a second misfortune."

"A second misfortune?" I inquired, astonished.

"There," said he, "that is what I have written to my mother; read this letter."

I took the letter from de Franchi's hand and I read it with growing astonishment:

"MY DARLING MOTHER,

"If I did not know that you were as brave as a Spartan and resigned as a Christian I should use every means possible to prepare you for the terrible news that is in store for you; when you receive this letter you will have one son only.

"Lucien, my dear brother, love my mother for the two of us.

"The day before yesterday I had an attack of brain fever. I did not take much notice of the first symptoms; the doctor came too late! My dearest mother, there is no hope for me, short of a miracle, and what right have I to expect that God will work a miracle for me?

"I am writing to you in a lucid moment; if I die, this letter will be posted within a quarter of an hour of my death; for, in my whole-hearted love for you, I should like you to know that I die regretting simply and solely your affection and that of my brother.

"Farewell, mother.

"Do not weep: it is my soul that you love and not my body, and wherever it may be that soul will continue to love you.

"Farewell, Lucien.

"Never leave our mother, and remember that now you are all that is left to her.

"Your son,
"Your brother,
"LOUIS DE FRANCHI."

When I came to the end of the letter, I turned and looked at the man who had written it.

"Well," I said to him, "what does this mean?"

"I am going to be killed at ten minutes past nine."

"You are going to be killed?"

"Yes."

"Why, you are mad! What puts such an idea into your head?"

"I am neither mad nor frightened, my good friend. . . . I have been forewarned, that is all."

"Forewarned? And by whom?"

"Didn't my brother tell you," asked Louis, smiling, "that the male members of our family enjoy a special privilege?"

"True," I answered, shuddering in spite of myself; "he has spoken to me of apparitions."

"Exactly. Well, my father appeared to me last night; that is why I am so white: the sight of the dead blanches the living."

I looked at him with astonishment, which was not devoid of fright.

"You saw your father last night, you say?"

"He told me of my death."

"That was just a terrible dream," I said.

"It was a terrible reality."

"You were asleep?"

"I awoke. . . . Don't you believe that a father can visit his son?"

I bowed my head; because, at the bottom of my heart, I myself did believe it possible.

"What happened?" I asked.

"Heavens! In the simplest and most natural manner possible, I was reading, waiting for my father, for I knew that if I was in any danger he would appear to me, when at midnight my lamp dimmed, the door slowly opened and my father appeared."

"In what form?" I inquired.

"Just as he was when alive; dressed in his ordinary clothes; only he was very pale and his eyes had no expression in them."

"Oh! In the name of heaven . . ."

"Then he came up to my bed very slowly. I raised myself on to my elbow.

"'Welcome, father,' I said.

"He came up to me, stared at me, and it seemed to me that the dullness in his eye was lighted by the strength of his fatherly love."

"Go on . . . it is . . . this is fearsome . . . !"

"Then his lips moved, and strange to say, although his words were mute, I felt them resound within myself, clear and vibrating like an echo."

"And what did he say?"

" He said to me:

" ' Think of God, my son!'

" ' Shall I be killed in this duel?' I asked.

" I saw two tears fall from his sightless eyes upon the pallid face of the apparition.

" ' And at what time?'

" He pointed with his finger at the clock. I looked to where he was pointing. The clock said ten minutes past nine.

" ' Very well, father,' I then said. ' Let the will of God be done. I leave my mother, it is true, but I shall join you.'

" Then a faint smile crossed his face, he made a sign of farewell and went away.

" The door opened of itself before him; he disappeared and the door shut of its own accord."

He told the story so simply and so naturally that it was obvious that either the scene which he described had actually taken place, or that he had been, in his perturbed state of mind, the plaything of an illusion and had believed it true, which in truth was as terrible to him as if it were.

I wiped my forehead, for it perspired.

" Now," added Louis, " you know my brother, don't you?"

" Yes."

" What do you think he would do if he heard that I had been killed in a duel?"

" He would instantly leave Sullacaro to come and fight the man who had slain you."

" Just so, and if he in turn got killed, my mother would be three times over a widow, widowed of her husband, widowed of her two sons."

" Yes, I realise, it is terrible!"

" Well, we must avoid it. That is why I have written this letter. Thinking that I died of brain fever, my brother will not want to revenge himself on anyone, my mother will be more readily consoled, believing that I am taken by the will of God rather than struck down by the hand of man. Unless . . ."

" Unless what?" I echoed.

" Oh, no . . ." answered Louis, " I hope that will not happen."

I saw that he was referring to some personal fear, so I did not press him further.

At that moment the door opened.

" My dear de Franchi," said Baron de Giordano, " I have respected your order as long as possible, but it is eight o'clock;

the appointment is at nine. We have four and a half miles to go; we must start."

"I am ready, my good fellow," said Louis. "Come in. I have said what I had to say to monsieur."

He put his finger to his mouth as he glanced at me.

"As for you, my friend," he added, turning to the table and taking up a sealed letter; "here is your part of the business. If any mischance befalls me, read this letter, and carry out, I beg of you, what I ask you to do."

"Absolutely."

"You were to find the weapons?"

"Yes," I said. "But I noticed as I came away that one of the dogs did not bark properly. We'll get a case of pistols at Devisine's as we pass."

Louis smiled at me and shook my hand. He realised that I did not wish him to be shot with my own pistols.

"Have you a carriage," asked Louis, "or shall Joseph go and get one?"

"I have my coupé," said the Baron, "and, at a pinch, it will hold three. Besides, as we are a little late, we shall go more quickly with my horses than with cab horses."

"Let us start," said Louis.

We went down. At the door Joseph was waiting for us.

"Shall I come with monsieur?" he asked.

"No, Joseph," Louis replied, "no, there is no need. I shall not want you."

Then, dropping a little behind:

"There, my friend," he said, pressing a little packet of louis into his hand; "and, if occasionally, in my moments of ill humour, I have been curt to you, forgive me."

"Oh, monsieur!" exclaimed Joseph, his eyes filling with tears, "what does this mean?"

"Hush!" said Louis.

And, jumping into the carriage, he sat between us.

We pulled up at Devisine's, just to get a case of pistols, some powder and bullets; then we set off again at a brisk trot.

CHAPTER XVII

We reached Vincennes at five minutes to nine.

Another carriage got there just at the same time as ours: it was M. de Château-Renaud's. We made our way into the woods by two different paths. Our coachmen were to pick us up in the Grand Avenue. In a few minutes we got to the appointed spot.

"Gentlemen," said Louis, as he alighted first, "remember I cannot come to terms with him."

"But still . . ." said I, going up to him.

"Oh! my dear friend; surely, after the story I told you in confidence, you would be the last person to suggest such a thing or agree to it."

I bowed to his inexorable will, which, to me, was a command. We left Louis near our carriage and went to meet M. de Boissy and Viscount de Châteaugrand. Baron de Giordano carried the case of pistols. We bowed to one another.

"Messieurs," said Baron Giordano, "in our present position I think it is best to cut short the paying of compliments; because, at any moment, we may be interrupted. It was our business to bring the weapons, here they are; will you kindly examine them? We have just bought them from the gunsmith's and we give you our word of honour that M. Louis de Franchi has not even seen them."

"This assurance is quite needless, monsieur. We know with whom we are dealing."

And, taking one pistol, whilst M. de Boissy took the other, the two seconds tried the cocking-springs and examined the bore.

"These are ordinary pistols which have never been used," said the Baron; "now, is it permissible or not to use the double-acting trigger?"

"Well," said M. de Boissy, "my opinion is that each should do as best suits him, and as he is accustomed to."

"Very well," said Baron Giordano. "Everything that equalises their chances is agreeable to us."

"Then you will explain it to M. de Franchi and we will tell M. de Château-Renaud."

"That is agreed upon. Now, monsieur, as we have brought the weapons," added Baron Giordano, "it is for you to load them."

The two young men each took a pistol, measured the charges of powder very carefully, took, haphazard, two bullets and rammed them home with the ramrod. During this operation, in which I did not wish to take part, I went up to Louis, who greeted me with a smile.

"You will not forget anything I have asked you to do," he said, "and you will get from de Giordano, as I have also begged him in the letter I gave him, a promise not to say anything about this business to my mother nor to my brother. Take care, also, that the papers do not mention the affair, or, if they do, they leave out the names."

" You are still thoroughly convinced that this duel will be fatal?" I asked.

" More convinced than ever; but you will at any rate do me this justice, won't you? I look upon approaching death like a real Corsican."

" Your coolness, my dear de Franchi, is so great that it buoys me up with hope that you are not quite sure about it yourself."

Louis took out his watch.

" I have still seven minutes to live," he said; " here you are, here is my watch; keep it, I pray you, in remembrance of me. It is a very good watch—a Bréguet."

I took the watch and grasped his hand.

" In eight minutes," I said, " I hope I shall give it to you back."

" Don't say any more about it," he said; " here come the others."

' Messieurs," said Viscount de Châteaugrand, " there is, I think, near here, to the right, a glade which I used on my own account last year; shall we go and find it? It will be better than in an avenue where we can be seen and interrupted."

" Show the way, monsieur," said Baron Giordano Martelli; " we will follow you."

The Viscount led the way and we followed in two separate groups and found the place after going about thirty yards down a gentle slope to the middle of a clearing which formerly, doubtless, had been a pond, just as at Auteuil, which had dried up, forming a kind of marsh, hemmed in on all sides by gently rising banks. The spot seemed as if it were expressly made as a theatre for a scene of the kind that was about to take place.

" Monsieur Martelli," said the Viscount, " will you measure out the distance with me?"

The Baron answered with a nod of the head, then, walking side by side, they stepped out twenty ordinary paces.

I, in the meanwhile, remained a few seconds alone with de Franchi.

" By the way," he said, " you will find my will on the writing-table that I was writing at when you came in."

" Very well," I replied; " I'll see to that."

"Messieurs, when you are ready," said Viscount de Châteaugrand.

"I am ready," Louis replied. "Goodbye, dear friend! Thank you for all the trouble you have taken for me, not to mention," he added with a smile, "all that I shall still give you."

I took his hand; it was cold, but quite steady.

"Come," said I, "don't think about the apparition of last night, but aim your best."

"Do you remember the 'Freyschutz'?"

"I do."

"Ah, well, you know, every bullet has its billet. . . . Good-bye."

He met Baron Giordano as he went, who had in his hand the pistol that was for him; he took it, cocked it and, without even glancing at it, went and stood on the spot marked by a handkerchief.

M. de Château-Renaud was already at his position.

There was a moment of grim silence, during which the two young men saluted their seconds, then the seconds of their opponents, and finally one another.

M. de Château-Renaud seemed quite accustomed to these kind of affairs and he smiled like a man confident of his skill. Maybe he also knew that it was the first time that Louis had handled a pistol.

Louis was calm and collected; his fine head looked like a marble bust.

"Well, messieurs," said Château-Renaud, "you see we are waiting."

Louis gave me a last look; then, with a smile he raised his eyes heavenwards.

"Very well, messieurs," said Châteaugrand, "get ready."

Then clapping his hands:

"Once . . ." he said, "twice . . . thrice. . . ."

The report of the two shots rang out simultaneously.

At that very instant I saw Louis de Franchi turn round twice and fall on one knee. M. de Château-Renaud remained standing; only the lapel of his coat had been shot through.

I rushed up to Louis de Franchi.

"You are wounded?" I asked him.

He tried to reply, but he could not; blood-red froth came to his lips. At the same moment he let fall the pistol and put his hand to the right side of his breast.

One could scarcely see the hole in his coat, which was hardly large enough to put one's little finger in.

"Baron," I exclaimed, "hurry to the barracks and fetch an army surgeon."

But de Franchi pulled himself together and stopped Giordano with a shake of the head, meaning that it would be useless. At the same time he fell upon the other knee.

M. de Château-Renaud immediately withdrew, but his two seconds came up to the wounded man. During this time we had opened his coat and torn aside his waistcoat and shirt. The bullet had entered his right side, just below the sixth rib, and had come out a little above the left hip. At every breath of the dying man the blood spurted out of the two wounds. It was obvious that the injury was mortal.

"Monsieur de Franchi," said Viscount de Châteaugrand, "we are distressed, believe me, at the result of the unfortunate affair, and we trust that you do not bear malice towards M. Château-Renaud."

"No, no," murmured the wounded man; "I forgive him . . . but he must go away . . . must get away." Then,, turning with an effort towards me: "Remember your promise," he said.

"I swear to you that what you wish shall be done."

"And now," said he, smiling, "look at my watch."

And he fell back, heaving a deep breath.

It was his last.

I looked at his watch: it was exactly ten minutes past nine.

We bore the body back to his rooms, and while Baron de Giordano went to make a declaration to the head of the police in the district, I carried him with the help of Joseph up to his room.

The poor boy wept bitter tears.

As we went in my eyes involuntarily fell on the clock. It said ten minutes past nine.

Doubtless it had not been wound up and had stopped just at that very time.

A moment later, Baron Giordano came back with the police officers who, having been informed by him of what had taken place, had come to put their seals on everything.

The Baron wanted to send letters to notify his friends and relatives of his death; but I begged him first of all to read the letter which Louis de Franchi had handed him as we started off. This letter contained a request to hide from Lucien the cause of his death and, so that no one should know, that the funeral should be conducted without pomp and circumstance. The Baron acquiescing in these requests, I myself went to pay visits to MM. de Boissy and de Châteaugrand to beg them to keep silent about the unfortunate affair, and get them to promise to persuade M. de Château-Renaud, without telling him the reason why, to leave Paris, at any rate, for some time.

They promised to do what they could to meet my wishes, and whilst they went to see M. de Château-Renaud I went to post the letter telling Madame de Franchi that her son had just died of brain fever.

CHAPTER XVIII

Contrary to custom in such cases as these, the duel made very little stir.

The newspapers even, those noisy misleading trumpets of publicity, were silent.

Only a few friends followed the body of the unfortunate young man to Père-Lachaise. In spite of the entreaties that were made to M. de Château-Renaud, he firmly refused to leave Paris.

I had a passing thought of following up Louis's letter with one from myself: for, although the purpose was good, this lie about the cause of his death to his mother and brother was hateful to me. I was convinced that Louis himself had thrashed it out thoroughly, and had felt it necessary to do it for the serious reasons he had given me.

I had, then, at the risk of being thought indifferent or even ungrateful, kept silence, and I was convinced that Baron Giordano would do the same.

Five days after the funeral, about eleven o'clock in the evening, I was working at my writing-table near the fire, quite alone, and in rather an ill-tempered mood, when my servant came in, shut the door hurriedly, and, in an agitated voice, said that M. de Franchi wished to speak to me.

I turned round and stared at him: he was deathly white.

"What did you say, Victor?" I asked him.

"Oh! Monsieur," he replied, "to tell you the truth I scarcely know myself."

"What M. de Franchi are you speaking about? Come!"

"Why, Monsieur's friend . . . the gentleman who has been here several times. . . ."

"You are out of your senses, my good fellow. Don't you know that we had the misfortune to lose him five days ago?"

"Yes, monsieur; and that is why monsieur sees me so upset. He rang; I was in the hall, I opened the door. When I saw him I shrank back.

" Then he came in and asked if monsieur was at home; I was so upset that I said ' Yes '. Then he said to me: ' Go and tell him that M. de Franchi wants to speak to him '; so, after that, I came."

" You are mad, my good fellow. The hall is poorly lighted, there's no doubt about it, you didn't see properly; you must have been half asleep and did not hear correctly. Go back and ask him his name again."

" That's no good, for I swear to you, monsieur, that I have not made a mistake. I saw and heard quite well."

" Then tell him to come in."

Victor went to the door trembling from head to foot and opened it; taking care to remain inside my room.

" Will monsieur please step in," he said.

Immediately I could hear, in spite of the carpet which deadened the sound, steps crossing the salon and coming towards my room; then almost at once I clearly saw M. de Franchi in the doorway.

I admit that my first sensation was one of terror; I got up and took a step backwards.

" Forgive me for bothering you at this hour," said M. de Franchi, " but I arrived ten minutes ago, and you can understand that I did not want to wait until to-morrow to come and see you."

" Oh! my dear Lucien," I exclaimed, rushing up to him, putting my arms round him; " it is you, then!"

In spite of myself, tears came into my eyes.

" Yes," said he, " it is I."

I calculated the time that had elapsed: the letter could hardly have reached Ajaccio, much less Sullacaro.

" Then, good Heavens!" I exclaimed, " you know nothing of what has happened."

" I know everything," he said.

" Victor," I said, turning to my servant, who was still very perturbed, " leave us, and come back in a quarter of an hour with our meal on a tray; you will have supper with me, Lucien, and you will sleep here, won't you?"

" With pleasure; I have not had anything since Auxerre. Then, as nobody knew me, or rather," he added, with a sad smile, " as everybody seemed to recognise me at my brother's flat, they refused to let me in and I went away leaving the whole place in a turmoil."

" The truth is, my dear Lucien, your likeness to Louis is so great that I myself just now was quite taken aback by it."

"Oh, is that it?" exclaimed Victor, who had not yet left the room. "Monsieur is his brother?"

"Yes; but go and get our supper ready."

Victor went out leaving us alone together. I took Lucien's hand and led him to an arm-chair and sat down near him.

"But," I said, being more and more astonished at seeing him, "you were on your way here then, when you heard the fatal news?"

"No, I was at Sullacaro."

"But it is impossible! Your brother's letter has hardly arrived yet."

"You have forgotten the words of Burger's ballad, my dear Alexandre, the dead travel fast."

I shuddered.

"What do you mean?" explain yourself. "I do not understand!"

"Have you forgotten what I told you about the familiar spirits peculiar to our family?"

"You have seen your brother?" I exclaimed.

"Yes."

"When?"

"During the night of the 16th and 17th."

"And he told you everything?"

"Everything."

"He said that he was dead?"

"He told me that he had been killed: the dead never lie."

"And he told you how it happened?"

"In a duel."

"And by whom he was killed?"

"Yes, by M. de Château-Renaud."

"No, it can't be so," I said; "you have heard in some other way."

"Do you think I am in the mood for trifling?"

"Forgive me! But, really, what you tell me is so strange, and what happens to you and to your brother is so outside the ordinary laws of nature . . ."

"That you cannot believe it, eh? I understand. But see," he said, opening his shirt and showing me a blue mark on his skin just under his sixth rib on his right side, "do you believe that?"

"In truth," I exclaimed, "that is exactly the spot where your brother was hit."

"And the bullet came out here, didn't it?" he added, putting his finger above his left hip.

"It is miraculous."

"And now," he went on, "would you like me to tell you the time he died?"

"Yes, tell me!"

"At ten minutes past nine."

"Stop, Lucien; tell me about it exactly as it happened; my mind gets bemused questioning and hearing your strange replies. Give me an exact simple account of what took place."

CHAPTER XIX

Lucien leant on his elbow in the armchair, and looking me straight in the face went on:

"Good heavens! it is quite simple. The day my brother was killed I was out riding very early in the morning. I was on my way to visit our shepherds near Carboni, when, just after I had looked at the time and had put my watch into my pocket, I got a blow on my side that was so sharp that I fainted. When I came to and opened my eyes I was stretched on the ground in Orlandi's arms, who was splashing my face with water. My horse was about four yards away, his neck stretched out towards me, snorting and sniffing.

"'Well,' said Orlandi, 'what happened to you?'

"'My God!' I said, 'I don't know myself; but didn't you hear a gun-shot?'

"'No.'

"'It seemed as though I had just been hit with a bullet here.'

"And I showed him the spot where I felt the pain.

"'To begin with,' he answered, 'no one has fired either a gun or a pistol; and besides you have not a hole in your coat.'

"'Then,' I replied, 'it is my brother who has just been killed.'

"'Ah, well—that,' he said, 'is a different matter.'

"I opened my coat and found the mark that I showed you just now; only at first it was inflamed and looked as if it were bleeding.

"For the moment I was so shattered by the pain, both moral and physical, that I felt inclined to go back to Sullacaro; but I thought of my mother; she only expected me at supper time; it would be necessary to explain the reason of my return and I had no explanation to give.

"Further, I did not wish, without confirmation, to tell her of my brother's death.

"I continued my journey and only returned at six o'clock.

"My poor mother received me as usual; she obviously suspected nothing.

"Immediately after supper I went to my room.

"In going along the corridor, which you know, the wind blew out my candle.

"I started to go downstairs to re-light it, when, through the chinks of the door, I saw a light in my brother's room.

"I thought that Griffo had been doing something in the room and had forgotten to take away the light.

"I pushed open the door; a wax taper was burning near my brother's bed, and on it my brother was lying, naked and bleeding.

"I stood, I confess, for a moment transfixed with fear; then I went nearer.

"I touched him. . . . He was already cold.

"He had received a bullet wound through the body at the very place where I had felt the blow, and some drops of blood were trickling from the purple lips of the wound.

"It was perfectly clear to me that my brother had been killed.

"I fell on my knees, and resting my head on the bed I said a prayer, shutting my eyes.

"When I opened them it was pitch dark; the taper had gone out, the vision had vanished.

"I felt the bed: it was empty.

"Listen: I admit I think I am as brave as any other man: but when I groped my way out of that room my hair stood on end and sweat stood on my forehead.

"I went down to get another candle; my mother saw me and uttered a cry.

"'What is the matter,' she said, 'why are you so pale?'

"'Nothing,' I replied.

"Then, taking another candle, I went upstairs again.

"This time the candle did not go out, and I went back to my brother's room. . . . It was empty.

"The taper had vanished: no weight had pressed down the mattress of the bed.

"On the floor was my first candle which I re-lit.

"Notwithstanding the absence of any new proofs, I had seen enough to be convinced.

"At ten minutes past nine my brother had been killed. I went back to my room and got into bed in a very agitated state of mind.

" As you may imagine, it was a long time before I could get to sleep; at last weariness overcame my agitation and sleep overpowered me.

"Then things happened in my dreams: I saw the scene as it took place; I saw the man who killed him; I heard his name mentioned: he is called M. de Château-Renaud."

" Alas! It is all only too true," I replied; " but why have you come to Paris?"

" I have come to kill the man who has killed my brother."

" To kill him?"

" Oh! rest assured, not in the Corsican way behind a hedge or over a wall; no, no, in the French way, with white gloves, an embroidered shirt with frilled cuffs."

" And does Madame de Franchi know that you have come for this purpose?"

" Yes."

" And she allowed you to come? "

" She kissed me on the forehead and said: 'Go!' My mother is a true Corsican."

" And you came!"

" Here I am."

" But, when he was alive, your brother did not wish to be avenged."

" Ah, well!" said Lucien smiling bitterly, " he will have changed his mind now he is dead."

Just then my servant came in with the supper; we sat down to table.

Lucien ate like a man free from all worry.

After supper I showed him up to his room.

He thanked me, grasped my hand and wished me good night.

It was the calm which, in strong wills, follows a vow irrevocably taken.

The next morning he came in to see me the moment my servant told him I was ready to receive him.

" Would you mind," he said, " going with me to Vincennes? It is a pious pilgrimage that I mean to undertake. If you have not the time I will go alone."

" How can you go alone! Who would show you the spot? "

" Oh, I should know it quite well. Haven't I seen it in my dream?"

I was curious to know how far this singular intuition would take him.

" Certainly, I will go with you," I said.

"Very well; will you get ready whilst I write to Giordano; may I ask your manservant to take a letter for me?"

"He is at your disposal."

"Thank you."

He went out of the room and came back ten minutes after with his letter which he gave to my servant.

I had sent for a cab: we got into it and started for Vincennes.

When we got to the cross roads:

"We are getting near, aren't we?" Lucien said.

"Yes, twenty yards from here we shall be at the spot where we entered the forest."

"Here we are," said the young man, as he stopped the cab.

It was the exact spot.

Lucien entered the wood without hesitation as if he had been there scores of times. He walked straight to the glade, and when he reached it he took his bearings for a moment; then going straight up to the place where his brother fell he stooped down, and seeing a red mark on the ground:

"That's the spot," he said.

Then he slowly bent his head till his lips kissed the turf.

Then, getting up, his eyes flashing, he walked the length of the glade to find the place where M. de Château-Renaud had stood to fire:

"It was here that he stood," he said, stamping his foot, "and it is here that you will see him lying to-morrow."

"What do you mean," I said, "to-morrow?"

"Yes, either he is a coward or he will give me my revenge to-morrow."

"But, my dear Lucien," I said, "the custom in France is that a duel does not carry with it any consequences beyond the natural consequences of the duel itself. M. de Château-Renaud fought with your brother whom he had challenged, but it has nothing to do with you."

"Ah, really. Then according to you, M. Château-Renaud had the right to challenge my brother because he offered his arm to a lady whom M. de Château-Renaud had grossly misled. Monsieur de Château-Renaud has killed my brother who had never used a pistol; he killed him with as little danger as if he were firing at that deer that is staring at us, and I—I—I have not the right to challenge M. de Château-Renaud? We shall see."

I bowed my head without speaking.

"However," he went on, "you have nothing to do with all that. Don't be uneasy; I have written to Giordano this

morning, and when we get back to Paris all will be arranged.
Do you think, then, that M. de Château-Renaud will ignore
my challenge?"

" M. de Château-Renaud has, unfortunately, a reputation
for courage which does not allow me, I admit, to have the
least doubt in that respect."

" Well, that's a good thing," said Lucien. " Let us go to
lunch."

We returned to the avenue and got into the cab.

" Driver," I said, " rue de Rivoli."

" No," said Lucien; " I will take you out to lunch. . . .
Driver, go to the Café de Paris. Didn't my brother usually
dine there?"

" I think so."

" Besides, it is there I have arranged to meet Giordano."

" Very well, to the Café de Paris."

Half an hour later we were at the entrance of the restaurant.

CHAPTER XX

The appearance of Lucien in the restaurant was another
proof of the extraordinary likeness between him and his
brother.

The news of Louis's death had spread; not with all the
details, perhaps, it is true, but at any rate it had leaked out,
and the appearance of Lucien seemed to stun everybody.

I asked for a private room, as Baron Giordano was going
to join us.

They gave us a room at the back.

Lucien began to read the newspapers with a coolness which
seemed like indifference.

In the middle of the lunch Giordano came in.

The two young people had not seen one another for four
or five years; however, a shake of the hand was the only mark
of friendship that they showed.

" Well, everything is settled," he said.

" M. de Château-Renaud accepts?"

" Yes, on one condition, however: that afterwards you
will leave him in peace."

" Oh! he may put his mind at rest on that score: I am
the last of the Franchis. Did you see him or his seconds? "

" I saw him. He will send word to MM. de Boissy and de
Châteaugrand. The weapons and the time will be the same."

"Splendid . . . sit down and have some lunch."

The Baron sat down and we talked of other things.

After lunch Lucien asked us to introduce him to the police officer who had sealed his brother's things, and to the landlord of his flat. He wished to spend the last night before his vengeance in Louis's own room.

All these arrangements took up most of the day—it was only at five o'clock that Lucien was able to go to his brother's rooms. We left him alone; grief needs privacy and one ought to respect it.

Lucien asked us to come to him next morning at eight o'clock, and begged me to try and get the same pistols, and also to buy them if they were for sale.

I went at once to Desvisne's and bought them for six hundred francs. The next day, at a quarter to eight, I was at Lucien's rooms.

When I went in he was sitting in exactly the same place, writing at the same table, that I had found his brother writing. He smiled, but he was very pale.

"Good morning," he said. "I am writing to my mother."

"I hope you are sending less sorrowful news than your brother sent her a week ago."

"I am telling her that she may pray peacefully for her son, as he is avenged."

"How can you speak with such certainty?"

"Didn't my brother speak beforehand of his death? I, beforehand, speak of M. Château-Renaud's."

He stood up, and touching me on the forehead:

"See," said he, "I shall put my bullet there."

"And what about you?"

"He will not even touch me!"

"But wait at any rate for the result of the duel before you send the letter."

"There is no need."

He rang. The manservant came in:

"Joseph," he said, "take that letter to the post."

"Then you have seen your brother?"

"Yes," he said.

It was a strange thing, that in these two duels which followed one another one of the combatants should be doomed in advance. Just then Baron Giordano arrived. It was eight o'clock. We started off.

Lucien seemed anxious to get there, and so urged the coachman to hurry, that we arrived at the appointed spot ten minutes before the time.

Our opponents arrived exactly at nine o'clock. They came on horseback all three, and were attended by a groom, also on horseback.

M. de Château-Renaud had his hand in his coat, and I thought at first he had his arm in a sling.

Twenty yards away, these gentlemen dismounted and gave their horses' bridles to the servant.

M. de Château-Renaud kept in the background, but glanced at Lucien however; even at the distance we were I saw that he was very pale. He turned away and, with the riding-whip that he had in his left hand, amused himself cutting off the heads of the flowers growing in the grass.

" We are here, messieurs," said MM. de Châteaugrand and de Boissy. " However, you know the conditions : they are the same as in the last duel, and whatever may be the outcome, M. de Château-Renaud will not hold himself responsible for the result in either case."

" That is quite understood," Giordano and I replied.

Lucien bowed to show his assent.

" You have the weapons, messieurs?" Viscount de Châteaugrand asked.

" The same ones."

" They are new to M. de Franchi?"

" More so than to M, de Château-Renaud. M. de Château-Renaud has used one of them once. M. de Franchi has not even seen them."

" Very good, messieurs. Come, Château-Renaud."

We immediately made our way into the wood without speaking a word : each of us had hardly got over the effect of the scene enacted in this same theatre, and we felt we were going to see another such scene take place there which would be no less terrible.

We arrived at the glade.

M. de Château-Renaud, thanks to his will-power, appeared calm; but we, who had seen the two meetings, were able to notice the difference.

Every now and then he cast a furtive glance at Lucien, and the glance showed nervousness that was very like fear.

Maybe it was the extraordinary likeness of the two brothers which disconcerted him and he thought he saw, in Lucien, Louis's shadow of vengeance.

While the pistols were being loaded, I saw him at last take his hand from his coat; the hand was wrapped in a wet handkerchief to keep it steady.